MADE BY DESIGN

BLOOD BOUND SERIES BOOK TWO

J.L. MYERS

A NEW ADULT PARANORMAL ROMANCE

MORE BOOKS BY J.L. MYERS

THE BLOOD BOUND SERIES

(New Adult Paranormal Romance)

What Lies Inside

Made By Design

Web Of Lies

Born To Die

~

OTHER BOOKS

Nerve Damage

(A Chilling Psychological Thriller)

~

FALLEN ANGEL SERIES

Ashes of Eden

Dawn of Reckoning

Breaking Lucifer

Cold-Blooded Fate

Falling Stars

BECOME A VIP AND GET A FREE BOOK!

J.L. Myers is giving away a free short prequel to the Blood Bound Series.

Use this link to get the your free copy.

http://bit.ly/JLFreePrequel

~

Dedicated to my special boy and baby girl.
You are the shining stars in my life and everything that makes my
world go round.
Forever a part of my heart, I love you both to the ends of this earth.

CHAPTER 1

My eyelids fluttered as my vision cleared. Through the disappearing haze I could see a row of thrones illuminated by the dancing candlelight of a chandelier. The reigning royals occupied them, cloaks draped over formal attire. Muted whispers rose behind me, the sound coming from countless people. Yet there was no scent of human blood. An audience of vampires…

I shot a glance down and my heart stopped. *Elevated on a dais?* I was kneeling, dressed in a white bodice and thin billowy skirt that pooled over my legs.

Approaching footsteps across planked wood drew my sight up.

Panic sliced through my chest, liquefying my insides. Caius stood before me. In one hand he held a scarlet-painted sword, the tip biting the wooden floor like a pointed cane.

What he held in his other hand would have made my mouth water in any other circumstance. It was a gold chalice coated with jewels…and filled with the peppery, metallic aroma of a vampire's Pure Blood.

Caius smiled and held out the chalice. "Take it, Amelia."

Instinctively I went to bolt, to escape whatever heinous act he was about to pull on me. Only my body refused to move. I wasn't in control.

As I fought harder my hands rose against my will. A moment later the chalice was in my grasp.

Stop, I screamed internally, unable to force my lips to move. But it was no use. Inch by slow inch the chalice lifted until its cold edge grazed my lower lip.

There was an instantaneous hush around me and I wavered. Had my scream gotten through? Was I resisting Caius's poison?

The sudden slice of metal cutting air broke the silence. Gasps erupted as Caius's sword arched towards my heart. His eyes gleamed, incredulous and crazed.

"Traitor!"

I BOLTED UPRIGHT, flinging my blanket across my dark bedroom. My tank top and cotton shorts were plastered to my body with cold sweat.

"It was just a dream."

My words didn't relieve the panic still drumming my heart. Because I knew better. My dreams were never just dreams, not anymore. They were part of The Sight; a Pure Blood ability that I'd somehow come to possess after whatever Caius did to make my blood immortal.

I snatched my iPhone with its new Icon For Hire case from the bedside table to dial Marcus, and cringed. The last phone had been obliterated by Caius moments before he'd stabbed his fangs into my neck.

"Amelia, hey," Marcus answered on the third ring.

"Where's Caius?" My grip tightened on my phone, while my other hand toyed with the amethyst pendant tied at my wrist. It was cool to the touch. There was no immediate threat. Pain twisted my gut as the fear of my dream ebbed. I clutched my stomach, my hunger growing. "Has he left the Armaya?"

"Why? What's happened?" Worry dyed his words.

"Oh, it's nothing." Marcus didn't know I had The Sight, and I didn't want to get into that with him now. "I just have a bad feeling."

"Amelia, he hasn't been anywhere near you. I'll kill him before letting him harm you again." The fierceness in Marcus's voice surprised me, forgotten under the weight of his next words. "Though you should know, he has left the Armaya."

I began to hyperventilate and Marcus cut in. "You're not in any danger…"

I jumped up and started to pace, my stomach grumbling with growing hunger. "Yeah, right."

"Look, I've been with him every time he's left," Marcus said. "There have been a few *incidents* in Anchorage."

Incidents? The word and the way he'd said it had my suspicious mind kicking into overdrive. "What kind of incidents?"

"It's nothing you need to concern yourself with," Marcus snapped. "Stay where you are and I'll let you know if anything changes."

When I began to argue the line went dead. I tried to re-dial, but after two rings it went straight through to voicemail. My stomach began clenching, over and over. The pain of my growing hunger knocked me back on the bed. I clutched at my stomach, hearing a distant rushing noise.

The next second my bedroom door flew open. Hall light streamed in as Kendrick rushed to my side. His hands came up to cup my jaw, still feeling my pain and panic through our bond. "Are you okay?"

His close pounding pulse thrummed in my ears. The smell of his peppery blood flooded the room. "So thirsty." My fangs broke free, face turning without thought to seal my mouth over his wrist.

Before I could break his flesh, Kendrick flattened me against the mountain of pillows. His arm braced against my shoulders and his hips pressed into mine. I thrashed against him, unable to think past the lure of his blood. Unable to see through the bloodlust.

"Amelia, stop!"

Something wet and chilled hit my lips. My need to escape dimmed as a steady flow of blood poured into my mouth. I reared up and the source was pushed into my hands, my lips finding the top of a bottle. My fangs clinked against the glass as I sucked down the dead blood.

With my crazed hunger sated, my vision returned to reality.

Kendrick slid off me and held out a tissue. "You got some…" He gestured to my chest.

Face ablaze, I snatched the tissue and wiped erratically at my chest, neck, and face. My eyes darted to the Ducati posters plastered across my wall and stayed there. What I wouldn't give to escape this awkward mess on one of those bikes. "Kendrick…I uh…*shit*. I'm so sorry."

Kendrick pried the bottle away and took my hands. "It's okay. It wasn't your fault."

After everything I'd been through since becoming a functioning vampire, I thought I'd mastered control over my hunger. Well, mostly. Ty, my irresistible boyfriend with his seductive werewolf blood, was still a temptation that was hard to ignore. My desire for his blood aside, I'd still made huge progress.

Angry at failing myself, I tugged my hands free. "I don't need you to lie to make me feel better."

"I'm not," Kendrick said. His next words weren't spoken, they were thought. Delivered from his mind to mine via our blood bond. *It's a symptom of The Sight. An after-effect following a vision.*

I knew why Kendrick was speaking through the bond. The connection had formed after my 'uncle' Caius tried to kill me. Kendrick had fed me his lifeblood to resurrect me. Since escaping the Armaya and Caius, he'd warned me to keep my supposed-to-be Pure Blood only ability a secret. Until now I had assumed the reason was to keep me from becoming a vampire experiment. Being a turned vampire, I shouldn't have an elemental ability. But now that I sensed him sifting through my vision's details, probing my brain like a pincushion, I knew there was more. Kendrick was worried about what Caius might be up to, but that wasn't all.

"What aren't you telling me?"

Kendrick took a slow, deep breath, and then blew it out. "That white dress you wore in the vision…it's ceremonial. You were on stage at the Portsmouth Vampire Council."

I felt sick thinking over the details of my dream. There had been an audience behind me, watching and waiting for something… monumental. "Oh my God. A sacrifice? What kind of sick race—"

"No," Kendrick cut in. "Vampires don't operate like cults. We don't take lives for a made-up cause." His expression became a mask I couldn't read. "Though we do have rituals. What happened in your vision I've only ever read about in vamp history. The Sight is so rare, an Oracle naming ceremony hasn't occurred for centuries."

"Oracle?" I clutched a pillow, letting my nails slice through the purple material. This ability to foresee the past, present, and future already felt like a curse. "I'm a vampire Oracle?"

Kendrick shook his head. "Not *an Oracle. The Oracle.* There's never been more than one at a time."

Swallowing the spike of bloody acid that came up my throat, I shuddered at the thought of Caius killing me in plain sight. "He needs me alive for his ritual. He wouldn't kill me like that."

"You're right." Kendrick stood and began to pace alongside my bed, raking his fingers through his golden-brown hair. "He calls you a traitor, which must mean he's challenging your ability. As a traitor you'd be imprisoned."

"In a place Caius rules," I whispered. My hand went to the bedside drawer. I pulled out a block of chocolate and shoved it into my mouth. "A place where he'd have easy access to me," I spoke around the melting mint chocolate. "A place no one can keep me from conveniently disappearing."

Kendrick stopped pacing and knelt by my bed, capturing my face with his hands. His eyes pleaded, a silver spark shooting through his blue irises. "That's why no one can know about your visions. Please, Amelia, promise me. Apart from Dorian and Ty, you can't tell anyone." His fingers pressed harder into the hollows under my cheekbones. "Promise me."

I bit my lip and nodded. If Caius got his way I'd lose everything: Ty, Kendrick, my family…and my life. Keeping this secret wouldn't stop him, but I wouldn't be handing myself over on a silver platter. "I promise."

I ENTERED the St. Volaras High School front gates with Kendrick, heading for the student parking lot. Fog surrounded us, thick and hazy. Just like my mind. Dorian had left early for swim practice, so with one car between us, we'd been reduced to walking. Not that I'd minded at first. The chilled air and open space gave me room to think. Too much room. After a few minutes the knowledge of being the secret Oracle was weighing on me. On top of that was the fact that I had just escaped Mom's dreaded talk on Ty. Plus today—the second to last day of school—would be the first time Kendrick and Ty had seen each other in person since our return. This was not going to be easy.

I glimpsed Ty through the swirling fog. He leaned against his bright blue Subaru WRX, his hands pressed into his jeans pockets. His wet hair was proof that he had been at swim practice with Dorian, and it was clear he was waiting for me. I tried not to sigh. Or let my heart flutter at seeing him in a white muscle shirt and black leather jacket. But that sexy smile under his black Oakley sunglasses made my heart skip. I smiled and waved. Instantly Kendrick's mood dropped, spreading through me like poison through our bond. A surge of anger, guilt, and hopelessness poured through me. And lucky me, the fun had just begun.

With great effort I capped a lid on my emotions and tried not to resent Kendrick as I made my way to Ty. Inside I wanted to sprint through the students and parked cars until I could leap into Ty's arms. But I couldn't. Kendrick's emotions were pulling me down, and despite my irritation I didn't want to hurt him.

Ty's focus shifted to Kendrick as I neared, then became cocky as he pushed off his car. His arms wrapped around me, rough hands squeezing my sides as he lifted me up and spun me around. His actions gained a parking lot full of gawkers as he breathed into my neck. "God, it's good to see you."

Ignoring the ogling students, I hugged him back before he lowered me to the asphalt. I wanted to say how much I'd missed him, even though I had seen him the other day. I wanted to tell him I loved him. Even more than that, I wanted to drink him in with my eyes, touch his chest, and lean up on my toes and take his lips between my teeth. Instead, I smiled and took his hand. "I missed you, too."

I sensed Kendrick approaching from behind as Ty directed a stunning yet cocky smile his way. Feeling like I'd done something wrong, I went to step back.

Ty caught me by the waist and planted a hungry kiss against my lips. The world around us disappeared and my toes curled at the taste of his mouth and the scent of his irresistible aroma. My hands shot around his neck, pulling him closer and holding tight. Ty's arm became a crowbar against my back, forcing our chests and racing hearts to meld together.

Sudden anger spiked through the bond from Kendrick. *Jackass,* he mumbled without speaking.

The world returned with a crash, like a shattering mirror breaking a beautiful view's reflection. I cursed and broke free from Ty, failing to control my breathing as I frowned at Kendrick. *Be nice, pleeeease.*

He's the one pushing it, Kendrick shot back.

Knowing Ty's kiss had been his way of laying claim on me, I shook my head. *You can't blame him. He knows everything.*

That doesn't mean that I have to be happy about this. Kendrick folded his arms over his chest. *If you want to be with him, fine. I can't stop you. But you know when it comes to you, I can't control the way I feel.*

It was the hard, honest truth. He couldn't control his love for me or the emotions that spiked when he saw Ty and me together. I reached out to grasp Kendrick's hand. *Sorry. I'm not trying to hurt you.*

"Huh hm." Ty cleared his throat, his hand on my waist falling away. "Am I interrupting something?"

I jumped at Ty's sudden voice. It was so easy to get lost in Kendrick's mind where everything around me could disappear. I forced my gaze up to Ty. "Sorry…" Thinking back to the plane trip home, I'd predicted I would be saying that word a lot. I hadn't been wrong. Sadly, this was just the beginning.

Kendrick coughed purposely, cutting me off by extending an arm toward Ty. "Truce?"

Hushed whispers erupted around me. Almost every remaining student's lips flapped at the surprising scene. But I didn't take any notice. I stared at Kendrick as if he'd suddenly grown a second head. What was he up to? Searching his mind I found nothing but a genuine gesture. An unselfish need to make the development of our bond and friendship as far from a burden as possible.

Ty lifted a single eyebrow, head tilted at Kendrick's hand as if it could turn into a striking snake at any moment. His golden irises lifted, peering over the black frame of his Oakley sunglasses. "Sure," he said with a shrug. "What could it hurt?"

"Not Amelia," Kendrick said. "And that's the point."

Ty shook Kendrick's hand with a tight grip I could feel through the bond. "Then we have a truce."

The bell rang and Kendrick gave me one last strained look before walking away. I watched him as he bled into the cluster of students heading for the main building. Somehow I felt relieved and terrible all at the same time.

Ty's hot calloused hand clasped mine, tugging me forward. I resisted and yanked him to a standstill. Emotions fired through my heart, responding to more than Kendrick's selfless gesture. I knew my reaction to Ty's enthusiastic kiss had hurt Kendrick, but I also knew Ty's display hadn't been for my benefit alone. Holding onto anger that sat like a hot poker in my gut I said, "That wasn't very nice."

Ty shot me an innocent *I don't know what you're talking about* look. "What?"

"You know what."

"Hey." Ty shrugged. "Just showing him where I stand."

I began to walk, all the while expecting Ty to chase after me. "And where might that be?"

Ty took an exasperated breath as he caught up. "With you and by your side. *Always*."

My anger fizzled and my stalking steps stalled. This was harder on Ty than his cocky attitude let on. He knew I had almost died, that Kendrick was the one who'd saved me. Doing so had bound our souls, making us soul mates in a non-romantic but everlasting way. And Ty still wanted me, only me. All of this was hurting him too. "I'm sorry. This is new to us all." I took his hand and squeezed. "It's going to take some getting used to. But we'll get through it, right?"

Ty curled a hand around my neck and dropped his forehead against mine. "Together we can get through anything."

I LEFT the warmth of the main building, meeting the freezing cold of a winter's day. I scanned left to right, back through the glass doors, then over at the gazebo. Ty wasn't here yet. Without any real time together, we'd agreed to have lunch alone.

I sighed, tearing open my chocolate bar and taking a bite.

Light rain fell from a deep gray canopy of growing clouds. In my wannabe biker jacket I could hear each drop patter as it landed on my shoulders. I sidestepped a puddle, one that in the past would have surprised me by soaking my Vans and jeans. Evidently my vamp senses and awareness were developing.

As I reached the gazebo centering the grassed space between the main building and art center, I looked around again.

Then I froze.

A blade of cold slid down my back and my vamp senses shot into overdrive. The amethyst pendant around my wrist blazed like a hot coal, a warning of approaching threat. Someone was watching me.

Fear hammered through my body as the hairs rose across the back of my neck. *It can't be him. Not Caius. Not already.*

That two-faced creep hadn't accomplished his goal to steal my immortality, but Marcus had insisted Caius was lying low for now, far away in Alaska.

So if it wasn't him, who was it?

The color drained from my face. The thought that Caius had sent someone to finish what he'd begun was paralyzing. Still, I wouldn't give in easily.

Heart pounding, I spun on my heels to meet the threat. If someone were here to take me, I'd fight like my life depended on it.

Behind me there was no one, not a soul, just the art center and a lush thicket of trees beyond that.

I squinted, trying to make out anything through the thick greenery as the sky darkened to purple-black. Sharpening every one of my senses I spun around. There, a dark figure edged the corner of my vision.

I whirled, eyes wide. But the space between the trees was empty. Nothing but moving shadows created by dancing treetops in the escalating bluster of wind.

A footstep from behind had me turning around, only to find Ty heading over from the main building. Paranoid much?

I forced a smile and waved, about to walk over to him, when a bright flash of light boomed like an explosion behind me.

My supernatural reflexes kicked into action. In a millisecond I spun.

Lightning had struck the solid oak a few yards from where I stood. A large branch split from its trunk and hurtled my way.

There was no time to move. I braced for the punishing impact. Something rock solid slammed into my side. The hot and powerful mass wrapped around me as we crashed to the ground. We connected with the pavement as the branch flew over us, grazing my cheek as it passed.

I tried to move but was locked in an iron grip. "Are you hurt?" The grip around my body loosened. Rough hands scoured my flesh, inspecting me.

Ty's face was panicked, the look easing as the stinging gash on my cheek healed. I moved to sit up. "I think I'm good."

Puddle-splashing footsteps raced up behind us. Kendrick knelt in the mud, clutching my wrist. "Amelia, are you okay?"

The concern in his expression, voice, and mind overwhelmed me. I nodded and glanced at my hero. "I'm fine. Thanks to Ty." I frowned at Kendrick. "What are you doing here?"

"I was walking across the oval and felt your fear." Kendrick cast his eyes down. "I-I got here as soon as I could."

"Not to break this bond moment," Ty said, getting to his feet. He held out his hand and pulled me up, putting his arm around me. "But what the hell just happened? I've never seen lightning like that in my life. And we get some pretty wicked electrical shows when training in the forest."

"The lightning isn't the issue." Kendrick got up, ignoring his muddied jeans while dislike for Ty struck through the bond at how close Ty held me.

"Are you delusional?" Ty's irises flashed gold and he released me, stepping closer to Kendrick. "That lightning almost decapitated Amelia."

I darted between them. "No, Kendrick's right. I mean that lightning was freaky, but there was something else. Someone was watching me...I think."

"Caius?" Ty's body became instantly taut with power, ready to fight. His eyes darted.

"No," I said, resting a slow-moving hand on Ty's forearm and feeling cords of muscle bunch underneath. "He's still in Alaska."

"That doesn't mean he doesn't have eyes watching." Keeping his gaze locked on Ty, Kendrick swiped at the mud on his jeans.

"I don't want you to be alone," Ty said suddenly, voice sharp and demanding. His eyes became lasers on mine. "You should always have someone with you."

"What?" It took a second for his alpha-like command to register. My expression became incredulous. "You want me to be chaperoned?"

As much as I'd rather not agree with his Neanderthal demands, Kendrick began through the bond before continuing out loud. "He has a point. This is for your own safety."

"It's to keep you alive." Ty clutched my shoulders. "I can't lose you. Not again." His eyelids squeezed shut for a brief moment then opened. "I'm not trying to control you. I just couldn't live with myself if I let someone get to you. If I let someone...kill you."

My heart ached at the true fear in Ty's eyes and the matching feelings from Kendrick through the bond. For my safety and happiness they were willing to set aside their differences and endure each other.

I took Ty and Kendrick's hands and sighed. "Then we're in this together."

CHAPTER 2

"*R*eady?" Dorian smiled at Kendrick and me.

There was a light of excitement in his silver irises and I wondered what was behind it. I headed for the other side of the parking lot and the entrance to Mt. Major. "Let's go."

Dorian took off toward the thicket of trees and we sped after him, darting around trunks, boulders, and ditches with ease. It was freeing to be able to run like this as the world flashed past in a blur. And with the shelter of countless trees, it was the perfect place for Dorian and Kendrick to evade direct sunlight. All royals felt uncomfortable when exposed, which included Dorian after what Caius had done to us. Though for some reason, I was still immune.

I tried to shut off the internal dialogue plaguing my mind about everything Caius could be up to, and concentrated on maneuvering past the lush green and snow-speckled scenery.

"Who's faster now?" Kendrick shot past me and jumped off Dorian's back. He launched himself into the air and landed on a thick tree trunk, then leaped down twenty feet ahead of us.

Letting the exertion distract me, I sped up with Dorian, closing in hot on Kendrick's tail. I bounded over a crackling river and passed my brother as I caught up to Kendrick. I pushed myself forward, the feel of the cold wind across my face exhilarating as I took the lead.

When we entered a clearing by a stream that had begun to freeze in from the edges with the onset of winter, I pulled to an abrupt stop. The icy water reflected the sky, showing every ripple and dark swirl from the clouds above. I'd been here before, at this exact location. Through my bond with Kendrick I received brooding confirmation. He had been here too, the day Ty had transformed in front of me and Kendrick had caught us. That event had changed my life forever.

"So this is our spot?" Dorian asked from beside me, pulling me out the beginning of a bucket load of painful memories.

Kendrick nodded, his rising guilt covered by his words. "As good as any. Let's get started."

Our trip deep into the forest hadn't just been for fun or to help me get away from Mom. With the last school day before winter break now over, my excuses to avoid her were running low. No, we'd come here because Dorian had something he wanted to show us. And from the look on his face, it was epic.

I elbowed Dorian in the ribs. "So we're here now. Let's have it."

"Yeah," Kendrick said. "What's the big secret?"

Dorian blew out a breath, rolled his shoulders back, and cracked his neck side to side. He said nothing as he crouched before Kendrick where a single tiger lily stood firm through a break of snow. Slight wilting showed at the tips of its orange petals. Dorian's hand rose over the flower, not quite touching it, just hovering, fingers splayed and tense. "Check this out…"

I stared as his fingers began to tremble, the veins across the back of his hand bulging. But nothing could have prepared me for what came next. There was no sound apart from the whistling wind through the forest, rustling leaves and creaking tree branches. But there *was* movement. At first it was slight, and if I hadn't been staring so avidly, I would have missed it. A tiny drop of water emerged from one of the six petals, turning plump and glossy before rolling down the petal and dripping onto the snow.

"You can manipulate water," Kendrick breathed. "You have a Pure Blood ability."

My reserved-only-for-Pure-Bloods spirit ability, compliments of Caius's experiments on me as an infant, had given me The Sight and all the visions that entailed. It had also created the blood bond between Kendrick and me, joining our souls and minds. Connecting with the dead was another trait of the spirit ability, one which I seemed to have escaped. Thank God. Dorian developing his own ability was just more evidence of how he too was affected by Caius's experiments.

"That's…" I wanted to say scary, terrifying, and proof that Caius used Dorian to experiment on too, but the accomplishment on Dorian's face made me reconsider. I crouched to get a closer look, seeing the water line left along the petal's length. "Amazing."

Dorian's smile grew wider. His hand still holding its place above the tiger lily trembled more violently than the second before. Frustration creased his face. "Come on," he said through gritted teeth. His eyes strained, their whites beginning to tint red from the outside in.

Just like when I had visions.

I went to grab his arm, to tell him to stop, but stalled. Another drop of water emerged from the same petal, then another in a consecutive clockwise motion from each of the other petals. Each drop grew larger than the last, each falling faster as more and more drops emerged and fell. The flower's vibrant orange shade began to dull, turning moss-colored then brown. There was an audible crackling as the tiger lily wilted, drying in on itself until it became as dry as parchment paper.

I reached out to touch the scrunched tip of one of the petals. As I did the entire flower came apart, turning to dust in the breeze.

"AMELIA ATHOBRY-LAMONT, it's time for that chat." Mom's stern voice called through her open office door as I entered the house with Kendrick and Dorian.

I stalled and winced, feeling as though someone's hands were wrapped around my throat. Usually Mon would have already left for The Council. Had she waited back for me? Through the opening I couldn't see her, but I could practically feel the invisible tension thickening between us.

"Good luck," Dorian shrugged before turning to walk into the kitchen.

Kendrick bit his lip, wavering. *Want me to stay?*

I sucked in a deep, rattling breath and shook my head. *No, it's okay. I need to do this alone.*

I'll be here if you need. He squeezed my hand then followed after Dorian.

I gulped, trying to loosen the grip around my throat as I stepped into her office. Time to meet the thing I'd been dreading since our return from the Armaya. "Look, Mom..."

"Close the door behind you." Dressed in sleek black pants and a lacy top, her desk an organized mess of post-it covered piles of stapled papers, her eyes tracked me. "I'm already late for work, but this must be dealt with."

Irritation made my forearms tense and my hands curl into fists.

Forcing them open, I closed the door and took one of the two seats across the glass-topped desk. Foreboding ran up my spine. Being closed in in this office, with busy book shelves and light-shielding drapes, reminded me of being back at the Armaya and sitting opposite Caius. The thought of him, more than knowing what was to come, twisted my stomach. But I wouldn't let him or anyone dictate my life, not now, not ever.

"I know what you're going to say and it's not going to change a thing," I said before she could talk. "I still want to be with Ty and I won't stay away from him, for you, Caius, or anyone. I'll be seventeen soon and I am old enough to start making my own decisions."

"That is Uncle Caius to you." Mom crossed her arms over her chest, scowling.

Huh, what a crock! My fingernails dug into my thighs. "He's not our freaking uncle."

Mom gasped, hand going to her throat.

Of course the statement was true, but she didn't know what fueled my hate-drenched words. She had no idea why I would respond this way, had no idea that Caius had tried to kill me to become immortal. Even before my attempted murder, he'd rendered me into a comatose state nightly through compulsion, so that his fangs could pierce my neck to test my blood. Instead of the pleasure a human feels when bitten, pain I couldn't consciously respond to had followed, searing through me as he drank my blood. That same pain had flooded my body when Caius had drained me to the point of death, or so he thought.

"How can you say that, Amelia? After everything he's done for our family, we owe him our lives."

The belief in her face at her own words and clear trusting devotion to Caius shot daggers through my heart. *I don't owe that creep anything!* I held my tongue and pinned my lips shut. The urge to storm out of my mom's office was overwhelming, to scream the house down over everything that monster had done to me.

Amelia, chill, Kendrick voiced through our bond. *She doesn't know, remember?*

I know, I hissed internally.

I wanted to tell her so bad. Only, doing so would put her life in danger. Caius had made that vividly clear.

I took a few deep breaths, forcing myself to calm down. "Mom, I know. I didn't mean anything by it, and I am sorry. But my feelings for Ty stand. I won't stay away from him. I can't. And besides, you're the one who wanted us to live normal lives. Well, I'm sorry to say but this is as normal as it's going to get. At least you don't have to worry about me killing him. He's stronger than me. And he knows what I am. And Mom," I said, reaching out to take her hand across the desk, "he accepts me, regardless."

Mom shook her head, a blond lock falling from her tight bun before she drew her hand free to push it back. "You've always been so headstrong, Amelia. So much like your father…"

The mention of the father I never knew spiked unusual sensations within me: sadness, regret, and most of all, anger. Caius had admitted to murdering my father in cold blood, solely so he could infect us like lab rats for his malicious plans.

Mom shook away the reminiscent expression from her face and lifted her glassy eyes to me. "So, I guess there is nothing I can say to change your mind about Ty?"

I shook my head.

She stacked her hands on the desk. "Well, I still believe you will grow out of this, out of *him*. It is only a matter of time before his life begins to fade while yours surges on. I am sure I don't need to tell you that you'll out live him ten times over."

I dropped my gaze, frowning at the indents my fingernails had left in my thighs. "Yeah, I know, but I don't care."

"The Council would not tolerate this," Mom continued. "As long as you're involved with him they must never know."

I already knew what The Council's punishment was for forbidden love. Even if I wasn't a Pure Blood, my association to Caius put not only me but also Ty at risk. "I want nothing to do with The Council or vampire politics." I was about to tell Mom she was right for trying to keep us human and away from everything vampire for as long as she could when her words hit me. "You're going to let us be together?"

Mom heaved a sigh and began sorting a stack of papers. "Love is never perfect, Amelia. After losing your father I know that better than anyone. So, for now, I will allow it." Her gaze returned to me. "Under strict guidelines, of course."

Waiting for the *I can't believe you bought that* moment, I clutched the desk's glass edge. "And they are?"

Mom leaned back in her white-padded office chair. "If The Council in any way becomes suspicious, your contact is to end. Immediately. I will not let you risk your life for this. I will take you away if necessary."

"That won't happen, Mom," I said. "I want nothing to do with their racist laws."

"Furthermore." Her hand came down on the desktop. "I trust you have not slept with this boy?"

My jaw fell to the carpet in complete horror. Embarrassment burned my cheeks. "I—uh..."

"And don't lie to me, Amelia. You're terrible at it."

I dragged my jaw off the floor and forced myself to speak. "No, of course not. And I would rather not talk—"

"What you would or would not like to talk about," Mom said

cutting me off, "is irrelevant. I am the parent here. If you cannot agree to my terms I will force you two apart. Don't think I don't have the means to do so."

I swallowed hard at the deadly seriousness on my mom's face. Would she try to force me back to the Armaya and Caius? There was no way in hell I would go, but then what would she do? Force the whole family to move, again?

"It is never to happen," she warned, wriggling a finger at me. "It's far too dangerous. The wolves are reactive creatures. They can't always control their animal side. After this boy's daytime transformation in the forest that you stupidly tried to witness, I know he can transform on demand. And you must know a wolf's bite is deadly to us." Mom stood up, graceful and willowy while looking anything but soft. "No transformations. No sex. No exceptions or the deal's off."

Like we were even close to that anyway. With Kendrick clouding my mind with jealousy and revulsion through the bond, being intimate with Ty wasn't an option. At least not anytime soon. Still these conditions aside, I wondered why she was giving in so easily. Was there more behind this agreement than I was aware of?

Mom cleared her throat, waiting for my response. Ulterior motives or not, the faster I got out of this the better. "Alright, I promise," I said, nodding. "Anything else?"

"You will invite Ty over here. I think it is time we all got to know each other a lot better."

Knowing I had no option, I shrugged in defeat. "When?"

"Next Tuesday for dinner," she said, her silvery-blue gaze piercing. "I have the night off. So no excuses. If he doesn't show, all bets are off."

I THREW open my bedroom window and jumped onto the sill, sitting with my legs dangling outside. My iPod hummed with Skillet's rock words from my bedside table. Outside it was already dark with night, the fattening moon rising into the sky. My new iPhone was clutched in my hand and pressed to my ear. After two rings the line picked up.

"Hello beautiful," Ty answered.

I swallowed my mouthful of chocolate, anxious to reveal the outcome with my mom. "Mom caught up with me."

"Hmm," Ty's deep voice buzzed. "Should I brace myself?"

The news wasn't bad, except for the *I can't sleep with you ever* bit, but he still had to endure an evening with my mom. And who knew what she was up to for that formal introduction. "No. It went quite well, I guess."

"But…"

I took a deep breath, clutching the sill with my free hand. "She wants you to come over for dinner so she can get to know you better."

"Now?" There was movement through the speaker. "I can be over in about ten minutes."

Shocked by his eager outburst I rocked forward, quick fingers clutching the sill to keep me from falling to the garden below. "You're okay with this?" I thought back to my total reluctance to meet Ty's father while knowing our races were born and raised to be mortal enemies. "With meeting her and being in a house of vampires?"

Ty laughed. "Well unless there's going to be any surprise appearances, I think I can handle Dorian and Kendrick. And besides, mothers love me. Plus I was the one who wanted us to come out in the first place."

"Well yeah, I guess…"

"Amelia, look," Ty went on. "I'm not worried. I want this. I want us to be out in the open, together. Not hiding our feelings from everyone who matters to us. Deep down I know you want that too. So, when is this dinner?"

"Tuesday night," I said. The enormous elephant of my promise to never go all the way with Ty lingered in the back of my mind. With the bond keeping a gulf between us, it didn't need to be said. Well, not yet.

"I wouldn't miss it. And I'd love to sneak over now to see you," he said, a clank and clatter vibrating through the speaker. "But my father's scheduled training for the next few hours. Call me tomorrow?"

"Yeah sure. Tomorrow."

I hung up, swinging my legs back over the sill—and almost jumped out of my skin. Kendrick sat waiting on the foot of my princess-style bed. With our bond I could usually tell where he was at any time, but somehow he'd managed to surprise me.

"So, the talk with your mom went well."

Of course he'd had a front row seat in my mind's eye during the entire discussion. Thinking back now, it was amazing that I hadn't sensed his pained emotions at my insistence to stay with Ty. "How did you do that?"

Kendrick smiled and patted the purple comforter next to where he sat. "Do what?"

I blew out my breath and dropped down next to him. "You know what. Block your thoughts from me. And it's not the first time. You've slipped away before. I've felt it. Tell me how you did it?"

"I'm not sure," Kendrick said, leaning back on his elbows. "I guess I tried to focus on something small and mentally tried to form a barrier around it. I had no idea it would work, but I figured it was worth a try."

I knew the real reason behind his efforts. The inner turmoil he suffered at seeing and feeling Ty and I together crushed him. In all truthfulness he had been extremely well behaved considering what he was subjected to. If the positions had been reversed I doubted I would have taken everything this well. "Can you teach me?"

"It's worth a try." Kendrick got to his feet, pulling me up beside him. "Try this. Stand with your back to mine, close your eyes, and focus."

I followed his instructions and faced away from him. Leaning against him I could feel the bones and slight muscles of his back through the thin material of his polo shirt. Kendrick breathed in at the touch of our naked arms. A split second internal image of his hands and long fingers running along my arms before settling at my neck scored my mind. My cheeks grew hot as I realized I'd just witnessed his physical desire for me. Oh God. What else had he imagined doing to me? The possibilities tied my stomach in knots and made me want to somehow escape.

Kendrick cleared his throat, his arms retracting enough to break the physical connection. "Um…keep your eyes closed," he instructed, thoughts snapping shut like a vault. "Imagine you're building a wall around your mind. Once you've done that, hold up a number of fingers."

Trying to forget the internal imagery of Kendrick's hands on me, I closed my lids, straining to focus on creating a solid wall. I imagined building it with bricks, piece by piece with cement until my mind was locked away inside. It was the same brick wall that had been created around my memories at the Armaya by Caius and Marcus through compulsion. But rather than fighting to break through the barrier, I was laboring to build it up. "Okay." I lifted my hand to hold up two fingers. "I'm ready."

A strange sensation tickled beneath the solid plates of my skull.

Kendrick's mind pushed against mine, harder and more determined with each nudge. The wall inside my head began to shake and crack. Then it fell, crumbling to pieces. I felt Kendrick smile. "Two fingers."

I slumped my shoulders and crossed my arms over my chest. "This is crap. And the only other ability I have is a nightmare. I can't do this."

Kendrick spun and caught my shoulders, turning me to face him. His irises—more silver than usual—contained a fierceness that locked our eyes. "Yes you can, Amelia. You *can* block me. Now try again." He released me and turned back around.

After turning and with my back resting against his, I closed my eyes and rebuilt the crumbled wall inside my mind. *I can do this,* my internal voice reassured with a resolve that was impossible to ignore, one that lit determination in my veins.

Ready? Kendrick questioned without a word.

As I held up my hand again with all five fingers extended, I imagined they were locked inside the solid brick wall. "Ready." Just like before, I could feel the unusual sensation of Kendrick prodding my brain, but I held my focus, refusing to let even one brick fall. After a minute the sensation eased with my internal wall still fully intact. I leaned harder against Kendrick's back. A wave of fatigue washed over me as the wall dropped. "I did it?"

Yes, you did, Kendrick replied wordlessly, turning back around. His face was marred by a look of accomplishment and worry at the same time. Because he had achieved something too.

I pushed my mental fatigue aside. "You compelled me? What the hell, Kendrick?"

Fire boiled in my veins and it felt like my head wanted to explode. Kendrick had compelled me to kiss him back when Ty and

I were broken up. My reaction had been livid at the time, not knowing that he was in love with me. And now he had done it again.

"I'm sorry. Seriously." Kendrick's hands came up like waving white flags. "I wasn't trying to manipulate you, I swear."

I stepped forward to shove him, and the walls between our minds came down. Through our bond, I understood why he'd done it. Manipulation had never been his game. He wanted to help us get back to normal, or as close as we could get. My anger fizzled and I clutched his hand, hope surging through me. "Can you make it permanent?"

"Huh?" Kendrick stared at me like I'd asked him to fly. "Amelia, no. I'm glad you don't hate me, but that was small. Long-term compulsion takes years, even decades of practice. Most never master it on anyone but humans."

My shoulders slumped, defeated.

Kendrick lifted my chin with his finger. "Hey, you still blocked me. This proves it's possible. You just need more practice. Okay?"

I sighed, far from convinced. "I hope you're right."

CHAPTER 3

A whimsical chiming echoed off the foyer's polished marble, up the stairs, and down the hall to my room. I ignored the interruption and kept trying to pull up the walls around my thoughts and emotions. Kendrick was in his room, rifling through a box of books he'd had shipped from the Armaya. One whole box was filled with boarding magazines. The rest contained compulsion and ability books, ranging from how-to guides to recorded feats in each ability —though none mentioned being able to dehydrate plant life yet. The whole time, Kendrick's thoughts were an open book. Not a single block to break. Yet pulling up my own barrier was wearing me out and getting me nowhere. As soon as I gained any ground, my curiosity in what he was reading would override my concentration and any walls I'd forged crumbled. Twenty-four hours of practice and nothing to show for it.

And now the doorbell was chiming again. *Damn repetitive sounds!*

I scooted off the end of my bed and shot down the hall, jumping down the tall arc of marble stairs to land with cat-like grace before the solid, double front doors. A twinge of paranoia crept in. Had whoever was out there seen me through the glass-lined entrance? I peeked out and saw no one, nothing but the deepening purple of a fast approaching twilight. As I reached for the handle my paranoia grew to suspicion. We never had visitors. So who was on the other side of the door? Someone harmless…or someone sent by Caius?

In the same instant, I sensed Kendrick's approach. Not from his room or the stairs, as I would have expected, but from the kitchen. His right hand brandished a thick kitchen knife that gleamed against the crystal chandelier light. *I've got your back.*

With a quick deep breath, I swung the door open as the chimes began to sound again.

Back-bordered by sheets of snow that blanketed every tree and hedge, stood an elderly man. He wore a blue uniform marking him as a delivery man and had a clipboard under one arm. In his other hand was an envelope. It was thin and cream in color with an embossed stamp in the corner.

The man's aged expression froze at the sight of me, perhaps seeing something in me that was distinctly different to regular human beings. Then it was gone and he held out the clipboard. "Delivery for Miss Amelia Lamont."

"For me?" As I took the clipboard the man stepped back, rigid and wary. I frowned and glanced down at the papers. My name, address, parcel tracking number, and a space for me to sign were in the gridded lines. No sender details. Kendrick shrugged at my side, the knife concealed behind his back. "Who's it from?"

The old man glanced sideways to his black, unmarked delivery van, as if wishing he were there rather than here. His shifty gaze returned to me. "I just make the deliveries, Miss."

His uneasy stance relieved my paranoia. There was no way he

was sent by Caius, no way he was here to cause any trouble, and no way he even had the ability to defend himself if he needed to. All this man could be—even though he seemed a little old for the position—was an underpaid delivery man.

I plucked the pen from the clipboard and signed my name before handing it back. The man folded the clipboard under his arm and handed me the envelope. The instant my fingers gripped the paper, the man spun on his heel, darting down the steps and disappearing into the driver's side of the black delivery van. In seconds the engine rattled to life, and the tire tracks left in the snow-littered driveway was all that proved he'd even been here at all.

I passed the envelope from one hand to the other. It was light, almost weightless. There couldn't have been more than a single sheet or two inside. My curiosity dared me to rip the envelope open. My paranoia feared it was from Caius; a promise that he was watching and closing in. My hands began to shake. "You open it."

Kendrick reached for the envelope when Dorian blew in through the front gates like a gale-force wind. He stopped right before us, snatched the envelope and ripped it open. "What do we have here?"

Surprised at his sudden appearance, I scanned my brother over. He was bare chested and wore a pair of sports shorts. His dark hair was slicked back and damp from melted snow. "Where have you been?"

Dorian shrugged and removed a single sheet of paper from the envelope. "Running on the beach." His eyebrows arched.

"What is it?" Kendrick abandoned the knife on the foyer table and stepped outside.

Dorian handed the sheet to me. "It's the results for the vial contents."

Anxious anticipation swirled through my stomach like a whirlwind. Caius had forced the vial's contents on me so he could steal my immortality by draining me to death. After escaping and returning home, we'd express posted the vial and a note straight to the Analyst. Every day since, my expectation of the results had grown, my need to know what Caius had poisoned me with always edging the back of my mind. Now the waiting was over. The information I so desperately needed to see was here.

My eyes focused like lasers, drinking in every piece of information. An emblem centered at the top of the page read, *Simon Beatty, Blood Analyst*. Below was a table that identified each element that had been found to make up the silvery liquid: Pure Blood and silver nitrate. But that wasn't all. There was a third, unrecognizable substance. According to the summary footing the page, this substance had been tested repeatedly. There had been no substantial results that could prove what it was or how its inclusion would affect the named substances. The mention of Pure Blood wasn't a total surprise. Caius had claimed the silvery substance to be ancient vampire blood. This finding gave us a reason why Dorian and I were experiencing Pure Blood abilities even when we were turned vampires. Yet it didn't explain how my blood could be immortal, or how this silver liquid could repackage this so-called 'gift' to anyone who drained all my blood.

I backed up, slumping against a porch pillar. "This is useless. It doesn't explain anything."

"Doesn't silver kill vampires?" Dorian pointed at the sheet.

"It's supposed to," Kendrick replied, frowning at the page in my hands. "Which makes its existence with Pure Blood impossible. Unless…"

Kendrick took the page from my hands and eyed the diagram showing how the two elements along with the third unidentified one connected to one another. The silver nitrate seemed to create a barrier between a single Pure Blood cell and an unidentified

32

compound, separating the two while acting as a bridge between them. He skimmed over the report below the diagram. "Instead of destroying the other cells, the silver nitrate has bonded to them. It doesn't make sense."

"Hey, what about that?" Dorian pointed at the table siding the diagram. In the table, percentages for each substance were listed, marking its potency within the silver liquid. "Could that make a difference?"

The table showed that the Pure Blood and unidentified substance each made up forty-five percent of the total liquid, while the silver nitrate made up ten percent of the total. "That's it!"

Kendrick voiced what we had already confirmed through the bond. "The silver nitrate level was so low that somehow the Pure Blood has managed to remain intact, bonding to the element, rather than being destroyed by it."

"And the unidentified element," I said finishing our explanation, "has to have similar deteriorating qualities to have mirrored the Pure Blood bonding."

"So what's the unknown element?" Dorian questioned.

"I don't know. But I'm betting it's blood." A shock of realization ran through me. I took the paper from Kendrick's hands and slid it back into the envelope. "What if it's werewolf blood? What if we're part—"

"Werewolf?" Dorian shook his head. "We're nothing like them."

"Then why is Mom letting me be with Ty?" It made perfect sense. "If our father was…"

"So, how do we get answers?" Kendrick asked.

I shrugged as Dorian spoke. "Mom's told us he was human before, and we know that can't be. If we want the truth, we have to compel her."

33

After being used and manipulated through compulsion, using it on our mom felt wrong. "There must be another way."

"Right now there's not," Dorian said. "Plus it's not like it'll hurt her. She won't even know she's being compelled. We'll get in and get out."

Decision made, we stormed into Mom's office. Perched behind her desk she was staring at the computer screen. Her cell phone was pressed to her ear and she was in the middle of saying "another one?" when her words snapped off at our intrusion. Her hair had been pulled back into a French knot, but was now messy and loosened as if she had been scratching her head in frustration or thought. She untangled her free hand from her messy tresses and impatiently motioned for us to wait. "Look, I'm going to have to call you back." She hung up and narrowed her gaze at the three of us while turning off the computer screen. "Well, you all look very serious. Where's the fire?"

Kendrick and I dropped into the two seats in front of the desk, while Dorian moved to stand before our mom. He took hold of her hands and squatted beside her. "Mom," he said, his silvery-blue eyes focused on hers and his pupils dilating. "Who was our father? What was his name?"

"I've told you…" Mom broke off, her face turning expressionless. The light in her eyes dulled, staring into Dorian's which were now entirely extinguished of color by enlarged, glossy-black pupils. The compulsion was working. "Athobry," she said without emotion. "Your father was John Athobry."

"Ask her what he was," I whispered, fearing I'd break his hold on her.

Dorian's gaze didn't shift from hers but the set of his jaw tightened as if to say, *shut up, I know what I'm doing.* Then he smiled. "Was John Athobry a vampire…or a werewolf?"

Mom's brows pinched. "Your father was human. He..." She inhaled sharply and her blank stare broke from Dorian's, shooting to Kendrick then me. The color drained from her face.

Kendrick leaned forward. "What is it, Ms. Lamont?"

"Oh no," she breathed, hands pulling from Dorian's to grab for the framed photo, before pressing it to her chest. It was the one of her cradling us as infants. "He's dead."

"Who killed him?" I demanded, clutching the desk's glass edge.

"What?" Mom replaced the frame on the desk as the light returned to her eyes. "Why are you asking me this? You all already know the answer."

"Good one, Amelia." Dorian shot me a glare. "You've got like the opposite of compulsion. Anti-compulsion or something."

"Dissuade," Kendrick said. "It's the opposite of persuade."

"Compulsion?" Mom reared, looking shocked and incensed all at the same time. "Were you—?"

Dorian's hands cupped her face, forcing her to look at him. "No. We would never compel you, Mom. We would never manipulate you like that."

Mom shook her head, blond tresses fanning around her oval face. "My children would never manipulate me."

At her compelled words a twinge of guilt squeezed my heart. Had we gone too far? Was there another way?

I got to my feet, about to air my doubts when Kendrick's voice spoke in my mind. *You know she'd never tell you the truth. She probably doesn't even know it herself. And we need to know what happened. Right now this is the only way.*

Dorian glanced my way. "Is there a problem?"

Unsure, I shook my head. "No. Let's get this over with."

Dorian's intense eyes returned to our mom. "The story you believe of how our father died, and how we were all turned into vampires, is a lie. You were there. You saw everything that happened. Now I need to you remember that night. Not what you were compelled to believe happened, but what really happened. What you saw with your own eyes. Dig into your memory. See the truth."

"The truth," she said in a quiet but level voice. "I saw it all; a monster in our home, starving for blood with sharp and deadly teeth." She broke off with a gasp, terror transforming her beautiful face. "No," she said, beginning to sob. "No."

I reared off my seat and leaned across the desk. "You remember," I said, trying to keep my voice from startling her.

She was still under Dorian's compulsion, but her gaze shifted to me. Her eyes were wide, too much white surrounding the terror in her pupils. Those were the eyes of someone who knew something almost too horrific to accept. The eyes of someone who knew the truth.

"You know who did this to us. Don't you?"

Tears pooled and she blinked, plunging them down her cheeks. "Yes," she whispered, making no move to wipe away the wet streaks. "A vampire killed your father, tore him to bloody shreds. Then he attacked me. I was left for dead."

Dorian gave her a slight shake, forcing her to look at him. A muscle ticked in his clenched jaw. "No. That's what you were compelled to believe. That's not what happened. Think harder. Who attacked you? Who killed our father?"

"A rogue vampire," Mom said in monotone, her expression blank again. Her hand lifted, fingers slipping inside her blouse and nails worrying at her shoulder blade. "I did it to keep you and Amelia safe."

"It's no use," I said. "We can't break through what Caius compelled her to believe."

Ignoring me, Dorian repeated the question, pulling on Mom's arm. As he did, her hand over her back shifted, drawing her blouse's thin fabric to the side and exposing her bare shoulder. I skirted around the desk and studied her flesh. There, on the pale, poreless skin was an intricate gold symbol that glimmered even in the room's low light.

"An alchemist mark," Kendrick said, coming up behind me. He'd never seen one in the flesh, but through my memories, he knew what they looked like.

Dorian's gaze found me over our mom's shoulder and slid sideways, as if to say, *we'll talk out there.*

I nodded and pushed Kendrick toward the door, stepping out into the foyer as Dorian replaced Mom in her office chair. His voice was audible as we hovered outside. "Mom, once I leave you'll resume whatever you were doing before we came in. You won't remember our interruption or anything we discussed." The light touch of his lips meeting her cheek reached my ears. A moment later he closed the door behind him and directed us upstairs to my bedroom. Once inside and with the door shut, Dorian asked, "The mark, do you know what it means?"

"No." I shook my head, and Kendrick, already knowing what I was going to say, threw me my iPhone from the bedside table. "But I know who will."

I RUSHED through the open gate fronting our property and over the quiet road that saw only a car or two every half-hour. It was late in the evening, not quite midnight but close enough that commuters had long since found their way home from work. Any lingering beach bums had bailed with the arrival of another freezing winter's night.

My bare feet bounded over the gravel beyond the diagonally painted parking lot and hit the soft, grainy feel of dry sand. Reaching Ty and what I hoped was an explanation of Mom's alchemist mark filled me with nervous anticipation. A wide path bordered by a wooden railing and beach flora led the way down to the gently crashing waves. The water lapped in slow repetition, silver lit in ripples by the moonlight from a cloud-streaked sky. The beach was almost abandoned, bar a small bonfire to my left before a rocky incline. Crouched on a piece of driftwood was a guy. His black hair whipped with the intensifying wind, but he made no attempt to push it back. Instead, he glanced up, a lingering smile painting his perfect lips.

As he rose to full height, I rushed forward and leaped over the crackling fire to land in his arms. He held me tight around my waist, his free hand pressed into my back. Then my feet met the cold grain-iness of sand as Ty's arms released. With a blank look on his face, he glanced out at the rolling of tiny waves. Nervous at his body language but unable to hold back, I let my fingers trail down his bare chest before hooking through the loops of his jeans. "I'm always happy to see you, but why couldn't you explain the mark over the phone? Couldn't you find out what it meant?"

Ty sighed, shoulders rising and falling. "I have someone I need to introduce you to." His focus shifted from the glittering water to glance over my shoulder.

At that moment, I heard footsteps crunching in the sand behind me. My head twisted, following his line of sight over the fire. Wind batted at me, flinging my hair over my face. I pushed it back impa-tiently, twisting it to one side.

There were two people walking along the beach toward us. They weren't hand in hand or anything, but there was a close awkward-ness between them as they walked, shoulders not quite touching. Under a red skirt the girl wore black leggings and ankle boots. A fur-lined jacket covered her top half with a hood that sheltered her face from view. The boy was... I squinted, making out his dark hair and the familiar lines of his face as he glanced up, blue irises shining silver against the moonlight.

"Dorian?" I threw a glance to the empty beach behind him, and then to the girl he was with. He'd known I was meeting Ty here to figure out what the mark we'd found on our mom's shoulder meant. And he was using the same space to hit on a girl? "What are you doing here?"

Dorian half waved, but his face remained impassive. "Sorry we're late."

The girl beside him lifted her pale hands, freeing her tangle of red curls from the seclusion of her fur-lined hood. She shook her head and smiled, releasing a cascade of red over her shoulders. "Hi, Amelia. Ty."

"Vanessa?" I almost choked on her name. She was an inquisitive and intelligent girl, and way too smart to fall for Dorian's single-minded charms. So what was she doing here? Why had Dorian brought her into our secret meeting? "Um, hi." I shot a quick glance at Ty. He was even tenser than before. I frowned back at Vanessa and Dorian. "What are you two doing here?"

Ty's broad hands found my shoulders and squeezed. His lips met my ear, his hot breath tickling my neck. "I need to introduce you to an alchemist. The one who marks my pack."

So, Vanessa knows who the alchemist is? I already knew she'd been marked to hide her blood's scent, but I hadn't given much thought to how much she actually knew about it all. She'd confessed to knowing about werewolves, but had seemed oblivious to the existence of vampires. "Okay," I said slowly. "So where is he?"

Dorian shook his head. "It's not a he. It's a she."

Vanessa walked around the crackling flames and held out her hand, as if we were meeting for the first time. "Hi, I'm Vanessa Aquinas. The alchemist assigned to Ty's pack."

I stared at her hand for a long moment, frowning as if it were the strangest thing I had ever seen. *Vanessa's Ty's alchemist?* In the past I had wondered how this pixie-faced girl had fit into the strange pack of werewolves, how much she knew about them—and about us.

Vanessa's hand dropped, and she crouched back onto a piece of driftwood. "Don't be mad at Ty," she said. "He wanted to tell you before you went to the Armaya, but I made him promise not to. I was still suspicious of your motives, even though Ty swore you had none. I just didn't want to reveal all my cards without being sure."

Ty pulled me down with him onto the driftwood behind us. Warmth from the fire coated my face as I frowned at Vanessa. "My motives?"

Vanessa bit her lip, but it was Dorian who spoke as he sat beside her. "She knows we're vampires."

I spun on Ty. His close nakedness distracted me, and I shook my thoughts clear. "You told her?"

Ty shook his head. "I didn't have to."

"Look," Vanessa's voice forced me to turn back and face her. "Alchemist children are raised with full knowledge of werewolves and vampires. Our purpose is to keep a balance, to hide both races' existence from human knowledge by helping the wolves to keep rogue vampires from drawing attention. My family comes from a long line of alchemists and raised me to follow in their legacy." She tugged at the edges of her jacket, drawing it together as if chilled despite the fire's heat. "That's the reason I warned you against Ty before Marika's, uh…involvement. I know the dynamics of each race and the feud that's bred into them. Your feelings for each other aren't normal. So I had to be guarded. I had to make sure you weren't plotting some kind of race revenge."

I remembered Vanessa's warnings and her attitude changing from friendly but intrusive to prickly and suspicious. She'd never lacked confidence in shutting down Ty's pack. Even Troy, who hated authority as much as he hated vampires, always backed down at her icy stare. I thought again of the mark across Marika's neck, and the flash of gold which I later realized was an identical mark along Vanessa's neck. A mark to block her blood's scent. Something inside me clicked, remembering how Marika had used the mark while imprinting me to seduce Ty. "*You*," I said, narrowing my eyes at Vanessa. "*You* marked Marika. Without you she wouldn't have been able to trick Ty."

"I did," she said, red curls blowing across her neck and looking like a vibrant, living scarf. "Though I didn't know marking her would create such drama."

My gaze became incredulous, but before I could speak Dorian cut in. "Vanessa told me what happened and I believe her." They exchanged a quick look before glancing away from each other.

"Why didn't you tell me?" I asked Dorian "You're my brother."

"I promised I wouldn't." Dorian shrugged, but wouldn't meet my eyes. "And I didn't want you to hate Vanessa like you did Marika. Especially when what happened wasn't her fault."

"Vanessa thought," Ty said, "that Marika wanted to keep her growth into a lycan to herself. She would never have interfered if she'd known what her plans were."

Remembering her harsh tone and skewering gaze as she reprimanded both Troy and Marika after the fact, I guess I believed her. I

41

sighed and pushed the memories of Ty and Marika almost naked in my bed to the back of my mind. "Fine. Whatever. It's in the past, and we have bigger things to worry about now."

Ty caught my hand with his, the look on his face questioning. Realizing his previous tension had been over keeping something else from me, I squeezed, lifting my free hand to rub up and down his scarred bicep. Of all the things I knew about Ty, there was one thing I couldn't question. Ty was nothing if not loyal to the end. That was a trait I loved about him, and one I could never blame him for. "So, do you know what my mom's mark means?" I asked Vanessa.

She stopped biting her lip and smiled. "It's a corruption of a mark that wards against a vampire's compulsion—this version makes vocal compulsion possible. Though the compelling vamp would need to be pretty powerful for the embedded belief to remain so intact like with your mom. Being a vampire opportunistic mark, I've never given it anyone before. Given my alliance with the wolves, I never would."

Dorian, Kendrick, and I didn't doubt that Caius was behind this mark that kept his lies as the truth that Mom remembered. Defeat weighed down my shoulders. Knowing the danger, we'd previously decided to keep Caius's attempt to kill me from Mom. We'd even planned to erase any memories Dorian had stirred through our earlier interrogation.

Would she ever be able to access those real memories, to see Caius for the monster he truly was? "So, as long as Caius is compelling her she'll never be able to remember the truth?"

"No, that's just it," Ty said. "That mark is temporary. It would have to be re-administered to keep working."

"It must last for a long time then, right?" For some reason I felt like everyone around me knew the answers and was holding back in telling me.

"No," Vanessa said. "Each mark's lifespan differs depending on who's marked and the technique of the one doing the marking. It could last days, a week, sometimes even a few weeks. But no more."

My head shook back and forth. None of what they'd said made sense. Caius had always been there while I was imprisoned at the Armaya. There hadn't been any time where he could have left and gotten back without me noticing. Weight filled my stomach, making me feel sick. "It's not possible. Marcus said he hasn't left." I sucked in the sea air and clutched Ty's forearm. "How could Caius have been here since Kendrick and I got back?"

"Amelia," Dorian said. I spun to see him shifting awkwardly on the driftwood. The light from the bonfire's flames cast an orange glow over his pale face. "Caius hasn't been here."

"He sent an alchemist," Vanessa said.

Ty's rough hand squeezed my thigh. "Which means he's got others doing his dirty work. And I think you were right. Someone was watching you the other day."

Amelia, the deep sound of Kendrick's urgent voice spoke through our bond. *Get back here, and bring Dorian. There's something you need to see.*

I tried to source the problem, but his thoughts were foggy. All I knew was that he was standing behind my mom's desk with something vital clutched between his fingers. *Okay.* I pursed my lips and patted Ty's thigh. "Dorian and I have to go. Kendrick's found something."

"Is everything alright?" Dorian questioned.

Instead of replying to Dorian, my focus centered on Ty. Stiff alarm had frozen his expression and his hand released mine, moving to my hip. "I'll come with you."

No, Kendrick said with total conviction. *Just you and Dorian.*

Even though I had no idea what Kendrick had to reveal, I could read into his emotional state. There wasn't any immediate danger. I glanced up at Ty through thick lashes, a rich caramel that was a few shades darker than my blond hair. "No, there's no danger," I said, then motioned to Dorian. "He's in Mom's office and there's something he needs to show us."

Dorian glanced at Vanessa, and then shifted his gaze swiftly to Ty. "Guess we'll catch you guys later." He rose and began moving back up the beach.

"I better go," I said to Ty. I felt bad for leaving but I needed to know what Kendrick had uncovered. "I'll call you later?"

Ty pressed his lips together, a shadow of a smile curving them. "Sure, later."

Ty leaned in and joined our lips. The light touch sent a flood of desire through me. It dared me to say, *the hell with Kendrick's secret reveal,* while wrapping my arms around Ty's neck and drawing his body against mine, matching his gentle kiss with one fueled by unrelenting passion. In the split second of my conjured desires, Kendrick's stomach knitted at those very thoughts, making me feel terrible and a little nauseous. Apart from that, Vanessa was right there, arms folded over her chest and watching after Dorian. As if she wanted to have as much space between us as my brother had already gained. I let my lips brush against the stubble on Ty's cheek. Then before I could waver, getting distracted by the pulse of blood coursing through the fat vein along his neck, I stood and bounded after Dorian.

No longer needing to hide our vampire speed from Vanessa we shot up the rail-bordered path and through the pooling light across the vacant road. In seconds we had covered the driveway and exploded through the front door, stalling only once our feet had met the soft carpet in Mom's office.

Kendrick sat at her desk chair. "What took you so long?"

I raised a brow at the cupboard's open roller doors that lined the right wall. The shelves were in disarray compared to their normal neat stacking and filing. Lucky for us, Mom was out with one of her socialite charity friends, otherwise she'd flip out. "You went snooping." Kendrick's thoughts were blocked as I walked around the desk. "What'd you find?"

Kendrick held out two sheets of paper and Dorian shot in front of me to snatch them. He frowned as he scanned over the first, the lineless planes of his face creasing as he scanned over the second. "His name's not here."

"Whose name?"

Dorian handed them over. It took a second for me to understand what his comment had meant. The documents were Dorian's and my birth certificates. Each listed our birthplace as Anchorage and our mom's maiden name, the name she still went by, Lamayli Lamont. Next to the details for the mother of the child was space for the father's information. Name. Address. Phone number. The address and phone number fields were blank, but the block next to 'Full Name of Father' wasn't. It was filled in with typed letters, rather than the handwritten ones that had clearly been our mom's handwriting.

"No father listed?" My throat felt dry, and I swallowed, looking from Dorian to Kendrick. "Why wouldn't she write his name?"

Dorian laid a cold hand on my forearm. "Well, she did tell us his name under my sparkling ability to compel her. Maybe she never intended for us to know his name."

"Or," Kendrick said pushing the chair back to stand. "Maybe John Athobry isn't your father's name."

I leaned against the edge of the desk. "But how could it not be?"

"She was compelled to believe that other stuff," Dorian said. He went to the cupboards and began straightening the contents. "Caius could have compelled her to believe his name was John."

As I shifted my weight, the glass lamp cast a glow over the framed photo below it. I picked it up. The photo was so old, the colors faded even though they rarely saw sunlight in this curtain-shielded room. Mom barely looked a day older than the day this photo had been taken. It couldn't have been more than weeks after our birth, judging by the two babies she held in her arms. I was on the left, white blond hair and pale as a ghost. Dorian was on the right, equally as pale but with a thick halo of chocolate-brown hair.

"Where was that photo taken?" Kendrick asked, seeing through my eyes. Although he didn't need to, he took the frame from my hands and studied it. The internal stone walls resembled the Armaya's castle decor. "Looks like you've visited the Armaya a few times before...well, you know."

"Before Caius made a meal out of me?" Flashes of that night struck my mind like electric probes. I slid a hand down my face, wishing Kendrick could compel the memories away permanently. But forgetting wasn't an option. I blinked hard and pushed off the desk. "But that's not at the Armaya. Mom's never been there."

"So where was this photo taken?" Kendrick shoved the frame back into my hands.

Dorian abandoned the cupboard and moved to stand beside me. In the photo our mom sat in her green armchair. It was the very same one she'd kept for all these years, which now stood out of place in the opulently decorated living room beyond the wall of this office. Behind her was a wall that was made up of a mixture of stone and horizontal set logs. There was an ice-crusted, glossy window, reflecting the pitch black of a night-darkened forest.

"That's at the cabin," Dorian said, face lifting as he shrugged. "Why?"

Kendrick arched his brows at me. "Do you still have that picture of Caius with you and Marcus as infants?"

I nodded, unable to sort through the clatter swirling through his mind. "It's in the jewelry box in my room."

In a blurred rush Kendrick disappeared from the office. A few seconds later he reappeared through the doorway. The black and white photo he held out to me was difficult to look at. Caius appeared much the same as he did now, except his hair was less salt and pepper and paler than it was these days. His face was a proud beam, the smile of a man who had taken this photo as a kind of trophy of the experiments he had succeeded in. Kind of like a serial killer keeping a lock of hair. It was a memento, a keepsake.

"Do you remember how I said this photo was taken at the Armaya?" Kendrick asked.

Fingers prodded over my brain. Somehow I understood that the sensation was the insertion of information rather than the retrieval of it. My eyes widened, darting up from the photo to my best friend. "You were wrong."

"Wrong about what?" Dorian stared at the photo as if trying to decipher a puzzle.

"Dorian," I said, pushing the photo back into Kendrick's hands. The longer I stared at it the sicker it made me feel. "This photo was taken at the same place as the one on Mom's desk."

"The cabin." A light behind Dorian's eyes went off, beaming like a torch. "Whatever Caius did to us all, was done there," he said, pointing at the photo of Caius.

"You know what this means?" Kendrick said.

Unfortunately I did. "The answers we need are linked to the cabin." Ice shards undulated up my spine, making me shiver. "We're going back to Alaska."

CHAPTER 4

I wriggled in the passenger seat of our rental car, feeling like I was sitting on a bed of spikes. This trip was taking forever. With Kendrick in the backseat and at least forty minutes to go, the tension had reached breaking point. Staring blankly at the increasing rush of snow that blanketed the forest bordering the winding road only did so much.

After three connecting flights and two days, we were on our way to the cabin. Dorian had volunteered to remain at home to keep an eye on our mom and monitor her calls, just in case Caius tried anything. He'd also stayed back to cover for Kendrick and me not being around for the hours she was at home and awake.

I sighed and Ty's hand broke from the steering wheel, his hungry eyes catching mine as he cupped my thigh. The heat of his firm hand traveled through the thick denim of my jeans. Without meaning to I imagined his palm sliding upwards and my face grew hot. Instant resentment squeezed my heart and I felt the undeniable urge to smash Ty in the face. "Dammit Kendrick!"

"What?" He tore his glare from the side view of Ty's face and clamped his arms over his chest.

We'd kept any previous tension throughout this long journey hidden between our bond, but the constant intrusion of his emotions was wearing thin. I twisted my neck to glower at him. "Can't you at least try to control yourself?"

"What's wrong?" Ty asked, patting my thigh.

The venom lancing from Kendrick to me shot faster, poisoning his words. "You think I'm enjoying this? You think I want to see the way he touches you? The way he looks at you?" He beat a hand against his chest as if trying to rid the pain that crippled his heart. "The way you respond to him?"

"You're a dick," Ty snapped. "Amelia hasn't done anything wrong. We haven't even kissed. And I've tried to be respectful, for her sake, not yours. But you're being a total jerk. She picked me. Not you."

"Yeah, and that's gonna last," Kendrick muttered, his tone dripping with arrogance. "Your life is a blip compared to our extended life spans. Who do you think will still be there once you're dead and gone?"

Kendrick's last words hit a nerve, flooding my body with frustration. They reminded me too much of Caius's words back at the Armaya—that Ty would die before I'd even lived out a tenth of my life. "Shut up!" I spun in my seat to smack Kendrick in the face. The shock rather than the force of the hit made him rock back. "You," I said pointing a thin finger at him. "Don't get to speak anymore."

"But," Kendrick said, about to apologize. He felt bad for what he'd said, even if the words did hold mountains of truth. The last thing he wanted to do was cause me pain in any way.

"No." I blew out an exacerbated breath, holding tight to a sliver of frustration. "I don't want to hear it."

Ty removed his hand. "Amelia, I didn't mean to start anything."

"I don't want to talk about it," I said. Part of the anger I felt was reserved for Ty. When he touched or kissed me, I knew that apart from it being a way to show me how he felt, how much he wanted me even with my link to Kendrick, that it was also a way to show Kendrick that he had won. That he had me, and Kendrick didn't. "Not now."

My head lolled back against the headrest, eyes blinking away the rush of white covered green outside my window. Without sight I plugged in my iPod's earbuds and pressed play. The piano intro to Write This Down's song *Citadel* calmed my anger and ignited my need to not give up. Love and life were a war, and I wasn't going down without a fight.

I turned everything inward, focusing on the brick wall I needed to block Kendrick's thoughts. Right now they were guilt-riddled and weighing against my heart, like a smothering blanket that made my lungs tight and my head heavy. And I couldn't stand it. One by one I imagined my thin hands placing bricks in a line then stacking one row after the next. It was a tediously slow and exhausting process. Behind the wall was a translucent image of Kendrick's face, his expression speaking of the regret he felt. As the wall grew higher and the view of his face became blocked by bricks, the weight of his emotions eased. With the last brick of this enormous wall that towered over my mind, the last sliver of his emotions shut off.

The weightlessness that rolled down my entire body was calming, letting my exhaustion become the only thing I felt. My own exhaustion, not someone else's, and my own thoughts, free from his.

Without opening my eyelids, my hand lifted from my lap, reaching across the center console to find Ty's warm forearm. I let my fingers slide along his arm, basking in the feel of his scarred skin which clung tightly to the muscles that ran down to his wrist.

Ty's hand opened as my fingers slid over his palm. There was a little intake of breath at my touch, before my fingers threaded through his. My lips lifted at the sides. "Wake me when we get there."

Despite the thoughts spinning through my mind, the exhaustion of our complicated threesome was enough to knock me out. As the conflict of their argument washed away, I found myself in a place I hadn't seen for years.

Dorian and I sat on the single bed upstairs in his room, playing a fast-paced game of Uno. His face was rounder than it was now, blue eyes large and filled with childhood innocence. Wooden logs made up the walls along with a number of rocks. A single six paned window bordered a snowy landscape of pine trees. Each tree's branches hung heavy with a collection of white dust.

A young pale girl's reflection stared back at me, matching blue irises to my brother's, but with white-blond hair. I blinked and so did the girl. *She's me*, I realized, *a younger version*. No more than six years old.

I'd seen photos of Dorian and me during our younger years, but those memories, the early years we had spent at the cabin before moving to Anchorage, had always seemed a fog. Most of the time it was a few snippets here and there, but nothing concrete, nothing as clear as what I could see now. I wondered if Kendrick's compulsion to remember at Marcus's command was clearing out more than what Caius had covered up at the Armaya.

I lifted a small child-sized hand to my cheek. As I did, something traveled across the soft snow below. It was a man, a man who was familiar, but different. His hair was lighter than it was now, more light brown with natural blond highlights than its current salt and pepper. His face was less wrinkled too, though he still appeared old. Caius.

I wanted to suck in my breath, but I wasn't really there. The little girl who had been me was. And Caius wasn't alone.

His hand was curled around the back of another man's neck, forcing him to stumble forward through the sinking snow. The man was very pale, sickly looking. Thick chains connected his wrists and ankles, like an inmate on death row. Except these chains weren't dark and dirty, they were shiny and silver in color. Blistering welts were left across the man's flesh where the metal touched. He stumbled when Caius pushed him harder, a gleaming dagger jabbing the guy in the back. He hissed as red wetness blotted the back of his dirty and torn shirt.

A little squeal escaped my throat and Caius's silver-gray eyes shot up. Fear rocketed through me and I sprang, flattening Dorian against the bed.

"Hey, what are you doing?" Dorian demanded in a boy's voice. He pushed himself free and sat up.

I scrambled to the window and peered out. "Didn't you see?" My own childlike voice surprised me.

Caius forced the man up the steps and through the front door. Then the heavy steps stalled.

"Oh dear, what happened?" Mom's startled voice drifted through the floorboards.

There were more steps then Caius spoke. "You saw nothing, and you will hear nothing. Go to bed, Lamayli."

As my mom's shuffled steps moved away, I heard something shift, sliding. More footsteps sounded as the shifting repeated. The noise I heard next lasted a second, before being cut off with a thud. Hair rose across the back of my neck and my small forearms prickled. It was the sound of cries and chains being rattled, of snarls and the threats of desperation.

"What's going on, sis?" Dorian peered out the window and down at the disturbed snow that was swiftly being covered by a thicker fall of snowflakes.

"Unky Caius had a man," I said, voice so young and terrified. "He had chains on him."

"It's not Halloween," Dorian said.

Before I could speak, I heard the sliding again, followed by the distinct tone of booted steps climbing the wooden stairs.

The door to Dorian's room swung open and Caius strode in. He took hold of Dorian who cried out at how tight Caius gripped his shoulders. Caius stared into my brother's eyes. "You saw and heard nothing."

Protectiveness surged through me, and my small child's body lunged at Caius. I landed on his arm and tugged with all my might. "Stop, Unky Caius. You're hurting him!"

Uncle Caius dropped Dorian and threw me off. I flew, hitting the toy box across the room with a cry of pain. I stumbled to get up, terrified eyes wide. But I was too slow. Caius was already before me, strong hands curled around my upper arms and lifting me from the ground.

Dorian stood still as a statue behind him, his face an empty mask.

I struggled, knowing I needed to get us away, then whimpered. Caius squeezed harder, shaking me until my eyes met his. "Amelia, stop moving. I do not want to hurt you."

Out of my own volition, my child-sized body ceased struggling.

Uncle Caius lowered my bare feet to the ground and touched my cheek. It stung for a moment and his hand came away with a smear of scarlet. He frowned. "I am so very sorry, my dear. I never meant to…" He broke off and shook his head before staring into my wide eyes. "You have been up here all night playing with your brother. You even tripped while running up the stairs and cut your cheek. But it is only a small cut. There is no pain. You will forget ever seeing me and that other man outside, and any noises you may have heard. Amelia, I wish it did not have to be this way. But it does. Please know that I love you."

"Get the fuck off me!" I gasped, shocked by my suddenly normal and un-childlike voice and language. My eyelids fluttered, the cabin room warping into moving white-laced plains behind a red lens.

"Whoa, what's going on?" Ty stared at me curiously from the driver's seat. "What's wrong?"

Kendrick sat forward to see me through the center console. "She had a vision, genius."

Ty ignored Kendrick and went to grab my hand. My knees shot up and I shrunk back against the car door. There was way too little space in this car. Blood dominated the air. Ty's and Kendrick's. The thrumming of both their pulses pounded in my ears. "Don't." I batted Ty's hand away as my fangs shot free. "Stop the car."

"Why?" Ty saw my fangs but didn't even flinch. "Amelia, what's going on?"

"She's starving." Kendrick scooted back to untie the knot on his backpack. "It's a vision thing. The reactions are getting worse."

Ty glanced away from the straightening road and held out his hand, wrist up. "Take my blood."

Kendrick snorted and I cringed, blurry vision darting to see that Ty's driving had slowed. Jumping out of the car wouldn't cause much damage at this speed.

I groped for the door handle, but before I could escape, the smell of peppery blood invaded my nose. Unable to think, I snatched the source and pressed my lips to its cool round edge. About half way through I realized I was draining a bottle. Right in front of Ty. I hunched away, increasingly aware of Kendrick's and Ty's voices.

"She still could have drunk from me." Ty yanked on the steering wheel, rounding a bend sharper than necessary.

Kendrick snorted a laugh. "Yeah, if you're into beating down your own girlfriend."

Ty punched the clutch and shifted gears. "What's that supposed to mean?"

"That she wouldn't have been able to stop." There was a clank from the backseat as the red left my vision and my voice started to return. "And I sure as shit wouldn't have stepped in to save your pretty-boy ass."

"Stop it," I croaked, blinking away the last of the red. "Please don't fight. Not about this."

Ty smiled at me but kept his hands to himself. "You're alright now?"

I nodded, wondering if he was worried about my still extended fangs or if he was trying to keep the peace.

My brain tingled and Kendrick eased back into his seat. "Wanna tell him what you saw?"

After reliving my vision through the bond, Kendrick knew what I'd seen. I sighed, glancing away from the thickening fog and snow-fall through the windshield to look at Ty. "Caius imprisoned vampires at the cabin." I shuddered, hearing even now their cries and the rattling chains. "He was experimenting on them too."

"Shit!" Ty slammed on the brakes and flung his arm across my chest as the car screeched to a skidding halt. Snow fell even harder than a minute ago, the wipers flinging back and forth at full speed.

I squinted through the shield of white. Something was blocking the car. It was wide enough and long enough to cut off the entire one lane road. "Is that a tree?"

I lifted my hood as we all exited the car. The air was chilling, the thick forestry bordering the narrow winding road showing no evidence of its lush foliage. Instead it was a frosted white expanse that was deathly quiet.

Kendrick made his way to the roadside and jumped onto the base end of the fallen mammoth-sized tree. Then he faced us with a look I couldn't quite read. Still the reason behind the look wasn't a mystery.

"The tree was cut?" I strode forward to see for myself.

Ty was right behind me, head poking over my shoulder to catch a glimpse. "That was done with a chainsaw."

"Loggers?" Kendrick questioned, surprisingly without an ounce of condescension as he looked to Ty.

Ty frowned past the felled tree, running a hand over its rough bark. "Loggers would never leave a road blocked like this. And don't they usually mark the trees they take down?"

"Trees?" I followed Ty's line of sight past the log Kendrick stood on to the road ahead. Through the thick fall of white was an obstacle course of felled tree after felled tree, disappearing only with the bend in the road. "That's not loggers."

Dread pooled in my stomach, making my ears open while my eyes darted. The road we were on was familiar enough for me to know that it was the last stretch before the cabin. No other properties came off this road and hadn't done so for the last twenty or so miles. This road never saw unexpected traffic.

My fingers curled, toying with the amethyst pendant at my wrist. It was cool to the touch without even a hint of warmth to indicate encroaching danger. "Whoever did this is gone now. But they did it on purpose."

"To keep us from the cabin," Kendrick finished for me, jumping off the log.

"But no one knew we were coming," Ty said. "Only us three knew, and Dorian."

Except that wasn't exactly true, and Kendrick knew it now too. While he and Ty were picking up the rental car back at the airport, I'd called Marcus and mentioned our location when checking on Caius's whereabouts.

"You told Marcus," Kendrick said, a hint of accusation in his tone.

"So what?" I zipped up my hoodie, feeling a chill that had nothing to do with how freezing it was. Had someone intercepted our arrival? Were they still there somewhere, watching, waiting? "You know Caius can't compel Marcus..." I broke off, feeling Kendrick's speculation. "You have gotta be kidding."

"What's going on?" Ty questioned.

Kendrick leaned back against the fallen log, face hardening. "I'm not kidding, Amelia. And you shouldn't be so trusting. He knew Caius planned to kill you, and instead of stopping him, he let it happen. Let that sorry excuse for an uncle drain your blood until you died."

"Hold on," Ty said, eyes shifting to me. "You said Marcus had no choice, that he did what he needed to do to save you."

"He did," I said. "Marcus's plan to resurrect me could only work if Caius's attempt on my life stayed on track. He needed to know when Caius would come for me."

"That doesn't make sense." Ty ran a hand over his face. His irises had become gold and intense, no longer set on me but staring at the car's snow-dotted headlights. "If you'd been warned and had fled that place, resurrecting you wouldn't have been necessary. And I'm sorry, Kendrick," he said glancing up at him, "but if not for her death, Amelia wouldn't be connected to you, or anyone."

Except you, I thought, guessing the words he didn't say. Because if I hadn't been bound to Kendrick, the new conflict of our love triangle wouldn't exist in such an imposing and unavoidable state.

"Ty, you don't get it. Believe me, I can see your point of view, but it's wrong. What Marcus did brought me back to life. If everything had gone according to his rescue plan I would have been..." My words died and I clenched my fists to stop my hands from flying to my mouth.

"You would have been what?" Ty moved forward to tilt my face up, forcing me to look at him. "Amelia, what haven't you told me?"

I bit my lip, dreading what I was about to say. Kendrick spoke before I could muster the nerve to blurt out the words. "Amelia would have been bound to Marcus, forever."

Ty's irises flared and he jumped over the log to stalk up the beaten road.

"Ty, please." I caught up and tried to catch his wrist, but he crossed his arms and picked up the pace.

Kendrick collected his backpack from the rental car and followed at a distance.

I cleared another fallen tree, hand levering against the rough bark to keep pace with Ty. "Look, I'm sorry. I didn't think it mattered. I mean, it didn't happen. I'm not bound to Marcus."

Ty's stalking steps stalled and he spun, his breath fuming. "You think that's what I'm mad about?" His expression was incredulous. "Whether it's Kendrick or some other guy, it doesn't matter. That fact that you're so..." his jaw clenched, "*trusting*, is what scares me. You knew this guy for a few weeks. That's it. And you believe every word he says. What if he's in league with Caius?" He strode forward, catching my wrist with tight fingers. "What if everything you've been relaying to him has been passed straight on?"

I snatched my wrist free. It felt like my insides were being tugged in opposite directions and were beginning to tear. "Marcus wouldn't do that."

Overhead, the sky darkened as the sun dipped behind treetops.

The snow began to pelt down like heavy rain while a gusty wind built. The swift weather change was unnatural, as if it were a sudden extension of my torment. I gritted my teeth and a flash of light struck overhead. I wanted to scream that I knew Marcus would never betray me. Because of the connection I felt to him and him for me, I knew that he would never endanger my life.

I wouldn't do that, Kendrick's voice warned through the bond. Now that we weren't walking he was gaining on us. *He already feels like he's sharing you. And it sucks. Believe me, I know. Learning that you feel connected to another guy is only going to make him feel even more like shit.*

Ty caught my hand, drawing it up to the wild flutter of his heart. "Amelia, this is your life we're talking about here. And I can't lose you." He glanced to Kendrick, almost nodding approval. "We know who we can trust in our group, and Marcus isn't part of our group." His mouth opened but nothing came out, his nostrils flaring, testing the air. "Do you smell that?"

I could smell it now too, the dense smell of a raging fire that had recently been doused. "Smoke." Above the tree line I could make out a spiraling column rising into a thickening cloud of menace. "It's coming from the cabin!"

CHAPTER 5

endrick shot past us, feet pounding up the beaten road, and Ty and I took after him. With our supernatural speed we blazed over the remaining miles toward the cabin, clearing each dropped tree while minding the snow-hidden potholes. The smoke intensified as we neared, growing dense and adding to the fog as the snowfall eased.

After painfully long minutes the narrowing road ended, opening onto a small area bordered by a thick circle of pine trees. Delicate gray confetti sprinkled down around us, looking like dirty snow. I sucked in a breath and spluttered. Smoke joined the ash here, making it impossible to breathe or see clearly.

I pushed forward, arms waving to clear some air…and froze.

Centering the circle of pines was an uneven patch of charred and still smoking remains. A corner beam to the front and back left were still standing, along with a crumbled fireplace in the center. For a long moment I just stared, not wanting to believe what I could see. But the evidence was as clear as the lifting smoke. The skeletal remains before me were all that was left of the cabin. Someone had burned it to the ground.

Kendrick met my side and touched the cool amethyst pendant at my wrist. "Whoever did this is long gone."

"I'm not taking any chances," Ty said, then took off past the barricading pines.

Not really listening or taking notice, I fell to my knees. "It's all gone."

Everything was charred black, nothing surviving the inferno. There was no second level. No window to see down to the wooden porch from Dorian's childhood room. No stairs that Caius's booted feet had climbed to erase his actions. There were no standing walls, just stone remnants leading up to the remaining corner posts. Bar the fireplace, which only resembled its former cavernous glory because of the small boulders that made up its structure, there was nothing else. Nothing that even closely resembled the home I'd been born in and had trouble remembering from our first six years of life.

I rushed forward and Kendrick called out for me to stop. I spun past his extending arm to land in the center of the ruins. Charcoal dust puffed up from my Vans, making me want to cough. I screamed instead, throwing myself against the fireplace and belting my fists against the stones. Each hit sent throbbing waves through my knuckles and up my arms. I felt the stinging of the cuts first, and then the wetness of blood as it left spattered marks against the rocks. I went to hit harder, needing to let the rage in me out. It wasn't just about this, another dead end in our quest for why, but everything before and since our return.

As my fist drove forward with enough force to crack bone, Ty's hand shot out to wrench me back. Kendrick caught me around the waist, hauling me back too.

The rational part of my brain knew they were helping, but I

didn't care. Holding onto my rage, I tried to pull free. When that didn't work, I kicked out, my feet hitting the fireplace one last time.

Rumbling rose all around us as the rocks began to fall. The ground below quaked violently, as if earthquake tremors were ringing out. The capturing hands holding me back let go. Caught off balance I fell to the ground. Between the crumbling rocks and the creak of charred wood, I heard a splintering crack. Complete quiet followed for an eerie second.

Then the ground beneath me opened up like the jaws of hell.

"AMELIA!" Ty shouted above me somewhere, his voice muffled by debris being ripped away. "Amelia, can you hear me?"

"I'm—" I gasped in a breath and felt weight push back against my chest, crushing my lungs. Everything was dark and the air tasted of charcoal. My lids fluttered through the dust, and I felt grains across my eyeballs. There were more shouts from Ty and Kendrick. My lips parted to call out but choked closed as sharp pain struck my chest.

"Screw this," I heard Kendrick say. "I'm going down."

Creaking vibrated around me, the debris threating to release as more than one person descended into this dark cavern. There was a sharp crack, and I followed the sound. In the darkness, I saw Ty had half fallen through the staircase's decrepit remains. Ty grunted, but couldn't lift himself from the small landing he'd fallen through.

Kendrick stepped before him and held out a hand. "Here."

Even in the lack of light Ty's grimace was clear as he swung a hand up to clasp Kendrick's. "Don't think this means I owe you," Ty grunted as his body came free.

The aroma of his blood bloomed on the thick air. A second later I knew why. The jagged wooden planks he'd fallen through had rent a long gash in his side.

"Ouch," Kendrick said. His mouth watered and he almost ran down the rickety stairs. "Bloody werewolf."

For a moment I laughed. Kendrick was drawn to Ty's blood too. Not as bad as I was, but with how much he detested him, it was still funny. The silent vibration of my laughter caused me to cough. Fresh bolts of pain tracked outward from my chest.

"Amelia?" Ty called out again, but it was Kendrick who reached my side first, feeling his way through our bond to the heap of debris I was prisoned beneath.

"Found her!" Kendrick began tearing the concealing layer off me. A split second later Ty was there, his hands helping to make light work of the debris. With each piece removed, the weight against my entire body lessened. Still the pressure against my chest didn't fade.

When my body was free Kendrick frowned at me. "Are you okay?"

I reached for my chest and gasped. A splintered plank of wood protruded from my ribs, poking up and underneath them. "I—" I coughed and winced at the lance of fresh pain.

"The wood's pierced your lung," Ty said, kneeling at my other side. "We need to get it out so you can heal."

I nodded through the pain as Ty leaned over me. My free hand found Kendrick's. "Squeeze as hard as you want. Break a bone or two if you need."

Ty watched me as I glanced back to him, his face a stiff mask. I bit my lip and nodded, as if to say, *I'm ready.*

Ty wrapped his broad hands around the thick splinter of wood as it rose and fell with my uneven breaths. Then he yanked it free. Crimson spurted from the gaping hole, spraying out to splatter across Ty's T-shirt. His hands came down to press against the opening.

I gasped at the jagged bolts striking through my chest and pinned my lids shut. Red and white flashes danced across the backs of my eyelids as my vision rolled, my head becoming light. I was about to faint.

Willing against the sensation, I focused on the smells of my own blood mixed with Ty's in the air, fighting my way back to consciousness. My gums prickled and my mouth became as dry as hot sand. Then there was nothing but the smell of *his* blood.

And I was starving.

Without thought my body took over, needing blood to repair itself. The desperation was similar to waking after Caius had drained me at the Armaya. But this time I knew what I was doing, and what I was about to do. Still, I didn't care. Instinct had taken over.

I flung Kendrick's hand away and sprung, blindly knocking Ty down and trapping his warm body with my hands. My fangs closed in on their destination, but they never met flesh. Kendrick took hold of me and hauled me off Ty. His arms were like bars around my body, and with my unhealed injuries and inability to breathe properly, he had the upper hand.

"Amelia, stop it," Kendrick rasped in my ear, fighting to contain me. His next words were only for me to hear. *Do you want him to see you like this?*

Before me, Ty had gotten to his feet and was taking slow steps toward us. His expression wasn't horrified, as I guess I'd expected it to be. Instead it was surprised, and maybe a little disappointed. "It's okay." He wasn't looking at me but at Kendrick. "If she needs my blood to heal…"

"Are you kidding?" Anger flared from Kendrick through the bond. "She just…and you?" He shook his head and glanced up to the edge of the cavernous hole we stood in. "Never mind. There's another full bottle in my backpack. It's up there. Go get it."

Given his condescending and demanding tone, I expected Ty to argue, but he didn't. "Sure. Whatever." He shrugged then leaped, clearing the debris and landing on the opening's edge. In seconds he maneuvered his way back through the obstacle-filled descent and held out the full bottle, an unreadable expression blanketing his face.

Kendrick released me and took the bottle, thrusting it into my hands. "Drink it."

I took the bottle and turned my back. I didn't think Ty seeing me drink blood like this would turn him off, but after attacking him I just felt too exposed. With a few pain-filled gulps, the glass bottle was empty, the hunger sated. The sharp lancing of my breaths began to ease. The flesh below my ribs and that of my own lung rushed back together in a thatch-work that stretched and bound. I gasped at the sensation, able to breathe again. All my wounds had healed.

I ran my tongue over my teeth, still able to taste the blood. It was peppery and somehow familiar. Suspicion dawned on me. "What kind of blood was that?"

Kendrick crossed his arms over his chest and shifted his weight from one leg to the other. "I brought it as backup. I never thought you'd need it."

Ty looked from me to Kendrick in confusion. "What's going on?" he asked. "What's the problem?"

I invaded Kendrick's thoughts to find the answer. My jaw clenched and I hissed through gritted teeth. "Say it."

Kendrick stared at me, half apologetic and half irritated. "It's mine."

"You ulterior motive dick." Ty grabbed a fistful of Kendrick's shirt. His free hand was tense at his side, trembling as canine-like nails grew from his fingers. "It's not enough that you're in her head every second of every day, you have to trick her too?"

"It wasn't a trick." Kendrick tore Ty's fist from his shirt and pushed him back. "She needed to be healed, and we already know what my blood can do for her."

I wanted to step in and put an end to this, but I was pissed too. Kendrick deserved the backlash, and Ty was giving enough steam for the both of us. Besides, I was so over the complication of our threesome that I just wanted to ignore the issue. "No punches. No drawing blood."

With a hard look at them both I strode away, focusing past their continued arguing and at the cavernous space we stood in. Most of the room was charred from the fire. Still there were remnants of what had been here before. Shackles lined the sooty walls, much like the ones that had entrapped me at the Armaya. A shudder ran through me and I picked up the closest one, studying it. There was an engraved marking, a symbol that was crossed through with a single line. An alchemist mark.

"You just couldn't stand to see her drinking from me."

Ty's venomous words drew my attention. He kicked debris from his hunting boots, clearing a path between him and Kendrick. Through the dust settling at Ty's feet, I saw something that wasn't entirely blackened with the charcoal dust left from the fire. Something had semi-survived the flames.

"And you know this wouldn't have been the first time," Ty added. "She's tasted me before, and it wasn't because she was dying."

Kendrick let out a scream and ran at Ty. I leaped between the two, strength renewed by Kendrick's blood as I shoved a hand at either guy's chest. The connection was so strong they flew backward, hitting opposing walls before falling into a puff of ash.

"Whoops." I almost felt bad, except I knew the force hadn't really hurt either of them. Still, I retained a crisp edge to my voice. "Enough with the pissing match."

Kendrick and Ty got up, glaring past me at each other. They moved closer but it was clear the threat of physical violence was over.

"Tick magnet," Kendrick sneered.

"Third wheel," Ty rebutted.

"Seriously?" I demanded. "Name calling? I think I liked it better when you were silently loathing each other. At least I didn't have to deal with *this*." Ty's jaw parted as if he were about to speak, and I could already feel an apology brewing through the bond from Kendrick. "No. I don't want to hear it. And we've got better things to do than kill each other."

I bent to grab the thing I'd seen at Ty's feet, a book. The front cover was missing and many of the pages had been burned away. The back cover was leather that was split in various places from age, and the binding was cracked and separating. It looked and felt incredibly old. Of the remaining thick and discolored pages a handful were left marginally singed. Patches of handwriting had survived, but were messy, making it difficult to read in the darkness.

"This should help," Kendrick muttered. A light beam flared over my shoulder, coming from his boarding cased iPhone.

We all studied the page. Scrawling calligraphy written with the inked tip of a quill stood out in the sudden light. Most of it seemed to be notes of experimental procedures, exposing subjects to UV light, silver, and other various substances. It went into detail on the rate at which each subject deteriorated in physical appearance. In the case of silver powder applied to the skin, it detailed how long subjects lived before either regenerating or dying from blood poisoning.

I panned around the room, imagining vampires trapped by chains and screaming out as their flesh was eaten away. I swallowed bloody acid, remembering the desperate cries I'd dreamed as Caius forced another prisoner down into his secret death chamber.

Kendrick flicked ahead, nearing the book's center. My eyes widened.

- *Test subject 1/Day 7 – Any physical signs of vampirism are still undetectable. The infection of solution 1 seems to have a continued nullifying effect. Any need for blood, human or otherwise, is still controlled. Preparing the blood through exposure to UV rays prior to infection seems to have achieved optimal results, with the subject still displaying no signs of discomfort when exposed to direct sunlight.*
- *Test subject 3/Day 7 – Infection minutes after birth seems to have influenced the solution's effectiveness. Although signs of bloodthirst and fangs seem dormant, the infant screams when exposed to direct sunlight, though is not physically burned.*

There was a space between subjects *one* and *three* that was too burned to make out, but something about what I could see captured my attention. "Caius wrote this," I said, certain beyond a doubt.

After that followed a stack or charred pages, too singed by fire to be legible. I flicked ahead finding more of the same, until I hit the back cover. A glossary was printed on the inside in the same inked handwriting. The writing confirmed my fears that Dorian and I were subjects one and three. Marcus was subject two. Capital letters were jotted next to each of our names. *IBB* was next to Marcus's and mine. I wondered if that somehow explained the connection I felt toward him, but I kept my mouth shut. With Ty standing over my shoulder, bringing Marcus up after what he'd learned would just be stupid. Next to Dorian's name was *IAB*. Following that were two sentences.

- *Solution 1 – Combination of ingredient X and silver nitrate, exposed to ultraviolet light then mixed with Pure Blood.*
- *Solution 2 – Combination of Pure Blood boiled with silver nitrate then mixed with ingredient X2.*

"This is rubbish." I sighed. "It's the same as the vial substance report. It still doesn't tell us what the third ingredient is."

"What vial substance?" Ty asked, snatching the book from me. "And how can Marcus be a test subject?"

Fan-freaking-tastic. Not only had I not mentioned the report to Ty, but I'd also kept my suspicion of Marcus being an experiment subject from him too. "Uh, yeah. Marcus gave me the empty vial that Caius used to drug me before we fled the Armaya. There was a card for an analyst to test the residue. Plus I found a photo," I kind of lied, knowing Marcus had given me the photo with the manila folder. "An experimental memento of Caius with Marcus and me as infants."

"Why didn't you tell me?" Ty dropped the book, looking wounded.

"Ty, I'm sorry." I reached out to take his hand. He took a step back, avoiding my touch. I instantly felt cold. "It wasn't intentional. There's just been so much going on."

Ignoring the rising tension, Kendrick cut in. "You didn't tell her about Vanessa, so get over it. Now back to this." He picked up the book from between two planks of charred wood. "The ingredients were the same, Pure Blood and silver nitrate with one unidentifiable substance. Though," he said sounding more hopeful, "the way they were combined is new."

"Yeah," I said, trying to focus on this rather than Ty. Right now he was staring into space, totally closed off. "But we have no idea who was infected with what, or when, or even what the extent of the infection is. This gives us nothing to go on."

"Almost nothing..." Kendrick opened the back cover and pointed to the bottom right-hand corner. There in small inked handwriting different to the experimental notes was *property of E.B. 1604.*

"The book belonged to someone before your uncle," Ty said, the hurt from his expression dissolving.

I gulped, knowing that what I was about to say matched Kendrick's own suspicions. "Caius was continuing someone else's experiments."

CHAPTER 6

An exhaust rumbled as Ty's WRX rolled up the driveway. My heart rate spiked. It was the following day after back-to-back flights home. Now Ty was here for my mom's mandatory dinner. Chomping into a fifth piece of chocolate from my bedside table, I tugged on a fresh tank top and jeans and shot downstairs, flinging open the front door.

Ty froze then smiled, finger retracting from the doorbell. "I didn't even hear you." Even in my casual clothes his eyes drank me in.

I smiled back and couldn't help checking him out too. Ty looked the perfect gentleman, in black cotton pants and a pinstriped black shirt with the top two buttons undone. The setting sun and purple-glazed horizon in the background added to the view, making his tan skin bronze. My pulse thrummed and I glanced at his lips, so badly wanting to kiss him. Now wasn't the time. Instead, I wrapped my arms around his muscular neck and breathed him in. My mouth watered. "You smell amazing."

Though it had been just over an hour since Ty dropped us home from the airport, he said, "It's good to see you, too."

"Oh good, you're here." Mom's sudden presence and sharp voice sent a spasm through my bones.

Trying to keep the irritation from my face, I released Ty and took his hand before turning back to my mom.

Ty bowed, casting a fisted hand over his chest. "Good evening, Ms. Lamont. Thank you for the invitation tonight."

Mom stood so still she almost resembled an angelic statue, her long dress stunning but face frozen with guarded curiousness. Her icy stare traveled up and down Ty. This was the first time she'd seen him since finding out the truth. Now it was like the veil of his true identity had been lifted and she was trying to figure him out, picking up on the subtle differences that had been there all along. "Well, it's arctic out here. Please, come inside." She spun and glided back through the house, leaving us to follow after.

Inside the dining room, Dorian and Kendrick were already seated. Dorian seemed his regular, carefree self, while the tension coming off Kendrick poisoned the air.

Dorian smiled. "Hey, Malau."

Kendrick made eye contact, not bothering to cloak his true feelings. "Ty."

At least he didn't call him fleabag.

Mom stood at the head of the hardwood table that matched the hutch and tall wine rack along the back wall. "Take your seats. Dorian, will you assist me with dinner?"

Mom disappeared from the room with Dorian bounding after her. Moments later Dorian reappeared with four full plates, expertly balancing two on each arm. The smell of colorful food hit me, making my stomach grumble as steam rose from the delicate china. I knew what Mom had prepared, her favorite dish; orange-stuffed turkey served with orange-glazed garden vegetables. Instant relief washed over me. For some reason, even though it would be crazy, I had kinda expected her to serve blood soup, or a leg straight off a deer. Though I'm sure Ty wouldn't have minded the second option.

Mom glided through the doorway then and my relief vanished. She carried her own full plate and a decanter brimming with chilled blood. So that was her plan. Turn Ty off me by blatantly displaying our differences.

"Mom, come on," I said. Evening meals in our home were served with blood, but we never drank it around anyone other than vampire. "You're just doing this to—"

"To show Ty exactly whom he's involved with," she interrupted. She set her plate at the head of the table and filled her wine glass.

Ty cleared his throat, his hand squeezing my knee under the table. "It's fine Ms. Lamont. I don't have a problem with any of you drinking blood. It's part of being a vampire."

Mom's gaze narrowed for the briefest moment at Ty. Then she raised the crystal glass to take in the blood's aroma. "How under-standing of you." She lowered the glass to her mouth to take a sip, and then licked her red-tinted lips clean. "Ah, AB. My favorite." She looked pointedly to Ty. "Pre-packaged, of course. Although nothing beats fresh from the source. What type are you?"

Ty didn't even flinch. "Well, if you must know, I'm—"

"Don't answer that." I glared at my mom. Her question had momentarily shocked me into silence. Now I couldn't believe how out of line she was. "Mom, seriously? Cheap tricks?"

"Yeah, Mom," Dorian spoke up. "Even I know you're fighting a losing battle."

She waved us off. "I am simply trying to get to know the *boy* you refuse to abstain from, Amelia." Her tone was condescending and dismissive. "If he *is* going to be part of your life, and subsequently ours, then he needs to know how we live."

"Can't argue logic," Kendrick nodded at my mom.

Ty's heated hand slid from my thigh to take my hand. I peered up to see him looking past me at my mom. "Ms. Lamont, I want you to know that I am devoted to your daughter in every way. I accept all the things that mark her as a vampire. When it comes to Amelia, there has never been any question in my mind about who she is or how I feel about her."

Butterfly wings batted through my heart at Ty's heartfelt words, while Kendrick's mood became stormy. He already knew how I felt about Ty, but hearing how deep Ty's feelings ran for me was hurting him. After Mom's actions, even though he'd known it was unlikely, he'd hoped Ty's feelings for me would turn. The opposite occurring only showed him how much Ty truly cared.

Mom pursed her lips. "So I see." She motioned to the decanter. "Would you do the honors then, Ty?"

Ty stood and grasped the decanter without pause and proceeded to fill our glasses. To show Mom how true Ty's words were, I picked up my glass and sipped.

Dorian pulled a bottle of red from the wine rack behind him and held it out to Ty. "Red wine?"

Ty shook his head. "No, thank you. The blood is fine."

Scarlet spurted from my mouth, spraying across my plate and food. Around the table Kendrick's eyes narrowed at Ty, Dorian stood frozen with the bottle of red in his hand, and Mom stared with wide eyes.

"Ty, you don't..." I began.

Ty filled his own glass and sat back down. "Amelia may not have yet mentioned it," he said, glancing at my mom. "But I'm a hybrid. Mostly lycan, but there's still a bit of vamp in me. I don't require blood like a full vampire. That's been bred out. Still, I do enjoy the taste of a good chilled AB."

Mom sat frozen for a few long moments while Ty's words webbed into my mind. His confession had shocked me too, and worry at Mom's reaction had my hands shaking. Of course I'd known he was a hybrid, part lycan and part vampire. The one time we'd spoken about it was when I'd recalled the horrific tale of the vampire heir who fell for a werewolf. Ty's grandmother was that werewolf. That union had caused the wolves to rebel, abandoning their roles as guardians and slaves when the heir had been burned alive with the pregnant werewolf to be executed next. The battle saw Ty's grandmother escaping intact.

I thought back to my dreamscape with Ty. He'd said he didn't need blood to survive. He'd never said he still drank, or even enjoyed the taste of human blood.

"Have you tasted my daughter's blood?" Mom asked suddenly.

Before I got the chance to answer, Kendrick's strained but sure voice rang out. "No! Of course he hasn't." The thought alone made him feel like barfing.

Ty spoke up. "No, I have not, Ms. Lamont. And I understand your concern. I want to assure you that I would never bite Amelia. Being a hybrid, my bite isn't fatal unless I've transformed, or have my canines extended." He opened his mouth, lifting his upper lip. Small and sharp vampire teeth grew from his flat human ones. Then his irises rippled gold and a separate, larger set of canines slid free, not from existing teeth, but straight from his gums. Both sets retracted and Ty released his lifted lip. "As you can see, I control both sets. Still, I would never take the chance of hurting Amelia."

With the infinite silence that followed, our immaculate dinners were going cold. Finally Mom drew back her shoulders and took a deep breath. "I—this is a lot to digest. I do appreciate your honesty,

Ty. Though I am sure you can understand that I am still concerned." She clasped her hands together on the table. "So I want to be as clear as possible. Hybrid or not, The Council will not accept your relationship. But apart from my position, that is a world I'd prefer my children not become involved with. So as long as that remains the case, and there is no suspicion on their part, I won't send Amelia away."

"Wow," I couldn't help saying. "Mom, thank you."

"I am not done." Her steely gaze turned on Ty. "Amelia knows my restrictions and she can relay. But this one I want you to hear from me. Under no circumstance are you to transform with my daughter present. No exceptions. And you are never to taste her blood, canines absent or not. If I find out even one of my conditions have been ignored, you will never see her again."

Ty stood and fisted a hand over his chest. "I swear on my blood that I will never endanger your daughter. If there was ever a choice, I would risk my life to keep her safe."

LATER THAT EVENING I ventured down to the beach with Dorian and Kendrick. With my mom accepting our relationship for now, Ty thought it was time to bridge the gap between his pack and us. Even with his confidence, I was full of nerves. The wolves hated us, and his pack was born and raised to kill our kind.

I gulped as we trekked along the sandy path to the beach. Dorian jogged ahead, not concerned in the slightest. Kendrick remained close, feeling as uneasy as I was. Past the railed path, the glow of a roaring bonfire added light to the night, its crackling and spitting almost extinguished the shore-kissing waves. Dorian had already met the group, waving hellos before squatting beside Vanessa on a thick broken log.

Ty stood as we made our way across the cold sand. He wore casual pants and a Skillet shirt matching the tunes coming from the small boom box beside him. One hand was bent behind his back, and the grin on his face was infectious.

What was he up to?

Kendrick, who had been eyeing the group with a look that could crack a mirror, glanced at me. "Fire *and* wolves? This should be fun."

"It'll be fine," I reassured. "They won't try anything with Ty here."

"We'll see."

I waved as we met the group.

"Hi, Amelia, Kendrick." Vanessa smiled, the picture of perfection in knee-high boots over black jeans and a designer jacket. She sat separating Dorian from Troy and Marika, confident but on guard.

Marika sat hard up against the tall, dark, and built to fight Troy, with her hand in his lap. She looked me over, disgust plain in her golden sneer.

Troy's loathing look shifted from my brother to us. "Great. Now there's three."

Vanessa clapped. "Wow, you can count. What an achievement."

With Troy's glare redirected, Kendrick reluctantly took a seat on another log across the fire.

Ty took my hand and pulled me down too, the fire's flames heating my face. He then drew his arm from behind his back, presenting a single long-stemmed white rose. "For my beautiful girl."

"Poser," Kendrick mock coughed.

Marika *huffed*, flinging her black hair over her shoulder while

Troy lifted his chin in defiance. "You let that leech talk to you like that?"

Ty's irises flared, the look on his face a direct command for Troy to butt out.

To avoid the possible alpha/beta showdown, I grasped the rose, breathing in its perfumed petals. The only flowers I'd ever been given had been from Caius. The memories made me feel nauseous, while Ty's gesture warmed my heart. I'd never received any kind of flower from a guy before, let alone one as hot as Ty. "You shouldn't have."

Ty wrapped his arms around my waist and pulled me close, taking my bottom lip between his. "You taste like mint chocolate."

Feeling everyone's eyes on me, my face grew even hotter. At the same instant, Kendrick's stomach churned. Ty may as well have kissed him for what he experienced through our bond. I tried to pull up the walls in my mind even though the damage was already done. But being like this with Ty killed my concentration to the point of nonexistence.

"So what should we get up to over winter break?" Ty lifted a brow, the insinuation in his words and expression unmissable.

I frowned and shrugged. "I don't know. What did you have in mind?"

Ty flashed me his perfect smoldering smile, one that if I'd been standing would have brought me to my knees. "Oh I have a few thoughts," he purred, running his hand down my arm and grazing the side of my breast suggestively.

My breath caught and my foot slid out, Vans catching flames and melting at the tip. I glanced around. Across the fire, Marika had begun whispering in Troy's ear, while Dorian and Vanessa spoke quietly. Kendrick was staring out at the waves, jaw clenched. The thought of intimacy and sex with Ty had my face burning brighter than the roaring fire. My body ached for his touch but my thoughts spun, mirroring Kendrick's dismal mood. Though not for the same reason. I had promised my mom as part of her letting me see Ty that I wouldn't be intimate with him, ever. And with Kendrick watching and feeling through our bond, I couldn't even consider the act, let alone anything leading up to it. I for one couldn't put Kendrick through the agony of feeling me with Ty. On top of that, I had never given myself to anyone. Bar that one dreamscape with Ty, I hadn't even come close. It was an epic step.

Kendrick chuckled and shifted his attention from the waves. "Get your mind out of the gutter, Ty. It's *never* going to happen."

Ty looked like he wanted to hit Kendrick. "Was I talking to you?"

Kendrick smiled with victory. "Hey, I'm only saying what Amelia's afraid to tell you."

All other chatting fell silent, gold and blue eyes now regarding the three of us. Vanessa's gaze was curious, Dorian's knowing, and Troy and Marika's smug.

Sweat dampened my face and hands and coldness settled in my stomach. I felt like I'd swallowed a fistful of ice cubes.

"Ah," Troy barked. "Trouble in paradise."

Marika *tisked* her tongue. "What a surprise."

Vanessa got up. "Both of you cut it out."

Ty ignored them all. "Amelia?" He laced his fingers through mine. "What's he talking about?"

Unable to make eye contact, I hauled Ty up beside me. "Come with me?"

"Hey, don't leave," Troy said.

"Yeah," Marika called. "This was just getting interesting."

"Would you both shut up," I heard Dorian say.

Ty shot them a glare but allowed me to pull him up the beach toward the shadows cast from a rising rocky cliff. *Should've When You Could've* by Skillet faded like the memory of our close physical encounter back when I'd been forced to live at the Armaya. The one time when we'd almost forgotten we were in a dreamscape and were ready to go all the way. The whistling seaside breeze replaced its taunting lyrics as our distance grew.

I trudged around the side of a huge boulder and leaned against its pitted surface. Unable to bear the look on Ty's face, I stared down, kicking at the sand with my Vans. "Ty, we can't be together like that."

Ty folded his arms over his chest. "Because of *him*?"

Arrogant jerk! Kendrick's voice shot through my mind.

I shook my head, throwing off Kendrick's snarky words. "Yes and no. It's not like I don't want to, I do. It's just…"

"Just what?"

A long silent moment followed. "I've never been with anyone before you," I whispered. "I mean you're the first guy I've ever dated. This is new to me. All of it. And I don't want to share our time together."

Ty's expression became softer, flashing with guilt. He moved closer to cup my neck with a warm, rough hand. "I know these are all firsts for you. And I don't want to share you, either." He sighed. "I'm sorry. I didn't mean to pressure you. Really, I didn't. Kendrick's just been getting under my skin with this whole bond and knowing you better thing."

Tears pooled in the corners of my eyes. The next part of the conversation to come filled me with dread. Kendrick wasn't our only physical obstacle, and Ty deserved to know the truth. "Ty, when my mom agreed to let us see each other, she forced me to make a promise."

Ty's hand slid from my neck and gripped my forearms, looking into my teary eyes. "You promised her you wouldn't sleep with me." At my shocked expression Ty laughed. "I figured as much. And that's okay, Amelia. My father asked me to make the same promise. Told him where to shove it, though. Lycans are considered adults at sixteen, so he can't control what I do."

"Did he say why we shouldn't?"

"No. I'm guessing it has to do with my mom being a hybrid. Oh, and he still thinks you're a royal."

Royal vampires could reproduce, unlike turned vampires. So his warning made sense if he thought there was a possibility Ty could get me pregnant. As a turned vampire my mom knew better. Though with the other royal traits we were displaying, fertility may not be entirely impossible. Not that I wanted to get into that with Ty now.

Feeling uncomfortable with the subject I said, "Oh."

Ty reached up to brush the hair from my face. "She can't control you forever, you know."

He was right. Plus I was still learning to control the bond. Until I had a handle on that, we'd have to wait. A hopeful idea occurred to me. "I want to try something. You need to stand still. I mean really, really still."

Looking curious Ty nodded, becoming the hottest living statue I'd ever seen. I placed my hands on his shoulders before closing my eyes. I imagined Ty standing before me, with his perfect features and gleaming irises. The two of us, alone and facing each other. One by one, I began building the same brick wall from my earlier attempts around both our bodies. It grew higher and higher until everything and everyone was separated from us. All that remained visible in my mind was the two of us, sheltered and hidden by an impenetrable force field. There was a slight internal prod from Kendrick, but I pushed back, holding the fort. Then I leaned up on my toes and met Ty's hot lips.

"Kiss me."

Ty responded with instant hunger, arms wrapping around my waist and lips moving over mine. He pressed me back against the boulder, his hard body against mine. I focused on holding the solid wall intact as our tongues danced, my hands feeling their way down his defined chest and abs. A flutter of excitement took over. I was doing it. I was blocking Kendrick. There was a feeling of total vacancy, of not having him present.

Then the blocks began to crumble. Breathing hard I pulled back and peered up into the mosaic of Ty's glowing eyes.

"What was that for?" he asked just as breathless.

I smiled. "Our first kiss, alone."

CHAPTER 7

I'd gone back to the beach in the morning to practice with Ty, attempting to pull up a decent block from the bond. Now I was in my room, disappointed and rain-soaked. A three-second kiss was far from progress. It was two steps backward.

Irritated and over it, I tugged off my violet tank and jeans and torpedoed them onto the mess of my multi-toned purple bed. Annoyed with my continued lack of progress, I stomped into the bathroom. On top of bond issues, we hadn't had time to look into who E.B. was from Caius's experiment book yet. The pressure of everything we didn't know was building. I needed to unwind.

I reached into the open-walled shower, turned on the tap, and then stripped off my underwear and bra. Exposed and waiting for the water to heat up, my focus slid sideways to the floor-length mirror backing the door. Little to no curves and tiny boobs. No surprise there. A little lower was a starburst scar below my ribs. The injury from falling through the floor to Caius's torture chamber had completely healed. I touched the spot, feeling the smooth and rough texture of marbled flesh.

Then I froze.

A feeling of pure desire washed over me, of being aroused at the sight of my exposed body. Confused and panicked, I glanced around. Someone was watching me. I could feel the weight of their eyes taking in my mirrored reflection, and almost hear the intake of breath at the sight of my bare flesh.

I tried to shake off the eerie paranoia as steam grew like a living organism around me. The door to the bathroom was closed. There was no one in here but me. I was alone. I was sure of it. Still the feelings remained, raw and strong…and embarrassed? The desire at the sight of my own naked flesh flared like an inferno, warming between my legs. There was panic now too, a feeling of needing to escape a house on fire. No, not my feelings…*his*.

Heat flared across my cheeks, burning with sudden realization. I scrambled, snatching the towel from the rail and flung it around my body. "What the hell are you doing?"

Shit! Kendrick's panicked voice emerged in my mind. *I'm sorry. I didn't mean to. I mean…I didn't think you'd know.*

I shut off the water, any embarrassment instantly turning to resentment. *Didn't think I'd freaking know?*

It was bad enough that I couldn't be alone with Ty. Now I couldn't even shower in privacy? Plus I hadn't even known it was Kendrick watching me. Yeah, I knew I could catch glimpses of what Kendrick was up to or where he was, but this? It was an invasion of privacy. A full body invasion.

How long has this been going on?

Kendrick sighed. *Ever since we got back. I was going to tell you, but I knew how pissed you'd be. It's not like I was doing it on purpose.*

My stomach lurched. What else had he seen? What had he felt? I imagined Kendrick's awareness when showering before today, as my hands scoured my body with sudsy soap, washing myself top to toe, and all the intimate parts in-between. Had he felt that too? The thought made me cringe. My best friend seeing me naked was one thing, but feeling every inch of my body at the same time was a completely different shade of mortifying.

It wasn't like that. I swear. He began pacing, leaving track marks in the mink carpet in his bedroom. *I've caught you watching Vampire Diaries by yourself and sneaking chocolate like you're starving. But I've never seen you naked before. Well, not since I walked in on you at the Armaya by accident. I didn't...*

What? Enjoy it? Tempted to smash the mirror backing the door and the one above the marble vanity, I clenched my fists. Then I screamed, needing to release the violent tension that had my insides wound so tight they were about to snap. *Get the hell out of my head!*

The instant vacancy of Kendrick's mind was like a door being slammed in my face. Standing cocooned within a big fluffy towel, I knew there was no way I could shower now. Kendrick wasn't in my head this second, but he could reappear at any moment. If his inability to control his slips were anything like mine when I was around Ty, a slight flash of naked flesh is all it would take to bring him back.

There was no way in hell I was going to let this go on. It had to stop. Right. Now.

After dressing with my lids squeezed shut, I chucked on my new purple-laced Vans and tucked my iPod into my back pocket. Then I stormed out of my bedroom.

Opening my mind, I sensed Kendrick. He was out in the back-yard, and he wasn't alone. Not caring who was out there, I launched over the railing and landed in the foyer. I sprinted through the kitchen and out the terrace doors. "Kendrick, we need—"

My words cut off as a circular, polished, and almost transparent object flew at my face.

"Shit!" I ducked just in time, the orb hitting the door behind me. It connected with a splattering crash, sending crystal-like shards raining down around me and onto the footpath. The shards that touched my skin didn't cut like glass, but rather, they were cold…and wet.

"Ah, sorry," Dorian said, a smile painted across his face. He stood across the lawn, his fingers splayed while he tried not to laugh.

I stared at my brother while Kendrick shrunk on the stone bench to the side. My brain took a second to catch up to what had happened. "*You* did that?"

Dorian's smile widened, flashing his perfect straight teeth. "Who ever thought water ability could be so cool."

With my anger from a minute ago distracted, I took a seat beside Kendrick.

Kendrick cleared his throat. "I've seen water in action, and even I thought that was impressive. I mean, I've read about Pure Bloods moving large bodies of water. But freezing and throwing it? That's something else."

With new warmth growing across my face at the memory of Kendrick seeing me naked, I forced my attention onto Dorian. "Show me how it works."

"Sure thing." He stared at the ice shards on the paved footpath. His hand reached out, splayed fingers becoming tense.

For a few seconds nothing happened. Then I saw it. The ice was melting, each sliver liquefying until it was lost in the cracks between pavers. I was about to say, *is that it,* when the drops of water rose from the cracks. They began to move, slithering like water snakes until they all met, becoming a large puddle. The water bulged and began to lift, rising off the footpath and forming a liquid ball that rippled and spun. As the ball floated higher its surface changed, turning less transparent and more opaque. Cracking erupted, the sound of ice forming while the ball floated through the air. Then it stopped to hover above Dorian's hands, spinning and coiling as if of its own accord.

"That's amazing," I breathed. Dorian's power was cool, so much cooler and useful than my horrible visions. He could extract the water from living things, and manipulated it from liquid to ice into a throwable weapon. "So what's next?"

"How about we tackle the 'me seeing you naked' issue?" Kendrick said without preamble.

I coughed, choking on his unedited words. The last thing I wanted to do was talk about him seeing me naked, especially in front of my brother.

Dorian punched Kendrick in the arm, tight fist ready to throw another hit. "You saw my sister naked?"

"It wasn't intentional. It's a bond thing," Kendrick said as if that made it okay.

I glared at Kendrick, wanting to throttle him. The air suddenly became frigid, wind whipping cold as ice through my black top and jeans. With my brother here this was far from the time or place. I screamed internally, *Shut—Up!*

The protectiveness on Dorian's face fizzled. "Well, I'm glad you're bound to him and not me. The last thing I ever, ever want to see is you naked."

"Shut up. Shut up. Shut up!" I screamed out loud, jumping to my feet. "This may be startling news to you both, but I don't want to talk about either of you seeing me naked. This is *not* okay. I'll never be able to shower again in my life!"

"It doesn't have to be that way," Kendrick said, voice reasoning. "That's why I've been trying to block you out so much. Even though it wasn't on purpose, I felt like I was spying. With more practice you can keep me out too."

"He's right," Dorian added. "Do you think I just woke up one day able to manipulate water? No. When I sensed something there, I explored it. I've been practicing these tricks since you left. And I've had obstacles, but with practice I've found ways to overcome them."

"And you can too." Kendrick got up and took my hand. "You're strong, Amelia, whether you know it or not. You just have to let us help you."

I *humphed* and propped my free hand on my nonexistent hip. "Fine, I'll let you both help me, but only if you promise not to mention the *incident.*"

"What incident?" Dorian shrugged.

Kendrick nodded. "Forgotten." He led me into the center of the lawn, bordered by hedges that rustled with the dying wind. "I want to try something different. I think it'll help with the bond issue."

I searched Kendrick's mind. I know—counterintuitive, seeing as the point was to put a block between our minds. What I found almost floored me. "You want me to try to bring on a vision? Are you freaking insane?"

Each vision was shocking and debilitating, haunting my dreams and remaining after my eyelids snapped open. There had even been one, back at the Armaya, where I'd been mentally torn from Caius's office to find myself standing in the library, as a kind of astral projection that couldn't speak or be seen, but was forced to watch Marcus's plans going into action.

"Your power is so much stronger than anything I've read about. Is uncontrollable," Kendrick rushed, knowing I was on the verge of losing it. "But it shouldn't have to be. Dorian's learned to control his, and I think you can too."

"How will controlling Amelia's visions affect her ability to block you?" Dorian questioned, seeming genuinely interested.

Kendrick walked past the line of trimmed hedges and dropped back onto the stone bench. "Your visions are part of your connection to spirit, which also created our bond. Everything is interlinked. So I'm hoping if you can learn to control one ability, then the other will become less of a stretch."

"So why not practice bringing up the wall to block you," I said, seeing much more relevance in continuing that than his crazy idea.

"Because we've tried that." Kendrick ran a hand through his hair. "Plus we can practice that anytime. This idea is something we haven't tried. Imagine what could happen if you can learn to do this."

"It's worth a try," Dorian voiced, moving to take the spot beside Kendrick. "Besides, what harm could it do?"

A lot, but I was starting to see their point. The visions were uncontrollable in every way. I had never even considered that they didn't have to be. If I could hold them back, or will them on when I was prepared, then why wouldn't I be able to control the bond? I'd already had small successes in that department, which would have to be a walk in the park *if* I could master control of my visions.

"Fine." I hugged my arms around my body, not from cold, but in anticipation of the unknown. "So where do I start?"

"Focus," Dorian said, surprising me. "That's what I do. Concentrate on what you want to happen until your eyes and fingers tingle. Imagine the power is a part of you that you can control."

Feeling the overwhelming instinct to do so, I lifted my face to the sky, extending my hands towards the clouds. I imagined there was power out there, raw and tangible. Power that I could somehow beckon to me. After a few long moments, tingles cascaded across my arms and my eyes stung from not blinking. But nothing happened. I tried again, eyes watering and tears rolling down my face. Still nothing happened. Frustrated, I went to drop my arms when something made me freeze.

I could hear pattering rain racing our way as the wind picked up. All of a sudden the clouds brewed above, coiling around each other like violent waves. They became darker and wilder until any remaining blue and white was swallowed up. The feuding waves collided with force, looking like a stampede of rivaling armies meeting in the middle.

Lightning split from above and shot at the ground, and me!

I dove, barely managing to escape its path before it viciously struck the exact spot I'd been standing. Glorious blue-white light blinded me while the impact boomed through my ears. I curled over, hands covering my ears too late and eyelids pinned shut over starbursts.

"Amelia!" Dorian's voice echoed as his hand touched my arm. It sounded as if he were speaking through water. "Shit. Are you okay?"

Kendrick appeared at my other side and lifted me into his arms. Through the bond he could tell I wasn't injured in any life-threatening way. "She's just startled."

Blinking away the starbursts, I watched the clouds disperse to a light gray calm. There was no sign of any lingering electrical strikes.

"Yeah, I think I'm fine." I wriggled free from Kendrick's supporting arms and stood on wobbly legs. "Well, this was a complete bust." I brushed the wet grass from my butt. "Apart from attracting bad weather, I didn't even feel like a vision was coming on."

"This was your first attempt." Dorian released his hold on my arm, satisfied that I was okay. "You just need more practice."

"Yeah." Kendrick walked over to the terrace doors. "And maybe next time, try it inside."

I sensed the worry behind Kendrick's words, which matched my own. These freaky occurrences with bad weather and lightning had increased. And the common denominator? Me.

I headed in the opposite direction and Kendrick stalled. "Where're you going?

"For a run," I called back without turning. "I need to clear my head."

I plugged my earbuds in and blasted Offspring's *Rise and Fall* album on my iPod. If only the noise could drown out my thoughts of the bond with Kendrick, the weather attraction, Caius wanting my blood, and the identity of E.B. But nothing could.

Hoping the exercise would help clear my mind, I tore through the suburbs. After clearing countless roads, a familiar rise in elevation announced the entry to Mt Major. I took off up the mountain, hoping the blaring music, cold air, and open space would distract me from everything. My muscles lengthened and tingled as I surged through the unending thicket of trees. Waiting to dodge each fallen tree, boulder, and stream until I almost hit it felt exhilarating and distracting. But too soon I reached the peak of Mt Major.

With winter in full swing, the surrounding mountains were blanketed by glacial-white snow. I squinted as the sun peeked through fading clouds above. Light rays spilled onto the snow-covered peaks and glistened so bright the glare burned my eyes.

Appreciating the fact that I could endure direct light when other turned vamps couldn't, I lowered myself into the snow, crossing my legs in a clear patch of sunlight. Even Pure Bloods, although immune, would feel uncomfortable if exposed. It was another trait that made me different.

As the mounting issues crept back to mind, I made a decision. I was sick of letting my abilities and everything Caius had done to me interfere with my life. Right now it was time to take control.

Unlike earlier, I kept my hands down and closed my eyes. On top of all the poisoning and experiments, Caius had erased my memories. Important memories to cover his malicious tracks. But I wasn't oblivious or weak anymore. I had been given a gift. When Kendrick had compelled me under Marcus's control, the blocks had begun to crumble. Traveling to the cabin, a memory had resurfaced with my vision into the past. But it wasn't enough. I needed more.

With a deep breath, I relaxed. Wind whistled through the trees. Soft consistent rain fell, hissing as it melted the snow around me. Non-hibernating creatures foraged down the hill. Some birds chirped while others cut the air with strong wings. I remained still and silent for a long while, willing all the worry away as the sunlight faded.

When I began to nod off, a rush of images flooded my mind, a dam wall breaking its banks. There were so many faces, voices, and places that my brain began to throb. With a few deep breaths I willed the rush aside, grasping the edge of a single memory, somehow knowing this was the one I needed.

As the confusion cleared I found myself sitting on a round rug. Wooden planks and stone surrounded me, while an open fireplace warmed my back. My mom sat in her green armchair with Dorian curled up on her lap. The sight would have been totally weird, except he wasn't the size he was now. He was small. Just a boy. They were both sound asleep.

A deep voice drew my eye to a slightly younger version of a man I knew. The same man I wished I never had to see again. Caius. He sat in a mirroring armchair, his hands clasped in his lap. His dull, silvery eyes stared through a six-paned window to his left. Outside the air was calm, the lush forest green rather than snow-sheeted.

My instincts told me to scream. To get up and run as fast as… I peered down. My legs were small, my hands child sized. The solidity of everything had confused me, making me forget. But I knew now. This was a memory. And the child who was me sitting before Caius wasn't scared. She was curious and excited. She *loved* this story.

"Erzsebet was close to a breakthrough when the monsters stormed the castle." Caius slid his gaze onto the child version of me. His expression was kind, nothing like the last time when he'd tried to kill me. "But did they kill her?" He shook his head. "No. What they did to her was much worse. She was forced into darkness, left to roam alone and starving. She longed for the light, for a way to escape. But there was no one brave enough to continue her perilous work."

"W-what happened, Unky Caius?" my childlike voice quavered, despite having heard this story countless times before.

"The insanity crept closer and closer. She could not escape it." Caius sighed, deep-set eyes lost in thought. "Though by that point, she no longer wanted to. She was lost to the dark, sentenced to an eternity as one of the monsters she had worked to save."

"And then the prince came and he saved her!" the little girl exclaimed, bouncing on her bottom.

Caius stroked his chin. "Would that make you happy, Amelia?"

The way he said my name made the real me cringe, while the little girl basked in its love. "Yes, yes!" the little girl cried. "Can he? Can the prince save her?"

Caius smiled genuinely, lips parting to reveal harmless, human-straight teeth. "Then that is exactly what will happen. The prince will break the spell and he will not fail. He will find princess Erzse-bet, and he will save her."

I gasped for air as the memory dissolved into nothing. Caius's story spun through my mind. "Oh. My. God. Kendrick, did you see that?" I jumped up, my heart racing.

What? Is everything okay? A few seconds of prodding ran over my brain. Apparently Kendrick had been practicing blocking me out again. *Wow, that's huge. Are you thinking what I'm thinking?*

I bolted down the mountain at breakneck speed. "The person Caius continued his experiments after was Erzsebet. E.B. What if B stands for Bathory? She could have been his relative."

A twinge of excitement streamed from Kendrick. *I'll see if I can log into the council server from your mom's computer.*

"Oh crap," I said, not slowing.

What? What's wrong?

I dodged around a thick growth of trees and jumped a boulder. *I think I know why Caius needed to kill me. Shit! He said it in the vision... "The prince will break the spell and he will not fail. He will find princess Erzsebet and he will save her."* I struggled to control my breathing as I pushed on faster. *Don't you get it? I'm the link, his experiment from the start.* I cleared a wide frozen stream in one bound and my feet sank into dirty, melting snow. Irritated, I kicked my drenched Vans free, and kept running. *We thought Caius wanted to secure his position on The Council, to have immortality so he could rule forever.*

We were wrong, Kendrick said. *He needed your blood to save Erzsebet.*

SOGGY AND CHILLED to the bone, I shot into my mom's office, shutting the door behind me. Being comfortable and dry didn't even make the list of things to do now that we had this new lead. Kendrick was behind the desk in Mom's padded chair, tapping his chin in frustration.

I went to stand beside him. "Did you get in?"

Kendrick shook his head. "You're mom's computer is locked up like Fort Knox. I tried everything: your last name, hers, birth dates. Nothing worked." He pushed the button on his iPhone and the screen lit up with a snowboarding shot.

"So we've got nothing?" I leaned against the desk's glass edge.

"Not exactly," Kendrick said. "I checked the net and found this." He clicked the mouse and the screen came to life.

Countess Erzsebet (Elizabeth) Bathory was born on the 7th of August 1560, into a renowned Noble family in Hungary. As a child, she experienced seizures and uncontrollable fits of rage. Later in life she was branded the most prolific female serial killer in history and was later remembered as the "Blood Countess." Following her husband Ferenc Nadasdy's death, Erzsebet was reported to have begun aging prematurely. Her four children, three daughters Anastasia, Anna, Katalin and son Paul, were sent to relatives. In 1604 she and four servants educated in witchcraft performed dark spells to combat her premature aging. Virgins were strung above a bathtub and cut open so that she could bathe in their blood. Erzsebet and her servants were accused of torturing and killing hundreds of girls, amounting to more than 650 victims, though her servants were only convicted of 80. Erzsebet was never tried or convicted, but in 1610 was imprisoned in the Cachtice Castle in Slovakia, where she remained bricked in a group of rooms until her death on the 21st of August 1614.

"How could she murder so many people?" I slumped back against the desk. The visual of all those defenseless girls strung up to bleed out over a tub was horrifically disturbing. It would forever be imprinted on my mind. "Who was she, and how was she related to Caius? Why would she kill all those virgins? Was it part of her experiments?"

"Well she's not his mother," Kendrick said with a frown. "Her only born son was named Paul. Maybe his aunt, or a sister. Do you remember what Caius said in his story?"

I couldn't forget a single word. "He said she was close to a breakthrough. But I have no idea what that means. He also said that monsters forced her into darkness. Could he mean the people who bricked her in until her death?"

"Maybe," Kendrick said. "But what if the darkness wasn't literal, like a place? What if the darkness was in her mind?"

At that second Kendrick's iPhone sung out a Tony Hawk game tune and he picked it up. "About time."

"What's going on?" I slid a patterned seat around the desk as Kendrick read the screen.

"It's from Marcus. An override code to crack into anyone's account."

So he did trust Marcus. I sat down beside Kendrick. "You told him what we found out?"

"No," Kendrick said absolutely. "I said we had some kind of lead on Caius and needed access." He didn't look at me as he keyed in the code, though a muscle ticked along his jaw. "I don't want you telling him anything about this."

I began to argue as a click, like a vault opening, sounded and *Access Granted* flashed across the screen. My words cut off as anticipation tightened my ribs.

I slid the keyboard my way and typed *Erzsebet Bathory* into the search bar. A list of links flashed onto the screen. "What are all these?"

"The Armaya's archives," Kendrick said, clicking the first link. "Old texts that have been scanned for historical preservation."

The scanned pages were frayed and discolored, looking seriously old. We both edged in and stared at the screen, speed reading at a similar pace.

The first scanned text was a history of Erzsebet's life. A lot of the early stuff was similar to what we'd found on the Internet. But what followed was far from the Internet's knowledge of human history.

After the living death of three of her four children, Countess Erzsebet Bathory devoted her life to discovering a way to restore damned vampires to life. Her experiments were controversial and conducted in secret, against The Council's laws. Countless damned were captured, imprisoned, and drugged. Many nights the Countess would inject herself with various concoctions to scale the rejuvenating effects and UV resistance. Most of these tests, according to the Countess's own records, failed, either increasing resistance for a short time or doing the exact opposite and leaving her weak and sickly.

I shivered, thinking back to our conversation with Marcus before fleeing the Armaya. He believed Caius's plans were linked to the damned in some way. But the damned were extinct. Kendrick and Marcus had said so themselves. "How can Caius's plans be linked to the damned?"

"I don't know." Kendrick skimmed ahead and stopped a few chapters later.

The Countess's downfall was her own perseverance and determination to bring back her lost children. One night, after another failed experiment left her weak and almost immobile, one of her captives escaped. An alarm was raised, leaving enough time for Erzsebet to stow her son in a lockable cellar before the escapee attacked. The Countess's son was discovered the next day, though her body was never recovered.

Printed after that block of text was a black and white photograph. Pictured was a woman with fair hair, youthful features, and chalky white complexion. Countess Bathory. A boy with dirty-blond hair stood by her side. Her son, I guessed. Behind them was a table that bubbled with beakers and Bunsen burners.

Kendrick printed the photo and closed the archive. Then he opened another link. "It's another experiment book."

Hand drawn tables filled the worn pages with thousands and thousands of experimental procedures. Some consisted of drawing damned blood to boil, dry, burn, or mix with chemical or metallic substances. Others consisted of injecting manufactured concoctions back into a damned vampire. Then there were the experiments she performed on herself, and even some on humans. Everything was dated and timed. All the results were noted. They ranged from severe reactions to ultraviolet light, increased or decreased healing, temporary return of heartbeat, disfigurement, and even death.

"Hey, look." Kendrick pointed to the table on the next page. These ones had the subjects DOB.

What I saw made me sick to my stomach. "Oh God. She started experimenting on children." I reached for the mouse and clicked ahead a few pages. I gulped at what was written. "Babies too."

"Look, there's a table key," Kendrick pointed out.

I followed his pointing finger to see acronyms, along with their definitions. Two I had seen before. IBB and IAB.

"Infected before birth and infected after birth." Understanding rocked me like an avalanche.

"Caius infected you before and Dorian after birth," Kendrick said, confusion streaming through the bond. "How is that even possible?"

Thoughts of a giant poison-filled needle being jabbed into my mom's pregnant belly swarmed over me. Or could the meaning be less literal, like infecting us before our first breath of life? Either way, the image made something else very clear. "I don't know." I swallowed the need to gag and clutched Kendrick's arm. "But this proves he knew my mom before he attacked her."

Needing to know everything, I opened the last archive. This one was handwritten in flowing calligraphy with *Erzsebet Bathory* on the first page. What followed were full pages of notes, most on research into breaking the curse of the damned. From her research she had determined that an immortal's blood was the key to restoring them.

"This all happened before the Blood War," Kendrick said, leaning back into the padded seat. "When the damned were hunted to extinction."

"She's not dead," I blurted. Oh, God, this was huge. "Caius wants *my* immortal blood. He's still trying to save her, which means that the damned aren't extinct."

I read on, but the reasoning behind how she thought immortal blood could bring the damned back to life wasn't there. Past that page the scanned information ended. I removed the photo from the printer on the cabinet behind the desk and stared at the innocent-looking boy. "Why does Caius care? Who is she to him?"

My gaze slid past the boy and I noticed something. "Hey, look at this."

Kendrick frowned at the photo in my hands. "Is that what I think it is?"

I squinted, trying to get more detail. Not that squinting would help. My vampire eyesight was almost perfect, its ability to sharpen and zoom now happened without trying. But my eyesight wasn't the problem. The quality of the printed photograph was. Still, I could make out the granulated lines of carved roses in the small rectangular-shaped box.

I touched the paper, recognizing the intricate gold box with amethyst stones. I'd first seen the item at Mom's auction, and been so explicitly drawn to it. "That's the jewelry box Caius won at the auction. The one he gave me."

As I said the words the office door swung open. Mom glided into the room, stalling as she caught sight of us. "What are you both doing in here? You know my office if off limits."

I hated what I was about to say, but we needed to know the truth, not be left wondering if her explanation was honest or not. *Compel her,* I sent through the bond.

Kendrick hesitated, shooting me a sideways glance. *I wish this wasn't necessary. Your mom has always been so nice to me, but I'll do anything to keep you safe.* Resigned to the task, he shot around the desk and placed his hands on my mom's shoulders. His eyes captured hers. Instant lightning sparked across his irises and his pupils dilated. "Be still and do not speak." He paused. *What now?*

A small memory teased the edge of my subconscious as I studied the photo. It had been the week before my mom's auction. She'd been in her office on the phone, sourcing a special item. Strong suspicion bled into my mind. "Mom, the item you had to specially pick up before the auction, what was it?"

Mom didn't make a move or utter a word. She just stood there like a statue, poised and perfect in her stillness. Under my best friend's compulsion she couldn't.

Kendrick squeezed her shoulder. "Answer the question, Ms. Lamont. What item did you pick up before the auction?"

Mom blinked mechanically, her lips parting. "It was the gold jewelry box with purple stones," she said, her tone expressionless.

Ask her why that item was so important, I sent my silent words to Kendrick. The compulsion seemed to work better if he did the questioning.

"Ms. Lamont," Kendrick said in a strong but calm voice. "Why that item? Who had you source it?"

"It was a family heirloom," Mom said in monotone. "The auctioneer was told it was from the 1700s. That was false. It was much older than that. Its location was discovered at a curator's private residence in Hungary. The curator had been a descendant of one of Erzsebet Bathory's nannies. It had taken him centuries to find it."

"Taken who centuries to find it?" I couldn't help blurting out.

Mom frowned but remained under Kendrick's compulsion. "Your uncle Caius."

More than one thing didn't add up. "Then why auction it? Why not just give him the item?"

Locked under Kendrick's gaze, Mom spoke without looking my way. "He wanted to know if anyone else was searching for it."

"Why was it so important to him?" Kendrick pushed.

"The item belonged to her only living offspring. Her son, Paul Caius Bathory."

I stood frozen for a long shell-shocked moment, my thoughts running a hundred miles a second. Caius was Erzsebet's son, her one and only son. The jewelry box was implicit to his plans in some way. It had to be. And all this time I'd had the clue within reach.

I vaulted up to my room, causing my motorbike posters to flap with the wind my entrance stirred up. Kendrick remained downstairs, erasing our encounter from my mom's memory. In seconds the jewelry box was off my white, antique bedside table and clutched in my hands. I turned it over, studying its cool gold surface. Seeing nothing unusual I lifted the stiff lid. There had to be something, anything that could give us a clue. Its walls were lined with pillowy satin that was in great condition for its age. I removed Madam Rosalie's card and saw the key beneath it. Nothing unusual there. My gaze lifted. There. I zoned in on the carved flower pattern that continued inside the lid. Inscribed on one delicate petal was E.B. This had, without a doubt, belonged to Caius's mother.

Kendrick appeared in the doorway then, focus locked on the printed photo in his hands. "Hey, did you notice this?"

We met at the foot of my bed. My fingers curled tighter around the jewelry box. On the photo inside the box was a dark smudge with an almost invisible line coming off one side of the smudge. I sucked in my breath. The object was familiar, and something I could never forget. "I know what it is."

Fingers tickled my brain as Kendrick lifted the picture to his nose. "That's the vial?"

I nodded. "Maybe even the same one Caius drugged me with." I plucked the small key from the jewelry box and twirled it between my fingers. The clang I'd heard when I first saw the item resurfaced. Later that night I'd found the key inside the box. Back then I'd assumed the clang was the key hidden inside. But what if I was wrong? "What if the vial had been hidden in the jewelry box at the auction?"

"That would explain why Caius was hell bent on winning the thing."

I slumped down onto my bed, staring at the pretty jewelry box in my hands. Caius had already been plotting to take my life to steal my so-called 'gift' back then. The one he'd imposed on me at birth. Finding the vial had been a necessary step to achieving his goal. According to his confession, its contents alone could complete the conversion in my blood, so that my death would pass my immortality onto him. "I was drawn to the vial. That's why the connection was gone by the time he left the piece for me. He'd already taken it out."

Anger that I'd shoved down with every new challenge that had plagued me and the people I loved began to rise. Caius may have been doing this to save his family like his mother had done to save her daughters. But that didn't make ruining my family and friends' lives okay. Murder was still murder.

I screamed and squeezed both hands around the jewelry box, delighting in the creak as it bent under the pressure. In a twisted mess, I tore the lid free and scratched the satin away. I lifted my hand to pelt it at the wall.

"Amelia, wait!" Kendrick caught my wrist and brought my hand down.

And that's when I saw it. Inscribed on the inside base of the now warped and satin-free gold box was a symbol. A circle surrounding a jagged bolt that was crossed through the middle. It was the same symbol Caius had painted on the dank ground in the cell. The same symbol he'd held me inside while he drained me to death. "The symbol was part of Caius's ritual. A step to becoming immortal."

"What do you think it means?"

"I don't know." I pulled my iPhone from my jeans. "But I know who does."

Minutes later I'd spoken to Ty and updated him on everything we'd found. He was hanging out with Vanessa, so I texted a photo of the symbol to his phone for her to see.

Now we waited. Kendrick perched on the windowsill, his back against the glass while I stuffed another choc-mint cookie from my bedside into my mouth. I fell back on my bed and stared at my phone again. Each passing second made the devoured cookies feel like bricks in my stomach.

When the phone finally rang I jumped up and fumbled to put it on loudspeaker. "Ty, hello. What did she say?"

"It's Vanessa." There was a loud sigh. "And I haven't seen that exact symbol before."

My heart sank, at the news and because she was calling instead of Ty. After failing at bond-blocking progress this morning I felt even more separated from him.

"But," Vanessa added. "I know what parts of it mean. The line through the center can be used for different things, mainly blocking. Though it can also transfer."

"Like taking an aspect from one person and moving it to another?" Kendrick asked, now beside me.

"Oh hey, Kendrick," Vanessa said. "And you're right. The circle around the symbol is a binding. It locks whatever is being transferred into place."

My disappointment ebbed as understanding settled in. "So the jagged bolt must stand for immortality or something, right?"

"No." There was no doubt in Vanessa's voice. "That's the one part I haven't seen before, but it's not the sign for immortality."

"What about visions?" Kendrick curled an arm around my bed's mauve-wrapped corner post.

"Or blood bond?" I added.

"No." The turning of pages sounded before Vanessa spoke again. "The symbol for The Sight is an eye. And I can't find one for the blood bond, but I don't think it's that."

"But you're not sure?" I remembered the glorious light that had exploded as our minds and souls intertwined. That had been the light Madam Rosalie had been talking about, hadn't it?

"Not completely, but I'll keep digging. It'll take time though. There are so many symbols and I don't even have them all in books." There was a slight pause through the speaker. "I'll let you know what I come up with."

"Okay, thanks." I hung up and placed the wrecked jewelry box in my bedside drawer, then fell back onto the comforter. It felt like for every step we'd taken forward today, we'd taken one back. Christmas was two days away now, and I had no idea what to do next.

Kendrick fell back onto the bed beside me. "Bond block practice?"

I couldn't help the tiny smile that curved my lips. "Distraction and progress? You know me too well."

CHAPTER 8

*T*hrough the windshield the sky was a dark shade of slate, as messy clouds swirled in threat. Soon it would be pouring down, and I shivered at the thought of more lightning. In the past I could have watched an electrical storm for hours. But after my too-close-for-comfort encounters, hanging around now put me on edge.

After braving the rush of shoppers at the mall in Manchester—on the day before Christmas—and managing to find gifts for everyone except Kendrick and Ty, I was home. I drove Dorian's and my Cabriolet into the driveway, right behind a delivery van. Remembering my brother's guidelines on driving the car without him, I left the engine running. God forbid I not allow *her* to cool down properly. Even at the shops I'd had to find the most remote parking spot to avoid anyone accidentally denting the car. And the Manchester mall's parking lot was huge. No, this would not do. I needed my own wheels. I committed for the second time today to begging my mom for my own ride. A Ducati, my favorite bike, would do just fine.

Eager to get inside, I climbed out of the car and met the delivery man at the door. "Can I help you?"

The man turned to me, holding an express post envelope in his hand. For a moment I was surprised not to see the old delivery man who'd dropped off the test results for the vial. This man was middle aged and seemed much more the part. "Are you Miss Amelia Lamont?"

"Uh, yeah." I glanced around, my paranoia growing. Kendrick wasn't home, I knew that much. I could also tell that his mind was shut off from mine. I was completely alone. "Is that for me?"

The man handed me an electronic device to sign, then as I handed it back, he gave me the envelope. "Merry Christmas."

He tipped his head and strolled back to his van. This one was blue, not black, and printed with the company's logo. A minute later he was gone.

I looked the envelope over. Printed in block letters on the back was Marcus Vladimir. Breath I didn't realize I'd been holding whistled from my lips. My lungs ached at the release. Anything unexpected these days sent a bolt of fear through me, the expectation of something horrible to come. I tore into the envelope and slid free two sheets of paper. The first was a confirmation booking for Kendrick and Dorian to spend a week at a snow resort. The second made my eyes bug. "A 5-night cruise for two around the South Pacific Islands, departing Brisbane Australia!"

Even more shocking than the cruise and pre-booked flights was who the cruise was booked for. Me and one Ty Malau. I dug back into the envelope and slid out a printed white card. It read:

Amelia,

Caius is planning something. I'm not sure exactly what. You all need to lay low for a while, and what better way than this?

Enjoy the gift, Marcus

P.S. Your mom will be fine, but don't call me until you're back. He's watching.

I tugged my iPhone from my jeans and texted Ty. *'Can u meet me?'*

'Can't. Brother home. Dreamscape tonight?'

While I was locked away at the Armaya, Ty's induced dreamscape had been the only way we'd been able to see each other. A plane of existence between sleep and awake where Ty controlled everything, including when I could leave. It was as close to reality as possible, without being in a physical location. In this case it was better than relaying my surprise over the phone.

'Tonight it is. Can't w8.'

I glanced back to the idling car, and froze. Two figures were walking up the paved driveway. Through the fear I registered who it was and sighed. Dorian and Kendrick. "Hey, you'll never believe this…"

After showing them the bookings and card, Kendrick called Marcus, ignoring his warning. The call went to voicemail and his face hardened. "Call me ASAP." Then he hung up. "I don't like this."

"What's not to like?" Dorian snatched the papers, looking like he wanted to scream *hooray!* "White Mountains. Layers of thick snow. And we're lodging at Wildcat. They've got the biggest continual vertical track out there!"

Dorian's enthusiasm didn't surprise me. His biggest love, apart from girls, was any and all sports, plus any competition that came with it. On the flip side Kendrick's reluctance wasn't a mystery. "You still don't think I'm safe with Ty?"

A muscle ticked in Kendrick's jaw. "I'm not prepared to risk your safety with anyone. Besides, this whole scenario screams suspicious. Why would Marcus send you across the world with Ty and keep us in New Hampshire?"

"Well I'm glad," Dorian said. "The sun and me? We're not such great friends, but Amelia has no reaction to it. It's summer across the world, if you didn't know."

That made sense to me. Because of what Caius had done to him, Dorian—like any royal—was made uncomfortable and weak from direct exposure to sunlight. I, on the other hand, had no such affliction. So with Caius and whatever vampire minions he had coming for us, a sun-drenched ship was the safest place for me.

I caught Kendrick's hand. "Marcus knows about Ty. He knows I trust him completely."

Kendrick freed his hand, expression turning smug as he leaned against a porch pillar. "You think your mom's going to allow this?" He laughed. "Fat bloody chance."

"She will allow it." Dorian smiled, a devious glimmer to his silver-blue eyes. "Whether she likes it or not."

"You're going to compel her?" This was becoming too regular an occurrence for my liking. "This can't be our go-to all the time. And using it on pointless things like girls is *not* okay."

"Hey, when I started doing that I didn't even realize I was compelling Mom. When I did, I stopped. Since then I've only used it to find out information to protect us." Dorian handed me back the papers and went to retrieve the keys from our car. "According to Marcus, we're in danger. If Mom says no, then for our own good I'll make her change her mind."

"Amelia, I still don't like this." Worry streamed through the bond, matching the bleak look on Kendrick's face. "What about blood? And how can I keep you safe? What if something—"

"Nothing bad will happen, and I'll stash enough baggies in my suitcase to last." I wanted to hug him but held back. "Plus I need this. We both do. And whether you're physically with me or not, you'll always be able to reach me. We'll never be truly apart."

The darkness across his face lifted. "And don't you forget it."

THAT NIGHT I awoke at the lookout, standing against the railing and overlooking the town of Portsmouth. Excitement had my heart fluttering as a set of unforgettable warm hands rested on my arms. "Hey, beautiful," Ty breathed against my neck, making me shiver.

I spun to wrap my arms around his heated body. His chest was bare. Being in cotton pajama shorts, his sweatpants were soft against my legs. His scent was intoxicating. It made my head light and airy, and my mouth water. Even though I'd seen him yesterday morning, it felt like so long ago. I hugged him harder. "I've missed you."

Ty smiled down at me, the most genuine smile that caused my heart to skip a beat. He dipped his head to press a hot kiss to my lips.

I drew away and spun back to the city lights that beamed up at me, reflecting colorful prisms across sheeted snow. My body and mind braced for Kendrick's intruding emotions.

But there was nothing. No nudging inside my brain. No disgust. No revulsion. There were just my own thoughts and emotions. It was weird. This was my first dreamscape since being bound to Kendrick, and I wasn't blocking him in any way. Still the evidence was there—Kendrick wasn't here.

I stood on my toes and twirled, catching the back of Ty's neck with one hand. Our lips connected and I parted his, tongue brushing over his again and again. My free hand ran over his chest, while his covered my hips and pulled me close. Our lip action grew hotter by the second. When the scenery began to spin from lack of oxygen, I broke free, gasping.

"What," Ty struggled for breath, "was that for?"

"We're alone…"

Ty peered around the lookout's empty parking lot. "Were you expecting me to bring someone else to our dream?"

I smiled. "No. I mean he's not here. Kendrick's not in my head."

"Are you sure?"

I took Ty's hand and led him up the gravel path to a quaint gazebo siding the parking lot. The metal and wood structure didn't exist at the real lookout, but it was a nice touch. "I don't know how it's possible, but I'm sure. He's not here. I can't feel him."

Ty sat next to me on the bench and smiled. "That's huge."

He wasn't wrong. Since returning from the Armaya, any and all moments we'd had together had been shared with Kendrick, or should I say marred by. Apart from my dwindling success with blocking, we'd hardly had a single private moment. This revelation was more than huge, it was monumental. Kendrick couldn't share my mind during a dreamscape. Without knowing it, I had grown accustomed to his continued negative thoughts and persistent interruptions. And now he wasn't here. It was just Ty and me.

Sudden nerves washed over me in waves. With Kendrick's expected interruptions I had gotten used to restraining myself around Ty. To holding back my animalistic need to feel, kiss, and drink him.

"I—I have a Christmas present for you," I said suddenly. His naked chest, full mouth, and scent were too much of a temptation. If I didn't change the mood I'd be all over him like a rash. "It's a vacation to the South Pacific Islands. A 5-night cruise. The flight leaves in two days."

"You're serious? Just us?" Ty rocked back against the bench. "What about your mom? She can't possibly be allowing you to go. Not if she knows it's with me."

"She won't have a choice."

Although I didn't want to spoil the getaway, I told Ty everything. Secrets in the past had always caused more trouble in the end. He wasn't impressed Marcus had initiated the vacations, but he took the warning seriously.

"Wherever we are, I'll never let anyone harm you." Ty ran his hand across my cheek. "I'd die to keep you safe."

As I went to smile, a roadblock occurred to me. "Oh, I didn't even...your father. He won't let you go, will he?"

Ty laughed. "I'm an adult, remember? He won't like it one bit, but he can't control me." His strong arms wrapped around me. "This is going to be awesome." Ty paused, arms releasing a fraction. "Hey, what do you plan to do about, uh...blood?"

Kendrick had already brought up that issue. "I'm going to stash packs of baggies and bottles in my checked baggage. That should work, right?"

Ty's eyebrows lifted, considering. "What if you get a puncture? How would you explain blood leaking from your luggage to airport officials?"

Hadn't thought of that.

"What about this?" Ty lifted my hand and pressed it to his elevated heartbeat. "Drink from me."

I coughed, choking on my own saliva. "What!" I shook my head. "No, Ty. I couldn't do that to you." Firstly, drinking from Ty like that would make it feel like I was using him. Secondly? I still didn't trust my self-control one hundred percent. What if I didn't have the strength to pull away?

"I know why you're worried. But you don't have to be. I trust you, Amelia." Ty saw the doubt on my face and lifted my hand to his lips. "If I need to help you stop in the beginning, that's okay. I understand this is new territory for you. It is for me, too. But I want to do this. I want to be connected to you in a way that's special, that's just for us. Don't you want that too?"

I wanted that more than I'd ever wanted anything in my entire life. "I do." I took a deep breath, seeing the hopeful determination on Ty's face. No matter what I did or what I was, Ty trusted me. I had always trusted him too. "If you change your mind…"

"I won't," Ty vowed.

I took another deep breath. "Okay then. I'll drink from you."

MOM CLEARED HER THROAT, pushed the neatly folded wrapping paper aside then rose from her green armchair. Behind her, the ceiling-high Christmas tree sparkled with decorations and flashing lights. A card for a booked weekend spa treatment and a silk shawl were clutched in her hands. "There's one last thing." Her smile was angelic and infectious, the earrings I'd given her complimenting her designer sweats. "Dorian and Amelia, why don't you have a look outside."

Dorian tossed his gift from me—the new iPad—aside on the imperial, cloth and wood sofa. He was up and running through the living room's tinsel and holly decked archway and out the front door by the time I uttered, "Outside?"

On the other side of the sofa Kendrick was listening to the new Three Days Grace album on his iPod, which now had a glossy new boarding case. He put aside the boarding boots and bindings I'd gotten him after our vacation surprise and smiled at me.

Dorian hollered from the front porch. "Woo hoo!"

I shoved my own loot aside—new Vans from Dorian, and surprise, surprise, a cocktail dress from Mom that I didn't totally hate—and rushed out the wreathed front door.

Out here snow coated almost everything: driveway, trees, grass, and the stone boundary fence. Even the windows were coated in crystal snowflakes. Amongst the winter blanket, one object was clear of white dust. Our car was parked at the steps, and the change was a standout. Brand new, massive mag wheels.

"They're fricken mad!" Dorian came around the car and wrapped his arms around Mom. "Thanks, Mom." He released her after a moment and glanced at Kendrick. "We've gotta go for a drive, but first..." He wriggled a brow at me. "You might want to take a look in the garage."

Expression guarded, Kendrick caught my hand and led the way through a gust of snow-swirling wind. I tried to read his thoughts, but they were locked up tight. Then I saw it. My eyes widened and my jaw dropped. In the spare garage bay was the most amazing gift I could ever imagine. It was purple and glossy and had two wheels. "A Ducati!"

"Kendrick told me how much you wanted your own transport," Mom said, now beside me. She hugged me and kissed my forehead. "You deserve it, sweetheart." Her arms released and she smiled. "You'll need to get your permit, of course, but apart from that it's all yours."

Mom trekked over the snowy driveway and back into the house, leaving Kendrick and me alone.

Almost in a trance I gravitated toward the bike, running my

hands across its cool metal. There was a silver insignia painted into the purple. *Soul mates.* My cheeks grew hot. "*You* did this?"

Kendrick smiled. "Yeah. That's why I've been blocking you out. When your mom told me what she'd gotten you it was so hard to keep it hidden." His gaze dropped with vulnerable uncertainty. "Do you like it? The artwork, I mean…"

I bit my lip, feeling uncomfortable. Then that awkwardness dissolved. Kendrick hadn't meant to imply that we were 'meant to be' or anything. This was just his way of saying that bound or not, nothing would ever break up our friendship. I stepped closer and curled my arms around his waist, head resting on his chest. Kendrick was my soul's mate and he always would be. "I love it."

After checking out every inch of the bike and firing it up to rev the engine, we headed back inside. Today had been awesome so far, but it wasn't going to stay that way. We had the huge job of bringing up the vacations with Mom. Guilt pressed against my heart. After everything she'd done for us, the possibility of having to compel her ate at my conscience.

"Mom," I said as Kendrick and I re-entered the lounge. Sitting in her green armchair, she smiled at the digital photo frame Dorian had given her. Right now it was scrolling through photos of us all as kids, including Kendrick. Seeing our innocent and naive faces made me feel even more terrible about what we had to force her into. "We have something we need to ask you."

Back on the imperial sofa, Dorian looked less than carefree as I walked to our mom's armchair. Kendrick remained leaning against the arched entry.

Mom replaced the frame on the ornate fireplace. "What is it, sweetheart?"

After receiving the itineraries and deciding to compel our mom if needed, we'd also made another decision. With Caius able to control her through compulsion, telling her the locations we'd be heading to would be asking for trouble.

"We want to take off on a camping/hunting vacation to the White Mountains. Off the beaten track, of course." I expected this next part to backfire, but I'd made my mind up. Mom had accepted my relationship with Ty, and if I wanted her to continue treating me like an adult, I needed to be upfront. "Though you should know, Ty will be coming too."

By the time I stopped speaking, Mom's face had turned from contemplative to hardened stone. "You think I'll allow this?" Her steely gaze locked on me. "You think I'll let you go away unsupervised with that wolf?"

Her words scratched at my skin. Of course the problem was that Ty would be there. I'd even bet if the roles were reversed, she'd let Dorian go with Marika. I copied her stance, folding my arms across my chest. "You can't keep treating me like a child. I made a promise to you about my relationship with Ty, and I intend to keep it." *At least for now.* "Do you have that little trust in me?"

"This is not about trust, Amelia. This is about—" Her words died with the loud chiming of her phone. She frowned and yanked it free from the pocket of her zip-up sweater. The crease between her eyebrows grew and her hand covered the speaker. "I have to take this. Wait here. This isn't over."

As she stormed out to the hallway and into her office, I was met by Dorian. "You didn't actually expect a different reaction than that, did you?"

"No, maybe…"

"Well it doesn't matter either way," Dorian said under his breath. "She'll change her mind whether she likes it or not."

Kendrick remained silent against the archway. He still didn't like the situation one bit, but he'd resigned himself to accepting it for my safety.

I perched on the edge of the stone coffee table and kept my voice low. "I'm not sure we should compel her. I don't…" I broke off and froze.

"Another one?" Mom's words traveled through the foyer from her office.

Dorian began to argue when I *shushed* him. "Listen."

A few seconds later Mom gasped. "No, not him. And in our own backyard. How could this have happened?" Mom made a noise of agreement, and then there was a long silence. "Yes, I understand." Soft steps came our way and she re-entered the lounge, looking paler than usual and clearly distracted.

Kendrick pushed off the wall. "Is everything alright, Ms. Lamont?"

Mom shook her head, glancing to each of us. "It's a council matter. I can't elaborate." She reclaimed her armchair and leaned forward, hands clasped in her lap and deep in thought.

After a tense minute she peered up. "I will allow the vacation. Though Kendrick, you'll need approval from your mother."

My jaw fell open, mirroring Kendrick and Dorian's utter disbelief.

Dorian recovered first. "I don't mean to sound ungrateful, but why the change?"

Mom sighed. "There are some current security issues in the vampire community. So for right now it is safer for you all to get away."

"What kind of security issues?" Kendrick pried.

Mom sighed, long and hard. "I can't elaborate. I've already told you too much."

CHAPTER 9

I paced the front steps the following morning. My suitcase was against the pillar, packed since yesterday. I'd barely slept and was running on fumes, but I didn't care. Ty would be here any minute to whisk me away on our trip. Our cruise didn't leave port for two days, but we'd lose a day in travel to get all the way to Australia, then another in time difference. Thanks to the long council meeting last night, Mom had said her goodbyes and sternly reminded me of my restrictions before passing out in bed with the sunrise. Dorian and Kendrick planned to take off after us in his car to keep our shared destination white lie going.

After a few more minutes of wearing in my new Vans, Ty arrived, driving up to the house in his WRX. Light rain fell as he jumped from the car and I bounded down the front steps. A second later I leaped into his arms. "I can't believe this is happening."

Ty's scent invaded my nose and I wriggled free. He smiled. "Well you'd better, because nothing's stopping us now." He collected my suitcase and placed it next to his in the trunk. Then he froze. "Is that a Ducati?"

My bones turned brittle as I followed him through the open garage door. Why the hell was it open? "Ah, yeah. Mom's Christmas present. Now I've got my own ride and Dorian keeps the car."

Ty swung a booted leg over to sit on the bike then frowned. His scarred hand slid over the insignia. "This isn't standard issue."

"Far from it." Kendrick strolled in to stand beside me. "Cost a bit, but she's worth it."

"Soul mates because of the blood bond," I clarified, frowning at Kendrick. "It's not meant to be romantic in any way. Isn't that right?"

"Yeah, sure." Kendrick raised a brow at me as Ty dismounted the bike. "You're not leaving without saying goodbye, are you?"

Despite the tension now radiating off Ty, I glanced at Kendrick. He was smiling, but the look was frozen with strain, painting his emotions clear as day. He wanted me to be happy, but he hated that my happiness included Ty.

Kendrick coiled his arms around me, lifting me off the ground and burying his face in my neck. "I'll miss you." A long moment passed, then he lowered me back down, keeping one hand on my waist. "Even if we are still connected twenty-four/seven."

I tried to ignore his lingering touch and the *I'll always be watching* meaning behind his words. But I failed. Irritation scored through me, knowing my time with Ty would always be shared. "Like you need to remind me," I snapped. A pang of instant regret at my tone weighed against my heart. Because even with the bond, I was seriously going to miss him. The guy my soul would forever be connected to. I threw my arms around him. "It's only a week."

Ty cleared his throat, now standing outside in the hardening rain. "We should get going."

His voice caused me to jolt away from Kendrick. I forced a smile, feeling like I'd done something wrong. "Say goodbye to Dorian again for me," I said, moving to the car to get in. I'd already done the hug and tears thing with him this morning. And I was glad. Right now saying goodbye to Kendrick was already difficult enough.

"Will do."

I shut the car door and Ty gunned the engine, directing us out the front gates. The property and Kendrick's silhouette shrunk in the rearview mirror. I sighed and began tapping my leg. Apart from the rain pattering the windshield, the air was thick with silent tension. With the mood threatening to dampen our trip away, I made a decision. I placed a light hand over Ty's, which clutched the gear shifter. "You're annoyed with me."

Ty frowned, chin twitching. "No. Not you. I just…"

"You just what?"

"I see the way…" His jaw clenched then released. "I see the way your *friendship* has grown."

Ty was a touch possessive, I'd noticed since we'd returned. But he was also confident. He knew where I stood and exactly how I felt about him. He knew he was the one. "You're not jealous are you?" my tone teased.

Ty's expression darkened and my breath caught. "Would you blame me if I were?"

Shock and defensiveness rocked me. "We're friends. That's it!" Hearing my sharp tone my lips snapped shut. I took a deep breath and ran my hand over his cheek. "I love *you*."

Ty's eyes closed as he grasped my hand from his cheek, pulling it to his lips. "I know you do. It's just difficult to watch you two sometimes. The bond that you share, that closeness…I see it changing." He dropped my hand and clutched the steering wheel as we veered off Ocean Boulevard. "I don't want to ever lose you."

"You will *never* lose me. I'm never letting you go."

Ty smiled at that, the tension from his body and hands releasing. "I have something for you." He reached for the inside pocket of his leather jacket. "It's your Christmas present. Though it's nothing as flashy as a cruise…" The next part was said under his breath. "*Or personalized bike artwork.*"

His heart began to pound. I could hear the increased drumming as he freed a small square box from his pocket. A velvet box.

My heart skipped in my chest, giddy and nervous all at the same time. I'd never been given any kind of jewelry before, well not from a guy I was in love with. Suspicion struck through me, turning any and all giddiness to full-blown panic.

Oh God. Don't be a ring. Don't be a ring.

The panic wasn't a commitment thing, not really. I knew I wanted Ty and that I would love him as long as I lived, which could be a seriously long time. Still, I was only sixteen, and with everything we were learning I had no idea what my future would hold. Would I even be alive in a year's time? Would Ty still want me? And what about The Council?

Unable to speak while trying to keep myself from hyperventilating, I stared.

Ty flicked open the box, seeming perplexed and nervous at my frozen, horrified expression. I gasped. Inside was a stunning heart-shaped amulet. Made of a red stone it was neither clear nor perfect. It was speckled with darker and lighter red spots with a hint of black grains. Silver molded around the stone's heart shaped edges, hanging from a long chain.

Ty grasped the thick chain with his free and shaky hand,

allowing the weighted stone to dangle before my eyes. "Do you like it?"

I exhaled the breath I'd been holding. "Like it?" I took the amulet in my hands and Ty let the silver chain drop. His intake of breath was audible as he watched me between checking the road. The stone was heavy, even heavier than it looked. The silver was cool to the touch. It wasn't purple, but it was the most beautiful thing I had ever seen. "Ty, I love it."

"It's a bloodstone. It belonged to my mother," Ty said quietly, glossy gaze staring out the windshield at the thickening traffic. "The morning after she was killed I found it under my pillow. Back then I thought my father would take it off me. I thought he wouldn't want me to have something so precious of hers that I could lose. So I hid it."

"Oh, Ty." My heart tugged, feeling like little hooks were pulling at it. I picked up the empty box and placed the amulet back inside, closing the lid. "I can't accept this. You should keep it."

Ty frowned at me. "No. I want you to have it." I began to argue, but Ty wasn't finished. "I've kept it all this time knowing that one day I would give it to the one girl who owned my heart. Amelia, *you are* that girl. Connected to Kendrick or a hundred guys, I don't care. I love *you*. Please…" He took the amulet from the box and caught my hand, the cold stone pressed between our palms. "Please say you'll keep it. Say you'll wear it as a symbol of my love, my heart in stone against yours."

Sniffing back sudden tears, I nodded. How could I say no to that? The guy of my dreams—or should I say, dreamscapes—was professing his limitless love for me. Solidifying the fact that nothing could ever get between us.

I took the amulet and fastened the chain around my neck, letting the heavy stone fall between my minimal cleavage. "I'll never take it off."

Ty smiled and laced his fingers through mine. "By the way," he said. "I kind of suspected, though I didn't know for sure..." His words ended as he maneuvered around a slow-moving car.

"Didn't know what?"

"If what Caius did to you had provided immunity." At my stumped frown he explained. "The chain and the edging around the stone are silver. You're immune."

Now in Australia, the cab passed by the Portside Wharf in Brisbane with its strip of boutique shops to pull around the bend at a huge shed-like building. Despite the jet lag radiating through my body, excitement streamed through me as I jumped out. The humid heat of summer hit me. I sucked in a lungful, trying not to cough at the heavy dampness of it. Even with my thick vampire skin, sticky moisture began to bead across my face and back. Appreciating how human this made me feel, I took in my surroundings while Ty removed our suitcases from the trunk. Beyond the huge building was the water where the massive cruise liner waited. People buzzed everywhere, the smell of salty sweat and blood mixing in the air as they dumped their luggage at the open roller doors. My stomach grumbled. I hadn't drunk any blood in over twenty-four hours. Still, I wasn't about to let that bother me. Not yet.

I grabbed my suitcase then caught Ty's hand as he paid the cabbie. "This is really happening!" I said, dragging him toward the bag drop.

Ty smiled, hauling his suitcase alongside as if it weighed nothing. "I know." He peered over the frame of his Oakleys, his golden irises rimmed with dark circles. "I keep wanting to pinch myself."

We checked our luggage and headed inside through the glass doors. The place was packed with people, all lining up to get their boarding passes. And there it was again. The heady smell of human blood. I groaned inwardly, gums prickling as I struggled to hold back my fangs.

Ty squeezed my hand, frowning. "You okay?"

I didn't want to tell him why my face looked so pinched. Unfortunately after agreeing to drink from him, being discrete on the whole blood thing wasn't going to work. "I'm a bit..." I lowered my voice. "*Thirsty.*"

Ty shot a glance over the heads of people to the male and female restrooms. "We can, you know, fix that issue now..."

Horrified at doing something as intimate as drinking from Ty in a public restroom, I shook my head. "Oh, no. It's not that urgent. And I'd rather not... Never mind. It can wait."

Ty shrugged and curled an arm around my waist. "If you say so."

Thirty torturous minutes later we finally reached the front of the line. I shoved our itinerary and passports into the woman's hands and tapped the counter. With Ty's hunting travels and my mom's tendency to prepare for the unexpected, we'd both already had our passports. The woman ran her fingers along the computer keyboard and frowned. "That's strange," she said, her accent Aussie. "Your booking states that you're both eighteen, but your passports don't." She lifted a brow at Ty. "Yours makes you seventeen." Then her brown eyes slid to me. "Yours, sixteen."

"Oh, it must be a clerical error," I said, wondering why Marcus would have used the wrong dates.

The woman glanced over the itineraries. "Well, if that's the case I will need to speak with my supervisor."

Over the collective noise of everyone else talking inside the huge shed Ty asked, "And why is that?"

"Being under eighteen makes you both minors," she said, eyeing him then me. "All minors must be accompanied by an adult on board."

The woman began to rise from her seat behind the counter, and it seemed like time had literally slowed to snail speed. Her hand rose in slow motion in the direction of an older man assisting another teller further down. Then her lips began to part. Shit! She was about to call him over. About to bring the guillotine down on this whole dream vacation with the guy I loved. After everything I'd done to get here, I couldn't let that happen. Plus I was starving, and if I couldn't be alone with Ty soon I was going to lose it.

My hand shot over the counter, catching her rising arm. The woman looked at me, startled. "We are eighteen." All the desperation I felt to make her believe streamed from my eyes and into hers. "Our passports match the booking details. Look again and you'll see it."

Still pleading with my eyes, I released the woman's wrist. The red press of my firm grip was painted across her arm and I cringed. The one other time I'd successfully compelled someone was back in Anchorage when I almost killed the school quarterback. I didn't like my odds. But at the same time, that desperation of needing something was there, so maybe I had a chance.

The woman reopened both our passports and frowned. "Oh dear, my mistake. Yes, you are right."

When her fingers slipped across the keyboard my insides felt like they were doing backflips. A few minutes later the woman gave back our passports and booking itinerary. "These are your cruise cards," she said holding up two plastic cards. "You'll need them to access your cabin and to purchase anything on board. Crediting the cards can be done here or after boarding."

After handing over some cash, the woman gave us our cruise cards. "Being eighteen, your cards are blue. So when buying alcohol or smokes you simply have to present this card to prove your age."

Ty's brows lifted, gaze shifting from his card to the woman. "Eighteen-year-olds can drink?"

The woman smiled. "Unlike the United States, our drinking age is eighteen. Enjoy."

"You're amazing," Ty said as we rushed up a set of stairs to a corridor, heading for the cruise ship. "You compelled her!"

"I can't believe it worked." With Ty's hand fastened in mine I didn't want to look back or slow down. "Let's just get on board. I don't know how well that's gonna hold."

As we rounded a corner we almost ran into four red-faced and sweaty men carting two fridge-sized crates between them. The crates were big enough to fit a body and were covered in colorful courier and airline stickers. We darted around and kept running. "Sorry," I called back.

Another bend later and we had to slow. We were a few steps from embarking, but a man with a high-tech camera prompted us to wait. "You must take a boarding photo."

Not hearing any shouting about the minors who'd somehow tricked their way through check-in behind us, I nodded. "I think we're safe." Besides, I wanted a photo of Ty and me. In all our rocky time together, we'd never had the opportunity.

We stood on the marked spot with a welcome aboard screen behind us. Ty wrapped me in his warm arms and pulled me so close that the amulet pressed between our chests. His lips brushed mine and the camera clicked.

"Any pictures taken will be available on the promenade deck at the photo gallery for purchase." The photographer waved. "Enjoy your cruise."

Once on board we were like kids in a candy store, tearing around every inch of what would be our home for the next five days. The boat was beautiful and massive. There was an Oasis up top with surrounding views and a hot tub. Inside on different levels there were boutique shops, restaurants, clubs, a show lounge, a casino, and even a spa that offered a full pampering experience. The outside deck housed a pizzeria, along with the dining lunch crowd, two pools, and two bars.

Ty nudged my shoulder and pointed to the colorful drinks fit with paper umbrellas being prepared at the bar. "Wanna get a drink?"

My stomach tightened. I was thirsty…for so much more than alcohol. But this drinking from Ty thing was new. Never been done. Well, except for the time I lost control at Troy's party and attacked him. And what about this time? What if I couldn't stop?

Ty took my hand and began leading me away from the bar. "Come on."

"Why? Where are we going?"

Ty draped his arm around my shoulders and pulled me close to kiss my hair. "To our cabin. You need blood."

Despite the panic that had my heart racing, I clutched Ty's side and kept walking, unable to think of a single thing to say. When we reached deck 12 and our suite, Ty let me go to open the door. I backed up against the corridor and sucked air, unable to clear his scent from my nose.

The door swung inward. Ty remained quiet, smiling as he caught my hand and led me inside. Trying to distract my sense of smell, I scanned our room. There was a small dining table, a couch, a personal bathroom, and a glass sliding door that led outside to a private balcony. But I didn't care about any of that. A queen-size bed jutted out from one wall, taking up half the floor space and filling me with anxiety. For some reason, the sleeping arrangements had never crossed my mind. Now they were all I could think about.

"I can sleep on the couch," Ty offered, squeezing my shoulders. "I don't mind."

I shook my head. "No, it's okay." Ty knew we couldn't 'sleep' together while I was still unable to block Kendrick, so that wasn't a real issue. "I just hadn't thought about it. It's fine, really."

"Well in that case…" Ty swooped me up and threw me onto the bed. He leaped on top of me in a flash and captured my lips. His hard body lowered against me. The suggestion in his movements had me tingling all over, and my fangs peeking through my gums. Alone together I kissed him back with force, lost in his scent and moments from biting down on his lip. But we weren't really alone. Kendrick's repulsion etched into my own emotions. Ty drew away before I got a chance to and reclined on his side.

I shifted to face him. "W-why'd you stop," I stuttered, struggling for breath.

Ty let out a long breath and rolled onto his back. His arm reached out and pulled me in close beside him. "We have plenty of time to be alone together. Well, mostly alone," he said. "And I know we can't…you know. But we can take our time exploring other options."

I curled into Ty, laying my hand against his hot chest. The black covering of his T-shirt irritated me. "Other options?"

"Well, I'm sure your thirst hasn't just vanished," Ty said. "You're going to have to drink from me sooner or later." He sat up and tugged his T-shirt over his head. Then he glanced back at me, touching my cheek. "I know you're nervous. But you don't have to be. If you need help to stop, I'm here."

I reared up on the bed and took Ty's hand in mine. His heartbeat had elevated at his last words and I struggled to think past the flutter...not to mention his bare sexy chest. "Are—are you sure about this?"

Ty removed his Oakleys and tilted my face up with his hand and looked—really looked—into my eyes. "Yes."

I took a deep breath, scrambling to pull up my mental blocks from Kendrick. When it was as solid as I could make it, I nodded. "What now?"

Ty cupped his hand around my neck and pulled me forward until our lips met. The touch was electric, making my body hum as my fangs broke free. I lapped over his tongue, again and again, getting hotter, losing restraint. His pulse throbbed through his bottom lip. It was too much to take, too much to wait for. As my lips tore free I froze.

"Wait!" I jerked back and my fangs ached in protest. "Won't this hurt you?" Vampire bites were meant to elicit a sensation of ecstasy with a flood of dopamine to the system. Except not when the donor was vampire too. "I mean, because you're a hybrid."

Ty reclaimed my lips hungrily. "The pain is nothing compared to the pleasure. Now stop stalling."

Worry sated, I met his lips again, reigniting our fire. I trailed kisses along his jaw and up its sharp curve to his neck. His scent was like a drug, tempting, alluring, and addictive. I kissed his neck with parted lips, tongue testing the vein that pulsed beneath. Oh God, I could practically taste him. Parts of my body warmed and my breath came in desperate pants. Then it was too much to withstand. Too much to hold back from.

"Ty," I managed to rasp, "I can't hold on any longer."

Ty's answer was a warm calloused hand at the back of my neck, and the distinct tilt of his head that exposed as much of his neck as possible. With my fangs in place I slowly bit down, hoping I wasn't hurting him. Ty groaned, hands hauling my body closer as his sweet, fiery blood pooled in my mouth. The taste was a thousand times better than his scent, and I drew harder. His quick pulse changed, somehow blending with my own.

As that sinister sensation of needing more and more grew, like no amount of Ty's blood would ever fill this hungry void within me, a sudden chill shocked me. My eyelids flung open. Surrounding me from all angles were snow-covered peaks. Panic swept through me. My legs were dangling fifty feet above an ice-capped slope. My brain screamed to grip the chair rail, but my body refused to respond.

Calm down, whispered a familiar voice.

Kendrick? Irritation frayed on the edge of my mind. *What the hell is going on?*

Anxious energy swirled through Kendrick's chest as if it were my own. *I'm sorry. I didn't know this would happen. I just didn't want to feel you...drinking him.*

You felt that? Nausea churned my stomach, exacerbated by Kendrick's repulsion. Still, overriding his discomfort was the phenomenon of suddenly being in the snowfields in New Hampshire. *How did this happen? What is this?*

You're in my mind, Kendrick answered. *Seeing what I see. Experiencing what I'm doing.*

Feeling the confusion building I wanted to frown, but I wasn't in my body. It was like I was locked inside Kendrick's shell, a meat suit that didn't encompass my own form, just a soul. *How is that even possible?*

I could sense Kendrick's response without him having to speak. He had experienced this before, many times in fact. Sifting through his memories I realized how devastating this had been for him. On many levels I had already known this, but I hadn't understood the full extent until this very second. He had been in my mind, in my body, seeing through my eyes when I'd been naked and caught him. And every time I sensed his depressed emotions because of what I was feeling for or doing with Ty, it had been emphasized by the fact that he was, in fact, seeing and feeling everything as I was. *I'm so sorry, Kendrick. I didn't know.*

It's okay. His arm clung tighter to his Burton snowboard. *It's not so bad now anyway. I'm getting better at controlling it most of the time. Though I never thought wanting to escape your mind so bad would draw you into mine.* Kendrick took a deep breath. *Ready?*

For what? I asked as Kendrick pushed off the chair lift. His board connected with the snow below. The wind whipped past as he plunged faster and faster down a steep and rock-riddled slope. The experience was exhilarating and didn't seem to go for nearly long enough with Kendrick reaching the bottom in record speed.

That was awesome!

I could feel Kendrick smiling. *That was a warm up…*

So, I questioned. *How do I control this, well, whatever you call it?*

Astral projection. He shrugged, unclipping his boots and picking up the board. *Well it kinda happened for me naturally, where I can now come and go as I please…well usually. But in the beginning, I guess I focused on my body and being connected to it rather than yours.*

I focused on my own physical body and where it was. *Oh shit!* I had been fangs-deep in Ty's neck, drinking his delicious blood.

Do you have to think so loud? Kendrick's stomach twisted.

Sorry. I don't know how else to do this.

Kendrick began trekking back up to the snow lift as I concentrated. He mounted the chair lift and I focused all my mental energy on the bed I was sitting on. On my fingers threaded through Ty's hair. On the taste of his blood as it filled my mouth. Then it happened. Darkness grew from the edge of my vision until everything became black. The taste of Ty's blood returned to my mouth and my fangs retracted.

Worry stirred up my stomach. I'd continued to feed from Ty while being absent. Had he noticed the change? Would he have any blood left? I edged back and licked my lips clean, watching as the punctures on his neck closed up.

Ty's head rocked up, burning gold irises shining. A sleepy smile played across his lips. "Told you there was no need to worry."

He had no idea. I sighed, knowing I wasn't about to tell him and feeling shitty for it. "You were right." Then I frowned. After donating his blood to me, Ty looked exhausted past being jet lagged, and even a little pale. How much had he let me take? "How about a cat nap?"

Ty reclined against the pillows and pulled me down against him. "You read my mind."

CHAPTER 10

Ty stirred as I drew away from his chest. He seemed so peaceful and content sleeping beside me, his breathing slow and rhythmic. His color had returned too after my feeding, his werewolf healing replenishing his body after I'd taken so much blood earlier.

The sun had set beyond the glass doors, leaving our room bathed in growing shadows. Needing to figure out how to reveal the new bond link, I rolled off the bed and tiptoed out onto our own private balcony. I stood at the rail and peered out over the black-rippling ocean. Apart from the whipping sea breeze, it was peaceful out here with the sound of the ship slicing through the reflective ocean.

"Here you are." Ty's familiar voice behind me almost made me jump. His breath was warm on my neck as he wrapped his arms around my waist. His chest molded against my back and his lips brushed my shoulder. The slight but imitate touch sent undulating goose bumps over my body and caused a shiver to run up my spine. "I've been meaning to talk to you about something."

I shivered again, not in reaction to his touch but because of the seriousness in his voice. Maybe he had noticed me slip away when feeding from him. Without turning I tried to control my voice. "What about?"

Ty loosened his hug to run his hands up and down my cold arms. His obvious nerves spiked my own panic. "About us," he whispered. "About my dismal lifespan, and your extended, maybe even eternal one."

So not about the bond. Instead, I knew Ty was referring to my immortal blood, and the possibility that this immortality could extend beyond my veins to my whole body. I could live forever... well, unless killed.

Ty gripped my shoulders and forced me to face him. There was a fragile hardness to his face. "You expect to live for a millennium, at the very least. But my lifespan, since the vampire part of our line has been mostly bred out, isn't expected to exceed much more than a hundred years."

I nodded and raised my hand to touch his face. A sinking feeling in my stomach told me I wouldn't like where this was heading. "What are you saying?"

Ty's gaze pleaded. "Amelia, I want to be with you for as long as inhumanly possible. One hundred years will never be enough. Not when you deserve someone beside you for your lifetime."

I blinked back the beginnings of tears. It was our first day away together and already the daunting topic of our relationship's lifespan was creating waves. As I read between the lines, a shocking realization sent my heart racing. Ty believed I deserved someone for my whole lifetime, or as close to that as possible. He personally would never come close. The only beings that could even compete in life years were other royal vampires. Was Ty about to release me? To let me go so I could have what he thought I needed? I stared down at the deck. "You can't leave me." My voice was shaky. "You promised."

Ty wrapped his arms around me and held me close to his chest, the amulet trapped between our hearts. "I'm not leaving, Amelia. I'll *never* leave you."

A sigh escaped my lips and I hugged him tight. I squeezed my lids shut while dread pooled in my stomach like hot lava. "But?"

"I want to offer you more. I know I could never give you a millennium, but…"

I pulled away. Sudden intensifying wind whipped my hair over my face. I yanked my hair back and twisted it over my shoulder. "Ty, what are you saying?"

Ty smiled, resting his palm against my cheek. "I want you to turn me. Reignite the vampire part of me that's been bred out. I know it's possible."

My jaw fell open. In theory the option was almost a good one, but in reality? It could kill him. "Ty, we can't. You can't. I won't—"

Ty raised a finger to my lips, silencing my words. "We can have a real life together, Amelia. You and me. Five hundred years to a millennium together, depending on how my royal wolf blood deals with the turn. Don't you want that?"

I dropped my now clenched hands to my side, feeling my nails biting into flesh. "Of course I want that. All I want is you. But I won't risk your life. I can't."

Ty slumped into the plastic deck chair behind him and rubbed his forehead. "I know the stats. Fifty percent of infected humans live. Fifty don't. But I'm *not human*. I'm already part vampire. And the lycan part of me is strong, stronger because I'm a hybrid."

"Exactly," I shot back a little too loud. Turning Ty was a risk, a risk that could give him what he wanted at best. Alternatively it could change him, the person he is. And what about his feelings for me? Would turning him change that part of him too? Would it harden his emotions or swamp his mind with bloodlust, extinguishing his humanity? Worst of all it could kill him, taking him from me. Forever. I knew if I went ahead and this backfired, I would never forgive myself. "Ty. It's far too dangerous. We have no idea what could happen."

Ty peered over the railing, where twinkling stars reflected light over the dark water. The look on his face was distant and cold.

I lowered onto his knee and lifted his chin, forcing him to look at me. "Please, Ty. Don't ask me to do this. I would rather have you now, than dare to risk it all." I swiped at the tears rolling down my cheeks. "Ty, I can't lose you."

Ty ran his hand up my back to stroke my hair. The distant coldness melted from his blank features. "You won't lose me. I'm not going anywhere. We don't have to decide anything this minute." I went to argue, to tell him that there was nothing to decide. Before I could, Ty pulled me down to his waiting lips. "We can just live in the moment," Ty said between the kiss, "for now…"

LATER THAT NIGHT we got pizza up on the deck after missing the dinner service in the dining lounge. We ate in silence, Ty scanning over a ship map while tension rippled between us. Our minds were distracted, but neither of us dared to bring up the elephant in the room.

When Ty finished the last pizza slice he sighed. Then he peered up. His irises were now deep brown with contact lenses to mask the gold from human sight. "Wanna get hot and sweaty?"

The image of me naked and crushed beneath Ty back in our

room flashed through my thoughts. Rapid heat burned my face. "Um..."

Ty winked. "You know, in the Oz bar." He pointed to its location on the map in his hands. "On the dance floor."

My lips curved into a cheeky smile. I had always loved dancing, and before all the stress of my new life had started, I used to rock out to pop songs. Now my playlists were inspired by more serious music that reflected my feelings of being different. Of being a monster. Except here with Ty, I wasn't a monster. I was accepted and loved. It was time to live a little, to let go and loosen up. "You couldn't hold me back if you tried."

After a quick stop at our room to change—me in the bathroom while Ty dressed in the main room—we were ready to burn up the dance floor. Wanting to keep Ty distracted from our earlier discussion, I'd pulled out my most daring outfit. The short ruffled skirt and bright purple top left just enough to the imagination. I was far from comfortable in it, but with Ty already stealing peeks, I knew the distraction would hold. As usual, Ty looked perfect and sexy in cotton pants and a black collared shirt.

The Oz bar was raging as we pushed through the glass doors. There were tables that glowed from lights beneath their glass tops. Benches surrounded them, jammed full of humans, drinking and chatting. Bodies flooded the dance floor, sweating and gyrating to the blaring pop music.

I waited by the entry, adjusting to the loud onslaught of DJ-spun music pounding through my ears. Then, letting my worries melt away, I lured Ty onto the dance floor. A Kesha song was blaring, the bass thumping through my body. Ty curled one arm around my waist and held me close. The touch of his hot body against mine, along with the energetic beat of the music, had my blood thrumming through my veins. We moved together, our hips joined by an invisible force, the heat and sexual tension growing with each flirtatious second. The seconds turned into minutes and the minutes into who knows how long as we continued our seductive dance. Songs passed and the dancing crowds dispersed and built back up with the humans needing a break from the energy-draining movements.

After a countless number of songs, I shot a glance at the bar. Glass shelves lit by blue light and stocked full of alcohol spanned the wall behind. Thirst dried my throat and for a moment I wished I were at *Bite* at the Armaya, where blood was the number one drink. All the close dancing had left me craving Ty's vein. Still, I didn't want to leave this bubble of energy and weightlessness to drink from him. Hopefully alcohol would buy me some time. "Wanna drink?"

Ty smiled before bringing his lips to mine. "Thirsty again?" His words were a rumble before he smiled and winked. "Come with me."

"Where are we going?"

Ty led me from the dance floor. "You'll see."

We continued past the busy drinkers, stopping when we reached a dark corner that escaped the green light coming off surrounding tables. Ty backed into the wall and drew me in with his arms, eliminating all space between us. He tilted his head to the side, exposing the pulsing vein at his neck. Sudden realization dawned on me. Ty wanted me to drink from him here, in front of all these people.

I inched back, mouth watering even though my head was shaking. "Ty, no! Someone will see."

Ty's hands were still on my hips as he panned left to right over my shoulder. "See for yourself. No one's even looking. And even if they were, their human eyes can't make out enough detail in this dim lighting."

"Ty, I don't know..." Looking around I found no one even glancing our way. The offer of his blood and the scent that had been tempting me since we began dancing had my body sure of what it wanted. But this was still public. What if I couldn't stop? "I don't think…"

Ty lifted my hand while I continued scanning the crowd. Then his scent bloomed. My focus shot back to see my nail tipped with crimson. A small cut along the side of his neck was already beginning to heal. Blood had dripped from the tiny cut to pool along his collarbone.

The trance-inducing puddle begged me to lap it up.

Through a primal need, I leaned into Ty. One hand curled around his neck and the other pressed against his chest, feeling his heart flutter. His hands encased me, holding me against him. My lips found the curve of his collarbone, lapping up the pooled blood from his salty skin. Then they rose, kissing his neck and finding the right spot. My fangs slid free of their sheaths and broke through his skin. His blood mesmerized me, still my paranoia of being caught resurfaced.

Drinking carefully so as to not make a mess, I scanned left. People still sat at tables, drinking and talking. To my right I could see the dance floor, which was still packed with an erratically moving sea of people. The bar was also packed. No one was looking our way.

I was about to let my paranoia recede when a stalling sensation struck through me. Someone was watching me. Watching us. There, at the far end of the bar and bathed in shadow, was a guy. He had light hair and looked around twenty.

And he was staring straight at me.

A flash of strobe lit his face, making his eyes appear red and his pallor bright pink.

I let my fangs retract and did my best to cover my mouth as I drew away from Ty's neck. The guy smiled, looking pleased.

Instantly I spun away, covering my face with my hands. Having drunk live blood my irises would be piercing and silver, my whites red. Why hadn't I thought of that before? "Shit! Someone's watching."

Ty lifted his head and glanced around. "Where?"

I peeked through my fingers. A slow-moving group of guys with drinks in their hands blocked the view of the end of the bar. I held my breath, cursing as they shifted out of the way.

Behind them the end of the bar was empty. No guy. No one watching.

Plus no one was screaming down the roof at the monster in the corner making a meal of the hot guy. I felt relieved and a little stupid. Ty was right. Humans had terrible eyesight. Even if someone had been watching, they would have assumed we were a couple making out. "It was nothing. I'm just being paranoid."

CHAPTER 11

Ty rifled through his backpack. "I know you're immune. But just in case..." He held up a bottle of sunscreen, a mischievous smile pulling at his lips.

I tugged my loose beach shirt off, revealing a tight purple bikini. The urge to re-cover myself was there, but I held it back. Ty's hungry eyes drinking in every inch of me spiked my confidence. I shrugged meekly. "Better safe than sorry."

Today was our second cruise day and our first port of call at the Isle of Pines. It was a small island, requiring a motorized passenger boat from the ship to cart passengers to shore. Following the ride we exited onto the floating dock, which rose and fell with soft waves and led to the beach. A quick photo op with local islanders dressed in traditional tribe attire followed. Then we found a shaded spot bordering the soft sandy beach, with short trees hanging above us to spread our beach towels beneath.

With my face warming at Ty's lingering gaze, I lowered stomach-down onto the beach towel. At the same time I formed a wall around my thoughts and actions before Kendrick could intrude. Ty threw a leg over my back, straddling my hips. A squirt of cold sunscreen dropped onto my skin. His rough hands began massaging the thick liquid into my back and shoulders, warming the lotion as his palms slid in a circular motion. The touch of his hands on my naked skin had my blood rushing with heat. I rolled over with him still on top of me and smiled. Ty squirted another cold blob onto my stomach causing me to flinch, then another onto my chest. He wavered, his hands hovering above my pale skin.

Knowing where I wanted those very hands, I connected our palms and directed them down to my stomach. His hands and fingers massaged me there before hesitantly trailing up over my chest. His eyes found mine over his Oakleys and I smiled. Taking the invitation, he rubbed the sunscreen into the exposed flesh, careful not to overstep by actually touching my breasts. His breathing deepened as he leaned closer to me, but he didn't make eye contact. Instead, his focus remained on his hands, trailing from my chest, up my neck, and over my face.

Arching up from the beach towel I met his lips. I teasingly bit his lower lip before parting his mouth with mine. Our tongues met briefly before Ty drew away. He smiled and grasped my hand, jumping up and pulling me along with him.

"I need to cool down." His voice was rough with lust. He tugged me across the scorching hot sand and into the lukewarm water. He released my hand and dove under the surface. A moment later he re-emerged a few yards away.

I followed, loving the feel of the soothing water before rising above the surface to float hard up against Ty. Sexual tension grew between us like crackling static. Unfortunately the bond block was failing. So I decided to defuse the situation, for now. "How about we go for a swim around that." I pointed to a giant rocky mass that was covered by scrubby trees and bordered by water, connecting on one side with the beach's shore. "Check out the marine life?"

Ty grazed my face with his hand. "Good idea."

After checking out the colorful marine life and coral reef around the giant rock, we reclined back on our beach towels. With our arms grazing we lay quietly. Rhythmic waves lapped against the sandy shore, and a light breeze blew through the surrounding palm and pine trees. The relaxing sounds almost had me nodding off to sleep.

Then a sudden recognizable shift jolted my senses awake. I was sitting in a cozy cocktail bar, my back leaning against the cold glass window. It was the only thing that separated me from the freezing snow building against the glass pane. With a start I realized what was happening. In my relaxed state my mind had shifted into Kendrick's body. He was nursing a crisp brandy on the rocks and favoring his left arm which throbbed. *What happened?*

Kendrick stiffened in his seat, noticing my intrusion. *I'm fine. Just had a little tumble on the slopes.* He threw back his drink. *It's nothing you need to worry about.*

I searched Kendrick's mind, finding the replay of events that led to his injury. He had been attempting a double flip off a crest and didn't pull off the landing. I tried to push further into his memories but came to a dead end. *You're keeping something from me.*

Kendrick motioned to the bartender for another drink. *It's nothing. I've just been practicing blocking you...for both our sakes.* With a new drink put before him, he took a big gulp. *That's all.*

There had been less intrusions from him when I was with Ty. He hadn't even popped in when I'd fed from Ty in the club. So I supposed he was telling the truth. *Please be more caref—*

All thoughts shattered as I was ripped from Kendrick's mind. "Amelia!" Ty's voice was panicked, his calloused hands shaking my shoulders. "Shit. Wake up!"

My heart shot into my throat. My eyes flew open. Sunlight blinded me and I blinked back tears. Ty's shaking stopped and I leaned up on my elbows. Still clearing my vision, I scanned the beach. "What's wrong?"

Ty breathed out hard, scrubbing a tense hand down his face. "Shit, you scared me. We both fell asleep, but when I tried to wake you…" His face paled like he'd seen a ghost. "It was like you weren't even here."

Ty knew I'd slipped away. Fan-freaking-tastic! There was no keeping it from him now. I sighed, resigned to telling the truth. "I wasn't here," I confessed. I turned further on my towel and laid a gentle hand on his knee. "I was at the ski lodge…well, sort of. In Kendrick's mind. It's a bond thing. And I didn't mean to. It just kinda happened."

Irritation edged in on Ty's grim features. He looked away from me and out to the sun-speckled water. "How long has this been going on?"

I stared at my hand resting on Ty's knee, then let it slip away. "It happened for the first time yesterday. Well at least for me it did. Kendrick's been able to come and go since the beginning."

"So now the bond has grown between you two." Ty's voice was hollow, a shell without emotion.

I shook my head frantically. "No, I mean yes. But this doesn't change us. None of this has to change us."

"But it does." Ty's head twisted. The hurt plaguing his expression broke my heart. "You will *always* be connected to him. The bond between you continues to grow. As do your feelings for him."

I wanted to throw myself into Ty's arms, but held back, feeling the glacial turn this discussion was taking. "No, Ty. That's not true. I'm in love with you, not him!"

A muscle ticked in Ty's jaw as his contact-shielded eyes shifted to me. I swear I could see gold sparking from the edges of his irises. "You think I'm blind, Amelia? You may not love him like you do me, but you can't deny that your feelings for him have grown. I know you love him too. How am I supposed to compete with that, when you won't even give me a chance?"

"W-what do you mean, *give you a chance*?" My stomach dropped with suspicion that had my eyes tearing up.

Ty placed his palms on my cheeks and rested his forehead against mine. "Even the odds, Amelia. Level the playing field," he whispered, voice low and sharp. "Lengthen my life."

I yanked my face free, jumping to my feet. A flash of Ty cold and dead shone behind my lids as I blinked back tears. Complete with bloodstains over his face and bare chest, the image almost brought me to my knees. "Are you so freaking threatened that you would risk your own life to beat him? Is that all I am, a prize for you to win?!"

I sprinted away from Ty without a backward glance. Tears were streaming from my face now and I couldn't bear to show him how vulnerable he made me.

I SPENT the evening alone in the dining lounge. Now on dessert, I forked pieces of mud cake and pushed them around my plate. The fact that it was chocolate didn't seem to matter. For the bitter taste it left in my mouth, it may as well have been acid.

I sighed for the millionth time. *Lost In You* by Three Days Grace played through my iPod's earphones, only making me feel worse. My head was a mess. I felt sick over my fight with Ty. As usual, I had overreacted. Not that I didn't deserve the right to react. Turning

Ty could kill him, and I knew I wouldn't be able to live with myself if I had been the one to do it.

I rubbed my eyes, trying to block out the image of Ty cold, stiff, and dead. Then emptiness dawned on me. Kendrick wasn't in my mind. I sent out feelers through the bond but sensed nothing. No connection. No thoughts or emotions. Just me, alone. Normally I would have appreciated the privacy, but not now. Kendrick's injury from earlier and his recapped events didn't sit well. Remembering that memory block had my stomach churning. Something was wrong.

Leaving my mangled dessert, I headed for the cabin and my iPhone. When I reached the room I paused. Ty was probably in there and I knew I needed to talk things out with him, but a sinking feeling told me Kendrick needed me first. I opened the door to find the lights already on. Ty stood outside on the balcony, the sliding door closed and the drapes drawn open. He glanced back at me, and his face didn't change. It just remained frozen and blank. I looked away and grasped my iPhone from the bed, dialing Kendrick's number.

'Out hitting the slopes. So leave a message and I might call you back later.'

Kendrick's phone was either turned off, or worse…out of range. "Dammit."

The sliding door opened. "What's going on?"

"Oh." I spun and was met by a gust of humid sea air as Ty came in. "Kendrick's blocked me out, and—"

"Great." Ty yanked the sliding door shut. "Let's talk about your *soul mate* and how much you're missing him."

"Ty it's not like that. I'm worried something bad has happened."

"Like what?" Ty leaned back against the glass, crossing his arms over his chest.

I knew I could have gone into detail, but there was no point. Ty would only put these little glimpses down to being misplaced affection. So I kept to the facts. "Kendrick was injured earlier, when I, ah…visited him. He was keeping something from me, too. And now I can't even feel him. It's like he's not here anymore."

Ty's guarded face softened. He took my arm and pulled me down onto the foot of the bed. "He's not dead, Amelia. I'm sure everything is fine. He's probably just zonked out sleeping off a full day boarding. Can you, um, you know, visit him when he's sleeping?"

I frowned. Today had been the second so called 'visit' to Kendrick, but neither this one nor the first had been while he was asleep. "I don't know."

"Well, that's all it is then."

I clasped and unclasped my hands. "Ty, I'm sorry…"

"No. Don't be." His words silenced me. "I just took the new Kendrick link badly. I didn't mean to push the subject."

Feeling the walls between us fall, I wrapped my arms around his broad shoulders. "Ty, I don't want to lose you, ever." I hugged him like I'd never get the chance again. "But I can't risk your life."

Ty slumped as his arms curled around my waist. "Okay."

"Okay?" I arched away from him, peering into his now golden eyes. "You're humoring me?"

Ty's smile said it all. "We can spend the rest of my life arguing about this, or we could spend our time living it…"

The last of what Ty was saying died as my vision swam with black, the cabin light blinking out. Whipping wind rose, my hair flailing around my face like a living scarf intent on blocking my view. I glanced around, trying to see something through the darkness. A pair of glowing red eyes appeared, blinking from the shadows.

"Nice to finally meet you." The man's hissed words were cold and deadly.

I jumped upright, my heart hammering through my ears. Confused and feeling out-of-body, I wondered if this was somehow a vision of what Kendrick was keeping from me.

The guy moved from the shadows, killing my thoughts. The escaping moonlight caught across his chalky gray flesh and sharp glinting fangs.

Terror struck through me. "W-what do you want?" Though I said the words, it was like my voice and tone was mute. Still I took a step back, cringing at the radiating fear I felt in those words.

The guy's smile widened. "Just you."

He lunged forward faster than light. I turned to run. Too slow. The guy's ice-cold hands caught around my neck. I struggled as his grip tightened, pulling me back into the shadows...

SOMEONE'S HANDS held me down. The smell of sweet blood was thick in the air. And I was starving.

I thrashed to get free and broke away. Still blinded, there was only one thing on my mind. Blood.

Without sight my other senses directed me as I lunged, finding the source and knocking it down. A male grunted as we hit the ground, and I snapped my fangs, aiming for the neck. But this one was strong.

One hand caught my throat. The other pushed against my shoulder, spinning me over until he was on top of me.

"Amelia, stop!" The familiar voice rushed.

I was hardly listening. The pull to his blood was too strong. I snapped my fangs again, starving. I needed to tap a vein like a needed air to breathe.

The rose color began to fade from my vision. Cabin walls reformed, along with our bed and the balcony door. Above me, a black-haired and golden-eyed guy struggled to keep me pinned.

My thrashing vanished and my eyes widened. "Ty?"

Unable to help it, I zeroed in on the pulsing vein up his neck. Beyond the surprise of him, the need to attack was rebuilding with force.

I slammed my fists into his chest.

Ty's hold released and he fell back, knocking into the table.

Free, I shot into the bathroom and locked the door, slumping against it. Struggling for breath, I saw my reflection in the small mirror. My irises were shining silver, my whites crimson. Blue veins ran like spider webs across my face and down my neck and chest. They were all physical reactions that went hand in hand with having a vision.

Ty belted on door. "Amelia! Open up."

My stomach clenched in starvation. A sinister voice in my head whispered, *open the door. Take one little bite. You know you want to.*

"Amelia, what happened?" Ty sounded panicked and breathless. "Let me in, dammit!"

I clenched my fists to keep from sliding open the latch. I was going to attack Ty, again, and he was worried about me? I banged my skull against the door, once, twice, three times. "Ty, I'm so sorry. All I could smell was blood. I—I didn't know…"

"It's okay." There was a loud exhale and a thump as if Ty had dropped his forehead against the door. "You had a vision, right? That's why you're starving."

"And that makes it okay?" I bit out between grated teeth.

"It's a learning curve," Ty said, still right outside. "It doesn't make you a monster." After a silent pause he said, "Amelia, you need blood. Open up and let me help you. Let me *feed* you."

The shudder that ran down my entire body had my stomach turning and my fangs aching. "No!"

There was no way I was going to risk lunging at Ty like the monster I was, even if he could hold me back. *Monster* by Skillet started looping in my subconscious, a devious reminder of the thing that lived right beneath the surface. The thing I may never have full control over.

"I don't want you to see me like this. I just need…"

"Blood," Ty said. Footsteps moved away from the door. "Got it." A few long seconds later he returned and knocked. "There's a glass full right outside the door. Drink it when you're ready. I'll be waiting on the balcony."

When I was sure he'd left the room and closed the balcony door behind him, I cracked open the door. Ty's sweet-smelling blood waited in a topped glass beyond the barrier. My hand shot out and claimed the glass. In seconds it was empty. I took a few deep breaths, watching as the blood returned my features to normal and took the edge off. Then I meekly slid out to the balcony.

Ty smiled up from the deck chair. A small bulb on the wall lent light to the darkness of night. All that filled the night air was the roll of waves slicing around the ship. "Better?"

I nodded, still feeling shitty over what I'd tried to do to him. Thankfully, Ty changed the subject. "So what did you see in the vision?"

"I'm not sure." I sank into the spare deck chair, staring out over the railing. In the moving darkness of the surrounding ocean, I imagined those burning red eyes again. Their crazed hunger reminded me of how I looked just minutes ago. I shivered and blinked. "I think the vision might have been of Kendrick. Something with fangs and red eyes was about to attack when I—" I broke off not wanting to say, when I came to and tried to attack you.

Without hesitation Ty took my hand over the table. "Think back. Did you see snow? Was it cold?"

I remembered the cool gust of wind and shadows. "No. It had been cool, but not cold like being in the snow. And it was windy. So wherever this happens, it's outside." Relief washed over me. "It couldn't have been at the ski resort."

"Then it must happen once we're all back," Ty said. "And now that we know it's coming, we can prepare."

"How?" I asked, wondering if Ty planned to stake out this threat and take it down.

Ty stood, pulling me up before him. Anticipation transformed his face. "As soon as we get back, I'm going to train you to fight."

CHAPTER 12

"*A*re you coming?" Ty called out from the low rippling waves as a flock of gulls squawked overhead.

His voice pulled me from my distracted stare down at the yellow, gritty shore of Lifou, our second port of call in New Caledonia. Abandoning my unending worry over Kendrick's continued silence, I sighed, glanced out at the crystalline aqua sea…and almost collapsed to my knees. The sun dipped over the waves, defining each ripple that made up Ty's six-pack. Even lower was the indentation that ran diagonally from his hips to disappear below the waist of his board shorts.

I covered my lingering gaze by dropping my towel, revealing a skimpy purple and silver bikini with lace-ups fastening the bottoms around my hips. With all this sun and lack of clothing needed, along with Ty's approving glances, my self-confidence was growing.

"Coming," I called, wading through the salty water to join him.

With a smile I placed my hands on his shoulders. I leaned in to almost kiss him, a ploy before I pushed him under. The distraction caught him off guard and he laughed, spitting water as he broke the surface.

"You shouldn't have done that," he mock growled. A wicked smile curved his mouth as he grasped my waist, throwing me through the air to bomb through the swells.

I flitted back to the surface as Ty's familiar hands grazed my thighs and waist. He'd swum over to me in the time it took me to fall through the air. "You're quick."

He pressed a hot kiss to my lips. "Faster than you." His full lips smiled, teasing.

I glanced around, checking that the other cruisers weren't watching us. Then I challenged his words by saying, "then catch me," before diving under. In my full power I torpedoed through the thick seawater, out the protective alcove, and around the island. I peered back for a split second. Ty was right behind me, so close that he could almost touch me. I pushed on harder and swam up the river's mouth. In the shallower water I darted around boulders as well as fallen and submerged trees. None of it slowed Ty down. And soon I was running out of river. I twisted below the surface, slowing before coming to a dead end.

Ty's hands connected with my hips and pushed me up, breaking the surface. We floated there, my hips pressed to his chest. His irises blazed. "Caught you."

My cheeks heated up and I glanced around. Surrounding the lagoon on almost all sides was a lush tropical forest. It was vibrantly green, providing contrast to the gushing waterfall plunging right behind us from eighty feet above. It's clear, mirror-like surface was an awe-inspiring sight. "Wow, this is so beautiful."

The perfection of this natural setting amazed me. I had seen the most picturesque waterfall, compliments of Ty and his ability to create any setting in a dreamscape, with unbelievable perfection.

The smells, sights, and sounds made each dream with him so close to reality that I had, on a few occasions, allowed myself to get swept away with it all. But this setting we were floating in *was* a reality. And I was here with Ty. Alone.

"You're beautiful," Ty said. He lowered me to the rocky ground below until our faces were less than an inch apart.

Motionless, with our bodies grazing, we stared into each other's eyes. Ty took a few steps forward, submerging our bodies under the waterfall. Then he ran a hand up my side. A shock of electricity crackled along my skin at his touch, stopping as his palm met my cheek. The water tumbled over our bodies, each drop like massaging fingers. Ty's head dipped, his hair falling over his forehead. His firm hand connected with my waist. In preparation, I built up the walls around my mind. Kendrick was still absent, but that didn't mean I wanted him butting back in anytime soon.

Ty waited until I nodded and smiled. Then any and all restraint vanished. Our lips met with the hungry passion I'd been restraining since my close call with death. It was passion that had existed between us from the start. The same undeniable draw I had always felt since I'd fallen for him at first sight. And now with Kendrick absent, this *was* a completely personal experience. Knowing that had my heart drumming in my chest, in rhythm to Ty's hammering pulse. My entire body pressed harder against his, trapping the amulet between our hearts. Still needing him closer, my arm curled around his neck, my lips coaxing his to open. Our tongues grazed as Ty's hands folded around my back. His heated fingers slid over my cold body with hungry pressure. Within our kiss I sensed a pause as Ty lowered his hands. They hovered above my thighs before gripping tight to lift me off the ground. Gasping, I wrapped my legs around his body. Being this close to him heightened every one of my senses. Every stroke of his fingers ignited my flesh. His breathing raced along with his pulse. The scent of him overwhelmed even the taste of salt on his skin. Every heartbeat was clear and distinct, begging me to taste.

Lost in the moment, I tore my throbbing lips from Ty's, trailing rough kisses over his chin and along his sharp jaw line. Ty's arms tightened around me and his head tilted to the side. An unmistakable invitation. Feeling in control, I let my fangs extend as I ran my tongue over his collarbone. My grip on his neck tightened and I bit down. The second his fiery sweet blood hit my tongue, an uncontrollable surge began to throb through me. Ty groaned, sliding a heated hand roughly up my side. His touch softened, slowing as he cupped my breast. I gasped through embedded fangs, reveling in the touch of his strong massaging hand. An expectant bulge pushed against my pelvis, flaring a deeper yearning at my core.

Stop! a sudden and soundless voice screamed. Nausea, anger, and depression flooded me like a tidal wave.

I ripped my fangs from Ty's neck and froze. This had to be the worst timing ever. Kendrick had resurfaced and he wasn't just hearing my thoughts. He was inside my mind. Living *this* experience. *So now you're freaking back?*

Ty's hold on me remained tight, his hand still cupping my breast and his breathing as fast as mine. I closed my eyes, focusing everything I had on forming a block. I knew I needed to talk to Kendrick and find out what was up with the disappearing act. But right now he could wait. Ty, who still held me close, was studying my features. He deserved an explanation.

Once I felt our privacy in check I bit my lip, dreading Ty's reaction. But his face was curious, not angry or confused. I leaned my head back, allowing the water flow to wash away the traces of Ty's spilled blood from my mouth. Pulling my head back out of the water, I gazed into Ty's intense eyes. Mine were a sight I imagined, with gleaming silver irises and scarlet-stained whites. They were the eyes of a predator. But Ty didn't seem to notice. "You're not angry?"

Ty frowned in confusion. He breathed slowly, in and out, his hammering heartbeat at odds with the slow breaths. "Are you kidding?" His perfect lips twisted into a seductive smile. "You were amazing."

With Ty's blood surging through my body, I could feel my cheeks flare vibrant red. "But I..."

Ty raised a finger to my lips. "Shh." There was a knowing glint in his eyes as he shrugged. "I know. Kendrick's back." His voice was so soft and calm and not pissed in any way. "But we made progress."

I smiled. Ty was right. We had kissed and touched intimately, and I had even drunk from him without worrying that I couldn't stop. Until the last few seconds we had been alone, completely unrestricted and lost in the moment. It may have only been a few minutes of pure unadulterated bliss, but it was still progress. Most of our luck may have more to do with Kendrick blocking me, but right now I was keeping him out. Usually a flurry of emotions or desires would cloud my ability, but in this moment I was succeeding. A surge of hope lit my heart. Perhaps one day I would have enough control to block and keep Kendrick out completely. Maybe even long enough to truly be with Ty. A triumphant smile spread across my face. "You're right."

Ty pointed to a large flat rock centering the lagoon. "Let's cool down."

My body was still humming and I needed to talk to Kendrick. "Good idea."

We swam over and pulled ourselves out of the water. Ty reclined on his back, closing his eyes as the sun coated his body with golden light. I drew my knees to my chest and let the walls in my head fall.

Where the hell have you been? I demanded, trying to keep the fury from my body language. I probed into Kendrick's memories. I wasn't in his head, *thank God,* but I could access his mind. He had been snowboarding, day and night, apparently having a ball and getting to know... *You met a girl?*

Kendrick didn't answer.

Dammit, Kendrick. Do you know how worried I've been? I wanted to shake him, the glowing sunlight bearing down on me further boiling my blood. *I thought something had attacked you. Hell, I even thought you could be freaking dead!*

Regret poured from Kendrick. *Sorry. I didn't expect to....meet someone.*

I slapped my forehead. Ty had said that Kendrick was probably having fun, but I had kept my skepticism. Never for a second had I expected Kendrick to meet someone. Not when his feelings for me were so strong. A pang of jealousy flooded me, like water filling my lungs. It wasn't because I couldn't imagine him with someone else. Well not really. I had always thought of Kendrick as mine, my best friend, and now my soul's mate. Since his confession of love, the thought of him moving on had never even crossed my mind.

It's not like that. There was no uncertainty in Kendrick's voice. *We're just having fun. It's nothing permanent, nothing like that.* His emotions touched on a twinge of guilt. *My feelings for you haven't changed, but I need to live, too.*

And now I felt terrible. Had I actually expected Kendrick to stay mine, in the only form I would have him and not in the way he truly desired? His feelings for me had kept him from living his own life. It had created a dependency between us. But I couldn't give Kendrick what he wanted. It was out of my power. And he deserved to experience all that life had to offer, with whoever he chose. *I'm sorry. I didn't mean to pry. It's not my place and you should be having fun. I want you to be happy. I do.*

Kendrick covered his guilt, though a touch still remained, probably from worrying me like crazy. *I'm gonna go now. I feel dirty and I need a shower.*

Understanding that he wanted to cleanse himself after being part of what Ty and I had been doing, I nodded. *Sure. We'll catch up later.*

With that our link severed and I was alone again. Still beside me Ty was now reclined back on his elbows and watching me. "What?" I questioned, shrugging.

Ty sat up and leaned towards me. The streaming sunlight caught his irises, making them gleam like chips of gold. "I just find you...amazing."

I frowned and pursed my lips. I wasn't about to start lying. "You know where I was, don't you?"

Ty placed a hand on my thigh. "I know. You were checking in on Kendrick." The missing irritation from his voice surprised me. "Is everything alright?"

Ty was asking about Kendrick's well-being? Had I entered the twilight zone? Seeing the interest and perhaps even a pinch of concern in Ty's face, I answered truthfully. "He's fine, it would seem. Better than fine." I gave a nonchalant shrug. "He's met someone. That's why he's been blocking me."

Genuine surprise crossed Ty's face. "You're serious?" I couldn't tell if Ty was doubtful or relieved. After a pause he asked, "So, how does that make you feel?"

Now realizing his staid expression was a cover for possible insecurity, I put his worry at ease. "I think it's great."

~

TY'S BODY broke from mine, and I felt the loss of his bare chest against my bikini-clad one. The crowd surrounding us on the outside deck whistled and waved drunkenly as the next song started up. Tonight was island night and everyone was dressed the part. Every guy was bare chested and wearing board shorts, while the girls flaunted skimpy bikinis or coconut shells with sarongs or grass skirts.

Ty rubbed the material of my own sarong and leaned in close. "Drink?" he asked over the loud festive music.

Following Kendrick's interruption at the waterfall, Ty had insisted I take from him back in our cabin. Satisfied with my earlier taste of him, I knew he meant an actual normal alcoholic drink. Still I blushed at the memory. "Sure."

We pushed free of the close-knit dancers and found the bar. Leis, tropical flowers, and light-flashing glasses served as themed decorations atop the varnished wooden shelves behind the staff. As Ty edged in to order our drinks, I shivered, feeling exposed. There was that peculiar sensation of being watched again. It had been happening on and off since the first night. Though apart from the perv watching what he would have thought was Ty and me making out in the club, I hadn't caught anyone else. I glanced around, letting my paranoia bleed in.

"You alright?"

I jumped as Ty appeared before me, holding out a girly purple drink with a paper umbrella and glazed cherries. "Oh, yeah. I'm good." I took the drink while registering that no one was looking our way. "I uh…it's nothing." I took a long sip from the curly straw and my face lit up. "Purple and tastes like candy. What is this?"

Ty shrugged. "Fruit Tingle. I figured since you like vodka, a purple version would have to be better." He drained his own drink, a much more masculine bourbon on the rocks. Then he pointed across the net-covered pool to the bathrooms. "I've gotta take a leak, but…" His free arm captured my waist and hauled me close. "When I get back, we're burning up that dance floor. All. Night. Long."

I shivered at this hot, alcohol-rich breath, my eyelids shutting at the thought. When I opened them his heat, scent, and touch were gone. I backed over to the end of the bar, sipping while watching the growing mass of drunk dancers.

Cold air touched my shoulder, raising the hairs backing my neck. Then the pendant at my wrist warmed. I spun and snorted purple out my nose. A pale, lean-muscled guy was right behind me, so close our skin almost touched. "Ah, sorry," I coughed. "I didn't see you there."

The guy's black pupils tracked down my barely clothed body, taking in every exposed inch. A smile parted his lips, showing off glossy white teeth. "No," he said over the noise, his accent sort of Aussie. "But I saw you."

I took a step back and he caught my wrist. His touch was arctic and he let go, running his fingers through his spiky blond hair. There was something familiar about the calculated look in his eyes that chilled me to the bone.

"I have a boyfriend," I blurted.

The guy laughed, the sound like nails on a chalkboard. "And he left you…alone. A pretty piece like you."

He stepped closer and I didn't move, panic at who he was and what he wanted keeping me planted. Because I had seen this guy before. This was the perv who'd been watching us. Anger fired in my bones and sudden wind picked up around us. "I'm not interested. Back off."

The guy chuckled. "Spirit. I like it. Will make our encounter so much more…fun."

He came at me with open hands and I readied to fight. Before I got the chance to knee him where it hurts, someone darted between us and shoved him back. "Lay off my girlfriend or I'll rearrange your face," Ty snarled, baring human teeth.

The guy barely took a step back, his expression turning feral. "C'mon, mate. I just wanted a taste. Pretty thing like that must be used to handing it out."

Violent wind hit the deck and Ty roared. His fist flew out, cracking the guy in the nose. I cried out and grabbed at Ty as the guy spun from the force.

The dickhead deserved the hit, but letting Ty wreck the guy would cause more mess than it was worth. Dancers had already stopped to watch, and the drinkers at the bar had shuffled back. Security would be on us like a rash any minute.

"Ty, let's go." I tugged harder, wind whipping my hair. "He's not worth it."

The guy shot around, face unharmed and smiling. "Now the party starts."

He leaped at Ty and I cried out "Stop!" as girls in the crowd shrieked.

Then a blinding flash of light struck with a deafening BOOM. I hit the deck, the aftermath obliterating my eardrums. As the noise faded I blinked rapidly, clearing the blinding light from my eyes. Around me there were shrieks and screams, the scamper of people running.

A set of warm hands found my shoulders, lifting me off the deck. "Ty?"

"Yeah," he yelled, sounding far away. "Did you see what happened?"

"No," I said as the surroundings started to come back into focus. "Just light and that noise."

'This is a severe weather warning,' a crackling voice barked over the speakers. '*All passengers are directed to retrieve their life vests and report to their safety stations at once.*'

Right on cue, fat drops of rain started to fall, splattering across the deck which moments ago had been swarmed by drunk, sweaty dancers. The cruise ship began to rise and fall with violent thrusts.

"There was lightning," Ty said, directing me out of the open. "It couldn't have been a mile from the boat. We need to get inside."

Now able to see, my gaze shot behind us. There was no one there. "What happened to that guy?"

Ty shook his head, face hardening as he took my hand to drag me inside. Another boat-rattling rumble rang out as the door to the stairwell slammed shut behind us. "Disappeared with the lightning."

CHAPTER 13

*W*ith a continued warning the next day for all passengers to keep indoors due to the storm, we spent our time switching from our cabin to cozy corridor seats, just talking and holding hands. It had been nice. An honest telling of our lives from the beginning up until now. Ty's upbringing had been a course of harsh training and high expectations from his father. It was vastly different to mine. Well, except for the early years that were still coming back to me.

Now we were all talked out and contracting cabin fever. It was time to break loose *and* break the rules.

Feeling like a naughty kid, I let Ty pull me past the cordoning tape and upstairs to the Oasis deck. Ty dropped his backpack from his shoulder, causing it to clank as it hit the deck. Bar the gentle glow of a three-quarter moon peeking through thick clouds, the windy area was almost lightless. Not that my vamp sight needed light to see. There was an above ground spa and a bar. Square potted plants had been pulled up against the sides, and stacked plastic deck chairs had been tied down to brave the weather.

Feeling confident in this private Oasis, I allowed my towel to slip from my hips. Beneath it was an iridescent-purple monokini. The one-piece kind with large cut-outs along the sides. It showed off plenty of skin and covered only the necessary bits. I smiled, reveling in my new confidence.

Ty's lips curved up at the sides and he tore his muscle shirt off. He came forward, pressing his steaming body against mine before stealing a quick kiss and sweeping me off my feet. I giggled as he carried me into the spa, holding me so tight I could feel his hot breath on my neck and hear every beat of his pulse.

"You're more beautiful than even the heavens," he whispered into my ear.

I hugged into his broad chest, forcing up the blocks in my mind. With the overwhelming punch of Ty's scent, it took serious concentration. Still, I wasn't giving up. When I was ready I peered up to meet his vibrant eyes. The desire in them made my face hot. I planted a soft kiss against his lips. "You're making me blush."

Ty loosened his hold on me, allowing me to slide off his lap. "Will you wait here?"

"Huh? Why?"

Ty raised a hand to caress my cheek. "I have a surprise. I'll be right back." He leaped from the spa, dripping a trail of water as he disappeared down the stairs to the deck below.

Before I could wonder what Ty was up to, a shock of tingles swamped my spine. Unease washed over me and I attempted to shake off the foreboding sensation. But it wouldn't budge, and I knew why. I had felt this before. The pendant warmed as if in confirmation, blistering against my wrist even below the hot water.

Someone was watching me. Here on this abandoned deck. I wasn't alone.

Pulling my knees up to my chest, I peered around. The moonlight had vanished behind thickening dark clouds. Ominous shadows grew, tricking my heightened vision.

"Ty, where are you?" I mumbled.

With eyes darting from shadow to shadow, they settled into the blackness beside the unmanned bar. I stared intensely. Was that a slight movement within the shadows? My vision began to blur from staring so hard. I blinked, forcing my eyes to refocus. "I'm imagining things," I told myself. "I'm being paranoid."

Caius was still out there, somewhere, but we were on the other side of the world. On a freaking boat in the middle of the ocean. There was no way he could get to me here.

An almost inaudible sound redirected my staring gaze. It was a guy in his twenties with spiky blond hair. His hands were shoved deep into the pockets of his black pants. The guy's head was down, gaze focused on his bare feet.

Although I couldn't glimpse his face, even in the dark of night, one thing did catch my attention. The top buttons of his white collared shirt were open, revealing unusually pale flesh. I'd see this guy before. More than once. "You again. Didn't you get the hint? I'm—"

Any words I had died as the guy took a few short steps forward and peered up. I inhaled too quick, sharp pain exploding in my lungs like a bomb of pins.

Compared to last night, his face appeared drawn and sickly, tinted to an almost gray hue. Had he been sea sick all day?

The clouds above glided from the moon, releasing an eerie glow that spilled light down on us. I did a double take and scrambled from the spa, backing up and tripping over Ty's backpack. The perv's pupils weren't black anymore. They weren't even human. They were blood red. *Rogue vampire.*

A pleased smile flashed across his face, revealing razor-sharp fangs. "I'm Lukas." His hissed words were cold and deadly. "Nice to meet you, again…Amelia."

Jumping upright my pulse hammered through my ears. There was a primitive way in which he stood, every muscle tense in preparation. Even the thin muscles along his neck were taut. There was no doubt I was the hunted.

The walls in my mind dropped and I took a step back. "What do you want?"

The creature's smile widened. "Just you."

Panic had my heart racing with realization. This was the vision I'd had the other day…I was the prey.

Amelia, run! Kendrick's sudden panicked words shot through my ears. *He'll kill you!*

Bile spiked in my throat as Lukas lunged forward. He was faster than any vampire. Faster than me. Too fast to track.

I went to run, but it was no use. The vampire was upon me, his icy, rock-hard hands wrapped around my neck like clamps. I struggled uselessly as his grip tightened on my throat.

Then I was moving, being dragged back into the shadows as my air supply choked closed. Gasping for breath, my head swam, vision blurred. The fight in me grew weaker with every second of lacking oxygen.

Crippling fear turned my bones to jelly. I was about to pass out. Even Kendrick's shouts had died off. Why hasn't he bitten me? I wondered as my vision blackened. Why not kill me and get it over with?

Out of nowhere a force like a battering ram slammed into us.

Lukas's choking hold on my neck released and my oxygen

deprived body thudded to the deck. I gasped for breath, blinking against the black haze and clutching my tender throat. My body felt like putty, unresponsive and heavy.

Around me I could hear scrambling, growling, and hissing. Another loud thud vibrated the deck.

Get up and run! Kendrick screamed, his voice cutting through the haze.

I teetered, rocking forward as I tried to regain my balance. I blinked frantically to force the black fog from my vision. There was another loud blow followed by a bone-splitting crack. A screeching hiss followed.

Two dark figures grappled across the deck. One was my attacker. And the other? Was black as night and freaking massive.

Lukas hissed, priming his razor-sharp claws. The gigantic beast responded in a threatening growl that was too familiar to confuse.

"Ty!"

His gold wolf eyes shot straight to me. In the same second the vampire sprung forward, slashing his claws across the wolf's shoulder and chest. Ty snarled as glossy crimson spurted from the deep lacerations, striking to bat Lukas in the chest. The guy went flying, hitting the railing.

Ty bounded my way as Lukas shot up, deadly starvation in his red eyes.

"Look out!" I screamed too late, still struggling for more air.

The vampire shot through the air like lightning itself, and landed on Ty's back. His claw-like fingers punctured Ty's skin, causing him to howl. The wolf reared and darted, but it was no use. The other guy's hold was concrete, his fangs snapping again and again, trying to bite into Ty's shoulder.

Moving fast, the wolf anticipated and deflected each attempt, wheeling, bucking, and snapping back. But he was growing weaker.

I could see it. Blood poured from his wounds and his defense was slowing.

A grunt escaped my lips as I forced my recovering and heavy body from the deck. With all my might, I lunged. The plan had been to yank the vampire back in an effort to free Ty. But as my hands connected with his shoulders his elbow shot out, so fast I didn't have time to react. It connected with my cheek with a brute force that sent me flying. My body collided with a stack of plastic deck chairs, cracking them on impact.

Ignoring the pain, I scanned around for something, anything that could be used as a weapon. Before me, Ty had somehow managed to throw Lukas off his torn and bloodied wolf back to stand on his hind legs.

My fingers folded around a jagged piece of broken deck chair as both guys threw clawed punches while snapping their bared fangs. As I went to move, brandishing my makeshift weapon, something caught my eye. The moon had resurfaced from the clouds above, glinting against something by my side. Next to Ty's backpack was a smashed bowl of melted chocolate and scattered strawberries. The surprise Ty had left to get. But that wasn't all. A gleaming silver stake protruded from Ty's backpack. There was an inscription down the length.

Amelia, you have to kill it, Kendrick said, no longer screaming for me to run. *The heart. Aim for the heart!*

I dropped the plastic and grasped the cold silver weapon in my shaking hands. My mind shut Kendrick and his voice out. If this went wrong, I didn't want him to see it.

An agonized growl forced my attention from the stake. The vampire had landed another hit on Ty, cutting fresh scarlet valleys across his stomach. Ty snapped forward, wolf teeth bared. The vampire used his movement against him, gripping his shoulders and digging his fingers like knives into Ty's wounds. Ty's knees buck-led, bringing him to the floor as the vampire opened its mouth in anticipation.

With a split second to save Ty's life, I sprang from the deck. Both hands rose, clutching my weapon. The stake plunged in, hitting bone and jutting sideways through Lukas's back.

A strangled scream rang through the thick night air as he released Ty. He scrambled to clutch the weapon, but he never got the chance. Ty lunged, flattening the guy to the ground. Then his wide jaw and sharp teeth clamped around our attacker's neck. With a slight twist and a sickening crack, Ty ripped into the guy's jugular. A fleeting shriek escaped Lukas while blood that smelled like death coated the sea air. Life vanished from the vampire's face and his body became limp.

Ty fell onto his back, heaving and gasping. Erratic trembling claimed his body as he began to shrink and change. In a few heart-stopping seconds he was back to his naked human form. I watched in amazement then gasped. His life-threatening wounds were even more obvious against his human skin. He clumsily pushed off the deck and got to his feet, grasping my strewn towel to wrap around his naked waist. I stared, shell shocked as Ty leaned over the dead guy, groaning as he lifted the guy's weight and pried the stake from its back. With a fleeting look up at me, he dropped the dead weight, fell to his knees, and plunged the stake into the vampire's chest.

As Ty turned back to me with the stake in his hand, the body behind him disintegrated, turning into a smoldering pile of ash. He gripped my forearms, pain flashing across his face. "Are you hurt?"

Unable to move or speak, I just stood there. Too much had happened, and I didn't understand any of it.

Ty shook me. "Amelia, are you alright? Did it hurt you?"

"What?" I coughed then swallowed. Damn that hurt. If my windpipe were crushed I wouldn't have been surprised. "Um, no. I'll be okay." Deathly silence hung in the air as Ty's glowing gold eyes watched me. I peered past his wounded body to the disappearing ash behind him, floating away with the ocean breeze. "You had a stake...on our trip. You killed..." I paused, staring at the ash. "Is that supposed to happen?"

"It's a precaution. I always carry one close by." He shook his head. "And no. Death by stake doesn't cause instantaneous combustion."

"He wasn't a vampire, was he?"

"Not like any I've seen before." Ty craned his neck to take in the singe marks on the deck. "He was stronger and faster." His face was dire as he looked back to me. "Thank you. He almost had me there."

The billowing wind died down, the air turning calm. The potency of Ty's blood soared. I hadn't drunk him since this morning. Without thinking I stepped forward, touching his arm. He winced and my hand shot back. Had I seriously been considering drinking from him like this? I frowned at Ty's broken body and the many deep wounds still steadily dripping crimson.

Ty followed my gaze down to his slashed and bloodied chest. He staggered back, his face turning white. "Something's wrong," he said, his voice quiet and fading. "I'm not healing."

Then he collapsed to his knees.

CHAPTER 14

covered Ty's injuries with towels, hoisted his weight against my side and hurried downstairs and inside, heading straight for our cabin. With my bottom lip between my teeth I kept biting down, breaking skin to taste my own blood. It was all that kept me from burying my fangs in him. Lucky the halls were empty, thanks to the extended performance being held in the show lounge.

Finally reaching our cabin, I unlocked the door and kicked it open. A split second later I'd gotten Ty onto the bed. He grunted at my sudden release, rolling sideways as more blood gushed from his wounds. On autopilot, I snatched the wastebasket from the bathroom and filled it with tepid water, emptying the saltshaker from the dining table into it. Then I ripped a towel to shreds and dropped the walls in my mind.

You have to clean the wounds and stop the bleeding, Kendrick instructed.

"You think I don't freaking know that," I hissed then snapped my lips shut. The last thing Ty needed was to hear the panic in my voice. Besides, I'd picked up the basics of treating animal injuries during my I'm-gonna-be-a-vet stage while watching documentaries and Animal Hospital. So this process was routine.

I dropped beside Ty's trembling body. He flinched as I began dabbing a wet piece of towel across his many wounds, the salt and moisture stinging his serrated flesh. "It's okay. You're going to be okay."

As the blood washed away, every gouge and tear appeared more and more serious. Each one was jagged and angry, and every single one still oozed crimson. Covering my aching fangs with my lips, I tried to control my expression. Ty's wounds were life threatening. If he'd been human he would have already been dead. The fact that he was a werewolf and still alive, gave me some hope. But watching his body grow pale without any sign of healing, struck fear through my heart.

Rain began to pelt down outside, splattering musical drops against the balcony's glass doors. I placed a gentle hand on a slash-free part of Ty's chest and tried to mask the terror that spread through me like poison. "The blood loss is slowing, but not enough."

It was true. Ty's blood loss had slowed. Though the sight struck fear through my heart. After all his bleeding out there was very little blood still pumping through his veins. The bed—our bed—that he was lying on, vibrated along with his trembling body. The sheets were stained a vibrant red that was soaking down towards the carpet.

Fuck! He's lost too much blood, I rambled internally as Ty began to gasp in short, sharp breaths. *Kendrick, he's dying. Help me, please!* Tears blurred my vision and I turned away from Ty so he wouldn't see them. *Tell me how I can save him. I'll do anything.*

There might be one thing, came Kendrick's unspoken voice. There was hesitation in his next words. *Was he bitten?*

Feeling the urgency of time slipping away, I scanned Ty over, feeling with my fingers. Ty groaned in agony between panting breaths. I couldn't see any bite marks. Just claw gouges all over his trembling body. *I—I don't think so.*

Don't assume, Kendrick snapped. *Ask him.*

Why? What the hell does it matter?

Because, Kendrick replied sounding exasperated, *if you want Ty to live, you're going to have to feed him your blood. Like the vampires used to when the wolves were our guardians. It'll kill off the poisoned blood he's ingested. But if he's been bitten he could turn, or worse...*

"Were you bitten?" I blurted, noticing in horror the gold fading from Ty's irises.

"No," he rasped. In, in, out. In, in, out. His sharp breaths grew faster. "I w-wasn't...bitten."

I slashed a nail straight through my wrist, opening up a deep incision that swelled with crimson. Kendrick's consciousness left me, and I held my wrist up before Ty's mouth. "I know it's gross, but it'll help. Trust me."

"Nothing," Ty said then coughed, "ab-bout you is g-gross." His mouth parted as I lowered my dripping wrist to his lips. Then he raised a shaky hand to grasp my arm, holding it close as he began drawing my blood.

I almost expected him to cough or gag, but then I remembered his confession at Mom's dinner. Ty could and did sometimes drink blood. And now he'd tasted mine. Warmth colored my cheeks and my fangs retracted. The sensation was unusual, like nothing I'd ever experienced before. I cringed, remembering that only one person had ever bitten me. Caius. Back when he'd attempted to take my life through full consumption. The memory raised a chill over my body that I quickly shook off. This was nothing like that. Ty's teeth—vamp or wolf—weren't biting into me. There was no pain surging through my body. All I felt was Ty's warming lips and the strangest pulling sensation as my blood was drawn from my vein.

A warm smile spread across my face as the color began to return to Ty's pale skin. I ran my free hand through his slick hair. At my touch Ty's groggy gaze lifted. He released my wrist and smiled with bloodstained lips. "I've never had blood that tasted that good. But yours is…"

His words trailed off as I lowered my lips to his, kissing him and tasting my own blood from his mouth. I edged away and examined Ty's wounds. The bleeding had almost stopped, but every jagged wound remained open, now only beginning to crust in from the sides.

Ty leaned up from the red-puddled sheets and winced as he touched my face with a rough and slowly warming hand. His eyes were hooded and he looked like death warmed up. His lips parted and I *shushed* him. "Sleep now. All you need to do is sleep."

I leaned down and kissed him. When I drew back he was out.

WITH ONE LAST glance back at Ty, I slipped out to the corridor. He was sound asleep and healing slowly. I winced, remembering all that vibrant blood flowing out of him. I'd come so close to losing him. I slumped against the wall, hand palming the stake hidden in my hoodie. Thanks to Ty our attacker was dead. But were there more? There was no way I could feel safe if I didn't find out. And I wasn't about to let any further harm come to Ty if I could prevent it.

Amelia, you can't search the boat alone, Kendrick's irritated voice repeated. *It's too dangerous.*

I ignored him and began heading toward the Oasis deck.

Bloody hell, Amelia. Don't be stupid. Kendrick was starting to sound desperate. *At least wait until the sun's up and they're disadvantaged.*

I stalled, feeling a hidden meaning to his words and remembering the vampire's speed, strength, deathly complexion, and blood-red eyes. Then I thought of how it'd died. Even Ty had admitted our attacker wasn't any normal vampire. And he should know. His father had trained him to hunt down rogues from childhood.

You know something. Tell me now.

After an extended pause that had me about to scream, Kendrick spoke. *You're right. It wasn't a normal vampire who attacked you. It wasn't even a rogue.*

With Kendrick's thoughts now open, I knew his suspicion. Nervous tension forced me to keep on walking. *Pulseless and soulless. A damned vampire?*

Sunlight doesn't just drain or even burn them, Kendrick said. *It incinerates them.*

Like when Ty staked him. I shuddered, visualizing the moment Lukas had instantaneously combusted. That just didn't happen to regular vamps. Plus we had uncovered proof that at least Caius believed the damned still existed. Even with the mounting facts, I didn't want to believe it. *Why are you so sure that that's what he was?*

Because I've seen one before.

My knees threatened to buckle and I caught myself by gripping the door handle to get outside. Still the momentum was there and I stumbled out into post midnight darkness, falling back against the door as it sucked shut. I was at the bottom of the stairs that led up to the Oasis deck. Wind blasted my hair while sideways rain soaked through my hoodie and jeans. *What the hell, Kendrick? You saw one? How? When?*

Melting into Kendrick's consciousness, I felt him shuffle in his seat. He was in the corner of the cocktail bar, turning a glass of rum with edgy fingers. Then I noticed something. *Where's Dorian?*

The stitched emotions already flooding from Kendrick stirred and reared. *Asleep,* he replied vaguely.

And? I pushed, feeling a wave of nausea stream through me. Whatever Kendrick had kept from me had something to do with Dorian, and it was big. When Kendrick remained silent, the anger I'd felt at his earlier disappearance reared its ugly head. *Kendrick, don't treat me like a child. I'm not stupid. You're keeping something big from me, more than meeting a girl, and it has to do with Dorian, and...* I swallowed hard, feeling my conviction in what I was about to say. *It's related to the attack on Ty and me.*

Kendrick threw back his rum and sighed. *We were attacked, too. Here, at the resort.* As the invisible wall around a single one of his memories fell, I edged down onto the stairs. I could still feel the wind blasting through my hair, but I couldn't see the ship's deck. Instead my vision became internal, running through a terrifying sequence of events.

It was dark with night, distant lodge floodlights highlighting the ski slope. But Kendrick wasn't in the light. He and Dorian were over the ridge, using vampire night vision to take on the abandoned course.

And they weren't alone.

As Kendrick got halfway down the dangerous slope a figure shot out, catching his neck with a thrown out arm. Kendrick slammed back onto the snow, gasping at the hit that had crushed his throat.

Dorian called out from higher up as the guy pinned Kendrick down. The stranger's fanged smile was lethal, his eyes starving for blood.

Shock and adrenaline spiked through Kendrick's veins and he tried to fight back. But the thing was stronger, fangs now closing in on their mark.

"I said back off!" Dorian crashed into the guy, torpedoing him off of Kendrick. The thing recovered quick as a flash and claws began to fly, cutting into my brother who fought with all he had.

Wind pockets sprouted up from an approaching snowstorm, and Kendrick jumped into the fray. But even against two, the creature was making ground.

"Immobilize it!" Kendrick shouted, and somehow in the chaos Dorian understood the command.

He backed away—boarding gear dyed with blood—and left Kendrick to defend. With concentration his hand rose, straining with violent tremors. Then it happened. The snow below the attacker changed from opaque to clear. Ice to water.

Kendrick leaped away as the guy sank into the pond beneath him. He hissed and went to escape, but not quick enough. Like watching a documentary of winter progression on fast-forward, the water snapped back to solid, imprisoning ice.

The thing began sprouting curses as Dorian nodded to my best friend. "What now?"

Kendrick's face became grim as he strode forward. His hands gripped the flailing guy's skull, and held tight. "Silver or decapitation. It's the only way to kill the damned."

Then he twisted.

The vision snapped off like a door being slammed in my face. I gasped and tried not to gag as the wind-blown deck returned. I spoke around the spike of vomit in my throat. "When did this happen?"

Three days ago.

Three fucking days ago! I remembered that day. Kendrick had been at the bar and nursing a brandy, favoring his left arm. And I had seen the replayed events. A double flip off a crest that he hadn't pulled off the landing to. It was all made up bullshit to throw me off. But why not tell me? And what about the girl he'd been busy blocking me out to hook up with?

There was no girl. Kendrick answered my thoughts as if they'd been questions. *There will never be another girl. Deep down you knew that. And I hated lying to you. But I never thought you'd be in any danger. You're on a cruise ship. In the middle of the ocean. On the other side of the world where the sun is shining. How could he even get on board? It doesn't make sense.*

The one thing that made sense was that someone had wanted us all taken care of. And they'd gone to great lengths to make it happen. Plus our attacker hadn't tried to kill me. He'd merely tried to subdue me. There was only one person who needed to silence us, and who needed me alive to achieve his goals.

It had to be Caius, and this time I'm going to find proof.

CHAPTER 15

I stalled at the top of the stairwell. The crumpled deck chairs still made a mess to the left. To the right, my attacker's ashy remains had now been swept away by the unrelenting wind. Any spilled blood, from either Ty or him, appeared to have been cleansed from the deck with the downpour that was now starting to lighten. There were no red eyes or lurking shadows.

With Kendrick nervously watching through the bond, I began searching the deck. I knelt at a darker spot where the damned had burned to cinders. Unease over Kendrick's attack and lies weighed against my heart. *Why did you keep it from me?*

I guess I wanted you to have fun, Kendrick said. I vaguely noticed him motioning to the bartender for another drink. *After everything that's happened, you deserved to live a little.*

Although *living a little* meant me spending time with and getting closer to Ty, Kendrick's words were honest and sincere. He wanted me to be happy. The weight in my heart lifted, forgiving him for his lies. *I can't believe you invented some girl to throw me off track,* I said, letting my fingers brush the singed deck.

I can't believe you bought that, Kendrick replied. Then his mood turned serious. *Amelia, I will never feel a millionth of what I feel for you for anyone else. I know you don't want to hear this, but it's true.*

His words left me speechless, and I almost wished I could return his feelings. But I couldn't. My heart belonged to Ty…and it always would. I straightened beside the hot tub, scrounging for something to say that wouldn't make him feel bad. Then I paused. There beside my Vans was a glossy spot the rain hadn't washed clean.

What is it? Kendrick asked, his trepidation peaking.

I knelt and touched the wet spot, then rubbed it between my thumb and fingers. It was cold and tacky. "It's blood."

Except it wasn't red. It was black like old oil. I lifted my fingers to my nose, and then flung them away. It smelled as putrid as decaying flesh. I rinsed the black liquid from my fingers in the hot tub's water and washed away the evidence on the deck. Even with the source gone the stench was imprinted on my memory. In this windy area, I could even detect where Lukas had died and where he'd been loitering in the shadows. This was the clue I needed.

Amelia… Kendrick's voice warned. *Don't, please.*

I jogged to the stairs. *No, Kendrick. Nothing you say will make me stop. This needs to be done. I need to make sure we're alone. I'm going to find his lair.*

In the past, I had located Ty by the potent aroma of his blood. Now I was going to use my heightened sense of smell to uncover the damned's hideout. Following the slight remnants of decay, I headed down flights of stairs. The stench disappeared and I changed directions, picking it up further down another corridor. Past the almost endless stretch of cabin doors, I met more stairs. This time I kept going down until I reached the lowest level with rooms. The scent was more pungent here and I followed it. At the opposite end of the corridor it spiked.

Cabin 505. I clutched the door handle and my heart pounded, feeling like it wanted to up and leave. A group of tweens exited the room opposite, and my hand shot back, waiting for them to pass. When the corridor was vacant again, I faced the door. A *Do Not Disturb* slip took up the card slot.

You don't have that card thingy to get in. Kendrick sounded hopeful. *Do you?*

I curled my fingers into a fist. *Don't need it.* Then I smashed the card reader's metal plate. The light flashed then went out. The door creaked ajar.

Shit, Amelia. Be careful. It could be a trap.

I panned left to right down the hallway. The coast was clear. No witnesses. My free hand found the cold silver of Ty's stake while my other pushed the door wide open. Inside, the room was dark, backlit only by the glow from the corridor. No sounds filled the small space, no breathing, and no heartbeat. Which would have made me feel safer if not for Kendrick's next words.

They're damned, remember? They don't have hearts that beat. They don't even breathe.

Voices echoed from further along the corridor and I yanked the door shut behind me. Now I was surrounded by complete darkness. Heart pounding and sweat budding across my entire body, I flicked the switch. The lights blinked on, and I expelled a long held breath. The room was empty.

For good measure, I kicked in the bathroom door. It was empty too. Then I saw something that made me pause. This explained how a sun-allergic damned vampire had gotten on board during broad daylight. The wall on both sides of the cabin could be pulled down to create bunk beds, but these ones weren't pulled down. In their vacant spaces were two trunks. The same two I'd almost collided with when Ty and I had been rushing to get aboard before my attempt at compulsion could backfire. They were both bolted shut.

Fear spiked my adrenaline. One attacker, two crates. Fill in the blanks.

Don't open them, Kendrick said.

I swallowed my fear. *You know I'm not backing down.*

Wiping my sweaty palms on my jeans, I raised the silver stake. Then I kicked the bolt free on the first trunk and flung open the lid. The inside was padded. Like a coffin. And it wasn't empty. Filling part of the vast space was a generous supply of blood baggies. Every single one was drained.

What's that? Kendrick asked, his panic replaced by curiosity.

On the side of the first trunk were airline stickers. One struck me like a knife through my windpipe. "ANC?" It was the acronym for Anchorage International Airport. Our attacker had been from Alaska? "Oh shit!"

I dropped to my knees, weeding through the baggies. Hidden beneath them I found a stack of papers. No, not papers, photos, not only of me but of Ty too. They had been taken back home. There was one with me outside the art center at school, expression worried. It was the day I had sensed someone watching me. The same day a tree trunk that had been split by lightning had almost decapitated me. Another was of me sitting on my windowsill at home. And another showed Ty entering the front door of my house...and greeting my mom. The day he'd come over for dinner. I gulped, flicking through the stack. There were so many of Ty and me either at school, or at my house, or on the beach. There were even a few with us on the road to the cabin when we'd had to stop the car because of the dropped trees. When I got to the bottom of the pile, my heart started beating so fast I could hear it. The last piece wasn't a photo. It was much worse. A flat card with an Alaskan postage stamp and printed instructions:

'The girl, Amelia, must not be harmed in any way. You are only to subdue her. The werewolf is backup. Turn him if you can, otherwise kill him.'

I stared long and hard at the note, feeling the same realization from Kendrick snaking through my very core. The card was identical to the one Marcus had sent with the vacation bookings.

Marcus set us all up, Kendrick stated. Rather than gloating at having been right in his continued suspicions, all he felt was dread. ·

I wanted to argue. I didn't want to believe that Marcus—the guy I was so strangely connected to and who'd helped save my life— could have had anything to do with this. There was no motive. Was there?

A noise cut off Kendrick's need to convince me that Marcus must be in league with Caius somehow, or be up to something equally as devious. It was an almost squeak, a muffled cry. And it had come from the other trunk. I wasn't alone.

With Kendrick yelling at me to *get out*! I kicked the lock off the second trunk and flung the lid open. A figure sprang at me and I knocked them to the ground, more easily than I expected. I understood why as my hand clamped over her mouth to cut off her screams. Beneath me was a young woman. A human. And not just any human. She was a passenger. A cruise card hung from a lanyard around her neck, and she had on a summery dress that had been torn across the bust. Dried blood patterned the front of it and blotched her chest. The blood was her own, I noticed in horror, seeing angry bites covering her neck and chest.

She's their food. Kendrick's words sent roiling nausea through my gut.

From her pale, freckled complexion, and the dimness to her eyes, she was clearly blood deprived. She wouldn't have lasted another night of feeding. But Lukas had kept her locked up here, so he must have intended on killing her.

That's what the damned do, Kendrick said. *They drink to kill. I'm surprised she's even alive at all.*

The young woman continued struggling beneath me, but it was like a mouse trying to escape the paws of a lion. She was too weak. "If I let her go, will she be okay?"

You can't let her go, Kendrick said, a note of regret painting his words. *She's seen you. She knows a fanged monster attacked her. She's a liability. We have to—*

"Dispose of her?" The woman's eyes grew wider at my words and I shook my head. "I won't do it. I won't take someone's life. She's innocent."

If The Council gets wind of this—

"No," I said with absolution. "This is no different from covering our tracks when I attacked that senior from school. You compelled him to forget what I'd done, and I can do the same now. I did it with the check-in clerk the other day. She won't remember me or that monster."

Except that you'll be the one compelling her, not me, Kendrick said. *And you didn't believe you could compel the clerk permanently. How can you go from that to believing you can convince this woman that horrific things didn't happen to her?*

"'Cause I have to." I stared into the woman's terrified eyes, focusing on taking control of her mind. "I'm not going to hurt you. When I take my hand off your mouth you're not going to scream or lash out. Understand?"

The woman semi-nodded and her terrified expression relaxed a little. My hand came away slowly. Tears spilled from her eyes, leaving tracks through the patchy crimson that marred her face. "That thing…" She broke off sniveling.

"I know," I said in my most calming tone, releasing her wrists. "But he's gone now. He'll never hurt you again. And I'm going to let you go, but I need to ask you some questions first."

The woman nodded, brushing away her tears. "Anything, I'll tell you anything. Just please don't kill me."

"Are there any more of them?" The woman shook her head. "Did you hear the man who trapped you talking to or about anyone? Did he say anyone's name?"

The girl's eyelids squeezed shut and she nodded. "The monster talked on the phone heaps, reporting about a girl and guy. He always addressed the person on the line as Lord Bathory."

AFTER DOUBLE CHECKING the entire ship and picking up no other lingering putrid scents, I headed for our cabin. We were safe from further danger, and that girl, now in my blood-free clothes, was back in her room sleeping off what she thought was a massive hangover.

I stood in front of the stairs to level 12. My plan was to slip out of the girl's torn, bloodied dress and into a clean tank and jeans. But the strong smell of fresh blood stopped me. Ty's.

I shot up the stairs and almost collided with him. He'd somehow gotten board shorts and a shirt on and was clutching the railing for dear life. His skin was flushed, and sweat speckled his face and dotted his shirt. The damp patches mixed with red stains on the white material.

"Where have you been?" he grated out. His face twisted with

pain as he tried to stand on his own. There was a sickening wet sound of skin tearing and a fresh red line bloomed across the front of his shirt.

Tingles pierced my gums as my fangs shot forth. My arms came around him and I pushed him back up the corridor. Being this close had the animal inside me fighting to break free. Just like the song *Animal I have become* by Three Days Grace. I cursed and swallowed, holding back my violent urges. "Ty, you shouldn't be out here." Thank God it was after 2AM. The corridor was clear. But any surprise visitors catching Ty bleeding out, or worse…seeing the animal in me taking him like prey, was bound to create a total shit storm.

"You…" I punctured my own lip, letting the blood swell and fill my mouth. "You need to lie down." I snatched his room card and kicked open the door to our cabin, hauling him in.

"Tell me where you were." Ty pushed back out of my hold and I heard another tear. Fresh blood swelled across his shirt like he'd just been shot. "Shit…that hurts."

He swayed and fresh streams of sweat poured down his pale face. I caught him, stringing my arms around his body. Holding his entire weight, I edged him back onto the bed. I tore open his shirt and snatched a stray piece of shredded towel, dabbing at the oozing wounds. They weren't streaming scarlet like earlier, but they were still ugly and raw.

"The bleeding's not too bad," I tried to sound convincing.

Ty's chest rumbled as if to laugh. Then he grimaced, hands coming over mine to press against the wounds. He blinked up at me then closed his eyes. "Where. Were. You?"

Ignoring the instant demand in his voice, I pushed his hands away to inspect the openings. The blood loss had slowed. My blood was helping him heal. Still, a shiver crawled up my spine. The open wounds reminded me of the terrified woman I'd cleaned up. Her neck and chest had been a field of gruesome raw patches. Though a little of my blood at Kendrick's instruction had closed them up, leaving nothing but small scars marking her once shredded flesh. A desperate attempt at compulsion had wiped the horror from her memory. "I was making sure we're alone," I said, answering his question.

Ty's eyes shone with hardened gold. "You should have told me." He stiffened, teeth grating. Every movement, no matter how small, was torture. His next words were throaty. "I would have come with you."

"Like I would've let you. You shouldn't have even left this room. You need to rest." I sighed as despair crept in. Caius had ordered our attacks, which was more expected than a shock. But Marcus? What had his part in this been? Masking my inner turmoil with a smile, I ran a finger up Ty's forearm, dodging the sores that marked him there. "Besides, everything is fine. There aren't any more of them."

Ty raised an arm to caress my face, clearly trying to hide the agony of the movement. "So why do you look so worried?"

Ty's ability to read me had improved. I hadn't particularly wanted to reveal everything until Ty felt better. Right now he needed to rest, not worry about being hunted or turned. Not that I could understand a reason why they'd want to turn him. What could they gain from it? But Ty was watching me with those eyes, the ones that would always accept me and trust that I would never lie to him.

I stared at our spattered bed sheets, not wanting to meet his eyes. With the blood drying, turning from vibrant red to ruddy brown, the scent wasn't too overwhelming. "Okay, this is what I know."

Over the next thirty minutes I covered everything: Kendrick and Dorian's attack, the damned vampire's cabin, the trunks from

Alaska, the photos, and the blood baggies. Then the human blood donor who'd named Lord Bathory as the instigator. Lastly, I revealed the card with instructions to capture me and turn or kill Ty.

When I'd finished rambling and answering Ty's rapid-fire questions, I felt shell-shocked and drained. Saying it all out loud forced me to accept things I didn't want to believe.

Looking like rage was about to make him burst, Ty nodded at my iPhone on the bedside, next to the wastebasket and remaining shredded towel pieces. "Call him."

I nodded and grabbed my phone. "Please stay here." I had no right to demand anything of Ty. My trust in Marcus had almost gotten him killed. Not to mention my brother and best friend. Even so, Ty remained still, watching me as I slipped out onto the balcony and dialed Marcus's number.

On the side of the boat in the pre-dawn's darkness it was even windier than the Oasis deck. I gulped, remembering those blood-red eyes. Dread-poisoned anger coursed through my veins as the phone rang in my ear. The guy I hardly knew but had inexplicably trusted was about to learn he'd failed. That we were all alive, and that I knew the truth.

The ringing stopped as the line picked up. "Amelia, hey. How's it going?"

Tears blurred my vision and I caught at my flailing hair and twisted, tugging it down over my shoulder. "Alive, no thanks to you!"

"Whoa, what'd you say?" Panic tightened his deep voice. "What's going on?"

"Your goon failed. We killed him!" I began pacing, fighting the boats sway against rough waves. "He's nothing but dust, incinerated. Kendrick and Dorian killed theirs too."

My rant would have gone on, but Marcus cut in. "What goon? Amelia, what's happened? Did they come to your home?"

"Don't play innocent with me, you prick. You know they didn't!" I laughed mirthlessly. "But what a great plan. Send Dorian and Kendrick to the snow and me half way around the world on a tropical cruise, just to have us attacked by the freaking dead!"

"Send who where? The dead?" The surprise in Marcus's voice seemed so real. "Amelia, what are you rambling about?"

I wavered. The part deep down inside me that wanted to trust Marcus reared its stupid head. "The vacation itineraries you sent. The ones with the printed card claiming Caius was planning something. You sent us away so we'd be safe."

Marcus's next words stunned me, stripping any words from my mouth until he'd stopped talking.

I took a deep, shuddering breath. "I gotta go." I hung up, opening the door and stepping back inside.

Reclining back against the pillows, Ty's gaze locked on me. As mine lifted he lurched upright, grunting at the effort. "What's wrong? What'd the bastard say?"

I slid the door shut behind me. "Marcus isn't working with Caius. He wasn't behind any of this."

"Amelia, come on." Ty tried to swing his legs over the side of the bed and froze as another wound cracked open. His teeth grated. "He's lying."

"No, he's not." I crossed the short distance to drop onto the bed beside him. Thinking back now I should have been more suspicious. Because if I had, none of this would have happened. Dorian and Kendrick would never have been attacked, and Ty wouldn't have almost died. "Marcus didn't send the vacation bookings. He didn't even know we'd left. He's been too busy investigating other deaths. Vampire deaths."

"Vampire deaths?" Ty sounded skeptical.

"Full consumption, and the numbers are rising. He even suspected the damned too, but The Council doesn't want to believe it. There have even been a few royals taken out." I touched Ty's knee, minding the gash up his thigh. "We're not the only ones being hunted."

CHAPTER 16

I breathed through my mouth as I scarfed down the food I'd brought back to our cabin from the lunch buffet. Ty sat up on the bed against stacked pillows, finishing off a croissant. He reached for a blueberry muffin, his face twisting as he bit back the need to grunt. "Damn, I'm hungry."

Me too. That thick vein along his neck throbbed, demanding attention. It had been over twenty-four hours since I last fed from Ty. Normally that wouldn't have been so bad, but after feeding him my blood to heal, I was deprived and starving. I forced my eyes away and chugged down some orange juice. It tasted like poison. "Well, you do need your energy. A full tank should help you recover."

Ty laughed, then coughed, trying to hide his discomfort. "I never imagined the day where a vampire would be tending to me."

Feeling hangry—a collective mix of hungry and angry as a result —I crossed my arms over my chest. "This isn't funny, you almost…" My face pinched, unable to say the word let alone allow myself imagine Ty dead.

"But I didn't." Heat settled across my thigh, coming from Ty's hand. His scent swelled at the movement. "Hey, are you alright?"

I slid off the bed, putting space between us. Telling Ty I needed blood wouldn't do either of us any good. He was still healing and badly injured. Taking his vein wasn't an option. Plus with the dried blood all over the sheets, thinking beyond the smell was impossible. "I—uh. I need some air. It's been a really long night."

"I'll come." Ty reached for a clean shirt and a gash across his ribs split.

I shot forward and shoved him back against the pillows. "The hell you will," I tried not to hiss while covering my fangs. "You're in no shape."

With Ty's lids closed at the pain, he missed my dangerous expression and sighed. "Fine. I'll stay. But today is our last port, isn't it? Villa? I hear it's great for cheap shopping. You should make the most of it."

I wanted to stay and clean his newly open wounds. I cringed. With my tongue… I backed up and hit the door. "Sure, shopping. Just stay here."

I shot out the door and doubled over, sucking air. Then I headed for the stairs. Shopping wasn't a bad idea, but I wasn't leaving the boat. No, instead I was going to steal some new linen—right after I commandeered a stack of first-aid supplies. Covering Ty's wounds and removing the sweet aroma of his blood was the only way I'd be able to re-enter our cabin…without turning into 'Psycho killer monster.' Plus I hoped to find maybe a pack or two of stored cold blood. It was my only hope.

My stomach gurgled as I made my way to level six, heading for the medical center. Absently I noticed blue veins spider-webbing across my hands and up my arms. Every time a person passed me my stomach clenched. The smell of their blood enticed and allured, making my dark internal voice grow louder. I shook it away, struggling to hold back the dark desire to feed as I entered the glass door to the medical center. Thank God the place was empty.

I stepped around the counter and shot down the hall, breaking the locked handle to get into the storeroom. The room was stacked with syringes, needles, gauze, tape, ointments, and medicines. Lucky for me, it was also free of people. My relief dwindled. There was no fridge, and no blood.

I heard a slight noise outside, perhaps someone in a consult room down the hall. The faint beat of a human pulse and the scent of their blood reached me.

I hurried my movements, finding a plastic bag and shoving gauze, tape, and ointment into it. As I was about to fly out the storage room, a man's voice stopped me short. The smell of his blood almost floored me.

"Hey, what are you doing in here?" He was in his thirties and was wearing a white coat. The on-board doctor's heart raced with surprise at finding someone lurking in what had been a locked storeroom. He caught sight of the gnarled door handle. "Did you break in?"

The man began to move back. I shot forward, yanking him into the storeroom and slammed the door shut. I pinned him against the wall, eyes trying to hold his. "Don't scream." I almost expected Kendrick to appear in my head, demanding I stop. But there was nothing. I couldn't even feel him. Was he asleep? "I'm not going to hurt you."

"Let me go," the doctor demanded, fighting against my strength. The vein along his neck bulged from strain. "How are you this strong?" His eyes widened. "Are you high?"

Dammit! The compulsion wasn't working. I was too blood deprived.

My hand clamped over his mouth before he could scream out. Without thought I zoned in on the thick vein along his neck, pulsing and plump. That wicked voice in my head came alive. *Vampires need blood.* You *need blood.*

I thought of Ty, injured and in pain. More of my blood would help him heal. Wouldn't it? But I couldn't give him my vein if doing so swelled my thirst and made me attack him. No, I needed blood, now. Right now.

"This will only hurt for a second," I whispered, staring as my fangs ached, closing in on his neck.

The man fought with sudden renewed strength, that adrenaline spike people experience when they think death is imminent. But it was no use. He was still human.

A split second later it was too late. My fangs found their mark, puncturing flesh as my lips pressed to create a seal. The doctor's fighting stopped as my bite delivered a flood of dopamine to his system. His body became limp, his blood feeding my thirst and taking the edge off.

After a few more long pulls I drew back, satisfied and surprised. I'd just drank from a human for the third time since I'd become a functioning vampire. Being a lycan, Ty didn't count. The first time had ended in disaster and the almost death of Joel, a rock-star foot-baller from my high school. But this time, I hadn't even come close to taking life. I had been in complete control. It had been more like my chaperoned drink at *Bite* with Marcus.

Lifting the doctor's chin with my finger, I took control of his eyes, feeling strong and capable. "You never saw me. No one attacked you."

Like with the damned's victim, I pricked my finger on my fang before letting them slide back. Then I pressed the swelling scarlet drop to the two punctures along his neck. The holes closed up before my eyes, removing any and all trace of my feeding.

WITH MY BAGGED supplies and my body humming, I skipped back to the cabin. My veins rushed with the doctor's blood, making my skin feel alive and my senses alert and sharp. The reaction was nowhere near what Ty's blood did to me, but it was still illuminating. The fact that I took from a living person without even coming close to killing them, and had compelled the whole attack away, was more than exciting. It was progress. Now I was becoming who I was meant to be. A living vampire who was in control. Not a monster *or* a killer.

"I'm back," I sang as I skipped through the door.

Ty would know I hadn't been gone long enough to venture off the boat, but I didn't care. I had what he needed, supplies and new linen. More importantly I had veins filled with reviving blood that could continue his healing.

Ty was outside sprawled on a deck chair. He glanced over his shoulder through the sliding door and winced. "Hey, beautiful. You're back fast." He frowned, noticing the plastic bag. "What's all that?"

"I went shopping on board." I smiled and dropped the supplies and linen onto the round table before walking over. With a glance down I noticed his dressings were soiled and oozing. I knelt beside him, touching a light hand over one. "Why are you out of bed?"

Ty waved off my hand. "I'm not an invalid." A mischievous smile lit his stunning face. "Though I could use a shower."

The image of Ty naked brought fire to my cheeks. I smiled,

trying to hide my inexperience. "Okay, great. Uh, yeah…let's do this."

Unable to look him in the eye, I squatted, focusing on removing the soiled bandages from his wounds and willing the fire in my cheeks to subside. Then I hauled him to his feet and supported his weight back inside and to the bathroom. I slid the curtain back and flicked the shower tap on. Ty leaned into the wall, hand braced against the sink and breathing labored from the small distance. He was practically naked already, only wearing the pair of board shorts he'd managed to get on last night.

Ty began to tug the blood-spattered covering down, and I stilled his hands. If he bent over the wounds across his back would burst like a dam. "Let me help."

I built up the blocks in my mind. Kendrick wasn't here, but I didn't want him accidentally popping into my subconscious. With caution I lowered my hands, pulling down Ty's boardies while keeping my eyes cast sideways.

I shot back up to find Ty smiling at me. "You're blushing."

"Am not." I turned away, pretending to check the water temperature. Then my focus set on Ty's face, and I helped him into the shower.

I was about to step in behind Ty when he said, "You know you're dressed, right?"

"Oh, right."

I glanced down at the shorts and tank I'd put on earlier. The same clothes I'd worn while drinking the doctor's blood. A single drop stained the neckline. My heart galloped and I whipped it off. I hadn't mentioned my feeding, and I definitely didn't want to get into it now. Not when I could barely think past Ty being naked before me.

Willing my pulse to slow, I slipped out of my shorts. Then I went to unclip my bra.

Ty raised an unsteady hand, brushing my arm. "You can chuck on your bikini, if you want."

I appreciated the suggestion but shook my head. Ty was standing, well leaning, against the bathroom wall before me stark naked, wearing only a smile. Our relationship had been through so much, but it was clear that Ty was completely comfortable with me, in every way. With the walls up in my mind, there was nothing holding me back from this. Besides, it wasn't like anything was physically going to happen. Getting hot and heavy would just tear him open more.

In answer I unclipped my bra, letting the straps fall from my shoulders then down to the floor. Ty's eyes remained focused on mine, unmoving and soft. I pushed my underwear from my hips, letting them fall to the floor.

Ty smiled and held his arm out for me to stand under. With my help he pushed off the wall, groaning as we stepped into the shower. Ty's back was to the spout, and the second the water hit his flesh he let out a grueling growl. Agony twisted his face and he twitched uncontrollably as the water—now tinged with his blood—stung every inch of his cut flesh. I stepped closer to him, letting his body lean into mine.

After a few minutes the twitching stopped and Ty took a shuddering breath. His head hanging over my shoulder moved, planting a heated kiss against my neck. The touch of his lips sent a shockwave of tingles through my body. Lightness swept through my head, while parts of me grew hot.

I shook off the wonderful sensation, reminding myself of what we were doing here. Then I pushed Ty back against the tiled wall. Grasping the soap from the dish behind him, I began washing over the deep gashes, starting with his shoulders and chest. Ty winced, keeping his eyes fixed on my face. The action on his behalf made me feel much more confident in what I was doing, especially since we were both standing before each other totally naked.

When I'd finished cleaning the deep cuts on his shoulders and chest, I helped turn him around so I could tend to the wounds on his back. These ones were bad, the worst of his injuries being the deepest and longest cuts. With a shudder, I recalled the damned landing on Ty's back with claws that tore into his skin as he attempted to throw him off. I dabbed each laceration, trying to be as gentle as possible. Still, every muscle in Ty's back tensed with each soapy touch. Once that was done, Ty shifted back around with my help.

I turned my back to him and drew my hair over one shoulder, exposing my neck.

A frozen moment of silence passed. "What are you doing?" Ty asked, voice suddenly rough.

"You need to drink more," I said. I wondered now that my back was turned, if he was staring at my butt. And now I was blushing, again.

"Amelia, we don't have to," Ty said. "I'm healing, slowly."

"Too slowly." I lifted a nail and made a little slice into my neck. Blood trickled down my back. After almost getting Ty killed this was the least I could do. "I want to do this. Let me help you."

Long seconds passed, then a calloused hand found my waist, guiding me back until my shoulder blades met the solid lines of Ty's chest. Leaning forward must have taken him great effort. His lower body was close enough for me to feel its warmth, but it wasn't quite touching. His other hand brushed over my exposed shoulder, and then his mouth found my neck, kissing with soft lips before parting. My eyelids fluttered shut at the gentle draw of his mouth taking my blood. My own lips parted, dying to whisper *I love you.*

But Ty spoke first, lips breaking away from my flesh. "Your blood…it tastes *different.*"

Surprise bolted through me a second before realization hit. He could taste the doctor I'd drank? And we were naked in the shower. Not where I'd expected to tell him about my achievement. "Oh…yeah."

I got out of the shower and groped for a towel from the rail, throwing it around my body. Then I handed one to Ty. For some reason it felt odd. I'd never talked to Ty about drinking from humans before. He already knew about my first attempt, which had been a monster-like disaster, the one where he'd stopped me from killing. But I'd never told him about the donor at the Armaya. It hadn't come up in conversation. Generally my needs were filled by packaged human blood, and on the rare occasion, wild game at Mt Major.

"Well, you still needed to heal, and I was, well…" My heart raced. Sweat budded across my face and body. Why was telling him this hard? "Well, you know. But I—"

"You *drank* someone?" Ty's voice was incredulous, the look on his face just as crushing. He snatched the towel around his waist, grimacing at the movement. Though I noted not even one his wounds split as a reaction. Then he limped past me, standing at the sliding door with his back to me. His wounds were knitting together, but his sharp voice stole my attention. "Was it good? Was it worth it?"

"Worth it?" I didn't understand the fuming hostility pouring off him, the anger. "Ty, I needed blood," I began, feeling a rush of word vomit coming on. "And you were still so hurt. You needed more from me to heal. But if I'd given you mine, I think I would have lost it. And I didn't plan it. But everything was fine. I didn't hurt the guy. I even compelled him to forget."

"Can you compel me to forget, too?" The muscles along his shoulders and neck ticked.

"Compel you?" I was seriously lost. "Why would I need—"

"So the image of you," he almost snarled, turning and irises blazing, "fangs deep in some guy's neck can be stuck from my memory."

Then it hit me, the reason Ty was so pissed off. "You think I cheated on you?" I tugged the towel tighter around my body. I felt way too exposed and a little sick. "Ty, it wasn't like that. It was only blood."

"Is it only blood when you bite into *my* throat? When your hands are in my hair? When your legs are curled around me? When your body grates against mine? Is that just *blood*?"

"You know it's not," I snapped back. Irritation bubbled up inside me, threatening to overflow. My hands curled into fists. "It's different with you. You know it is. You're more to me than a meal. But I'm a vampire, Ty. And you said you accepted me. You said you accepted me for everything I am. Well, this is what I am. I need blood to live."

The challenge in Ty's ferocious eyes was clear. "And if the roles were reversed?"

"I—I..." Any words of rebuttal died on my tongue. Because Ty had a point. If it were his lips on some girl's flesh, food or not, would I be okay with it? The answer? Hell no! I would be livid.

With a clenched jaw at my deflated expression, Ty stomped to the wardrobe built into the wall, pulling out shorts and a T-shirt that he tugged on in a rush. The small amount of blood he'd taken had helped, but that didn't matter now. He shoved the door open and stepped out into the corridor. "I need some air."

I SHIFTED my weight from one leg to the other. Then I read the note in my hands again. It had begun to tear from the number of times I'd folded and unfolded it.

'Have dinner with me. I'll be waiting outside the formal dining lounge. Reservation's at 6:30.'

I scanned the crowd again. There were people lining up for couple and group portraits. Everyone else was being ushered forward through the twin doors to the lounge. My heart sank like a stone. It was past 6:30PM and Ty wasn't here. He'd changed his mind.

I faced the wall, blinking back tears as I tugged at the end of my braided hair. Earlier I'd left our cabin to search for Ty, needing to apologize and talk this out. But he was as absent then as he was now. A ghost on an inescapable ship. Unless he'd jumped overboard and swum for it… When I returned to our room, I found the note and his dress clothes missing. Relief had eased my guilt, though not anymore.

I tugged at my dress's hem. It was the one Mom had given me for Christmas, purple and not crazy short. When I put it on earlier I had actually felt pretty. And confident. Now I felt stupid…and alone.

Tears rolled down my cheeks as I sniffed. Then I sniffed again and spun, trying to pinpoint the direction of the scent. There. Panic and desolation fled my body, replaced by nerves that churned my stomach and made my heart race. Ty was descending the wide, carpeted stairs in a single breasted black suit and a black patterned shirt. The top two buttons were undone. My jaw gaped and I drew in a lungful, my body forcing me to breathe after holding my breath.

A smile played across Ty's lips while he drank me in. Still, I couldn't help notice his stiff hesitation as he stopped before me. Rather than drawing me into his arms, he stepped back, looking uncomfortable. "You look…amazing."

That foot of space separating our bodies was like an impassable ocean. Guilt crippled me, like acid being injected into my bones. "Ty, I'm sorry," I blurted, fiddling with my hands. "I didn't even think of it like that. And I didn't mean to hurt you. It meant nothing."

Ty sighed and then paused. An expression I couldn't read crossed his face. Then his hand came forward and he shrugged. "How about we talk about it all over dinner?"

I nodded and took his hand, unable to speak as we joined the shuffling queue. I hated not knowing where we stood. I hated wondering if Ty was calming the storm before the real shit started. The livid anger was gone from his expression. Still it was clear he wasn't okay. *We* weren't okay.

After an agonizing few minutes we cleared the line to the dining hall. Inside, a tower of sparkling crystal glasses had been set up for the champagne waterfall. The lights were also dimmed, creating a romantic atmosphere. We settled into our pre-booked table and ordered. Don't ask me what I chose though. I was so nervous that I couldn't even remember what I'd asked the waiter for.

The crippling silence went on until our appetizers came, and we ate without speaking. My thoughts raced with all the things I wanted to say, but I couldn't quite rearrange anything into words.

"I overreacted before," Ty said suddenly. "Just the thought of you with some other guy…" He trailed off, jaw clenching and teeth grating.

Instant defensiveness tightened my tone. "It wasn't like that."

"I know." Ty shook his head as if clearing the mental image from his mind. "I believe you. And for the record, I do accept you, *every-*

thing about you. But I know that's not something you do." He lowered his voice. "Taking from humans. Well not since *Pulse*, as far as I know."

Pulse was a popular vampire club in Anchorage, the one I'd gone searching for Kendrick in before knowing about its clientele. Before knowing why it was a frequent hangout for my best friend. A supermarket of fresh blood from unsuspecting humans. I nodded, about to confirm when I remembered the club *Bite* at the Armaya. Back then Marcus had introduced me to the custom of drinking from living and willing donors. That had been my second taste from a human. "There was one other." Ty's expression became cloudy, a thunderstorm ready to explode. "It was at the Armaya. I drank from a girl, a human."

The clouds were gone from his expression, replaced by contemplating surprise. "I didn't know you swung that way."

"What?" Had he just suggested that I was bi? "No. It wasn't like that. It was—"

"Like today?" Ty questioned.

I sighed and lowered my voice to a whisper "Yes. I won't deny that I wanted his blood. But it wasn't because I was into him. I was thirsty, and I wanted to give you mine again so you'd heal better."

Ty fell silent, looking guarded as the waiter brought out our main course.

I began eating and glanced around. Surrounding us, other happy couples dined with easygoing chitchat about everyday, mundane things. "Don't you want that?" I nodded at an old couple sitting at a booth hand in hand, content and talking about their normal lives.

"What?" Ty questioned. "That seriously old woman over there? Hmmm, not my type."

Despite everything, that made me smile. "No, I mean what they have. A normal life with someone you can build a family and grow old with." As the words tumbled from my mouth, fear of his response surged through me. If the answer was yes, that would be the end. I'd have no choice but to walk away.

Ty reached across the table to rest his hand on mine. "Amelia, I want you. Only you. Forever."

I pulled my hand from his and hurt flashed across Ty's beautiful face. "But I can't grow old with you. I can't give you a family," I said, knowing that only royal vampires could procreate. "I can't give you a normal life."

Ty mock laughed. "Ha, like my life is normal with or without you. My whole life I've been trained, conditioned so that I could one day protect the world from..." His words hung on his tongue.

"From vampires. From me." It wasn't a question, but Ty's head dipped anyway, glancing down. "So that's what you want to do with your life?"

Ty's head snapped up faster than lightning, vehemence radiating from his contact-shielded eyes. "It's what I was born to do."

"But your father's a senator," I replied. "Don't you want to be something, too?"

Ty folded his arms over his chest and leaned back. "I wanted to swim, to compete in the Olympics." His eyes lit up, then dropped to the plate in front of him. "Not that that's possible. With all their drug testing they'd find something odd with my blood. Besides it's unfair, given that all the competitors are human." Ty shook his head. "I've accepted my future long ago. I know what I am and who I'm meant to be."

"A protector," I whispered. "A warrior."

"And I could be an even better one." His hand found mine across the table again and squeezed. Hope shone even through the concealing contacts. "Turn me, Amelia. Level the playing field and make me stronger. Give me a life span that can compete. One that will make what I do significant, not a blip in time. One that will give us—"

"We're onto this again?" I snatched my hand free and began worrying the end of my braid with my fingers. Turning Ty wasn't an option. We'd already gone over this. I wouldn't risk his life. Not for me. Not for anyone. Capping my anger, I tried to keep my voice reasoning. "Ty, I'm sorry. I can't do it. I can't risk losing you. Please understand."

The waiter arrived then and took our unfinished but done with mains. A minute later he had delivered a slice of mud cake.

"I do understand," Ty said once he'd left. "Thought I'd give it one last go, but I already knew you'd say no."

"Oh," I said, confused. "Then why'd—"

"Because I want to barter." Ty forked a chunk of cake and held it out for me to take.

I closed my mouth over the delicious chunk and let the fork slide from between my lips. When my mouth was clear I asked, "Barter?"

Ty fed himself a piece of cake, looking thoughtful as he chewed. "How about this? I'll stop asking you to turn me, *if* you take me as your consort."

I coughed, choking on nothing but air. If I'd had another mouthful of cake it would've been all over Ty's face. Was he offering to be a prostitute? "Consort?"

Ty laughed, seeing the shock on my face. "I'm not offering to be your sex slave."

A few close dining guests gaped at his words. Their heads turned away a second later.

Ty lowered his voice. "Just your blood donor. If you're sick of baggies and bottled AB- and want to drink someone, I want it to be me. Only me."

Ty wanted to be my blood donor? Given how heated our

drinking encounters had gotten, I guess I shouldn't have been surprised. Thinking about it now warmed my body and made my toes tingle. There were probably a million reasons why I should say no. But right now I couldn't think of a single one. All I saw were the positives. I didn't want to hurt Ty by taking another living person's vein. Though I still didn't see it as cheating, it was clear that he did. And I would rather drink from Ty any day of the week, than attack and use some unsuspecting human.

No matter what way I looked at it, I couldn't think of any reason to say no. So I didn't. "Deal."

CHAPTER 17

The cruise concluded the next morning, and after a string of exhausting flights we finally touched down in Boston. Although it was over twenty-four hours later, the date was the same as when we'd left due to regaining time from overseas travel. When Ty drove his WRX up to my house, I still hadn't told him my plans.

We exited the car, pre-midnight darkness lit only by porch lights. Ty moved to kiss me goodbye, long and slow. With my heart fluttering erratically, I pulled back and tugged on his arm. "We're having a meeting about the attacks, and I want you to be there, too. I'm gonna need your help with something."

Ty raised an eyebrow but said nothing. Sharing space with Kendrick and experiencing our bond was the last thing he wanted to witness. Still, there was an air of determination about him as he slung his arm around my shoulder. "Let's get this party started."

My mind was closed to Kendrick as we walked through the front doors, but his was wide open. He was waiting upstairs in the rec room. Dorian was propped on the high-arched windowsill texting—probably a girl—and to my total relief, appearing healed of any injuries. Kendrick was perched on the arm of the leather couch, the desk lamp highlighting the contemplation across his face.

As I entered with Ty in hand, Kendrick sprung up. The instant smile on his face at seeing me dropped the second he spotted Ty. His eyes slid from Ty to me. "Good blocking."

"Hey, sis," Dorian said, sliding his phone back into his jeans and taking a spot on the couch.

Kendrick strode around the glass coffee table, face blank and stiff at the same time. I braced for the *get out, this doesn't concern you* to fly from his tight lips. But it never came. Instead he paused, rolled back his shoulders with a crack, and then held out his right hand. "Thanks for saving Amelia. I'm glad you were there."

My jaw dropped and I stared, shocked out of words.

After a long silent moment, Ty released my hand and clasped my best friend's. "I'll always protect her, no matter who or what comes hunting. Wolves always guard what they love with their lives." There was an underlying edge to his words and gold-pulsing gaze. A claim that I was his to love and keep safe.

Kendrick's lips thinned into a straight line, but he kept his thoughts to himself as he pulled his hand free. "Don't think this makes us buddies."

Ty smiled coldly. "Wouldn't dream of it."

Kendrick went back to his perch as I sent a silent *thank you* through the bond. "Take a seat." He nodded to the two leather armchairs and waited for us to sit.

"Now that that's over," Dorian piped up, leaning forward with his elbows on his knees. "Can we get to the damned attacks?"

There was a unified "yes" in response.

Dorian glanced at Kendrick, kicking his feet up onto the coffee table. "Have you told her what they are?"

Taking his drifting eyes from Ty, we shared a look. I blinked back the memory of our attacks and tried to focus on the facts. "Damned vampires. Red-eyed, faster than wolves and living vamps, with crazy strength and psycho thirst." My throat tightened at the rising block coming from Kendrick. "There's more, isn't there?"

"Yes," Kendrick said, clasping his hands in his lap. "They were once vampires. Alive like us. Now turned into pulseless beings with fractured souls. In vamp history we learned that a curse was created, making them slaves to the darkness with sunlight incinerating them on contact. It also plagues them with insanity that grows stronger with each consumption kill."

"Like we learned about Erzsebet."

"Who's Erzsebet?" Ty questioned.

I bit my lip as he lifted his brows expectantly. In our week away I hadn't brought up what Kendrick and I had found out. I'd wanted everything doom and gloom to be temporarily forgotten.

"She's Caius's mother," Dorian spoke to my surprise.

So Kendrick hadn't had the same reservations. In his time away he'd filled my brother in on everything. I quickly explained what we knew then looked to Kendrick. Ty didn't seem annoyed that I hadn't told him, but I still wanted to get back to the main subject. Plus a growing inkling from Kendrick had spiked my curiosity. "There's more about the damned?" I assumed.

Reluctance stormed across Kendrick's pale face. "They can live forever, unless killed."

Ice undulated my veins, making my blood run cold. "*Immortal?*" According to Caius and the experiments he'd subjected me to, my blood was immortal. Was there a link?

"And the other thing," Dorian said, knocking Kendrick's knee with his hand.

"There's more?" I sank into the armchair, hitting the roadblock in my best friend's mind. "What are you keeping from me?"

Kendrick fidgeted on the couch, cracking his knuckles. "Look, don't get mad, okay?"

I glared at him. "Patience is not one of my strong points."

"Okay, okay." He stared down at his tight hands. "I thought something was up before we left. Especially with your mom letting you go away knowing Ty would be there. So I kept checking in on her."

"What did you find?" Ty asked, his eager but calm exterior in stark contrast to how livid I felt.

"Nothing," Dorian answered for him.

"But you didn't stop there." I edged forward in my seat, fingers pressed through denim into my thighs.

"No." Kendrick glanced up. "I pulled a few strings and got some inside information. Marcus reported some unusual deaths in Alaska. A few humans, but mostly vampires drained of blood."

The image of dead bodies, gray and bloodless, quelled my anger. That part Marcus had volunteered over the phone. "That's terrible. But wait. Why would that influence our mom's actions?"

"Because there was another death," Dorian supplied. "In Manchester."

My jaw dropped. The morbid information had just hit too close to home. Manchester was about an hour's drive from here. A growing concern for my mom burned within me. "Why would she keep—" A flashback to Christmas morning stopped me short. That day we'd revealed the vacations with the fallback of compelling her to agree. But interference hadn't been necessary. A phone call had interrupted her flat-out refusal. Mom had talked to someone about a council issue, as she explained afterward. I remembered the words *"Another one..."* Then Mom had gasped and said something about it being in our own backyard. When she'd returned to the living room her face had been paler and her expression distracted.

"She let us go away because of the deaths," I said, certain I was right.

"Do you think Caius is behind this?" Ty asked.

"He sent our attackers," I said. "That's proof that he's linked to the damned. He's at least involved."

"We can't tell your mom then," Kendrick said. "It'll only endanger her, too."

"I know. And it's only a matter of time before Caius comes for us again."

Dorian got up, seriousness edging his normally carefree face. "So what do we do now?"

This was the moment I'd needed Ty for. I just hadn't expected it to come out this way. "It's time to prepare," I said, straightening from the armchair. Caius had made two attempts on my life now. Except this time he'd threatened my life and the lives of the people I loved most. We would not wait around like sitting ducks anymore. We would not be his prey.

"Abilities are not enough," I went on. "And our strength and speed can't compare to the damned. We all learned that the hard way." I turned from Dorian and Kendrick to face Ty, grasping his hand and pulling him up beside me. "You said you'd teach me. But I need more. We all do. I need you to train us all to fight like our lives depend on it. Like we're a pack of wolves that would die for each other. And you need to teach us to kill."

Ty's eyes flashed gold above smiling lips. "That's the hottest thing you've ever said to me." He glanced past me to Kendrick and Dorian. "Training starts tomorrow. 0700 at Rye on the rocks. Don't be late."

I MOVED from the front door after watching Ty drive out the property gates in his WRX. Training tomorrow would be interesting, and I didn't know what to expect. I yawned. I was in desperate need of a jet-lag catnap. I closed the door and started up the arching marble steps.

Then the glittering chandelier lights blinked out and everything faded to black.

Feeling out of body, my eyelids fluttered and my surroundings cleaved into focus. A rustic room of logs and stone with frosted windows surrounded me. Light and heat radiated from a crackling, open fire. A fluffy rug separated me from the flames. Atop the plush surface lay a heavily pregnant woman propped against pillows. She was breathing fast, the man kneeling at her side patting her forehead with a wet towel.

My eyes bugged, realizing the woman was my mom. Caius was the man. Mom's knees were propped up, sweat pouring down her red face. "Caius, please. We've discussed this." She cried out, clutching at her swollen belly. Her gray, human eyes became frantic and she snatched Caius's hand. "We're running out of time, and you promised. You said this would work."

"It will work," Caius grated. His expression was fierce and somehow resigned at the same time. "And if this is truly what you want—"

"It is," Mom snapped, cutting him off. She winced, leaning up to lift her loose-fitting dress to expose her swollen belly. A second later something long and slender glinted in her hand. A scalpel. She snatched the towel from Caius's hand and shoved it into her mouth, biting down. Stubbornness set her delicate features with harsh lines. Then she nodded.

Nausea roiled my stomach. What the hell was she doing? I wanted to scream, to blast into the room and somehow stop this terrible scene and what I knew was about to come. But this was the past. Not the present. Although I could see what was happening, I wasn't physically there.

Caius took the scalpel, meeting my mom's eyes and almost pleading with his own. Then he ran the sharp edge along the lower part of Mom's belly. She shrieked through the towel, instant tears spilling from her eyes as blood poured from the long cut. Caius moved fast and shoved his hands inside her. A blood-cloaked baby girl was yanked free. He dragged the scalpel along my tiny infant belly, and I winced, feeling the cutting pain. A glittering red vial appeared in his hand, and he poured the contents into the gash. Without waiting, he plunged his hands back inside my mom, tearing the second baby free. The cutting process was repeated. Except this vial was filled with a dark, silvery substance. The cut along my infant body was gone, and I watched as my baby brother's shrunk to nothing. I heard the second their tiny lungs inflated, instantaneous cries wailing from their throats.

We'd already been torn from our mom's womb before Caius poured the contents of the vials into us. So why was I labeled IBB? Did IBB mean infected before my first breath of life? And if Dorian was IAB, did that mean he'd already started breathing when Caius ripped him from the womb?

"Are t-they al-right?" Mom gurgled, eyelids drooping and head lolling back.

Caius wrapped the babies with white mink blankets and went to her side. "They're fine. It worked." Fear transformed his face as he bit into his wrist, before pressing it against her mouth. "Hold on," he said. "*Please* hold on." He lifted her upper body, causing more blood to gush from her carved belly. Then he sank his fangs into her neck. Long moments passed, the patter of my mom's heart fading to almost nothing. Caius tore his fangs free from her neck and bit into his bottom lip. He removed his no-longer bleeding wrist from her mouth. "Do not die on me!" he shouted, then pressed his lips to hers.

Crimson drops escaped from between their mouths, and then I heard it. Mom's dwindling heartbeat increased in strength then began racing.

Her eyes flung open, startlingly silver. No longer the eyes of a human, but the eyes of a vampire.

The first thing I felt as the vision faded was a cool hand against my cheek. "Are you okay?"

I was cradled in Kendrick's arms, my head against his firm chest. We were in the foyer at the bottom of the stairs. He frowned at me, stroking my hair back and looking worried. His pulse was elevated...and damn, he smelled good. I kicked free of his hold and stumbled back against the wall.

Dorian flew from the kitchen and steadied me before shoving a full bottle of blood into my hands. "What'd you see?"

After emptying the bottle I sank onto the lower steps, my knees still wobbling.

Kendrick took the glass bottle. "Did you see the damned?"

"Or Caius?" Dorian interjected.

With my brain beginning to throb, I rubbed my thumbs over my temples. "Mom forced Caius to infect us. It was her idea to have us all turned..."

The moment I'd finished recounting what I'd seen, the wooden front door swung open and Mom strolled in. She caught sight of us as she dropped her keys into a glass dish on the foyer table. "Oh, you're all home. I'm so happy you're—"

Dorian shot forward. His hands wrapped around her shoulders and his eyes captured her startled ones. "Why did you make him turn us?"

Kendrick and I crept closer but kept quiet. Dorian's compulsion always worked better without interference.

The shock left Mom's face, replaced by muted confusion. "Turned who? Where?"

Dorian's steel gaze narrowed. "You made Caius turn Amelia and me into vampires."

Watching the turmoil as our mom's eyes became distant, darting with memories, I held my breath. It felt like an ant nest had been obliterated in my gut, and a million ants were trying to crawl up my throat to freedom.

Finally Mom spoke and my breath released. "I never did that. It all happened when…when the rogue vampire attacked. His blood and venom mixed into mine to make you vampires, even before you were born."

Caius's compulsion is still holding strong, Kendrick said wordlessly. *The alchemist mark on her shoulder must still be working.*

I leaned forward and whispered in my brother's ear. He nodded and lifted Mom's hand over her blouse to the hidden scar across her now flat stomach. "Then why did you make Caius cut us from your body?"

Mom frowned, moving her hand back and forth over the long scar. She frowned, creating lines in her youthful complexion. "You were going to be born vampires. I didn't want that. I didn't want you to be forced into their world. I made Caius do it to keep you from them. To make you appear human. To keep you safe."

Dorian questioned our mom over and over. Still no matter how hard he forced his compulsion, the responses were the same. In the end we let it go, and after wiping the encounter and putting Mom to bed, Dorian met us back in the foyer.

In the time he'd been gone, my brain had been spinning on overdrive. Her turn of events just couldn't be true, because she was still human when Caius had torn us from her body. If the rogue vampire —who was actually Caius—had attacked earlier, she would already have been a vampire. There was only one believable explanation.

"Caius compelled her to think we were already turned, and the one way to keep us human was to poison us."

As Dorian directed his Cabriolet around the sharp bend of a cliff, the rising sun spread a rippling orange hue over small ocean swells. The anticipation on his face was unmissable. Today we were training at the beach. But not just any beach. Rye on the Rocks was secluded, and in these chilly weather conditions would remain abandoned.

After passing a few miles on Route 1-A, we arrived at our destination. Bone-chilling wind howled, whipping sand past us. Dorian replaced his car's hood as Kendrick and I got out.

Ty was already waiting and he pushed off the log-framed barrier to wrap me in his arms. "Morning, beautiful." His lips met mine for too short a moment, breaking away as Kendrick and Dorian sidled up.

Slight distaste swelled from Kendrick, but he kept a lid on his emotions. His hatred for Ty was slowly decreasing.

Ty's body straightened to maximum height and his gentle voice hardened. "Okay, let's get started."

Ty led the way down the rocky incline to the small sand and rock-filled beach. Then he nodded to Dorian and Kendrick. "Amelia and I will grapple. You two watch."

"I have to fight you?" I said as Ty pulled me into the sandy clearing. Although I'd known what we were coming here to do, I hadn't considered the possibility of forcefully trying to hurt him.

Ty smiled. "Experiencing your strengths and weaknesses first hand will give me the best idea on how to train you." He glanced over to the others. "After Amelia, I'll take each of you on."

Dorian and Kendrick took spots on a large, pitted rock in the shade, watching us.

I gulped when Ty turned back to me, not just because of what we were about to do, but also in morbid anticipation of Ty and Kendrick duking it out. "O-okay," I said. "What do I do?"

Ty leaned forward, lips brushing my cheek. "Try to hit me."

My eyes widened. "Hit you?"

"If you can."

Ty smiled in the way that always got my pulse racing. It raced now, but not for the same reason. Adrenaline flooded my veins as I let his arrogance grate on me. I pushed aside the fact that the guy I loved stood before me, and clenched my hands. Then I struck out, aiming for his stomach.

Ty reacted, catching my fist to shove me back. "Your eyes betrayed your action."

I stumbled at the force, the heel of my glittery silver Vans hitting a rock before I regained my footing. My knees bent and I lunged. Ty blocked my attack, bringing my feet back to the ground. I struck out, aiming for his face. His forearm came up in a flash, blocking my hit. I struck out again and again, but each and every hit was met with anticipation. Breathing hard, I stepped back. "I suck at this!"

"Not if I have anything to do with it." Ty clapped his hands together. "Go again."

Using all the strength I could conjure, the hits began to fly. Each time I would meet Ty's fist, or arm. Even more embarrassing was when I hit nothing but air, stumbling forward as he spun fluidly out of my reach.

Ty's expression remained focused, and he made no attempt to fight back. "You've got legs too," he said. As if I didn't already know that. "Use them!"

With a frustrated cry, I continued my attack, bringing my legs and knees into the action and aiming for any and every part of him. Even with the wind chill, sweat slicked my face and body. My hair stuck to my neck and arms, and my clothes latched onto my skin. This fight had been going on for ages. The cloud-cloaked sun was higher in the sky, a gentle glow of mid morning. When my stamina began to ebb and frustration at my lacking skill enraged me, I kicked for Ty's groin. He didn't even blink, catching my foot and throwing it away. I spun at the power of his thrusting arm, my back suddenly to Ty.

And then it was all over.

Ty had one arm around my waist. The other was clamped around my neck. "Never turn your back on your enemy," he said, vampire fangs grazing my neck. "Or you're likely to become their lunch."

Ty spun me out of his hold and I tripped on a rock. Challenge radiated from his eyes while his expression darkened. "Try harder!"

The harsh demand in his tone caught me off guard. His hard alpha stare made me pause. To me Ty had always been gentle. I'd never had this other side of him directed at me. The demand. The anger. The formidable hostility. I got to my feet, brushing the sand from my tank top and wondering if this was what he'd received growing up. Was this how real fighters were made?

"Take it easy," Kendrick called, rising from beside Dorian off the rock.

"Saving your skin isn't easy," Ty said, glaring at him. "I'm doing this to save her life. All your lives."

Kendrick stalked forward and I held a hand up. Regardless of my fatigue and initial surprise at Ty's harsh treatment, this is what we'd come here to do "No. It's fine."

Kendrick kept walking. "This is not fine. He's treating you like you're one of his pack. Like you're his to boss around." He pushed my arm away and fronted on Ty, shoving him in the chest. "Back off, tick magnet."

Ty smiled and the look had the lethal malice of a bloody dagger. "Don't hold back, vampire. I know you've been waiting for this."

"Guys, please," I pleaded.

Kendrick swung before I could stop him. The strike was quick as a catapult and connected with Ty's ribs. He barely flinched, making me wonder if he'd expected the landing. Then he struck out at Kendrick's face. The whipping breeze became glacial as they continued to lash out at each other. And I didn't step in. For one, they'd brought this on themselves. And two, with the whole bond threesome thing they both needed to blow off some steam.

Dorian met my side and nudged me with his elbow. "Want me to break it up?"

I caught my flailing hair and used the elastic around my wrist to tie it into a ponytail. "Not yet."

Kendrick had somehow gotten Ty in a headlock and was punching into his side over and over.

"Is that all you've got?" Ty laughed then threw Kendrick over onto his back. He landed on his chest and clocked him in the face. An instant bruise flared across Kendrick's cheek and around his eye.

My best friend screamed out as I yanked Dorian forward. "Okay. Now it's time."

Before we could reach them, a swirling gust of wind kicked up clouds of sand and knocked both guys onto their backs. It kept up a battering force, the thick windblown sand separating both guys and holding us back.

Then just as suddenly the wind was gone.

Ty sat up, wiping blood from his split lip with the back of his hand. At the same time, Kendrick rolled onto his knees and clutched his ribs. Purple and black bruises scored their bare arms and faces, turning mustard in color as they both began to heal.

"What's with the crazy wind?" Ty asked.

I shrugged, wrapping my arms around my body. "Don't know, but usually crazy lightning follows." I scanned above. Clouds slid like billowing smoke beneath a now slate-black mass. "Can we take off before that happens? Or are you two not done yet?"

Ty jumped up and Dorian hauled Kendrick to his feet. "Sounds good," Kendrick said, the puffiness from his eye receding.

Ty took my hand and began walking. He glanced over his shoulder. "Not bad, Kendrick. For a beginner…"

Kendrick ignored him with a grunt and jogged past us. Dorian took after him.

Ty squeezed my hand, full lips thinning into a straight line. "Sorry. I let that get out of hand." I began to tell him it was okay, that I understood, but he kept talking. "I know this wasn't easy for you. Seeing me like this. I wish I didn't have to be so tough on you. But I do." He released my hand and curled his arm around me, hugging me against his side. "You can handle it. I know you can. You're strong, Amelia." At my look that said, *yeah right,* he smiled. "Think about it. When the damned attacked us on the boat, you didn't run or hide. You risked your life to save me. You're a fighter,

Amelia. And with practice I know you can be as menacing as any opponent. It just takes time."

I put an arm around him and squeezed. "So I'm not a lost cause?"

Ty laughed, tightening his hold around me. "Far from it."

CHAPTER 18

I drove my Ducati up the long driveway to Ty's house on Friday. Mr. Malau was out of town, *thank God*, and after five days of beach and bush training, my alpha boyfriend had a new location in mind. The personal training arena below his house.

I stood before the formidable front doors, trying to force my racing heart to slow. Kendrick had had enough this week, but Dorian's car was already parked. If Mr. Malau were here there'd be no way my brother would hang around. I saw a note on the door and snatched it.

'Around back. Door's unlocked.'

Past the tall rendered walls and reflective windows that watched me like eyes, I found the door. I kicked snow from my Vans, which had begun to soak through, and went in. It was pitch black inside, my vampire sight leading me along the blank sterile corridor. At the end was an open trap door that led down a wooden ladder. I dropped down through the trapdoor, found the door handle, and pushed.

White light shot through the opening, taking my vision away as calloused hands found my waist. "Heard you coming. We'll need to work on that. But not today." Ty's hot lips brushed over mine. "Welcome to my training room."

My sight adjusted to the glow pouring off the multiple domed lights strung from ceiling beams. The room was big, square, and underground. Divots marked the wooden floors and there were darker stained patches.

Across the room my brother sat against the wall with a silly smile on his face. Beside him was Vanessa, dressed in black leather pants and a tight vest. They weren't quite touching, but Dorian glanced sideways at her slowly and obviously before standing up. "Great, you're here." He raised a brow at Ty, looking impatient. "Now can we get started?"

"Hey, Amelia," Vanessa called before smiling at my brother. "Don't see why not."

"Get started on what?" I asked, feeling nervous.

Ty cupped my shoulders and spun me to the back wall. My jaw fell open while tingles rippled down my back. The wall was strung with weapons. So many that you could barely see the white of the wall behind them. There were axes, picks, mallets, machetes, and a bunch of other items I didn't know the names to. Every weapon was silver, or at least tipped with the metal. Their surfaces glinted against the light, promising pain. A sparkling assortment in deadly sharp proportions. I'd known I was going to see his training room, but I hadn't expected this. This was the room Ty had been taught to fight in. The room where he'd learned to deflect the attacks of these very weapons at the hands of his father. It was also where he'd perfected wielding them himself.

Without thought my hand traveled up the many rough scars across Ty's arm. I cringed. The same scars covered his entire body. After seeing Ty transform in the forest, I'd guessed some of them had come from his bones splitting through his flesh. But the others? They had to be the result of constant years of war-like training. In many ways it was barbaric. Still, I wanted to hear it from Ty.

I traced one of the larger scars across his forearm. "Your scars... they were inflicted by these weapons? By your own father?"

Ty shrugged. His expression was flat. "The training has to be brutal. It has to be real. Fighting for fun with fake weapons will only get you killed in the field."

Imagining Ty as a boy, fending off weapons and battle strikes from his solid-built father seemed like abuse. Still, I could understand why it was done, and why it was necessary. If not for Ty's combat ability, the attacker on the cruise may have killed us both.

I exchanged a look with Dorian who seemed to be waiting for something in between watching Vanessa. They both came up beside us and Ty nudged me closer to the wall.

"Oh, shit," I said. "Don't tell me—"

"That we're training with weapons!" The excitement in Dorian's voice peaked. "Which one's mine?"

Vanessa clinked forward in black stiletto boots and unhinged a bow from the wall. "It's one of my favorites." Directing him to the other side of the room, she slid a target with a painted bull's-eye out from between a gap in the wall. "Target practice first."

"What do you like?" Ty breathed against my neck, his chest grazing my back.

I shivered and imagined his hot, broad hands touching places on my body that were hidden by clothes. An emotional spike struck my chest and I abandoned the fantasy. Kendrick wasn't here, but he was still in my head. I pulled up my blocks the best I could and glanced back at the wall of weaponry. Dorian and I were here to train, not fool around.

I studied each weapon. All the knives, machetes, and axes

looked so deadly…and messy. I couldn't imagine having to use them on any living, or non-living thing. It was too gruesome and violent. The spiked mallets and other pulverizing weapons made my stomach drop. But then I saw—

"What about this?" I ran my fingers along the links of an iron chain.

"Thought that might be your style." Ty went to the wall but didn't grab the chain. Instead he removed a shiny silver ring that was as big as my skull. I almost wondered if Ty was secretly into magic tricks until he uncoiled the thing. "This packs a bigger punch than any chain."

Entirely made of silver, it unraveled into a long, flexible whip. This was a serious and lethal weapon. I gulped when Ty cracked it out in the air. The ripple forced countless, inch-long, silver spikes to jut out.

"I—I don't think—" I stopped speaking as Ty curled my shaking hand around the silver handle. The whip was heavy, but not too heavy, and the way it sat in my grasp just felt…right. It was like this weapon had been forged personally for me. "Wow," I breathed, any other words lost to me.

Ty smiled, looking a little unsure. "I know I've been tough on you, and I know Kendrick thinks I get off on it. But I don't. I needed to push you to see your strengths. So when I saw how quick you were with your hands…I got the whip made. Its length, width, links, and weight are customized to fit you."

Warmth coated my heart and dyed my cheeks. "Ty, I—I don't know what to say."

"Say you'll use it."

I curled the whip back up, amazed at how the spikes fell flat before coming in contact with my hand. "How do I start?"

Ty pulled a bunch of target dummies out from a chest against the wall, and got to work stringing the human-shaped sacks from the ceiling beams. I peeked over at Dorian and Vanessa, wondering how his weapon of choice was working out. Right now Vanessa was standing next to him, her arm around his back and positioning his hold on the bow. There was a look on his face that I'd seen many times before. The one that meant he wanted to strip off her leather pants and have some fun.

I was almost about to warn Vanessa when Ty stepped in front of me. "All ready."

Wanting to test out my new arm-extension, I decided to leave the warning for later.

Ty was with me the whole way, barking pointers and tips to get the whip to do what I wanted. Time and time again the whip struck its targets, curling around limbs, torsos, and necks. A good hour later my targets were shredded. Sawdust piles—their stuffing—littered the floor and coated my sweaty tank and leggings.

Propped against the wall, Ty smiled. "Good job."

I smiled back. "Got any more dummies?"

Ty's smile changed, holding a hint of mischief as he shook his head. "Let's move on to the next step."

Before I could question what the next step was, Dorian and Vanessa strode over.

Dorian kicked at a heap of sawdust. "I'm gonna bounce. Got stuff to do, people to see."

"Yeah, I've gotta go too," Vanessa said, gaze not meeting ours but shifting to the exit door. "Experiments and study to catch up on, you know."

I shot a hard look at Dorian that said, *don't even try it,* as he backed up to the door after Vanessa.

"Later Sis, Malau."

As the door closed I asked Ty, "The next step?"

Ty moved to an area that wasn't covered with sawdust and removed his shirt. "Moving target practice."

Eyes transfixed on his sculpted chest, I stared. With Kendrick locked out of my mind, we were finally alone. If I could just touch —then his words registered. "Hold on. You want me to attack you?" I lifted the coiled whip. "With this? Ty, no. What if I hurt you?"

"Then I'll have trained you well enough to be able to stay alive and defeat an opponent." He came forward, arms pulling me close and lips pressing against my forehead. "Then I won't have to be as terrified every minute I'm not there to protect you."

Touched, I rose on my toes and captured his lips for a short, hot kiss. The temptation to stay was there, to distract him from our training. But Ty was right. "Be careful."

Ty released me and backed up. "Don't hold back."

I squared my shoulders and let the whip roll out, ignoring the clenching of my gut. Ty's stance was centered, his focus sharp, waiting for my strike. With a deep, dreadful breath, I flicked my wrist. The silver length strung out into the air at Ty's arm. I winced, but he ducked at the last second, evading its curling spikes. I struck out again, this time at his shin. Again I missed, hitting air as he launched six feet into the air. The next move was a sweeper, gliding fast as light to trap his torso. Ty evaded the needle-like tip, back rolling out of its path.

The strikes and dodges continued on. After what felt like hours my arm began to ache, and Ty's chest was slick with sweat and his face was red.

I reined in what little stamina I had left and compiled the moves I'd learned. The ebbing energy and growing fatigue made my attempts less precise, more desperate, and erratically faster. When my whole body started burning with exhaustion, I picked my last moves. Quick curl-out above the chest. Missed. Backward sweep for the waist. Missed. And wrist flick for the—

The whip met its mark, curling around Ty's leg, spikes embedding in his shin.

He fell backward and I rushed over. "Shit. Oh shit!" Red torrents leaked from the numerous holes now plugged by silver in his leg. "What do I do? *Shit*. Tell me what to do!"

Ty leaned up on his elbows, pain tightening his muscles and... smiling? "Calm down first," he said. "Believe me, these are just scratches. I've had much worse. Now twist the handle, jiggle, and pull back."

"Ty, no. It'll—"

"It's the same thing you did with the dummies." His voice was so calm, reasonable. "If you can't do this, you'll lose your weapon in battle. Plus taking it out myself will tear open the holes even more."

The panic left me with a rush of instant calm. Adrenaline faded while the smell of his dripping blood onto the wooden floor soared. I bit my lip and held my breath, twisting the whip's handle. A jiggle and a tug freed every spike from Ty's shin. The whip recoiled into a tight hoop in my hand. Now unplugged, scarlet poured from the punctures, streaming down Ty's leg. Fresh desire pumped through my veins, speeding faster with my bloodlust.

"Hold it back," Ty spoke without concern. His eyes caught my wild ones, burning with total belief. "You *can* control it."

Repeating *control it* over and over, I stared as the leaking blood began to slow. My mouth watered and my fangs ached, but I wouldn't give in. As the last drops fell, the holes closed over, crystallizing with scabs that smoothed to pink fleshy spots.

As I stared at his leg and the pool of scarlet beneath it, Ty moved to kneel before me. His irises glowed as he curled his fingers around the back of my neck. "You did it."

Overwhelmed by my achievement and the still-lingering aroma of Ty's spilled blood, my body took over. I flattened Ty against the wooden floor and leaped on top of him, bloodlust warping into desperate desire. His breath sucked in as my hands ran along the outline of his chest, my nails digging in just a little. I took a deep breath and let his scent fill my lungs. With the mental blocks reinforced in my head, I threaded my hands through his sleek hair and lifted his face up to mine. Met with hunger, his lips slanted across mine, over and over. His hands captured my hips, pulling me closer. Our tongues slid against each other and any space between us was lost. The scent of desire rose from both our bodies.

And still my bond blocking held. I lowered my hands, wanting to remove the material separating us. Wanting to see how far we could get this time. My fingers grazed the hem of my dirty, purple tank...

Then the door to the training room swung open.

Mr. Malau strode in, eyes registering me and turning incredulous. "Get. Up."

I scrambled off Ty, my face ablaze and my heart smashing against my ribs.

Ty sighed through uneven breath and leaned back on his elbows. "Father. You're back early."

The pissed off alpha let his glare slide from me, taking in the mess of sawdust and blood before narrowing at his son. "You're training her." It wasn't a question, and was spoken like an accusation.

Ty answered anyway. "I want to know she can protect herself." There was challenge in both their faces, but neither said any more on the matter. Instead Ty asked, "So, you have news?"

Mr. Malau's jaw clenched, a muscle ticking in his cheek. "There's been another one in Anchorage."

Ty jumped up, dusting off his hands. "Same location?" He pulled me up and smiled. Then he nodded at his father. "I'll make the arrangements straight away."

My brain raced with confusion, my lips speaking past the shock of Ty's father walking in on us. "What's going on? What arrangements? And another what?"

Mr. Malau's eyebrows lifted at me. "Nosey. Aren't you." His gaze narrowed and he *huffed*. "Since my trusting son's going to tell you anyway… There's been another rogue murder in Anchorage. Near the club you tried your luck at."

My gaze fell to my dust-caked Vans, my stomach twisting. Ty's father was referring to the time I'd almost killed a human. The first time I'd met Ty when he'd stopped my kill. Back then he'd thought I was the killer they were after. After that, his hunting expeditions had been to take out any acting rogue vampires. So he must have found and killed the one in Anchorage, right? "Does that mean there's a new rogue vampire?"

Ty ran a hand through his dusty hair. "Maybe. I'm not sure. We put down one in Anchorage back then. But there have still been victims, and the numbers are growing. The last time we interrupted two attacking one girl. One got away."

Imagining two blood-hungry monsters chowing down on a poor innocent girl brought acid to the back of my throat. "So what happens now?"

"I'll go on recon," Ty said. At my confused look he explained. "Check out the victim and murder scene. See what clues were left behind."

Like a menacing hulk Mr. Malau strode forward, his golden eyes sparkling dangerously. Ty blocked my body with his, a warning growl rumbling from his throat. My hand tightened on my whip.

Mr. Malau laughed, seeing the weapon. He sniffed the air. "You may have spilled my son's blood, but I've got decades on him." Ty growled louder as his father came closer, eyeing his son. "Stand down, before I knock some respect into you." When there was no movement he almost smiled. "Strong and fearless. I've trained you well." The older version of Ty slid his gaze my way, the expression on his face devious at best. "Since you, vampire, insist on remaining in my son's life, you may as well experience our world. Our lives."

"Father..." Ty's tone was warning, a challenge he was ready to take. "No."

"No what?" I tugged on Ty's arm. "What does he mean?"

Ty stared down his father who flashed canines as he spoke. "I think you should go on recon with Ty. If you're lucky you could witness my son disposing of a vampire. Or is that too *real* for you?"

I met his challenge head-on, expression set with absolution. "I know what Ty is, what he does. He's a hero, saving humans from, well...yeah, vampires. Bad vampires. And I have no issue with that. He's saved me more than once, too." I now knew what was out there, rouge and damned vampires, creatures that thrived on blood and death. I couldn't stand idly by and let Ty take all the risk. Besides, this could be linked to our attacks, and even Caius. I laced my fingers through Ty's. "I'm coming with you."

Surprise sparked across the older alpha's face. He half-smiled at his son. "She has fire...like your mother did."

CHAPTER 19

"Why do we have to see the body?" I asked. My skin crawled at the thought while my Vans made light squeaks across the linoleum floor.

In my short new life as a vampire I had already seen one damned vampire die. Well, almost two if you count Kendrick and Dorian's attacker being decapitated. In the way that ours had been killed, his body had instantly incinerated. Except this time we weren't going to see a damned vampire's body. We were here to see a human who'd been killed. Drained to death. I wondered what that kind of death would change in a decomposing body, and shuddered. I'd not so long ago come close to that end myself.

It was after 8PM, the day following my run-in with Mr. Malau. Now in Anchorage, we headed for the morgue on the lower level of the hospital.

Wearing a suit and tie, Ty ran a hand across my back as we headed down the off-white corridors. "Apart from the crime scene itself, a body can tell you so much about the killer. It could lead us to him or even his hideout."

I went to ask about the formal attire when something distracted me. The capital letters *MORGUE* headed the end of the hallway. There was no turning back now.

"Will they let us see the body?" I asked. We weren't related or anything. We didn't even know her name.

"I've got it covered." Ty sounded both cocky and confident. As if this was something he did on a regular basis. And here I'd thought he just put down murdering vampires. Apparently there was much more to being alpha of a werewolf pack than I'd ever thought.

Ty held open one side of the double doors for me to enter, and then followed behind. Inside was a glass-enclosed office manned by a male nurse. Corridors flanked either side of the office with swinging doors. One was unmarked. The other stated NO ENTRY.

The male nurse glanced up from his desk as we stopped in front of the glass barrier. "Can I help you?"

Ty withdrew a wallet from his pocket and flipped it open, displaying a badge. "Officer Scant. I'm here to pick up the murder victim's personal effects."

Somehow I managed not to blanch. So that's why he'd dressed in a black suit with a collared shirt and tie.

"Who's the girl?" the mid-twenties guy asked, more curious than suspicious.

Ty, or should I say, Officer Scant, glanced to me. "Right. Her." He gave me a careless tap on the arm. "Almost forgot you were there." His gaze returned to the male nurse. "Please meet our latest intern. What was your name? Oh that's it, Jenny, right?"

The nurse scanned us over and shrugged. "You types get younger by the year."

Ty smiled. "Yeah, and us newbies always get the mundane jobs.

Where's the action I signed up for?"

With a distracted noise the nurse went back to his computer screen. "Head on in, down the left. Second door on the right."

We began to move away, but as we reached the doors below the NO ENTRY sign the nurse called out. "Oh, and don't mind the body. It's still in there but it's covered."

"Sure thing," Ty called.

The doors creaked as he pushed them open. Less light brightened the hallway than the entry, and it was quiet as hell. Hairs rose up the back of my neck. At least I couldn't see dead people. That ability was part of the spirit gift, to see and speak with the dead. But so far I hadn't had any eerie spectral run ins. Hopefully that wasn't about to change.

We paused before a door with a square glass window. I peered inside. Beyond the glass was a sterile room. Cabinets and pigeonholes marked the right wall. Body fridge doors marked the back wall. A suspended lamp centered the room, flickering above a stainless steel table. A knot formed in my throat and I swallowed. A lumpy mass took up the table space, covered by a white sheet.

Ty squeezed my hand. "You ready?"

I feigned strength. With everything we'd been through and would have to deal with, this would end up being a walk in the park. Plus I needed the exposure. In the future, I may have to kill to stay alive. Seeing death without falling apart was a step in training. I nodded, feeling anything but ready. "As I'll ever be."

We moved to the table. Beside it was a trolley with a plastic bag on top. Inside appeared to be the victim's bloodstained things: a Lycra skirt, skimpy top, heels, and a purse. Below the table a bucket collected draining blood. It was a fair sized bucket, but hardly a drop filled it.

Ty noticed it too and frowned. "She was almost completely

drained before being dumped." He took hold of the edge of the sheet and uncovered her face.

I gasped and stepped back, hitting the trolley. The girl was young, maybe eighteen. Her auburn hair was tangled and wet, her pale face dirty. Her dead fish eyes were frozen in an open and eerie stare. But something about them stood out. Even though they were cloudy their silver-blue color was still visible.

"She's a vampire."

"You're right." Ty bent, pulling back more of the sheet.

I fought the urge to gag, even as the sight tingled my gums and made my stomach ache. The girl's neck was shredded. Chewed into so viciously that bone glinted through the mess.

"The attacker was newly turned, ravenous," Ty said. "Probably a first kill."

I clutched the edge of the trolley as he peered under the sheet at her body. "H-how can you tell?"

"He kept biting until he punctured a vein. That's why her neck's so shredded."

Glancing away, I opened the plastic bag to rifle through her belongings. I needed a distraction, and without chocolate, that bucket of blood drops was the only thing on offer in this room. The fact that I even thought about it made my stomach lurch. I reached past her soiled clothes to pull out her purse.

"Her name was Delina," I said, studying her pretty face in the picture I.D. Apart from that there were a few twenties and small change. There was a card for the local blood bank and one other. It was worn and tattered with a fold through the middle. She'd had it for a while. "She's been to *Pulse*, a lot," I said, putting the card in my back pocket. I grabbed the clipboard from the top of the trolley. Delina's body was found a few blocks from the popular vampire club. "But she wasn't killed there."

"Don't crap where you eat," Ty said. He replaced the sheet over her body. "It doesn't make sense. A new vampire wouldn't be able to think rationally enough to take his victim from the abduction site. What else doesn't make sense is…" He lifted the sheet from her thigh, exposing another vicious bite mark. "That she's been bitten in three separate places. A new vampire would latch on and not let go until their victim is empty. He wouldn't change positions."

I cringed at the memory of my own attempt to kill the school quarterback. I'd latched on too, fangs finding that spot and keeping a fatal hold. That had been the night I'd discovered I was a monster. *But you're not one now,* I told myself. Since then I'd come so far. Every day my control over bloodlust improved.

I dared to ask, "So what does it all mean?"

"That there were three attackers," Ty said, his voice grim. "And they were all starved. New vampires. Unless—"

"Unless what?"

A creak followed by footsteps cut off Ty's response. Someone was coming. Ty grabbed my hand to pull me from the room, but the door swung open before we'd even reached it. A blond guy strode in, flanked by two men in black gear. The men tensed and went to move in on us. The first guy held up a hand, freezing them in motion.

"Marcus?" I couldn't believe it. "What are you doing here?"

"Leave." The order in Marcus's voice was crystal clear, disobeying would mean punishment. Before we could react the two men with him vacated the room. He studied Ty, moving slowly from his face down, then up again. "Is that him?"

Ty tensed, a rumble vibrating from his throat.

I edged forward, blocking him from Marcus. "It is."

"Why are you here?" Marcus's nostrils flared as if scenting him.

Ty made fists of his hands and his lips curled back from canines.

243

"Stepping in because your 'powers that be' won't police your own kind," he snapped.

"Why do you think I'm here?" Marcus looked amused, unmoved by Ty's hostility. "Besides, when it's one of our own and not just a blood bag, we're a little more vigilant. Can't have humans running autopsies on vampires, now can we?"

His flippant tone and words shocked me. "Humans aren't blood bags. They're—wait. So you knew she was a vampire?" I hoped that wasn't the only reason The Council was stepping up. Though with how they kept their humans for food, it shouldn't have surprised me so much.

"Not just a vampire," Marcus said. "She was a Pure Blood."

"THERE'S NOTHING HERE," I said, kicking rubbish away with my Vans.

We'd left the hospital after Marcus's bombshell and checked into our hotel. Now we were down the alley where Delina had been drained to death. Marcus had, of course, ordered us to steer clear of Council business. Like that was going to happen. Ty was an alpha, and whether the vampires appeared to be policing their own kind or not, he wasn't leaving anything to chance. His integrity surprised me. After discovering the victim was a vampire, I half expected him to let it go. But it seemed that human or not, Ty didn't discriminate. Delina may have been a vampire, but she was still a victim.

"She wasn't killed here." Ty straightened from the wet asphalt, taking a deep breath through his nose. "I can't even pick up the scent of blood. With how badly she was chomped into, there should be at least some."

"So what now?" I asked.

Ty slid his hand around me and into the back pocket of my jeans. I held my breath at his closeness and touch. An alchemist mark on his chest blocked his amazing scent. Still that didn't mean I couldn't remember the delicious taste. Though in spite of my rising desire, this dingy alley was far from romantic. I hadn't even pulled up the walls in my mind to block Kendrick.

"Ty, uh…"

In a flash his hand left my back pocket, now holding up a card. It was the card I'd found in Delina's purse. "I need to check out *Pulse*."

"Oh, right." Of course Ty hadn't been about to get intimate in a disgusting place like this. His brain was on the job. Not that I could say the same for mine. "Let's go then."

Ty hesitated. "I'd rather you didn't."

"You don't want me to come with you?" Was my lack of experience getting in his way?

"No, it's not that. At least not in the way you think." Ty reached for the inside pocket of his jacket and withdrew two silver stakes. "I think the victim was abducted from the club. And she was a royal, taken out by new vampires." One stake was shoved into the back of his pants. The other one he slid into the front, concealed by his bomber jacket. "Normally new vamps target easy prey. They're not strong yet. Not until they've fed a few times. They definitely aren't as strong as a royal."

"So you don't want me there in case the killers come back looking for another vamp to feed on?"

"Yes," Ty breathed, almost looking relieved that I understood.

That look wasn't going to last long. "Well," I said. "Are new vampires as strong as the damned we took down on the cruise?"

Ty's response was hesitant. "No—but what if I'm wrong? It could be a damned attack."

Ty was right, it was a definite possibility—but that wasn't about to change the outcome of this discussion. "Well, aren't you training me to be able to defend myself against any evil creature that tries to kill me? Dead or not?"

Ty sighed and scrubbed a hand over his face. "You're coming with me, aren't you?" I nodded. "And nothing I can say will change your mind?"

"Nothing."

Ty bent and lifted the leg of his pants. Below the cover was another silver stake strapped to a holster at his ankle. Prepared for anything, as usual. He slid it free and held it out. "Then you may as well be armed."

A FEW MINUTES later found us in the alley behind *Pulse*. Being out here in the place I'd almost killed the first person I bit for blood made my chest tight. The dumpster was still here. The stink of rotting garbage hung in the frigid air. And there was the brick wall I'd pinned my prey against. I shivered, trying not to release my fangs at the memory of the quarterback's fresh blood. Trying to believe I wasn't anything like that monster anymore. This was also the place Ty and I first met. The night he'd stopped me from killing. The night he'd intended on putting me down. But he hadn't been able to. Something about my reaction to having almost killed a guy had reached his heart. He'd never seen a blood-hungry vampire repent and beg for death.

I looked at him, amazed. My would-be killer was now my boyfriend. But now wasn't the time for reminiscing.

Ty was jiggling a thin piece of metal in the back door's lock, grunting with frustration. When it clicked open he sighed and faced me. His expression fell with regret. "I can't believe I almost..." He stared at a spot of asphalt. It was the exact spot I'd begged for death from. "It would have been the worst mistake of my life."

I ran a hand down his face, lifting his chin. "But you couldn't do it. Remember? Even then you saw the real me. You saw right through my fear into my very soul. You saved me."

"Always," he growled. His fingers curled around my waist and he pressed a brief kiss to my lips, stealing my breath. "I can barely believe where we are now. That you're doing this with me. Just promise you'll stay close and be careful."

"O-okay," I said, blushing, my lips tingling with warmth as I followed Ty inside.

Past a dark narrow hallway the inside of the club opened up. The air was electric, buzzing with energy. It was past ten and the place was packed. The dance floor was filled with close-dancing bodies, hands groping and lips touching flesh. It was easy to tell which dancers were vampire, and which were human. Apart from their pale flesh, the way they moved was somehow primal. Their hands were rough and controlling. Their lips searched for the supplest blood-delivering spot to bite on their companion's necks and collarbones. Their irises were also charged, silver sparks ready to command their thirsty needs.

"They don't, uh...drink on the dance floor, do they?" I'd only ever been inside this club once. At the time I'd been so determined to find Kendrick while holding back my own dark desires. I hadn't taken any real notice of the clubbers.

"It's against house rules," Ty said. "On level one, that is."

"What?" My gaze slid upward. Beyond the strobe lit dance floor was what appeared to be a second level. It was hidden behind mirrored glass. A guarded, black stairway to the right led up there. I gulped as an image similar to the cavern below *Bite* at the Armaya resurfaced. Were there partitions with slumped-over feeder humans up there too? "They *feed* up there?"

Ty nodded. "Yeah. A vamp will pick out their *date* and compel them to comply. Then they take them upstairs. Afterward, their memories are wiped clean."

"How do you know all that?" I dared to ask, my skin crawling.

Ty took my hand and led me to the solid, black bar. He ordered a bourbon and cola for himself and a vodka-lemonade for me. After a quick sip he said, "Because, I've been up there."

I coughed, choking on my own drink. Ty had been up there? I knew he was part vampire and could drink blood. But as a were-wolf-hybrid he didn't need it to survive like the rest of us. So had he taken some girl up there to 'get on' with? The thought made me feel sick. "Oh, okay…"

"It wasn't like that." Ty leaned in to whisper in my ear. Over the loud thumping music no else would have heard his next words. "They only let vamps up there, a flash of silver eyes as proof. Which I can't do. So I imprinted a vamp that'd already left the club to gain access. Marika was my human prop."

I began to move away, not wanting to hear what he and Marika had gotten up to behind the privacy glass. Because this had to have happened before she'd moved away and come back. Which meant her and Ty could still have been together.

Ty's hand caught around the back of my neck. His eyes blazed behind brown contacts. "*Nothing happened.* We just needed to check that club rules on killing were being followed. That there wasn't a cover-up going on."

"And was there?" I downed my whole drink, wishing it were chocolate sauce. Thinking about Ty with Marika always brought back the memories of that night. Ty almost naked and ready to take someone else. Marika disguised by my imprinted flesh.

"No," Ty said. "Everything was above board."

He scanned the room, glancing from the occupied velvet lounges to the dance floor, then at the stairs. There was a stunning female vampire having words with the guard there. Her hands rested on her slight hips and she tapped a high-heeled foot impatiently. Beside her were two guys with their backs to us. Their shoulders were slumped and their stances docile. Even from this distance, I could detect the strong aftershave cloaking their bodies.

Irritated, the guard barked into the speaker at his shoulder. His face set with hard lines and a second later he stood aside, allowing the vampire and her company to pass.

"Well that's good, right?"

"Yeah." Ty took my hand, pulling me past the lounges strewn with intimate groping couples. "But that means that any victims picked from here are taken elsewhere. They'd have to go willingly or be under compulsion."

"So what do we do now?" I asked, seeing the guard at the stairs eyeing us as we neared.

"We're going upstairs."

"What?" That last thing I wanted to do was see a gang of hungry vampires chowing down on unsuspecting humans. At least at the Armaya those feeders were volunteers. Their hope was to one day be rewarded for their service by being turned into vampires themselves.

"It's against house rules to let a vamp take more than one *date* upstairs," Ty said. "The only exception is for royals." We were still a few yards away from the guard as Ty turned, his back facing the staunch-looking guy. "I'm your human *date*, and you're going to take me upstairs."

"That vampire was a royal?" Ty moved from in front of me and I wiped the shocked look from my face. "What now?"

"Take the lead," Ty said with a smile.

CHAPTER 20

The guard looked me over as we met his post. "Can I help you, Miss?"

My face was clammy and sweat trickled down my back. "I uh, would like to take my date…" My gaze glided up the black-carpeted stairs. Beyond them was a glass-mirrored door. "Upstairs."

"First timer?" The guard's gaze slid over Ty who stood lazily, shoulders slack and skull bobbing as if heavy. "Boy, what do you expect to happen up there?"

Ty blinked slowly, his mouth parting. "Want to make Samantha happy. Will be quiet and obey."

Somehow I kept my mouth from falling open as the guard moved aside. "Enjoy your *date*."

I took Ty's hand and pulled him up the stairs, wanting to get through the door as fast as possible. Once past the barrier I took a deep breath and slumped against the door. "Aren't you all surprises, Mr. Hollywood."

In contrast to my expectations, the area was dark and empty.

No partitioned feeding areas. No fang-to-neck action in plain sight. On our left was the glass barrier that peered down over the dance floor. On the right were entrances to rooms that were covered by mosaic curtains. All the curtains were drawn shut, except for one. More continued along a wide hallway. Rumbling music penetrated the space, blocking out any sounds of feeding. *Thank God.*

Ty shrugged. "Deception comes with the job."

He began moving along the closed curtains, listening before peeking inside at the vampires feeding on their humans. I followed close behind, hoping anyone inside wouldn't notice our snooping. When we reached the eighth entry Ty paused.

I held my breath.

Even with the pumping music, noises emanated through the curtain. Panting and moaning. I stepped closer to Ty and peeked through the gap. Inside the room, two people were colored by red light. There was a guy, fully naked and pinning a partly clothed woman to the wall. His fangs were buried in her neck as she moaned in pleasure. I jolted back so fast I bumped into Ty. Fire scorched my face.

I was about to babble something when another sound stopped me.

"You're not h-humans," a female voice rattled in alarm, coming from behind another curtain down the hallway. "You're not even alive."

Before I had time to react, Ty clutched my shoulders. "I knew it. The two guys are damned. I need you to go and pull the fire alarm. Then wait out here." He shook me a little. "Do you hear me? Wait. Out. Here."

Feeling shocked and unprepared I nodded, then I raced back down the hall. At Ty's nod I broke the glass and pulled the alarm. A split second before it went off a scream cut through the pumping music.

Then all hell broke loose.

Partially dressed humans and vampires spilled out of the rooms, yanking on discarded clothes as they ran out the exit.

My eyes darted back down the hall. Ty wasn't there. All I could see was a red glow casting shadows across the opposite wall. No one body visible. Just mashed movement. The alarm pounded through my ears, drowning out any noise coming from where Ty was.

I crept closer, heart pounding and body shaking. Now was not the time to freak out. Ty was in there trying to save that Pure Blood. And he was up against two damned vampires. If I didn't hurry up they'd kill him. Hell, they'd probably kill the both of us. Still, there was no way in hell I was about to let Ty go out alone.

My hand found the stake in my hoodie's pocket. My fingers gripped it so tight my bones hurt.

Feet pelting, I shot through the curtain into the room. Black smudges marked the wall and day bed. Aftershave clouded the room and a satin blanket lay on the floor. Slim legs and a heel-covered foot stuck out. Unmoving. I didn't know if she was already dead. And there wasn't time to find out.

Ty was pinned against the wall, growling and thrashing. The damned had its fangs extended, snapping for his jugular. Its irises flashed, as red as the blood pooling from beneath the blanket.

Fearing for Ty's life, I leaped for its back. Before I landed, the damned moved, cracking its elbow across Ty's cheek. There was a hideous crunch and Ty's body fell.

"No!"

The damned spun with enough time to catch me. The stake impaled its shoulder and it screeched in pain. But that didn't slow it down. Next thing I knew I was on my back on the day bed. The soft mattress absorbed me, making escape impossible, while puffs of ash constricted my lungs.

One hand scrambled to reclaim my weapon from its sizzling flesh. The other pushed against the creature's neck, trying to hold it back. But he was too strong. His open mouth reached for my neck. Crimson-tinted drool dripped from his fangs, patterning my chest.

I was seconds from death.

Then the damned's expression contorted in pure agony. A flash of pointy silver protruded from his chest. I waited for the instantaneous combustion, but it never came.

"Let go of her and stand up," Ty grated. His hardened face appeared behind the damned. "Slowly."

The damned stared down at me with venomous hunger as he released me and slowly backed off the bed. His lips curled back from his fangs and my trepidation peaked. But he didn't lunge. The stake Ty kept pinned through his chest from behind somehow restricted his obvious need to attack.

"Ty, you're okay." I held back the need to wrap my arms and legs around his body and never let go. Ty needed his attention locked on keeping the damned on a leash, and there was something I desperately needed to know. I rolled off the bed, dropped to the floor, and pulled back the blanket. The Pure Blood's eyes were open and lifeless, a life-sized doll frozen in time. There was no heartbeat. "She's gone." Guilt at not checking her earlier flooded me. "If I'd only—"

"No," Ty snarled. "There's nothing you could have done. The first one had already snapped her neck when I came in. That black smudge is all that's left of him."

I glared daggers at the second damned frozen with the stake in its chest. Burning flesh sizzled around the protruding weapon. "Why didn't he die? He's damned too, isn't he?"

"The heart's not pierced, but one quick shove can fix that." Ty took the damned by the shoulder and hurled him face-first at the wall, bearing down on the stake through its back. "Tell me who sent you?"

"Screw you," the damned spat, black tar streaming from its red eyes.

"Have it your way," Ty said, smiling dangerously. He twisted the stake and edged it sideways.

The damned shrieked, its claws rending down the walls.

"Feel that?" Ty asked, canines long and threatening. "That's the feel of your disgusting life on the brink of being snuffed out. That's just a fraction of what instant incineration will feel like. But since you don't want to talk…"

"Okay, okay!" the damned screamed over the still blaring alarm. "We're building numbers. Different groups get stationed at different locations, turning every vampire we find. Except for Pure Bloods. The order is to take them out."

I re-covered the woman's body and face with the blanket and stood next to Ty. "Why?" I demanded. "Why Pure Bloods?"

The damned's red gaze fell on me, hunger flashing like lust in his eyes. "To thin the blood lines." He sniffed the air then licked his pasty lips. "But I woulda kept you on tap."

Ty cracked a fist across the damned's face. "Look at her again, and I will end you. Now tell me who gave the orders?"

"Get fucked." He spat black. "I'm as good as dead if I tell you."

"Wrong answer." Ty twisted the stake and hammered it sideways. The damned's cry cut short as he burst into a human-shaped body of smoldering coals. When the coals settled into an ash pile on the floor, Ty grabbed my arm. "We need to leave," he said over the still wailing alarm.

I planted my feet. "I'm not leaving her." I knelt and peeled back the blanket from the woman's face. The dead fish eyes still shocked me. The chewed and gory flesh at her neck and wrist made little nips of pain touch my own flesh in those same spots. This woman wasn't a crowned royal—as far as I knew—so she'd have family. People who loved and cared for her. "Her family deserves an explanation. And The Council needs to know what we found out." I got up and pushed Ty past the curtain and out to the hall. "But you need to go. If they find you here and realize you're a—"

"No." The single word and his unyielding tone matched the fierce look on his face. "I'm not going anywhere." His unspoken words said more than his spoken ones. He didn't trust The Council for a second, and he never would. "I won't leave without you."

I shot a glance up and down the hall, expecting guards to swarm in at any second. I began to argue, fearing for Ty's life at The Council's hands if he stayed.

"Call him, if you must," Ty spoke over me, jaw clenched. "Tell Marcus what happened and where to find the body. You trust him with your secrets, your life. You should be able to trust him with this."

Ouch. Stuck by his dare, I yanked my iPhone from my back pocket and dialed. My sharp stare shifted from Ty the moment the line picked up. "Marcus, it's Amelia. Can you hear me?" The ongoing alarm bells echoed through the speaker. I grabbed Ty's hand, heading for the exit. "There's been another murder."

"Where are you?" Marcus's voice was sharp like a blade. He sounded seriously pissed off. "I said, where are you?"

The alarm suddenly died. Through the one-way glass windows the dance floor below was empty. "I'm—"

The glass door swung open.

Marcus stalked inside, face alight with indignation. His

entourage of two advanced at his signal, taking hold of Ty. One had him by the neck. The other restrained his lengthening claws.

Ty snarled, challenging their concrete containment. His body began to tremble, ready to release the wolf.

"Marcus, stop! Please." I tugged at his lean-muscled arms. "You don't know what's going on."

Marcus bared his fangs at Ty. "Stop struggling and I'll let you walk out of here. Although after trespassing and interfering in Council business, I'm within my rights to do the complete opposite. For her sake, however..." He eyed me with plain irritation. For some reason the expression reminded of the time Caius had regarded me like an unruly child. "I won't."

"Don't do me any favors," Ty said, but the trembling in his body recessed.

Marcus ignored him, nostrils flaring as he sighed. "Amelia, how many were there?"

"T-two," I said, caught by the sudden warmth in his velvet voice. Marcus was nothing like Caius. He'd saved me after Caius had tried to kill me. "Ty killed them both. We couldn't save the woman, another Pure Blood. The second damned said they're turning vamps, as many as they can find. Except for Pure Bloods. They're killing them. Thinning the bloodlines."

Surprise flashed across Marcus's face. Then it was gone, replaced by softness as he drew me into his arms. "You're so stubborn. Why didn't you listen to me." He released me and held me at arm's length. The teal flecks of his irises shone. "You could have gotten yourself killed."

Ty's breathing became hoarse. "Let go of her."

I stepped out of Marcus's hold. "I'm sorry I scared you. But I'm not the same girl I was at the Armaya. I don't need every guy in my life protecting me. Now tell your goons to let my boyfriend go."

Marcus smiled at the command. "No. You certainly are not." He waved his hand and the bodyguards released Ty.

He was at my side in a flash. A gentle rumble still vibrated his throat.

Marcus laughed. "A wolf protecting a vampire. Sure, it was the way centuries ago, but I never thought *I'd* see the day." He moved aside, leaving the doorway unblocked. "Now get out of here before backup shows. I can promise you they won't be as understanding as I've been."

Ty's arm claimed my waist, forcing us out the door to the stairs. "What about the woman's family?" I called over my shoulder. "You'll contact them, won't you?"

"Sure." Marcus motioned the guards down the hall. "Retrieve the body. Oh, and Amelia. Do try to keep out of Council business. Next time I might not be there to keep your pet from The Council's grasp."

CHAPTER 21

Two days later we were back home and back to training. Being the second week of January we were also back at school, which meant training after hours as the sun set and night approached.

On the beach and covered in gritty sand and sweat, Ty had already handed me my ass more than once. He took the whip from my hip and kissed me, hot, hard, and quick. "Practice your aim." He smiled, jogging toward my brother and best friend.

I was so relieved. One on one with Ty was a challenge and still somehow sexy and hot. Seeing the drive on his face and the power of his body as his muscles bulged while flattening me on my back was a serious turn on. The hours of hand-to-hand combat had bull-dozed my bond-blocking walls. I needed a cool down.

"Alright, time to put down the bows. You two are up," Ty called out to Kendrick and Dorian. He met them before the rising cliff where they'd been stringing out arrows at pieces of driftwood. "Though, instead of swapping offense and defense, I want you both to be attacking each other at the same time. Let's see what you've got."

Kendrick looked relieved. I didn't know if the expression was because he wasn't taking on Ty, or because he got a break from target practice. Dorian was a total natural, but Kendrick was better in unarmed combat.

They both nodded and took their stance in the clearing on the beach. Facing each other they stood only feet apart. After my long grapple with Ty, the sand had been left uneven and filled with divots. I rolled out my whip, weaving fast cracks out at a jagged cluster of rocks. My focus flicked back and forth, wanting to witness this head to head.

"Don't hold back," Dorian said.

Kendrick cracked his neck to either side. "Not planning to."

Ty was crouched to the side, watching as he always did when not in the melee himself.

Dorian crouched facing Kendrick, every lean muscle along his arms and legs visible. Kendrick's fists curled, ready and waiting. Without any warning Dorian sprang. Kendrick ducked out of his way. The two faced off, Kendrick throwing the first punch. It hit, but Dorian wasn't surprised. Instead, he was ready. His own fist connected with Kendrick's stomach. Then his other slammed into his cheek.

My iPhone buzzed, drawing my attention. I pulled it from my jeans to find a new text from Marcus. *'Will be OTG with council and family stuff UFN. Can't play lookout. Be on guard.'*

Taking the warning seriously, I returned my attention to my whip, lashing out, flicking, and sending figure eights at my target. Every second of practice could mean the difference between life and death. With each strike my aim improved. My ability to control the whip was turning it into an extension of my arm.

After taking a few hefty chunks out of the rocks, I paused to watch my brother and best friend. They were closer to the shore now. Swinging punches and roundhouse kicks tossed wet sand up into the air. Bruises marked their pale arms and legs, fading as new ones appeared with each connecting hit. Drying blood marked lines from Dorian's lip and Kendrick's temple.

Dorian connected with a pummeling hit at Kendrick's shoulder that spun him to his knees in the waves. Now facing the star-speckled ocean, he began to rise. But Dorian was already in the air and landed hard on Kendrick's back.

In blurred movement Kendrick's arms shot up, gripping Dorian's wrists. With a quick twist of his body, he spun on the spot. Dorian was thrown over his head to splatter into inches of seawater. Kendrick leaped forward, delivering a solid blow to Dorian's face. The force reopened his lip on impact and scarlet sprayed like a projectile from his mouth.

With a strike of blue blazing in his irises, Dorian thrust his hands up. At first nothing happened. He hadn't even made contact. Which he clearly could given how close they were.

Kendrick looked smug and Dorian smiled. Then a basketball-sized frozen orb lifted from the sea. It shot forward, slamming into Kendrick's face.

I gasped and dropped my whip. At the same time Ty twitched while Kendrick fell backward. None of us had expected Dorian's water ability to come out. And although I had mentioned it to Ty, he had never seen it in action before.

I replaced my weapon at my hip and jogged over. "That orb was massive."

"Cheap trick!" Kendrick used his elbows to prop himself up.

Dorian got up and wiped the blood from his lip with his arm.

Using his free hand he hauled Kendrick out of the shallow waves. "All's fair in love and war."

"He's right," Ty called, rising to full six-foot-plus height as they began trekking away from the lapping shore's edge. "Winning in battle means fighting dirty. Not fair."

I met his side as smugness crept over Dorian's face. "Well if that's the case..."

His words broke off with a flick of his wrist. Simultaneously a foot-deep wave climbed up the shore, surrounding Kendrick's feet. He went to move as the water rose, snaking up his legs, body, and up to his neck. But he couldn't. The water instantly snapped to ice.

Kendrick struggled, every part of him trapped except for his head. Cracks appeared in the ice. But escape was impossible. New layers of water kept rising with Dorian's coaxing hands, keeping their captor from breaking free.

Kendrick's face blazed red with fight, his eyes clouding. A surge of icy wind whipped, striking through my hair and batting my loose T-shirt against my body.

Then a human-sized tornado emerged from the sand.

It coalesced around Kendrick, the wind moving so fast that it sucked sand up until Kendrick was lost inside.

I rushed forward and Ty followed. "We have to do something!"

Dorian appeared around the tornado's edge, but he didn't look shocked. No, he was smiling. "I think he's doing this."

There was a pop as the twister sucked in on itself, imploding. Ice shards shot out like bomb shrapnel and I screamed. Ty's hand found my neck and forced me down as Dorian hit the sand beside us. The tornado died, violent swarming wind turning to quiet calm. We all peered up. Kendrick stood right where he had been, unharmed and free of Dorian's ice trap.

"That was mad," Dorian said, clapping.

Ty helped me to my feet. There was almost a look of awe on his face as he watched Kendrick. "*You* did that?"

The bond left no questions over what had happened. I stared at Kendrick. "You're affinity is Air."

Dorian laughed. "I knew it. And you're welcome. Forcing it out of you was fun."

Kendrick stared down at his body, then hands, like he couldn't believe it himself. "That was...awesome!"

TY JUMPED up from his perch on a fallen tree, clapping his hands. "Great work. You're all getting better at using your abilities in combat. Your reflexes have become more sharp and precise, too."

He extended an arm to pull me up from where he'd last taken me down. My butt was numb from snow and my jeans were wet and heavy.

"But most attacks will not be foreseen or obvious. Your kind," his tone held no resentment as he glanced back to Kendrick and Dorian, who both slumped down into the snow, "can be very calculating. And I am sure the damned will be much, much worse."

Dorian snatched his phone from the base of a tree and leaned back against the trunk. Kendrick stretched out his legs over his boarding jacket, looking just as exhausted.

It was the following afternoon and we were in the depths of Mt Major. With Mom concerned about the escalating murders, Dorian had told her we were going to hang out at Vanessa's house. She would have just worried otherwise. Or tried to stop us.

We'd been training at Mt Major for hours in one-on-one combat while practicing our vampire abilities. Well except for me, seeing as having a vision wasn't going to fend off any attackers. In my opinion, we'd had enough for today. Each of us was wet with sweat, rain, and snow. We were all exhausted. And with only a first quarter moon lighting the growing fog, it was getting eerie out here too. I'd had enough. But I wasn't calling the shots.

Ty spun back to me with anticipation brightening his beautiful face. His tan skin glistened with sweat, and I had to force my wandering gaze away from his muscle shirt. Not that I hadn't been checking him out the last few hours. "So, what's next?"

Kendrick made a small, irritated noise and tugged off his own damp T-shirt. Ignoring the jealous move, despite noticing how his muscles had filled out since we began training, I faced Ty.

He reached for my hand and led me from the sidelines and into the center of the now torn up and muddy clearing. The minimal moonlight and twinkling stars penetrated the space. Snow-draped skeleton branches danced in a gentle breeze. "I want to do a demonstration with you," he whispered in my ear. "Stand here. Close your eyes."

I shivered, my lids sliding shut. Then I heard the squish of mud as he turned from me to face the others.

"The damned, from what we know, will attack at night." Ty's voice was gravelly as he spoke. His words flooded my memory with the night we were attacked on the boat, dark and deadly. "Light and vision won't always be available. We must learn to use all our senses in case any are lost in combat." The squish of Ty's hunting boots came closer and he placed a rough hand on my shoulder. "I am going to come at you without you seeing," he said, voice now softer, almost gentle. "I want you to deflect me without sight." His breath cascaded over my neck as a kiss met my flesh with the brush of his lips. "Give me everything you've got. Don't you dare hold back."

Feeling irritation from Kendrick, I opened my eyes. Ty's heated hand grazed my cheek. Then he retreated for the trees, splashing through puddles before disappearing from sight. With a shrug, I closed my eyes again and tuned my ears, taking in every noise surrounding me. The gentle breeze had ceased, replaced by the pattering of soft-falling rain. Each drop against my skin was ice cold, feeling like tiny piercing needles. Time seemed to stand still, getting slower, becoming infinite. Each raindrop became audible against every surface it touched. They pattered against individual leaves. Tapped against larger exposed rocks. And almost sizzled as they hit the snow and turned to ice. The wind around me picked up. Surrounding trees began wailing in dance, harmonizing whooshes with the persistent rain.

An almost inaudible movement rose in the far distance. A whoosh of air followed by snow-crunching boots. Ty was moving faster and quieter than humanly possible. I held my ground and listened as each step covered an unspeakable distance. My shoulders hunched and I bent my knees to brace. He was close now, his heart's drumming breaking through an almost soundless descent. My lids remained shut tight as the air around me swirled. It was as though I could see everything surrounding me even in my blind state. I could hear, feel, and smell every movement, every change.

Ty exploded from the tree line behind me. In that moment I swore I could hear his muscles tensing as his arms reached for me. Instantly I launched off the ground. My body propelled up into the air and backward, landing on the thick branch of an oak tree.

I peered down at Ty as he smiled up at me. "That was pretty impressive."

I returned his smile and dropped from the branch. In one fluid movement, I landed on the ground twenty feet before him. The rain around us started to pelt down harder. The clouds above coiled and grew more black and angry. For some reason I felt cocky. "That was nothing."

Ty took my words as the challenge they were intended to be and took after me at a dead run. Each powerful running step created divots in the snow under the force of his hammering boots. He launched into the air again, arms outstretched, ready to take hold.

At the last millisecond I dropped to the ground, crumbling under his muscular form as he flew over. He landed as I leaped back to my feet, not hesitating to come at me again.

Just as Ty reached me I ducked. My arm shot up in the same instant and my fist connected hard with his jaw. Ty stumbled and actually looked startled. Instant guilt radiated like lava through my veins. "Oh shit. I'm sorry."

Without warning Ty sprang. His iron grip curled over my shoulders, flattening me to the ground. My back slammed into a rocky patch, radiating pain through my bones. The rainfall grew harder, drops turning into hail. I struggled to move against his brute strength, but it was useless. I was pinned.

Ty flashed me his cockiest of smiles. His hair blew back off his face with the wind's growing intensity. "Never underestimate," he said, loud enough for Kendrick and Dorian to hear as he glanced up at them. "The slightest hesitation could mean your life." He gazed back at me, loosening his grip. "And we can't have that, now can we?"

A sudden flash of blinding white light lit up the entire forest surrounding us, like an insane camera flash going off. At that exact moment a crack like splintering wood erupted through the trees. My hands shot up to cover my ears as another crack of light erupted. This one vibrated the ground beneath us while Ty still straddled my body. We leaped up as another went off. This one was so close we could see the strike.

"Get behind me," Ty yelled over the exploding boom.

Kendrick and Dorian ran straight for us. But the lightning was faster. It struck again, splintering light breaking out in forks that penetrated the ground. The force sent dirt flying up. My best friend and brother jumped back to keep from being hit.

Thoughts and memories rushed through my mind. Worsening weather had dampened each training session. Most accompanied by lightning that seemed drawn to our presence. Ty and I edged away from the continuing strikes.

"Why does this keep happening?" My scream barely registered through the shattering noise.

Even before our training, there'd been close run-ins with lightning. My first day back at school had almost seen me decapitated by a tree that had been split by a plummeting fork. On the cruise, a single strike had broken up the bar fight between Ty and the damned. And there was the lightning storm when I'd tried to bring on a vision.

Over the aftermath of another rumbling strike that kept Kendrick away, he yelled, "This is a sacred site—a beacon of power. Whatever is going on with this weather, the site is amplifying it."

"It's where Satan used his blood to create the first vampires," Ty added, keeping my body protectively behind his.

"Where the Dawn of Reckoning took place," Kendrick called out. "And where the damned were cursed to darkness and insanity."

As another strike hit the ground only two yards from the hunting boots on Ty's feet, something dawned on me. The first lightning encounter and all the others since had one thing in common. Me. I was the catalyst. The lightning was coming for me.

Knowing that in seconds Ty and I would both be fried, I shoved my hands into his back. Having not expected the attack, Ty flew across the clearing. Now the lightning had a clear path to take what it kept coming back for.

"No!" The screams came from all three guys. Ty was already

racing my way, but smaller forks kept Kendrick and Dorian back.

What happened next was so fast it was a blur. The energy in the air intensified, crackling with power. Then a new lightning bolt split from the clouds. It forked through the sky. Its thick center headed straight for me.

I braced for the impact, but it never hit.

Instead, crackling energy whipped around me and the tree I was backed up against. Ice raced up the trunk, freezing the wood while a twister appeared out of thin air. It surrounded the tree without touching me. Then a crunch of wood erupted. Ty's body collided with mine as another crack rang out. The tree came crashing down, absorbing the lightning and exploding in a shower of splinters. It landed like a demolished building, missing me only because Ty had cleared me from its path.

The lightning receded and Ty hauled me into his arms. His face was ghost-white. "What the hell were you doing? You could have died." The anger left his face and he gulped. "Oh, God, I couldn't lose you."

Seeing the fear all over his face stabbed pins into my heart. "I'm so sorry. I…" How could I tell him the lightning had been gunning for me without sounding crazy? The answer? I couldn't. Because it was crazy. "I didn't want you to get hurt." I wriggled free and pulled Ty up as Kendrick and Dorian reached us. My legs wobbled, but I managed to stay upright on my own.

Kendrick went to bring up the *me being a lightning rod* thing, when I gave him a hard look. "Well then, I think we should all take off," he said, unable to hide his frown. "Before the weather goes psycho again."

Fear and guilt grew like poison in my gut. I took Ty's hand and began walking. "I've had enough bad weather and training for one day, anyway."

CHAPTER 22

I bounded into the kitchen the following night, heading for the fridge. Mom would be off to her council meeting soon and we'd have the house to ourselves. Which was good, because Ty was on his way over, and he wasn't the only one. Troy and Marika were heading over too. The time had come to bring new challenges to our training, and his pack mates were more than equipped. But Ty wanted to try to smooth the vampire/werewolf feud beforehand. Which I guess was rational. Still, I didn't see it changing how much they despised us.

I took a glass bottle of blood from the stainless steel fridge and sucked it dry. Keeping my fangs retracted while being subjected to their potent wolf scent could only help the hopeless interaction.

As I placed the empty on the ivory limestone counter, going for another, the doorbell rang. My heart stopped. Shit, was Ty early?

"Will someone get that?" Mom called out from her bedroom down the hall. She sounded rushed, like she was hurrying to get ready.

Abandoning the full bottle, I shot through the archway into the foyer. Kendrick met me there, having raced down the stairs. "I thought they weren't coming for another ten minutes."

"They weren't." I peeked through the tall frosted window to the front steps. Outside it was dark, the marginal moonlight laced by thick, moving clouds. Though with the streaming porch light a car's outline was visible in the driveway. "And my mom should have left already."

Dorian strolled up behind us, mussing his hair rather than worrying about the situation. "So what if Mom finds out they're here? She's letting you see Ty. What are a few more wolves?"

"More sets of canines that can kill with one bite." The doorbell rang again and Mom called out. "Got it," I replied, unlocking the door and swinging it wide open.

I stepped back at the unexpected woman standing over the threshold. She smiled, looking regal in a floor-length, silk indigo gown. Her complexion glowed under the porch light and her loose golden-brown hair glistened.

"Mother?" Kendrick brushed past me as she stepped inside to embrace him.

"Hello, my son." Her voice was like wind chimes. She released him and stepped back. "You've grown." Her smile shifted to Dorian and me. "So lovely to see you both again."

We muffled surprised hellos, then Kendrick cut in. "What are you…" He shifted his weight, looking like he'd just dry-swallowed a pill.

Apart from when his mom dropped him over in the past, I'd never witnessed their dynamics. Although here and now the bond explained everything. Growing up, Serafina had always been too busy to make real time for her son. Without a father—as according to her he'd merely been a sperm donor—she was all he'd had. Still, The Council had always been her priority. The reason she'd had Kendrick was to continue her royal line. And since his stay here, their only communication had occurred when Kendrick could get hold of her on the phone.

"Why are you here, mother?"

Serafina swept her arms open. "I'm back from Russia and in town for the meeting. How could I be in town and not stop by to see you?"

Easily.

High heels clicking across the marble floor behind us interrupted Kendrick's unvoiced words. "So glad you could make it, Serafina," my mom said, bowing her head.

"We're glad we could, too."

"Who's we?" I butted in before anyone else could talk. A strain of anxiety swam up my chest cavity, but I wasn't sure why.

Serafina glanced back to the open doorway as a suited, dark figure emerged from the shadows, stepping into the light. Caius.

My heart jumped into my throat, pounding like it wanted out. Fear drove a lick of dead blood into my mouth. Kendrick stiffened, stepping closer to me. Dorian remained still, his silver-sparking eyes tunneling anger at our enemy.

A devilish smile lit Caius's face as he sauntered forward, his appearance youthful and bright. He embraced my mom, and I shuddered as his parted lips kissed her cheek. The same lips that had closed over my neck when he'd bitten down.

"Of course," Serafina said, looking curious, "Caius could not miss seeing his niece and nephew."

Caius's smile was calculated, revealing his gleaming white teeth. He held out a perfect black calla lily to me. "For you, my dear Amelia."

"Well don't be rude," my mom said, ushering me forward. "Welcome your uncle."

I exchanged a mashed look of concern with Kendrick and Dorian. *What the hell is he up to?*

Kendrick replied through the bond, eyes refusing to shift from watching Caius. *He won't try anything here in front of everyone. Too many witnesses. And too many of us to compel at once.*

I nodded and took a shaky step forward, burying the hate and fear I felt on the surface, at least. "How wonderful for you to grace us with your presence." My ability to hold a level tone amazed me, given that my insides felt like tearing themselves from my body to race in the opposite direction. I snatched the flower, holding back a shiver. This was the flower Caius always gave me when he visited. It was also the same type he had laid across my chest after killing me.

Dorian moved in front of me, blocking my body from Caius. He extended a firm and level hand. "Caius," is all he managed between gritted teeth.

Kendrick managed a nod, hand going around my waist. "Lord Bathory." As he turned to his mother the vehemence drained from his face. "I am glad you could come. Will you be staying long?" The question was a double-edged sword meant to track Caius's movements.

Serafina shook her head, somewhat apologetically. "We flew in for the meeting. Then I'm back to Russia, and Caius to the Armaya."

Mom eyed the three of us, picking up on the tension strangling the air. Though in her elegant *don't create ripples* way, she changed the subject. "Kendrick, did you tell your mom about your camping trip?"

Kendrick smiled and crooked his neck to face his mother. He began detailing all the fun we'd all apparently had while away, save for the part about being attacked by Caius's henchman. And while I could hear everything he said and thought, my own thoughts were elsewhere. The sickening feeling in my stomach refused to shift while I watched Caius from the corner of my eye. He looked so freaking casual, pretending that this was like any other normal visit. He even made normal conversation, questioning Kendrick and Dorian on the trip. Like any close family friend or true uncle would. Each answer they gave him was clipped and to the point, never encouraging any further discussion. To me the tension was obvious, but my mom and Serafina both seemed too interested in the details.

As the subject wrapped up, Caius caught my watching eye. His head twisted to face me. "So," he said, clearing his throat. "How did you enjoy your trip to the woods? Was it an *eventful* getaway?"

Caius's piercing gray eyes made me want to punch him. It was a confession without words. We all knew he was behind our attacks. His unprompted question would seem harmless to anyone not in the know. But we knew better. He was toying with us.

I reined in my blooming anger that made me want to take him on here and now. "Well." I fixed my steely gaze on him, wishing my hatred could melt him like a witch dipped in water. "If by eventful, you mean being able to relax in nature, hunt and kill..." I paused, ready to take my verbal punch. "Oh, and of course being able to spend my every waking minute with Ty. Then yes. It was *eventful*."

Instead of Caius's smile vanishing at the mention of Ty, it widened. "Yes, my dear. I know. And I am pleased you all enjoyed my Christmas present. Vacations can be so life altering."

"So you admit it?" Dorian fists clenched, his forearms corded.

"Of course I do. Did you not know?" Caius stroked his chin. "Perhaps I forgot the personal note." He chuckled, glancing at me. "It may also interest you to know, Amelia, that it was my advice that convinced your mother to let you go away with that *boy*."

I stepped back like he'd slapped me. Everything suddenly made sense. The call. Mom's sudden change of heart. Caius had compelled our mom over the phone to let us all go away. And he'd used the alchemist mark on her shoulder to do it.

"You—" Dorian's face fumed like he was about to out Caius in front of our mothers.

Caius ignored him and nodded to the town car idling in the driveway. "We best be off. The Council will be waiting."

Still oblivious to the tension, Mom retrieved her briefcase from the foyer table while Serafina hugged Kendrick goodbye.

Caius hovered behind as they got into the slick, black car. "Mind your tongue, boy." He stepped closer to Dorian who didn't even flinch. "Or the next ones will come for your mothers."

I WATCHED as the town car Caius and Kendrick's mother had appeared in rolled from the driveway and out the front gates.

Relief swept through me as the car disappeared down Ocean Boulevard. A body-convulsing shiver followed that chilled me to the bone. Our mothers were in that car too, alone with Caius as they headed to tonight's all-night council meeting. I loathed the thought of them near that monster, my mind ticking over all the lies he could be planting in their heads. Kendrick's mom was a royal, so compelling her would be harder than if she were a turned vamp like my mom. But if Caius needed to pull something off, I didn't doubt he would. And I wasn't about to let anything happen to either of them.

As I was about to close the front door, a familiar drone of an exhaust rumbled down the road. Knowing who was coming, Kendrick pulled a reluctant Dorian into the kitchen to stock up on blood before the other wolves arrived. A slight irritation vibrated from Kendrick, but our unexpected encounter with Caius overrode his dislike of Ty. He was thinking up what to do to help our mothers too. Dorian, on the other hand, was still fuming and needed to cool down.

Headlights shone up onto the house as a bright blue WRX veered up the driveway. Ty parked at the front steps. As he emerged, an impressive smile brightened his face and his irises blazed, taking me in. Without hesitation I ran and leaped into his strong, protective arms. My hold on him was so tight that if he were human I would have cracked a rib or two.

Straight away Ty tensed. His capturing, possessive arms released and he inhaled a deep breath through his nose. He untangled me from his body and pushed me behind him. Power poured off him as his eyes darted. "Where is he?"

His body began to quake, threatening to change forms. I darted in front of him, clutching his bulging biceps while trying to ignore the movement of his transforming muscles beneath my hands.

Kendrick blew into the foyer with Dorian. Through the bond he knew what was about to happen. His face was hard as he and my brother shoved Ty into the living room. He flicked on the chandelier that threw crystal light prisms over the imperial sofa, ornate shelving, and mink-soft carpet. "Bloody impulsive wolves," Kendrick mumbled, his eyes skewering me. "Calm him down."

Knowing how dangerous it was for a vampire to be near an out of control werewolf on the verge of transforming, my words rushed. "He was here. But he's not now. He left with my mom and Kendrick's. There's a full-on council meeting about the murders."

The trembling in Ty's body released, threatening cracks receding. Though his glowing irises remained, as did the taut strain of his muscles. At a moment's notice he could snap back into action. He looked at me, furious and worried at the same time. "Why didn't you call me?"

Kendrick folded his arms over his chest. "Because she had us to protect her."

"Like that would have stopped him," Ty snarled, taking a menacing step forward. "She's almost died once when *you* were the only one around."

"I saved her life!"

"Yeah." Ty laughed mockingly. "After drugging her. What a hero."

The death glare between both guys was acid-drenched. Dorian pulled out his phone and began texting. Of all the times for him to get distracted by a chick. What was he thinking?

Kendrick jabbed Ty in the chest. "At least I wasn't here sulking over being dumped."

Matched sounds of challenge came from both guys. I darted between them, a hand pressing on each guy's chest. "Both of you stop it! This is not helping anything." Right then we needed to plan a way to keep our mothers safe, not start another pissing contest. "If we're constantly at each other's throats we may as well give up now. And we can't." I pleaded with Kendrick. "C'mon. Our mothers are with that monster, and who knows what he's doing to them."

"What'd you have in mind?" Ty asked. His hand met my waist purposely, but his tension wavered.

I'd been brewing a plan in the back of my mind since our mothers had left. We needed to know what was happening. Waiting to find out wasn't an option.

"No way!" Kendrick folded his arms over his chest.

I bit down on my lip. The plan had been to gently reveal my idea, knowing he would be against it. But with Ty's reaction to picking up Caius's scent, my walls blocking Kendrick had come crashing down.

Kendrick stalked over to the wooden corner shelves, stacked with books. His hands tensed as if he wanted to tear it all down to the ground. He spun instead, glaring. "It's too bloody dangerous."

"What is?" Dorian questioned, peering up from the phone's screen.

Everyone was watching me. Ty and Dorian were waiting for me to explain. Kendrick just glared, spouting off reasons against my plan through the bond. But I didn't reply silently to him. There was no point in keeping this discussion between the two of us when we were all involved. "We have to do something."

"Not that. Not YOU!" Kendrick came forward and caught my hand, fingers squeezing.

Ty shoved Kendrick's hand from my arm. "Don't touch her."

Another fight was about to break out, and I couldn't have that. "Look." I cracked my knuckles. "Mom and Serafina are at The Council with Caius, and I know none of us are okay with that."

Dorian nodded while Kendrick remained stationary in front of me. His arms were like defiant bars over his broad chest. His glaring eyes remained zoned in on Ty who kept close to my side.

"So, I'm going to check in on their meeting," I continued. "Spy to make sure our mothers are safe. See what's up with the murders. And scope out what Caius is up to."

Dorian and Kendrick both shook their heads and replied, "No."

"We'll go instead," Dorian countered, nudging Kendrick.

I sent a silent message to Kendrick. *You know he would expect that. And what if he sends someone here? Besides, I won't be alone.*

Kendrick gritted his teeth, slumping back onto the imperial sofa. "No. Of course not." His acidic tone made Dorian and Ty look at him. "He," Kendrick spat, pointing at Ty, "will be going with you."

I planted my hands on my hips. "You know it's for the best."

"Well." Kendrick blew air out his flared nostrils. "Why don't you explain it to them."

With a deep breath I set out my reasoning for Dorian and Ty to hear. Through the bond I knew that Kendrick wanted to be the one to go, the one to protect me. But that wasn't safe or rational in this situation. A whole group going to spy was more likely to be spotted. Plus if one of Caius's henchmen did show up, who knew what could be tampered with. Besides, I didn't plan on getting caught. And I needed Kendrick here with our link wide open so that he and Dorian would be able to communicate with us. No other combination would work.

A motorbike followed by a car veered up the driveway, their headlights streaming through the bay windows lining the wall.

"I don't like this at all," Dorian muttered, heading through the archway to the foyer.

"Don't worry." Ty took my hand. "We'll keep her safe."

We? I threw Ty a questioning look as Troy and Marika strode through the front door without knocking, passing Dorian and heading into the living room. Vanessa was right behind them, looking party perfect in a black skirt, red top, and seriously high heels. Marika looked sultry as usual in skintight shorts and a boob tube. And Troy wore all black and a hard stare. No surprise there.

"You're all coming?" I asked. Troy and Marika had just arrived, but with their werewolf hearing and Troy's eyebrows lifting, it was clear they'd caught onto the thread.

Troy shrugged, wolf eyes flashing. "Going into the leeches' lair? Can't think of a better way to spend my night."

"And where my beau goes," Marika said, smiling at Troy. "I go."

"No," Ty said with a snap of his jaw. "Marika, you'll stay behind."

Marika's mouth dropped and Troy growled, but neither argued.

"You're staying here aren't you?" Dorian asked Vanessa who he'd moved to stand near. Hope transformed the uncertainty from his face.

"Sure am," Vanessa said, smiling at my brother without seeking approval from Ty. She wasn't a wolf, and as their alchemist was never given orders. "I'll put up some protective marks."

I bit my lip again, gaze sliding sideways to Troy who leaned against the archway. Having him along as well as Ty made my spy mission less dangerous. That is if Troy followed Ty's orders and didn't turn on me himself. He and Marika hated vampires as much as they hated the thought of Ty and me together. I squeezed Ty's hand. "Are you sure this is a good idea?"

"Trust me," Ty said.

"I'm pack beta." Troy's expression was challenging, as if it held a promise...or a threat. "Second in command and sworn to protect my alpha."

Yeah, but not me.

MINUTES later I'd redressed in black and was heading out front to Ty and Troy. I tugged on my zip-up hoodie, ready to feel the wind in my hair. "Let's go."

Ty followed me to the garage while Troy fired up his motorbike. It was a mean, beefy piece of machinery that matched his jacked body. But my concerns about him were forfeited, replaced by so much more.

Since moving to Rye my life had been turned upside down. The distinct changes had been irrevocable in so many ways. But, would I change any of it if I had the power? To be a normal girl who wasn't in love with a werewolf? No. I knew the answer without a shadow of a doubt. I would never exist without Ty. The danger and fear for my life were nothing compared to the thought of living without him.

With a deep sigh, I pushed the button on my keys and the garage doors curled up from the ground. A controlled smile spread over my lips. Standing in the shadows my Ducati waited. What little light there was caught on the chrome and purple panels, making them glisten. I swung my leg over the seat and fired up the engine.

Ty stood back, gaze shifting over the *soul mates* insignia. "How about I drive?"

Since being back from the cruise, I'd taken and aced my driving test. But that wasn't the point. Knowing his reluctance had nothing to do with my ability, I decided to lighten the mood. "Don't you trust my driving?" I quipped over the noise of the engine. "Or, does being a passenger with a female driver affect your tough, manly facade?"

Ty stepped forward to swing his leg over the back of the bike. "I'm tough whether you take the reins or not. I'm just not used to handing them over. But for you? I'll make an exception."

I smiled and pulled my biker glasses from the front pocket of my jacket, perching them on my nose. "Ready?"

Ty placed his hands on my hips in answer. I let the clutch out and pulled back on the throttle. The bike's wheels spun, screeching over concrete and out into the night. Troy pulled in behind us as we sped through the front gates, keeping one pace behind. The thin icy wind whipped across my face as we sped past the beach and adjacent mansions. It was exhilarating to move at this speed, as fast I could run. Still, it was distinctly different. Yes, I loved the feel of my tight muscles lengthening and retracting when I sprinted to any destination. But the feel of controlling this powerful machine beneath me—the grunt of the exhaust and maneuvering ability—was entirely foreign and thrilling.

As we cornered a sharp bend around the scenic park, I eased up on the throttle, veering off the unlit road and into a small parking lot. We ditched the bikes, concealing them behind a cluster of thick bushes, and continued on foot. The idea was to spy and find out what we could, not draw attention with the loud rumbling of our bikes.

We trekked through the thick trees before emerging on the other side of a large green field. Keeping to the bordering shadows, we crept closer. The council building appeared over the rolling hill.

When we reached the spiked fence surrounding the council grounds, Ty caught my arm. "Wait." He pointed to the square, brick columns that joined each spiked panel. "They're warded."

On each column was a symbol carved into the brick. It was an almost full moon that had been split in half on an angle. "What does it mean?" I whispered.

"It's alchemy," Troy said, glaring. "Any entering wolves will set off an alarm."

You're not going in alone. Kendrick's voice lifted in my mind at the same time Ty said the words out loud.

"Besides, me being part vampire means I won't trip their alarm. It doesn't react to hybrids." Ty nodded at Troy. "As for him, he'll need your blood. It'll temporarily mask the properties of his own blood."

"Like that's going to happen," Troy spat. Fire scorched his neck and face and his irises rippled gold. "Assisting your leech is bad enough. But taking her poison blood? No way."

"My blood?" I shivered, feeling cold. Kendrick's voice in my mind strung out curses and argument, and I agreed with them all. Neither of us trusted Troy. On top of that, the last time an enemy had drunk my blood they'd tried to kill me. I cringed, remembering all the times Caius had drawn back my hair and bitten into me. Then I shook it off, getting back to the issue. Troy hated all vampires. If his canines even poked out a little, his bite could kill me. "Ty, I don't think…"

Ty skewered Troy with a hard look. The tip of his canines peeked through his parted lips. "You will do as I order. Unless you want me to make Marika my second."

Troy's face turned to stone, chin jutting out. A second later his head dipped in the slightest move of agreement.

Ty took my hand, exposing my wrist. "I know you don't trust Troy. You have every reason not to. But he won't," he glared back a Troy, "try anything. If I even see a glint of canines—"

"I'm not fucking stupid," Troy grated. "If I'm going to challenge you as alpha, it won't be outside a house of vampires."

With that apparently everything was settled. Still, it didn't ease my trepidation for what was about to happen. I gulped as I ran a quick nail across my wrist. Then I held it out with closed eyes. There was a grunt, and then warm hands took hold of my arm. A hot, open mouth pressed against my flesh and I flinched, feeling long pulls as Troy drank my blood. In less than a minute it was over. I stepped away feeling dirty all over. Ty tried to catch my hand, but I sidestepped to the fence. "Let's go."

We all cleared the barrier and shot to the building's outer edge. Surrounding its base was a six-foot wide gravel path. Peering up I trekked over the stones, managing not to make a sound with my Vans. The pitched cathedral windows on the second floor were so high above the ground from where we stood.

I turned to Ty and Troy. "You two stay watch here. I'm going up."

Ty nodded, while Troy looked indignant at a vampire ordering him around. Still he complied, turning opposite to Ty and facing outward from where I stood. Without wasting a second I crouched to the ground, fingers pried on the stones below. Every muscle in my body snapped tight before I sprung, my legs extending with a powerful push. My arms simultaneously swung overhead, with my fingers outstretched to grip the window ledge's thin border. I swung up, pulling my body onto the poor excuse for a ledge, and positioned my back against the window frame.

The room below was bright. Enormous wrought iron chandeliers with thick white candles hung from the cathedral ceiling, lighting the huge hall. Banisters ran around the second level. All of which were vacant at the moment. On the floor, people clustered around a huge marble table. Some of their faces were strained, others anxious, and others determined. The discussion going on was definitely a heated one.

Without wanting to I caught sight of Caius. He sat on a throne of carved wood and red velvet, regal and important. My heart belted against my ribs and nerves churned my stomach. Forcing my lungs to breathe normally, I popped the latch and edged the heavy glass pane open an inch. A small creak rang out and I shrank back against the frame. When there was no break in the bickering below, I dared to peek. Silent relief escaped my lips. No one had heard. My ears pricked, listening to the unbroken, heated words.

"You cannot believe they have not returned," came an accusing voice from one end of the table.

The woman, who also sat in a throne, jabbed her index finger into the marble while staring across at Caius. The sight surprised me. I had never seen anyone talk to him like that in my life. Her porcelain-white complexion was red with frustration. It was almost the shade of her braided, fiery hair. I'd seen this woman before. Once in the dining hall at the Armaya with Caius and Marcus's father Vladimir. But I'd seen her before that, too. She was the vampire from the auction who'd bid against Caius for the jewelry box.

"And you, Uriel, my inexperienced young colleague, can?" Caius countered.

That was Uriel Aswind. The owner of the diary I'd discovered back at the Armaya which mentioned the damned. She was one of the reigning royals. That fact aside, it was obvious in Caius's tone and words that he held no respect for her in the slightest. He would never consider her to be his equal.

Uriel pursed her lips and crossed her arms over her chest. "Then how do *you* explain the murders?"

"Well," Caius began, "they have hardly been in proximity to one another. The attacks have occurred throughout the globe. And I doubt the damned, *if* they still existed, would possess the restraint to execute such atrocities."

"So you discount Lord Marcus Vladimir's report from Anchorage?" Uriel slammed her palms down on the table. "The ash remains left after one of our own was taken out?"

"Of course he doesn't," Serafina spoke up from her own throne. "That ash could have come from many other sources." Her pale hand covered Caius's.

The move spiked anger within me, not just mine but Kendrick's too. He was keeping close tabs on me and my spy mission, and paying little attention to Marika and Vanessa, or any possible lurking intruders. Seeing his mother's obvious trust in Caius had hate radiating through him. He had been used through Caius's strong compulsion, but we didn't know if that's what was happening here. Serafina may be a genuine ally to this traitor without knowing what he was up to.

"But the damned are extinct," Serafina added. "We made certain of that during The Blood Years."

"Without the assistance of the traitorous guardians, I might add," a middle-aged man in a charcoal suit voiced. "So far we have very few leads as to who has orchestrated these crimes. Although we do know a few things. Extended royals seem to be the main victims."

"Yes," my mom agreed. "And a majority of those victims were taken through full consumption."

Uriel eyed Caius. "So we're going to keep pretending that they can't come back. By heaven, we have become arrogant over the years, haven't we? We have come to believe that we alone are superior, invincible, and infallible. That we are without serious mortal threat."

"Uriel," Caius warned, glaring as he steepled his hands. "This is not the place."

Uriel rose to her full willowy height. "So apart from the few reigning royals, the rest of our kind should be left blind? No. That may be the old ways, but not anymore." Uriel glanced at all the faces around the table. With an inkling from Kendrick, I knew most were extended family to royals in power. My mom was one of the few exceptions. "Most of our race believes our only threat are the wolves. Yet there are much worse foes to have. Now this threat comes hunting for us all, and we're *vulnerable*." She grated over the word as though it enraged her. "Vampires vulnerable? I never thought I'd see the day."

Another council member spoke up, an old graying woman. "I presume this 'rant' has a point?" She leaned back into her seat.

Uriel pinned the old woman with a firm stare. "My fellow members of the Royal Council would have this stay between us seven, but I think the time for silence has passed—too many are dying. Extinct or not. It doesn't matter. Through full consumption a vampire is changed, cursed. The damned can be created."

CHAPTER 23

On that startling revelation a marrow-freezing shiver flooded my bones. I blinked, the light from the chandelier candles burning my retinas. My face felt like it was in flames as my blood rushed with my spiking heart rate.

Still blinking, now frantically, my sight blurred. Blackness sprouted in from my peripheral vision, eating away the light until there was nothing.

I lost my grip on the window ledge and fell.

A sudden shift blinked into reality, cutting off my scream before it could escape.

I was crouched atop a sprawling staircase that descended into the foyer of a grand manor. To the left was a ballroom filled with exquisitely dressed people, dancing and drinking champagne delivered by tuxedo-clad waiters.

My hands and arms were child sized, wrapped tight around the thick banister, as if trying to hold me back. I got the sense that I wanted to be down there, but knew I wasn't allowed. Which was strange. Because I'd never seen this manor with its carved ornate wood, wide domed windows, or any of the people inside the ballroom.

Chimes rang out over the gentle waltzing music, and a waiter went to answer the carved wooden front door. Just as he got there an elderly man intercepted him, dismissing the waiter with a waved hand. The waiter bowed, stepping back until he coalesced with the shadows on the opposite side of the foyer.

I took little notice, focusing on the old man. His hunched stance, thinning white hair, and height were familiar. I'd seen him before. Marcus's father, Lord Vladimir.

As the old man swung open the thick door, he clapped his hands together. The man on the other side was tall and lean, wearing raggedy jeans over shit kickers and a clingy T-shirt. From the top of the stairs his upper chest and face were cut off from view.

"Welcome, my—"

The old Lord's greeting stalled as everything turned black. The atrium lighting, foyer lamps, and ballroom chandelier had suddenly extinguished. An eerie moment of heart-stopping silence followed.

Then a woman's shriek permeated the air and all hell broke loose.

Bodies filed in through the front door and swarmed the ballroom, red eyes filling the shadowed space. Shouts and cries erupted with the sound of glass and ceramic shattering, and wooden furniture splintering.

A window shattered as a woman tried to escape, only to be dragged back into the frenzy. Her scream died with a gurgle as a red-eyed figure tore into her with gleaming fangs. The other screaming men and women began to fall too, silenced in death.

Frozen in terror at the top of the stairs, the child's eyes I saw from shifted. They were blurry with tears, her body shaking at the screams of sleeping children being woken and slaughtered down the hall behind her.

The man from outside now had Lord Vladimir pinned to the door, his forearm a crowbar against the old man's neck. His back faced the stairs. "End of your shelf life, old man."

The man's forearm released and he ripped out the Lord's neck with his teeth. The body dropped like a bag of stones, cold and dead. Glossy liquid pooled out of him over the polished wooden floor.

A shriek escaped the girl, the first noise she'd made.

In a flash of movement the man had her by the throat.

Through tearing eyes, she couldn't see his face clearly. But she didn't need to. She knew exactly who held her in a death grip. I felt her recognition as if it were my own, only I couldn't place the blurry outline of his face or his cruel voice.

"Why?" she mouthed too late, her vision fracturing as her vertebrae were crushed.

A RED-TINTED BLACK haze stole my sight. I was blind. A scream tried to tear from my mouth. But it never escaped my lips.

My throat was choked closed. The man still had me in his grasp. Hands crushing my throat in iron-clenched fingers before fangs bit into my flesh.

Somehow I managed to fight back, nails tearing flesh.

Someone shouted my name. The voice was rattled as hell. And so far away. Too far to see. Too far to touch.

My lids flung open, pain striking as I blinked. Still I couldn't see a thing. There was only terrifying darkness.

Fear struck through my body. "Let me go!" I screamed,

squeezing my eyelids shut. Panic exploded in my chest. My arms thrashed out in front of me, but something caught my wrists.

"It's okay," a familiar voice soothed. It seemed closer now. "Just breathe."

But I wasn't listening. I could hear the erratic beating of two hearts coursing with blood. Blood I needed bad enough to kill for.

Amelia, no! The desperate cry was smothered as the walls in my mind slammed into place.

I threw off the hot hands holding me and sprung. My body found its target, a built mass that I knocked to the ground. Gravel scraped my knees, cutting flesh, but I didn't care. With fangs unsheathed and dripping saliva, my jaw snapped. The smell was so good I couldn't stop.

Broad hands tried to hold me back. Still my hunger wouldn't give in. Just one more inch—

A force hit me like a train, barreling me off my prey. I landed on my back, skin grazing gravel and tearing my top. Pressure sat on my chest like a boulder. Calloused hands claimed my wrists, pinning them above my head. Another set caught my flailing legs.

I screamed and fought, fangs aching while my jaw snapped for flesh.

"Take her out," a hard-breathing voice demanded. There was a slice of unsheathed metal. "Or I will."

"Try it and I will kill you myself." The responding voice was low, but the promise edging his words were clear. One hand released my wrists, leaving the other to keep me pinned. Gentle fingers touched my hissing face, stroking back my hair. "It's me. It's Ty."

Over the pull of hot blood, I registered only that someone was trying to keep me from what I needed. What I would kill to get. I fought harder, my whole body convulsing and unable to think past the bloodlust. Nothing in this moment mattered more than what I could take.

A sudden release had me off my back, my arms and legs trapping a warm body. My fangs clumsily found their mark. I sucked greedily, reveling in the rich, potent taste of blood.

"You idiot," a male snarled. "Now you give me no choice. I won't let her kill you out of stupidity."

As boots crunched closer over gravel, another voice spoke. "Stand down and wait." Heat flared at the back of my head as a hand cupped my skull. "I love you, Amelia. I trust you. With my blood. With my life." The stroking continued, smoothing my hair down my back over and over. "I know you'll stop. I *believe* in you."

Rose-colored tears blurred my vision, the crazed spell breaking as they fell. Like waking from a nightmare, something was terribly wrong. My fangs were free, embedded in hot flesh. The taste of blood coating my mouth couldn't be confused.

"Ty?" I scrambled off his lap, stopping as my back hit a tree. It was one of the many trees that surrounded the parking lot where our bikes were stashed, all the way across the field, and well away from the council building. "W-what happened? Why—"

"You fell from the window ledge and I caught you, then I rushed you back here," Ty said. Then the walls in my mind dropped, and I heard Kendrick and Ty speak in unison. "You had a vision."

Troy flipped a stake in one hand, body tense and ready to fight. "And tried to fucking kill me."

I attacked Troy? Great way to mend mortal enemy bridges. "Troy, I'm sorry. I didn't know…"

"It's okay," Ty said, standing up and moving closer. "I stopped you."

In the gentle breeze their scents carried around me. Even after what I'd taken, the lust was still dominating, controlling. My crazed attack replayed in my subconscious. Self-loathing edged my words. "And that makes it okay? Attempted murder is okay, just because I had a freaking vision? What a crock of shit. I'm no better than—"

I froze, just flat out stopped speaking. Even the hate for myself ebbed a fraction. The horrifying vision of the manor filled with slaughtered vampires returned.

Amelia, has it already happened? Kendrick's words rushed. *Is it too late to send warning?*

Somehow I knew there was still time. "No. I'll call him now."

Ty stepped forward to take my hand. "What is it?"

I jumped back before he could touch me, hands raised to stop him. "No. I can't be near you right now. I'm too *hungry.*" Even as I said the word I zoned in on the pulsing vein along his neck. The marks of my attack had closed over, but scarlet torrents still marked a path down to his collarbone. My tongue ran over my teeth. "I need you both to leave so I can call Marcus. His family's in danger."

Troy came forward and pushed Ty back. "Come on." He jumped onto his motorbike, firing up the engine. His stare on me was full of loathing. "Time to go."

Ty nodded and I threw him the keys to my Ducati. "Here." Shaking restraint was fast taking over my arms and legs. There was no way I'd be able to drive home without crashing. "Take mine. I need the run, anyway."

"We'll wait back at your place."

Without waiting for a response I took off through the trees. In the background my Ducati's engine revved to life. I took a much-needed breath. The surging and painful thirst remained, although the distance from any living, breathing thing began to clear my thoughts.

You did well, Kendrick voiced as I cleared the park to take to the streets.

I wanted to kill my boyfriend, again.

All the progress I thought I'd made was nothing if every time I had a vision I lost all control. But my bloodlust was small fry compared to what I'd seen. The Vladimirs' lives were at stake.

I whipped out my iPhone, noticing scratches across the Icon For Hire case. All that thrashing had left more than a mark on Ty. *Shit.* I pressed down my similarities to the slaughterers, ran harder, and dialed Marcus.

You're going to tell him about your visions. Aren't you? Kendrick already knew the answer and he was far from happy about it. *What if he enlightens The Council to your ability?*

How else can I explain knowing his family is going to be slaughtered? Besides, whether you do or not, I trust him. He won't tell The Council.

The ringing stopped and the line picked up. "Amelia? Is everything okay? Caius is M.I.A. and I think he's headed your way."

"I know. But this isn't about him." I laid out everything I'd seen, including the replay of his father's gruesome death. I even detailed my ability and promised the vision hadn't played out yet. Hearing a speaker announcement over the line, I asked, "Where are you now? Can you get to them or send warning?"

"Give me a sec." The line went silent and a moment later Marcus was back. "Shit. There's no," his voice broke with emotion, "there's no answer. It's probably daylight there now."

I cleared Portsmouth's suburban streets, hitting the winding, tree-shrouded road that led toward the beach. "Daylight where?"

"Russia. I'm at the airport now, heading to the manor for a family reunion." He cleared his throat, forcing some control back to his voice. "Every Vladimir in existence will be there."

I gulped, wondering if Marcus had been in that ballroom in my vision. Had he been killed there, too? "Oh God. Be careful. Don't go alone, please."

Last call for American Airlines flight 6984, sounded in the background through the phone.

"I've gotta go. That's my flight." In the background a woman greeted him. "I'll keep calling from the plane. And don't fret. I'll be far from alone." The rush of his words subsided and his voice lowered. "Oh, and as always, your secrets are safe with me...Oracle."

BACK HOME I made for the kitchen and bounded around the limestone breakfast bar to the double-door fridge. I snatched a bottle of blood. The glass shattered in my desperate, clutching hands, shards falling to the tiles in a red mess. Fangs still aching, I went for another bottle, twisting open the cap. The glass was empty before the lid hit the tiles, the blood spreading quickly through my body. The last of my maddening thirst receded and I hurriedly mopped up the mess.

No longer a threat to everyone with a pulse, I hit the foyer and launched up the stairs. Everyone was waiting up in the rec room. I flashed fangless teeth as I entered. Troy kept glaring from the open, high-arched window.

Ty took my hand and led me to the leather couch. "Are you alright now?"

Far from it. After what I'd done to them, his acceptance made me feel like a fraud. "Sure."

Troy mumbled a curse, while Marika shifted to his side, eyeing me the whole time.

"Any more news?" Dorian asked. He looked up from the iMac

Vanessa was drumming away at as the screen flashed up a list of flight times.

"No," Kendrick answered for me. He sat forward in the armchair beside the coffee table and messed his hair. "You know there's not. The plane will be taking off by now."

Vanessa glanced up from the screen, the desk lamp making her red hair glow like flames. "He'll arrive in daylight. So even if he can't get through on satellite phone, as long as he can get out there with backup fast, they should be able to evacuate."

"Unless the attack happens while this guy's still in the air." Marika's tone was direct and without sympathy. She could clearly care less if a whole line of vampires were obliterated.

Ty began to reprimand her and I patted his hand. "No. She's right. I don't know when they'll make their move, only that no one is left alive. Not even children." I fought the need to scream out for all those innocent young souls. Instead I sent out a silent prayer to whoever would listen.

Ty grasped my hand and squeezed. A flare of jealousy streamed from Kendrick, but given the circumstances it was watered down. Still, he wanted to be the one to comfort me, the one to relieve my pain and guilt. Unfortunately nothing was going to help that. Not even one hundred blocks of chocolate could make a dent.

"And the attackers," Vanessa chimed in. "They were all damned?"

I nodded. There was a possibility that they were rogues. Though after everything we'd witnessed recently, I couldn't ignore the facts. Besides, during one of Marcus's lessons at the Armaya, he'd stated that rogues were solitary, not pack hunters. "Yeah, I'm sure."

A strangled smile fell from Vanessa's face. "The Council should have listened. So many lives could have been saved."

Everyone's eyes shot to her in question. She waved Ty and the others off, turning off the computer screen. "Even before your attacks, I'd expected their return for years now. The occurrence of human deaths and disappearances has been steadily rising. But vampires taken through full consumption? That's not rogues. They prefer easy prey. And still The Council refuses to acknowledge that they've returned."

"Wait," I interrupted. "You mean our council, the Royal Vampire Council?"

"Yes," she said as a matter of fact. "We have a long standing relationship with the RVC, among others."

"Not all the Royal Council," Kendrick added, kicking his feet up on the coffee table, "disbelieves the damned have returned."

At last, something that was news to Vanessa. Her sapphire eyes shot across to him. "Really?"

"I'm sure of it." I slumped onto the couch, pulling Ty down beside me. "Uriel Aswind was very clear. She believes they've returned. She also revealed something else. The damned can be created, and she didn't mean through bite and infection."

"No wonder the numbers have soared." Vanessa forked her fingers through her wavy hair. "Given you're all associated with royals, whether you're pure or not, you're clearly in serious danger."

"Hand-to-hand battle isn't going to cut it," Ty added. "The bow and whip are good, but not in short-range battle. You need something more." He caught Vanessa's eye and she nodded.

"Alchemists always assist the greater good."

Ty stood tall, the remnants of my attack still marking his neck. "Tomorrow we all meet at Vanessa's for supplies. Then it's on to the next step in training. It's time you all learn to kill."

∼

AFTER SCHOOL we made our way past a rickety gate and into a garden so overgrown that it resembled a jungle. Vines climbed trees and leaf litter was everywhere. After following the overgrown path, we mounted cracked wooden stairs to a dilapidated mansion's weathered double doors. The stained glass was coated in dust and a few panels were even cracked.

Ty eyed me, Kendrick, and Dorian. "Stand back for a minute... just in case." Then he raised his hand to knock.

Light footsteps across hollow wood rose beyond the barrier, growing louder as someone approached. The door swung open, revealing an old man. Vanessa's father, I guessed. Though something about him seemed familiar.

The man with white hair and wrinkled features smiled at Ty. Then his sapphire gaze registered me, Dorian, and Kendrick. His body stiffened, brittle bones creaking, and his eyes grew wide. "Code red!" he screamed over his shoulder and reached for the first drawer in a rickety cabinet.

Kendrick and Dorian tensed, moving to block my body.

The old man's fingers grasped a silver stake as Ty moved to catch his wrist. "It's okay, Tom. They mean no harm."

With much effort the old man yanked his wrist free and raised the stake.

Vanessa shouted out, emerging in body-hugging black from behind him. "Stop!" She glanced at Ty. "You're early."

"Only five minutes. You've had thirty minutes since school finished."

Looking confused, Vanessa's father backed up to her. His arms spread wide in protection of his daughter. She placed light hands on his arms and forced them down to his sides. Although he allowed the movement, his do-or-die grip on the silver stake remained.

"It's okay, they're kind of my friends," Vanessa said, apology staining her voice.

After a long-winded explanation Mr. Aquinas knew why we were here and what we were up against. Still, even after accepting our explanation, he refused to loosen his ready grip on the stake in his hands.

"Will you assist them, Grandfather?" Vanessa asked.

"Grandfather?" So this wasn't Vanessa's father. "Where are your parents?"

"Rogues killed her parents," Ty said, taking my hand. "Tom has taught her everything she needed to know to win out against the things that go bump in the night."

"Oh, I'm so sorry." I felt horrible. No wonder this old man feared us and wanted to drive that stake through our beating hearts. And he'd clearly taught Vanessa how to be strong. Even among the wolves she held rank. Troy and Marika never challenged her, and even Ty respected her opinion. I studied the old man's features. Apart from his white, thinning hair and aged face, he had an uneasy stance. Probably because he'd just had a bunch of vampires turn up to his home. Except...no. I'd seen those shifty eyes before.

"You're the delivery man!"

Kendrick moved closer to me while Dorian and Ty exchanged confused looks. Vanessa had on her usual cool, nothing-can-shock-me expression. Mr. Aquinas, on the other hand, looked like an animal that had suddenly been caged.

"What delivery man?" Dorian asked.

Kendrick flanked my side. "The one who delivered the vial results."

The old man's shoulders slumped. "I'm not a delivery man."

"You're an alchemist," Kendrick said. "Like your granddaughter. We know."

"That's not what he means," Vanessa said. She and her grandfather stepped aside to let us into the narrow entryway. With the door behind us closed, gentle sunlight filtered through the stained glass, highlighting dust motes in the air. "Most of our work is for the wolves. But my grandfather has a long standing alliance with the Vladimir line."

"Marcus's family?" My blood ran cold. If my vision came true that alliance would be as dead as every member of that Pure Blood line. Without being able to get through to Marcus's phone, I had no idea if any of them, including Marcus, was still alive.

Vanessa touched her grandfather's arm. "Please meet Simon Beatty."

"What?" The news was like a bomb blast in my mind, shifting the reenacting terror of my vision aside.

"The Blood Analyst," Dorian murmured.

Mr. Aquinas cleared his throat. "Yes, I am. So now that I know what you're facing, I will assist your group. First though, there's something you need to know."

The old man secured the silver stake in his belt loop and led us down the hall, past faded wallpaper hung with photos and shelves filled with musky books before pausing. Ty moved to slide a bookshelf aside, revealing a door in the wall. Mr. Aquinas used a large brass key to unlock it. The door creaked open and a light flickered on. The dull glow lit narrow steps leading below ground. He gripped the rail and descended, one step at a time. This old man, although he had seemed alert and prepared to fight when we'd first arrived, now revealed his true age in his shaky slow steps.

As we emerged below ground, a rectangular space opened before us. Another set of fluorescents flicked on, illuminating everything. I stared around the space. What a set-up. Workbenches littered the room. Some were cluttered with glass cylinders and test tubes, all filled with varying amounts of colorful liquids, bubbling and frothing. Their chemical smells married in the frigid air. Other benches housed metals and woods in all shapes and sizes. An anvil sat to one corner. And what appeared to be a cauldron hung by chains from a roof beam. Beside it was a small dirty alcove. A fire-place. The most eye-catching part was the walls. Similar to Ty's training room, they all housed hanging ancient and rusting weapons.

"What is all this?" I asked, my curiosity peaking.

Vanessa walked up beside me. "Our experiments. Our life's work."

Mr. Aquinas and Vanessa stood behind the workbench with bubbling beakers. "This is where I compiled the results for the substance you sent me." He took a dropper and filled it with a thick black liquid from a corked test tube. He squirted the substance into a petri dish. Then he lifted a UV lamp over the top of it. As soon as the light hit the edge of the liquid it burst into a flaming ball. A second later the fire died and the liquid was gone.

Kendrick's amazement seared through the bond while Dorian moved to take a closer look.

"What was that?" I asked.

"Damned blood." Vanessa shrugged, handing another vial to her grandfather.

This one was filled with a watery silvery liquid. Mr. Aquinas took the vial and repeated the process. This time when the UV light touched the liquid, nothing happened. No crackle. No smoke. No flames.

"Is that supposed to happen?" Dorian asked at the same time I said, "What was that?"

Mr. Aquinas re-capped the second vial. "This is the substance you sent me, in diluted form. And no, that is not meant to happen.

With the makeup of the liquid you sent me, it should burn like the damned blood. But it doesn't."

"Why?" Kendrick asked. "If it's Pure Blood and silver nitrate, why would it burn? I mean I know we can still feel the sun, but royals are mostly immune."

As I stared at Mr. Aquinas a glint of knowledge sparkled from his ancient eyes. "You know what the unidentified substance is."

He nodded. "I do. But I was under instruction to keep any mention of them from public knowledge."

"But since you all already know they exist," Vanessa interrupted. "There's no reason to keep it from you."

A shiver ran down my body, chilling past my bones and solidifying the marrow inside. At any moment I expected to crack into a million pieces. I knew what the third ingredient was. "I was infected with damned blood."

A LITTLE LATER Mr. Aquinas retired upstairs with Ty's assistance. When Ty re-emerged he rubbed his hands together. "Now for the reason we came here."

Vanessa smiled and strolled to the far right wall. Considering the other walls all housed hanging ancient and rusting weapons, this one appeared empty. She pressed her finger onto a silver button in the wall. With a click then clatter of rattling chains and cogs, an eight-foot-long section of the wall spun from the middle. "Think yourselves lucky. Not many have seen the extent of our hand crafted stock."

My mouth hung open at the hidden room inside the wall, fitted with floor-to-ceiling hanging weapons. But these weren't just any old weapons. These were shimmering and deadly weapons of all sorts. Like Ty's training room, these weapons were sharp, made to kill. Every piece was edged with silver, if not coated in the metal. There were guns too, automatics, semi-automatics, handguns, rifles, and shotguns. Dark metal glistened from guns of all shapes and sizes. So this was where Ty's stock had come from.

Kendrick's jaw hung open in shock, mirroring Dorian's. They hadn't expected this any more than I had.

Vanessa went to a stainless steel counter and slid open the top drawer. She rifled through with a clink and a clatter before both hands reversed, now filled with gleaming silver stakes. She handed me one first. "Ty tells me you're immune to silver."

Ty's and my encounters on the cruise and at *Pulse* when I'd used one of his silver stakes had proved that. Not to mention the silver amulet he'd given me that had belonged to his mother. My fingers toyed with the amulet nestled against my almost cleavage. I couldn't help thinking about the red, hungry eyes of the damned vampires we'd encountered. Their color was same as this hefty stone. And some of their vile blood was inside me, poisoning me.

Feeling ill and wondering what other side effects Caius's drugging would have, I nodded and took the stake. "Yeah, I guess I have Caius to thank for that. Kendrick won't be immune though, will he?"

"No, I'm not," Kendrick said out loud. But through the bond his words were more personal, picking up on my rising insecurities. *And being infected with their blood doesn't make you like them. Please believe that.*

"If that's the case..." Dorian held out his hand and Vanessa handed over another stake.

Without warning there was a sizzling followed by a shout of pain. Dorian dropped the stake like it was a hot coal. It bounced with a clank against the concrete at his shoes. The stink of burned flesh invaded the frigid basement air.

Dorian rubbed at his blistered and bleeding hand. "What the hell?"

Vanessa caught and inspected his hand, which was already smoothing over. A moment later only remnants of his spilled blood remained. "You're not immune."

I rubbed at my temples. The first thing I saw was Marcus, a silver-faced Rolex on his wrist. *Marcus is immune,* I passed my words and memory through the bond. Then I conjured up details of what we'd found under the cabin ruins in Alaska. The explanation hit me like a sonic boom. "Caius used two solutions in his experiments. Both had silver nitrate and Pure Blood, but one had ingredient X."

"Damned blood," Ty said.

I nodded. "Yeah, and the other had X2."

"The X probably means it's damned blood, too." Vanessa walked back to her workstation and flicked through a tattered notebook. "But my guess is that it was altered in some other way. Before being mixed with the other ingredients."

"It could also have something to do with the infected before and after birth stuff," Kendrick mused.

Dorian took all this information in his stride. Yet all I could think was that this was another thing that separated me from everyone else. Another thing that made me different. An outsider.

"So what's the alternative?" Dorian asked, sliding a finger along a mean-looking handgun. "I'm guessing your guns aren't made of silver."

"No, they're not," Vanessa said. "But our bullets are. Not great for killing unless you're a perfect shot and can fire off enough rounds to pretty much shred the heart. But seeing as the damned are so fast, they'll rip your neck out before you get the chance."

I heard Dorian mutter *"buzz kill"* under his breath which made Kendrick snicker.

"There are silver-coated machetes and swords." Ty pointed to the ones hung from the wall. "But with their size they're difficult to conceal. In the end a stake is the best weapon."

"But we can't touch them," Kendrick said, his tone screaming *dumbass*.

"No." Ty laughed. "Not those ones. But these…" He let the word hang in the air as he pulled two objects from the cabinet's second drawer. Each was a stake, but they were different from the others. These ones were silver, but their hilts were coated with a thick layer of rubber.

"Never thought I'd be giving those out." Vanessa sighed, resigned to the idea. After hearing about her parents' tragic murder at the hands of rogues, it was no wonder. Still, I wondered if her shift to help was more to do with something else. Something more than assisting the greater good. Like my charismatically charming brother who kept sliding her sexy eyes.

"If you don't stick yourself with the pointy end," Ty said with a smile, "and carry the stake in a holster or pocket, you won't get burned."

"Good to know." Dorian grabbed one by the rubber casing, testing what Ty said by sliding it into the back pocket of his jeans.

Kendrick muttered *"smart ass"* but did the same.

With each of us armed and enough bombshells to clog up my brain, I let my focus drop to the silver stake in my hands. It was unsurprisingly heavy and now the third I'd held. During our attack on the cruise, I'd grasped the one from Ty's backpack in a desperate effort to save his life. Though back then I had taken little notice of the weapon itself. I rolled the piece across my palm. A scrawling inscription was etched into the length. The flowing words weren't in English.

"What does the inscription mean?" I asked Vanessa who was still nose-deep in her dusty book.

She went to answer, but Kendrick replied before she had a chance to. "It's…" The next words he spoke were in a language I didn't understand. Maybe Greek or Latin.

"That's Greek, isn't it?" Dorian asked, surprising me. He shrugged. "What? It's my language elective at school."

"And it translates to mean," Ty added. *"Deliver back unto hell."*

My body convulsed at Ty's words, ice undulating my muscles. Then the world around me faded. The stake fell from my hand, rattling to the ground. I swayed, knees giving way as I fell.

In a flash of confusing light, I saw a man standing at the edge of a cliff backing a forest. Tattered clothes that appeared centuries old covered his body. His hands were outstretched, reaching for the raging electrical storm above. I tried to scream, to tell him to move. But I wasn't there. I was merely a spectator, eyes without a body. And then it was too late. A bolt of light split from the roiling clouds, plummeting at the man in the blink of an eye. The lightning connected with his hands, sizzling through his entire body as he crumpled to the grass.

"No!"

My body jerked back and forth and my lids flew open. My vision was hazy as a familiar voice registered in my ears. "Amelia. It's me. It's Ty."

Ty was cradling my shaking body in his arms. Dorian and Kendrick were kneeling around us. Vanessa stood behind them, her face showing the most shock I'd ever seen in her.

"I'm okay," I said. Ty tried to pull me up and I pushed him away.

I struggled to stand on my own and fell back on my butt. "I can smell blood." With blurry vision I scanned everyone in the room. "Everyone's blood."

As I blinked, lifting my lids, Vanessa gasped. Through Kendrick's sight I saw my red-tinted, bloodshot eyes. A sight Vanessa hadn't witnessed, having been absent during my other visions.

"Another vision," Kendrick guessed. He reached into his jacket and withdrew a bottle of blood. "Don't ever say I'm not prepared." At my hesitation he said, "And no, it's not mine."

Even though his preparedness came from not wanting to see me sink my fangs into Ty's neck, I accepted the bottle. A few seconds later it was empty.

As the blood sank in, taking the edge off, I shook my head. I needed to piece together what had happened, what it all meant. This vision had been different from the last. There'd been no death. No violence. And no bloodshed. But that didn't mean it hadn't been confronting. The images of this stranger being struck by lightning were hitting a little too close to home. Yet I had sensed his decision. He had wanted the lightning to strike him. *Who would purposely walk into that?*

For once Kendrick didn't have an answer to my unasked question. But there was something else different about the vision. It hadn't been an urgent warning of something terrible to come. It had been an insight into a past event.

"So what did you see?" Dorian, standing close to Vanessa, looked worried.

"It was a past event," I offered, sending *this stays between us* silently to Kendrick. "Not related to the damned or anything posing an imminent threat to us or anyone we know. Just some guy in old clothes in the forest."

CHAPTER 24

I skidded to a halt as the forest opened up into a winter wonderland. Kendrick and Dorian stalled beside me. "This'll be fun," Kendrick said dryly.

Dorian clapped. "Head to head with Troy. I'm psyched. Been wanting to knock that dick around since our last fight."

I groaned. Today we were training against the wolves. One on one while wielding stakes. How Ty saw this going well was beyond me.

I glanced around our usual secret training space. All the lush greens of white cedar and hemlock pine trees were lost to powdery white snow. The once dewy forest floor was a blanket of white just waiting to be torn up.

It was the following morning—Saturday, so we didn't have to wait for school to finish—and the wolves were already waiting. Ty was having words with Troy across the clearing, jabbing a finger into the guy's chest and flashing canines. Although indignant with his own canines peeking out, Troy nodded. Glued to his side, Marika sneered at Kendrick and me while ignoring Dorian's very existence. For once she was dressed in black, with most of her body covered.

Vanessa waved us over and tension fled Ty's warning expression. "As you all know, the most efficient way to kill a damned—"

"Or a vampire," Troy barked.

Ty glared but continued. "Is to stake them in the heart."

I had experienced the effectiveness of Ty's silver stake on the damned, which Kendrick had witnessed through my mind's eye. But Dorian had relied on his brute strength, speed, and a lot of luck to kill his and Kendrick's attacker.

I palmed the stake in my hoodie's pocket. The entirely silver stake that I, a vampire, could touch. An unexpected questioned rolled off my tongue. "What happens when you stake a living vampire?" The words tasted like acid in my mouth. But we needed to know. If it came to it, in the end we might have to kill Caius, a living vampire. All I knew so far was that we didn't disintegrate like the damned.

"They die a painful death as a result of the silver burning the heart and preventing repair," Vanessa answered sounding clinical. "If the heart doesn't stop from the damage, the blood loss will eventually have the same effect."

I swallowed, knowing that Ty had actual experience in this. The times he'd assisted his father in killing rogue vampires. Even more daunting than that was the memory of the night he had almost killed me, too. I would have been his first.

With an uneasy smile, I nodded to Ty. "Let's get started then."

We walked into the center of the clearing, leaving sunken boot and shoe prints in the snow. Light pattering rain began to fall.

Ty nodded to Troy. "First, you need to know where to hit." He motioned towards Troy who at Marika's curled lip removed his shirt to expose his buff torso. Ty took a stake from the back pocket of his jeans and directed the tip at his chest. "You need to hit here, before the base of the pectoral, between the 4th and 5th rib." His gaze narrowed. "If you misjudge even half an inch, you'll strike a rib, or worse, the sternum."

"Neither of which will kill or really harm your opponent," Vanessa chimed in. "But will more likely just piss them off."

Under Ty's direction, Dorian was set against Troy and Ty took on Kendrick. "Now this is training. Not battle. Hits are fine." He leveled flashing eyes at his pack. "But if any skin is burnt by silver you'll be answering to me."

With Vanessa separating Marika from me, we watched from the sidelines atop a fallen tree. The log was sheltered by a few oaks and almost clear of snow. First the wolves, still in human form, were armed, showing us in one-on-one combat how to hit our mark. Ty was all business, but you could tell Troy loved every time his stake hit the kill point on my brother. Kendrick was behaving too, for now.

Vanessa barked out tips throughout the sparring, not missing a single mistake by Kendrick or Dorian. I kept my focus on the guys, picking up weaknesses and strengths. What moves worked and which came up short. Beside Vanessa, Marika mirrored my intent observation.

After round one, the tables turned and my best friend and brother were the ones armed. Following an hour of that, their bodies dripped sweat and mud from the ground they'd shredded up. Kendrick's frustration every time he missed the mark on Ty was met with a curse. Though to his credit he got in a few wins. Troy reacted to every correct hit from Dorian with a roar of rage. Each time the outburst got louder, teetering closer to an unstoppable edge. As Troy was about to blow his top and actually take my brother down, Ty called a stop.

"That was good," Ty said, walking over with the others to the log where we sat. "But now…"

I pushed off my crouched perch, dumping my phone and iPod on the log. I knew what was next. "It's our turn."

Marika stood and dusted snow off her hands before pulling out her own stake. "Challenge accepted, leech."

She jogged into the clearing and I followed, pulling my own silver stake from my belt. With my pulse racing I grounded my feet as Marika launched at me. She moved like the wind. But her stance gave her away.

I dodged just in time, elbow jutting out to connect with her ribs. The hit made her snarl but she didn't falter, swinging out a leg as she dropped to the ground. Off balance, I staggered. The fact that I hadn't seen that one coming cut through me with irritation.

The rain began to pelt down harder and I spun on the spot. Free fist ready, I delivered a blow to her cheek. The hit caught her off guard for a moment. Which was all I needed. I threw my arm forward, directing the stake at Marika's chest.

Before I reached the kill spot her hands came up, knocking the stake free. It flew through the air into a wide oak. Its branches trembled at the embedding force, dusting snow like icing sugar through a sift.

Not stopping to berate myself, I back flipped to the tree. I tugged the stake free, but I didn't have a second to waste. Marika was coming for me.

As I spun to face her, a deafening crash rang out. A lightning strike plummeted straight for us. I leaped away as it struck the exact spot I had been standing. The force sent me flying straight at another tree and cracking it in two.

With a groan I stood on aching legs.

You must accept the light. Madam Dorothy's words blew through my ears with the wind. I fingered the amethyst pendant tied around my wrist, shivering at the memory of her cryptic telling of my future. For the first time ever her declaration made sense. I knew what I needed to do. The vision yesterday had painted a clear picture. At the time, I hadn't understood the vision or the strange man's will to get struck by lightning. I'd felt an unnerving sensation at my own close encounters with the storm-created force. That unnerving sensation was lost to me now. Right now, I knew what I felt. It was an unrelenting pull towards the storm, towards the power within the lightning's volatile strike.

"I'm over this crap," I spoke to myself, and I meant every word. I took off past the clearing and through the thicket.

"Amelia, stop!" Kendrick screamed, bounding through the trees after me.

I ignored his call, maneuvering through the incline of the thick, snowy forest, dodging, weaving, and jumping. I burst from the tree line, pulling to a stop at the edge of a rocky, plunging cliff.

"Come and get me!" I screamed up at the angry coiling clouds.

"No!" Kendrick's scream echoed. Other feet pounded along with his, but only he knew what I planned to do.

With my arms outstretched to the blackening sky, Kendrick sprinted past the tree line.

Too late.

A crack split the sky, blasting through my ears as a strike of lightning shot straight at me. It connected with my palms and surged through my body, turning every bone and muscle to liquid. Everything disappeared and I collapsed.

Somehow, even in this darkness, I wasn't unconscious. I could hear nearing steps. Smell the crispness of winter. Sense the storm receding.

I forced my lids open as Kendrick reached my side. He grabbed

my arm and recoiled as static shot free. I watched my arm in fascination as blue lightning danced over my skin.

Ty and Dorian met us on the cliff's edge then, and Ty dropped to
his knees, reaching out to take me into his arms. "Are you hurt?"

"Don't touch her!" Kendrick shoved him back. "She's a live
wire."

With shaky hands I pushed my body from the ground. "I think
I'm fine," I said, brushing myself off. The static rays had slowed and
now seemed to be sinking into my skin. They faded out, becoming
lighter and lighter until they all disappeared.

"What the hell happened?" Dorian asked as Marika joined us
along with Troy, who was carting Vanessa on his back.

I raised my eyebrows to Kendrick in question, hoping his
vampire knowledge would somehow explain this. He shrugged,
completely lost.

"The lightning," I said. "It's what I saw in the vision of the man.
I knew I needed to let it hit me."

"You could have gotten yourself killed." Ty's voice was rough as
he watched me, his face revealing the pure terror I'd just subjected
him to.

"I wasn't afraid." I recalled all the past close encounters. How
the lightning had reacted to my fear, anger, or a threat. It had always
been coming for me. "It was all leading to this. I knew I needed to
do it. I needed to seek it out."

"But why?" Vanessa asked, frowning at me like I'd gone totally
batshit.

"Aren't you the one who knows everything about creatures that
go bump in the night?" I quipped.

"I do. But *this*?" She waved her hands, indicating my entire
body. "It isn't in any book I've ever read. It's not normal."

"Nothing about any of you leeches is normal," Troy said.

"Amen," Marika added.

I ignored them both, feeling powerful and hollow at the same time. "What am I?"

Ty held his hand out for me to take. "Exactly what you're supposed to be," he said, now smiling.

I went to lace my fingers through his, feeling Kendrick's jealousy rise. But the moment our skin touched a spark shot from my palm into his hand.

"Ouch." Ty slapped his hand against his thigh. "That seriously hurt."

I saw the ghost of a smile on Kendrick's face and sensed his hope. Now a new obstacle stood between Ty and me ever getting too close. And I had brought this on myself.

"Fan-freaking-tastic."

WE RETURNED HOME LATE in the afternoon, the sun wilting behind snow-ladened clouds. The paved driveway and front steps were wet from rain and slippery as hell. I minded my step and stared down. My Vans reminded me of the pair I'd ditched before escaping the Armaya. Clogged with mud and drenched from melted snow. But at this point shoes were the least of my worries. Because after my reckless actions I was electric. Literally. A spark-conducting vampire with no control. Just what I needed.

Kendrick opened the front door, waiting for me to pass. "Amelia, you coming in?"

Hearing him through Red's song *Fight Inside*, I removed my earbuds. The sparks had died down since leaving Mt Major, enough that I wasn't worried about frying my iPod. So long as no one tried to touch me at the same time. During our journey home, I'd already gone through the whole album once. Thankfully Kendrick knew I was past the point of talking.

I peered up from my Vans to see him watching me. The pity on his face made me want to scream. Instead, I pulled my iPhone from my soggy jeans. "I'm gonna call Marcus again."

Since my vision of the mass slaughter, I'd called so many times. So far there hadn't been a single pick up. Not knowing was torture, and I'd tried not to dwell on the subject. Which was useless. Was Marcus even alive? Was his family? My worry and need to know trumped any new personal issues. It also made me feel like shit. How could I be so caught up in my own problems when other lives were at stake?

As the phone reached Marcus's voicemail, I hung up with a sound of frustration. "He's dead. Isn't he?"

"I'm sure he's fine," Kendrick said, going to embrace me. He stopped as sparks lit up my exposed arms like a glass plasma ball, the currents attracted to his nearing touch. He sighed. "Don't take this on. It's not your fault. You warned him. That's all you could do."

"Was it?"

As I edged away, Mom came out of her study into the foyer. Her phone slid back into her pants suit. "Oh good, you're home. I mean, no. Not good…" Her complexion was sheet paper white, her eyes glassy and bloodshot. She took small breaths, clearly holding back tears. "Where's Dorian?"

The sight of her sent morbid terror clawing at my throat. "Out at Vanessa's. Why?" I gulped. "Mom, what's wrong?"

She sat down on the padded bench beside the foyer table. Her back was posture-perfect straight, but her long fingers twined together, tight like a rope. "The Vladimirs…they're all dead."

The memory of spine-chilling screams rang through my ears.

The innocent girl, Marcus's cousin, choked to death at the top of the stairs, her vertebrae crushed like shells underfoot. His father's jugular ripped out, his lifeless body dropped like yesterday's trash. My legs gave out and my butt hit the marble. "Every one of them?"

"It was in Russia." She shook her head. "They were all there for a family reunion."

Kendrick sat beside her and unlocked her hands. He glanced at me, frowning as my entire body began shaking. "Ms. Lamont, was Marcus...was he...?"

"Marcus?" Her hand went to her heart, seeing the all over body quake and tears streaming down my face. "Oh, Amelia, your tutor. I'm sorry, no. I didn't mean to make you think..."

I stumbled forward, falling to my knees in front of her, careful not to touch. "Tell me. Please. Is he dead?"

"He arrived too late." Tenderness stole the despair from her face and she pushed my hair behind my ear. "He found them all...dead. He's the only Vladimir now in existence."

I fell back, cold marble coating my back while I just breathed. The whole Vladimir line had been exterminated, but Marcus was still alive. The relief at his survival over all the others, so many others, stung my heart with guilt.

I was so overwhelmed that I almost missed Mom saying, "The bodies are being flown to the Armaya for a royal funeral. Our flight leaves tonight."

WHEN THE COAST WAS CLEAR, meaning Mom had left to source suitable attire for the royal funeral, I stalked toward the backyard seeing red. I was beyond pissed. As usual, my stupid visions had failed. Showed me a future I couldn't change at the stake of others' lives. A whole line of royals extinguished, bar one sole survivor.

And now I had a new power. The ability to electrocute anyone and everyone. Yet another uncontrollable 'gift' that made me anything but normal. I was cursed.

My palms hit the terrace doors and static jolted them open like a bomb exploding. I screamed in frustration, the setting sun stinging my eyes. Snow no longer fell but it coated everything. Beautiful, pure…and natural. Everything I would never be.

I kicked at it with my Vans, the rubber buffering the built up current streaming to my toes. Crying out at the lack of release, I fell to my knees before the stone bench. Blue lightning danced along my arms, collecting at my clenched hands. The rest of my body tingled too, including my face and neck. A live wire, Kendrick had said. How true that was.

I was a freaking freak. A vampire with a power none had ever had before.

I screamed again and brought my fists down. As they met the stone the force cracked straight through, the voltage liquefying the snow coating.

"Amelia, stop."

With my vision blurred by tears, I shot up. Rage seared through my veins, lighting my skin on fire. "Leave. Me. Alone."

Kendrick came forward. "I'm not going anywhere."

Like a match setting off a firework, my hand shot up. My voice splintered with ice. "I said, leave me the hell alone!"

A blue streak shot from both my hands as I shoved Kendrick's shoulder. He spun, face-planting in the snow.

I rushed over, horrified at what I'd done, eyes glued to his convulsing body. As I went to reach out, my hands snapped back.

Constant static ran down my arms like waves, ready to let loose again. "Shit, Kendrick. Talk to me. Are you okay?"

"J-just. Ah, shit that hurts." With the tremors fleeing his body he rolled and used his hands to sit up. "You're a weapon."

I sank to my heels, imagining this happening anytime Ty and I tried to touch. "I'm a freaking live grenade with the pin out."

When Kendrick said nothing, I looked up. The prick was smiling. Freaking smiling. It was the same smile he'd had when I shocked Ty. Static surging, my hand rose in threat. "You better wipe that look off your face before I slap it off."

Kendrick's smile didn't falter. "Is that the way you talk to the friend who's going to help you control your newfound power?"

His words had my hand dropping to melt a hole in the snow. Teaching me to control the ability to electrocute people would remove the new obstacle standing between Ty and me getting closer. "Why would you do that?"

"I may not like Ty, but I still want what's best for you." He went to take my hand then thought better of it. "Besides, I want you to be safe. Learning to control this power, wherever it came from, will make you stronger."

"But—"

"You're not cursed," Kendrick cut in. "You've only looked at this gift from one angle. Only considered the *relationship* you have with Ty. Not the benefit of controlling your new power. Amelia, you could be a weapon."

I felt the truth of Kendrick's words in his unwavering stare. Even though he hated helping me remove what could potentially keep Ty and me physically apart, he truly wanted to help. "Okay, so what do we do?"

Kendrick walked over to the terrace, sheltered by a thatched roof twined with white-dusted vines. He pointed to a candle on the glass and wrought iron table. "Hold your hand out, palm facing down. But don't touch the candle. Concentrate on the energy and force it's power to your fingertips."

I followed his direction, my hand reaching for the object without touching it. As my fingers neared, a blue streak crawled across my skin, over my hand, and down my middle finger. While still attached it shot at the candle. It flashed again and again, trying to touch what was just out of its grasp. "Now what?"

"Touch it."

My fingers edged closer and closer, the blue electricity still reaching, wave after wave. I could sense the multitude of energy within my fingertips growing with every second. It was intense and powerful, unlike anything I had ever experienced before. The split second I touched the surface the built up power split from my hand. It plunged into the cylinder and shattered with an explosion of wax.

The thought of having almost done that to Kendrick had my heart racing. "I don't like this, Kendrick. It's too dangerous."

Kendrick crossed the stone pavers and disappeared through the terrace doors to the kitchen. A clink and clatter later he emerged with a stack of plates and glasses. "Not if you can learn to control it."

I reined in my growing despair. If I ever wanted to have any resemblance of a normal life, I needed to do this. No one else could. No one even knew why I'd been gifted this power, or where it had come from. Know-it-all Vanessa didn't even have an answer. I was one of a kind, a total freak of existence. Well, except for the guy in my vision who'd also been zapped. But who knew who or what that guy was, or if he was even alive. Or what his life had been like after the lightning strike.

On Kendrick's continued direction, I refocused the power to my fingertips and attempted to pull back the force as I connected with plate after plate. Each and every time the buildup was volatile, searing from my hand to obliterate its target. The terrace now resembled a bombsite. Porcelain, ceramic, and glass dotted the pavers and glass table, and fluff from exploded seat cushions swirled in the gentle twilight breeze.

Fed up and unable to hold back how pissed I'd grown, I stalked away. My inability to control this new shitty power ate away at me from the inside. Kendrick was in my head, trying to talk me down. But I didn't want to hear it. Instead, I kept on marching, skin tingling all over until I reached the biggest cherry tree in the backyard. In spring the tree was beautiful, decorated with pink blossoms and glossy cherries. Now it was a draping skeleton, its branches weighed down by snow.

Right now I hated the tree. Its natural beauty. Its predictability. Its strength. Standing ten feet back I concentrated all the pain, regret, despair, and anger down my arms and into my fingertips. So much built up that both my hands glowed blue.

With a scream and an instinctual whisper, I threw them forward. The blue propelled from my hands in streams, striking like lasers in the air until they connected with the solid trunk. A crack rang out, the tree splitting down the middle with a black scorch.

"Geez," Kendrick breathed, stumbling to a stop behind me. "Now that's a weapon."

Stunned, I fell back into the snow as my iPhone buzzed. I pulled it from my jeans and couldn't stop the tears that fell.

'We'll get through this. Just like everything else. U R my world. 4EVA Ty.'

APPREHENSION TIGHTENED MY CHEST, making it difficult to breathe.

Squeezed into a long, black slip of a dress and high-heeled shoes, we'd just been ushered through the Armaya's thick, iron-braced doors and into its Gothic foyer. It was 9PM and the long drapes were tied back to reveal pitch-black night beyond the soaring arched windows. Hundreds of candles decorated the space from sconces, their flames reflecting on the glass. Inside milled with royals, men dressed in sharp suits and women in decadent gowns and elaborate jewelry. The Armaya's local, less-prestigious residents crowded behind the pews. The atmosphere was more party-like than funeral. Except for the double row of shiny black coffins up front.

Mom caught sight of Caius standing before the dais and glided his way in her flowing black number. Dorian, all suited up, followed to keep an eye on her. As I tried to catch my breath, I scanned the crowd. Marcus had survived. Hadn't gotten there in time. I had to see him. Not that I knew how to apologize for my vision coming too late.

A smooth hand curved around my elbow. "It wasn't your fault," Kendrick whispered. "You can't control what you see and when you see things."

At his squeezing touch, I went to pull away. The static was already rising, and my emotions weren't helping. But separation wasn't necessary. Compliments of Vanessa and at Dorian's request, I wore a pair of satin gloves that stretched almost all the way up my arms. That was the reason Dorian hadn't come home with us. The insides were rubber lined, which with my below average body temperature weren't too uncomfortable. And a black shawl hid the rest of my exposed shoulders and neck.

I sighed, letting him lead me through the gatherers to our seats. Mom and Dorian were now positioned up front. Up on the dais before them, Caius was perched on his throne. He watched me like a snake preying on a mouse. I shivered. I hated being so close to him, but he wouldn't chance pulling a stunt here. Too many spectators.

We took our seats as the others rushed to theirs. Silence fell over the hall and the last royals took their places on their thrones. The one with Vladimir carved into the wood was glaringly vacant.

Caius rose, regal and strong, smoothing his suit before taking control of the gold-plated podium. "Today heralds a great loss to our race. The loss of our oldest crowned royal and all but one of his line…"

The speech went on, the words honest and heartfelt. Women sniffled, using black handkerchiefs to dot their eyes and save their makeup. The men offered consolation. If only they knew the truth. That Caius was somehow involved in this extermination. That he had damned vampires at his command.

I clutched my hands together as a ball of energy battered around beneath my ribs. I so wanted to do to Caius what I'd done to that tree.

Breathe. Rein it back. Kendrick's words flowed like a glacial gust over my burning insides.

Still that red returned to my sight, that fury that had to be unleashed. My clutched hands separated and I began to peel down my right glove.

A sudden shift in the air, like the quiet devastation in the wake of a tsunami, stopped me. My neck craned to see the open twenty-foot doors behind the pews. Organ music filled the air as Marcus stepped inside. He wore an all-white suit and his hands were above his head carrying…a solid gold casket. His teal-flecked gaze met mine, pain resonating from them before he resumed his blank forward stare.

Only living family members can carry in the coffin, Kendrick spoke somberly through the bond.

With every labored step forward my heart broke for him. His

expression was flat, unreadable, a strong facade masking any and all emotion. Tears pooled and I let them fall, not bothering to wipe them away.

Once Marcus had secured the coffin on a stand on the dais, he relieved Caius of the podium. His pale hands clutched the gold podium, fingers curled tight. "I stand before you all as the last living Vladimir. The only blood left to assume my father's throne. Lord Vladimir was a great ruler. And I will make him proud in death by filling his shoes and exceeding all expectations. Lord Vladimir lived a long and purposeful life." Marcus's hand swept across the rows of black coffins. "This is proven by the number of seeds his blood brought forth. Though they all now lay still alongside. However tragic, this will not be the end of his line. Nor will it be the end of his blood." His voice rose, becoming stronger and surging with determination. "Mine, now the last seed, will spread. It will create not dozens, but hundreds. The name Vladimir will never become one of those lost from the original twelve. On my father's death, I vow it!"

The crowd rose, clapping and cheering while I stared dumb-founded. This was my first ever vampire funeral, but it seemed so cold. So political.

My body started to tingle again, emotion at Marcus's strong words firing up the sparks. "Is that what—"

Words drowned in my throat, something else replacing it. Hunger and anticipation. Reality warped, strobing like a camera flash going off over and over. In the flashes I saw a stately house. A manor. My heart's beat was level and controlled. Just like my movements as I climbed the front steps. In the next flash my hand came out. No. Not mine. A man's. Young, unwrinkled flesh with a scar across the wrist. Then the wooden door swung open. Lord Vladimir stood on the other side, smiling. Welcoming me.

Another flash.

Now I had the old vampire pinned to the wall. The voice from my mouth was velvet and sinister. A promise that wouldn't back down. "End of your shelf life, old man." My mouth opened, fangs lengthened. Then it was all over.

I gasped as the Gothic hall slammed back into sharp focus. So much noise. So many people. Kendrick was holding me up, sitting back on the pew. Mom and Dorian were crowded around us. So was Caius.

"Amelia, sweetheart. Are you okay?"

Biting my lip, I kept my eyes down. Tasting my own blood helped a little, but it wasn't enough.

"She's low on blood," Kendrick said. "After the news, I don't think you drank any before we left."

"No," I croaked. I blinked away the red haze, knowing I needed to get out of here before I went primal. "I didn't."

Caius pushed past my mom, and in spite of Kendrick's glare, helped me up. With how badly I needed blood, I couldn't resist or ever remember how much I loathed him. "Take her to the kitchen. There's plenty there."

The genuine care in his voice surprised me. His stare wasn't quite hard, but it wasn't easy, either. It was somehow contemplative…maybe even regretful.

Holding me up by supporting a gloved arm, Kendrick led me away. Once out of the hall and down a dimly lit corridor he spoke. "Someone else led the attack on the Vladimirs."

My stomach felt like it was crammed with live bugs, crawling over each other without any space between. I remembered the murderer's steady beating heart. If only I'd seen his face. "Young. Male. A living vampire."

THE FOLLOWING NIGHT I stumbled into my dark bedroom and fell back onto the cloud of purple linen on my bed. It was midnight, and after the funeral, vision, and all the flights and driving to get home, I was bone-deep exhausted. Even the static in my body had receded. Rolling sideways I wriggled out of the slip dress. Then I lay back and peeled off the first full-arm glove. As I peeled off the second, something unstuck from my skin and fell onto the duvet.

I sat up straight as a board and my bedroom door swung open. The chandelier beamed to life, sending glossy rays across my wall of motorbike posters. Kendrick rushed forward and I snatched the duvet up to cover my black lace undies and bra. "Warning would be nice."

"I've seen plenty more than that." There was no comedy to his voice. Not even apology. All he saw was the small folded piece of paper with my name on the outside. "From Caius, I bet."

Kendrick plucked the note from my bed.

"No." I snatched it from his hands. The time for letting everyone protect me was far-gone. Time to toughen up. "I want to read it."

Ignoring my thumping heart and my shaking hands, I unfolded the note. A single message was scribbled across the paper. No name or signature. Still there was no doubt who had sent it. I knew my ex-uncles handwriting.

'I will not stop until I claim the power that is rightfully mine. You cannot hide.'

"Oh. My. God." My head became light and I leaned back on my arm. The hand holding the note kept the duvet covering my chest. A not so long ago memory teased the edges of my subconscious. The time I had slipped from the reality of Caius's office and seen Marcus compel my best friend to poison me. When I'd come to there had been a split second look of surprise on Caius's face. Because he'd seen my eyes change—blood-red whites and silvery irises—without tapping a vein. "Caius knows I have The Sight."

Before Kendrick could utter a word, Dorian shot into my bedroom. "I'll put you on speaker," he spoke into his mobile.

Kendrick slumped onto my bed, watching my brother. "What's going on?"

"My hard-working alchemist has figured something out," Dorian said pushing a button on his mobile.

"My?" I asked. Had I heard him right?

Dorian flushed. A sight I'd never seen in my life. "Ours, Ty's... whatever." He shook his head. "Go ahead, Vanessa. You're on."

"Okay, so after you lit up like a Christmas tree with that lightning strike, I went searching. My grandfather has some seriously old texts." In the background I could hear the slice of turning pages. "I'd seen the symbol years ago, but it was just a myth. I didn't even think about it when you asked. Not until two days ago."

Keeping covered, I snatched the phone from Dorian. "What symbol?"

"The one Caius used in his ritual when he drained your blood," Dorian answered. Judging from his answer and the look on his face, he knew what Vanessa was on about.

Kendrick went to place his hand on my shoulder but stopped. Blue sparks were dancing across my shoulders and down my arms. Instead he asked, "You know what it means?"

"Well, you already know what part of the symbol means. The circle with a crossed-through line is meant to take something," Vanessa recapped. "And the rest was the thing he was trying to steal."

My throat felt tight, my lungs punctured all over by spikes. There wasn't enough air. "The stepping stone he needed to save them." My voice emerged small as I remembered the jagged bolt centering the symbol. How could I not have puzzled this together before now? "Caius meant to steal my electric ability, before I even had it."

Dorian's voice was grim. "That means he knew you would get it."

Kendrick let a small spark shoot from my shoulder into his finger. "And that his experiments are probably the cause."

"Thanks, Vanessa." I hung up and handed Dorian the phone. "So does he need to steal my visions or my electricity?"

Resounding silence filled my purple room.

CHAPTER 25

*W*hen my eyelids cracked open I knew I'd woken in a dreamscape. The air was clean and crisp, blowing gently inside and curling the black curtains that framed an open window. Minimal light came from a ballooning moon beyond the wall of this room I'd never seen before. I turned to find Ty rising off the end of a king-sized bed that was swathed in black satin. "Missed you, beautiful."

It was the first time we'd seen each other since I'd shocked him with my new curse. Except Ty had never used this location before. I took a step closer but kept my distance, letting my curiosity override my battling nerves. "Where are we?"

Ty frowned at the space separating us. Then his lips curved seductively. "My bedroom."

"This is your room?" A long desk took up one wall. Topping it was a laptop and masses of stacked folders and books. The mantle above sported all his swimming trophies and medals. The opposite wall opened into a walk-in closet and personal bathroom. The remaining wall space was filled with objects and color. Weapons hung in a deadly collage in one area. The rest was taken up with pinned newspaper clippings, scribbled notes, and photographs.

I edged closer then froze. My heart skipped a beat. Near a clipping on unusual murders in Anchorage was a photograph. Pictured was a girl being led by a guy from a dark but multi-colored area. There was another of the same girl, pinning the solid guy against a brick wall. Then a third of her, crouched and crying crimson tears. The desolation and self-loathing that gripped her face was heartbreaking. I gulped, throat grating like sandpaper. The girl was me. And this is what Ty had seen that night. This is why he'd let me live.

"We usually take photos before making any moves."

I jumped at Ty's voice and spun. He was right behind me, and as usual, I hadn't even heard him move. I went to speak, but I didn't know what to say.

Ty's honey-glazed eyes stared into mine, cautious and guarded. "It's a precaution. In case your council has an issue with..." He stopped speaking and glanced away.

"With you killing one of theirs." I went to touch Ty and paused. Ty had been honest with everything he did and was trained to do. And I accepted him. All of him. "I guess it makes sense. I wouldn't want to be on The Council's bad side, either."

Ty's brows arched in surprise. Then he smiled. "I knew you'd understand. And for the record, I kept those photos because I didn't want to forget you, even when I didn't know who you were." He stretched his arms to wrap around me.

Alarm spiked my heart and I backed away until I hit the wall. Something sharp jabbed into my shoulder blade, cutting my skin. But I didn't let up. The last time I'd touched someone, Kendrick had been reduced to a convulsing lump. I didn't want to see what effect my power could have on Ty. "I can't control it," I whispered. "I don't want to hurt you."

Ty paused for a split second then took another step forward, then another. "I know you would never intentionally hurt me." That smile transformed his lips, making my toes tingle. "Amelia, you can't hurt me here. This is a dream."

All the alarm in me melted away like ice thawing after a frigid winter. Despite it all, the funeral, Marcus, being hunted, and Caius, I smiled. Ty was right. In a dreamscape I wasn't really in his room with him. I was asleep, at home. So any physical interaction was more like a seriously real figment rather than actual reality. I thought back to when I'd almost given myself to Ty while stuck at the Armaya. Heat dyed my face and neck. That encounter, imprinted on my heart and body, proved his words.

Unrestricted, I leaned into Ty, stretching on my toes to join our lips. Ty's were fiery and hungry, and his arms folded around my body. I melted into him, loving the familiarity of his scent, taste, and touch as warmth within me grew. It started at my core like a lit match. A ball of adolescent hormones ready to take over. Then it grew, snaking out in powerful streams that dominated every internal inch of my body. I kissed Ty harder, the warmth moving from within to coat my skin with the heat of the sun.

"Ouch!" Ty jolted away from me.

With my lids closed I hadn't seen the reason behind his knee-jerk reaction. But I felt it. What I thought was volcanic desire wasn't. Well not entirely. The warmth had shot without warning from my body to every inch of my cold skin. Rippled shockwaves had erupted to connect with every place Ty had been touching me. His fingers and hands pressed into my back. His arm encasing me. His chest against my own. And his lips and tongue lapping over mine. They had all caught the blow.

"Shit, I'm sorry." I went to touch him but restrained myself. "I didn't think…"

"I'm alright." Ty shook off the static. Then he peered up, his smile weak and filled with shattering realization. "I know you didn't mean to. And I don't know how…I mean, you shouldn't be able to."

I slumped onto Ty's bed, staring down at the receding blue sparks. "How could this happen?"

Ty dropped beside me, leaving almost a foot of air space separating us. My heart sank at the empty space and everything it meant. Reality or not, Ty couldn't touch me. And if I couldn't control this stupid power, he'd never touch or kiss me again.

"I don't know," Ty said, answering my question. "But I do know one thing. Your power isn't restricted by space."

I was about to ask what his words meant when I felt an uncontrollable pull from within. Ty and his room bled away from sight in a swirling blur, a spindle of black chaos that swallowed me like a sinkhole.

I fought the falling current, but it was no use. Everything was cold. Everything was dark. No shadow. No gray. No depth.

Without warning everything slowed. No longer in a dreamscape, it was clear I was far away from anywhere or anyone I knew. There was a damp, stale stink, and no air movement. Firelight grew around me, burning brightly from metal fire pits with carved flame edges. My heart almost stopped. Uneven walls caged me, made of rock and compacted dirt. I was underground in an enormous cavern.

But that wasn't the worst of it.

Standing before me was a league of damned vampires. They stood in uniform rows, crimson eyes staring at…me.

My first instinct was to run, to somehow get the hell out of dodge. And if that option failed, to fight. With everything I had.

Problem was my body refused to obey. Instead, I paced back and forth in front of soldier lines of horrifying creatures. Each glowing set of red eyes followed my every movement. But they didn't advance. They were watching, waiting for something.

Then a voice emerged from my throat. It was dagger sharp and lacked human emotion. It wasn't my voice, but one that sounded so unnervingly familiar. "The time is fast approaching for our plans to take effect. Our numbers must grow if we are to succeed."

The voice was male, deep and commanding, but still young. It struck fear through my heart. This voice wasn't Caius's. If only the vision would swing around so I could see his face.

"Why are you all still standing there!" he screamed at the damned. "You have your orders. Now go!"

He raised his hand, revealing a scar across his wrist as he pointed his index finger away. The same scar I'd seen on Lord Vladimir's murderer. The scar that belonged to a living vampire.

Feeling the challenge pouring from the eyes I saw from, every damned averted their glowing gaze and scurried away. At least forty of them disappeared into the darkness beyond the fire pits.

SUDDEN BLACKNESS ENVELOPED me and invisible cold hands held me down. One covered my mouth, muffling my scream. The damned had come and they were here to silence me. Terror clawed my soul, but I wasn't going down without a fight.

I thrashed against the force before thrusting my hands forward. Blinded, I felt rather than saw the thick blue bolts streaming from my palms into my attacker. They flew off me, colliding with a crunch across the room.

And then I was right there with them. No longer fearful, hunger squeezed my insides as the smell of spilled blood soared. Hands pushed me back and words I couldn't register hung in the air.

My live-wire body captured my prey and diffused their fight with shock after shock. As their lean body went limp, my fangs sank in deep, stealing what I needed.

Sudden pain sliced through me, setting my veins on fire. It was the same pain I'd experienced when Caius had drained me. Except this wasn't my pain. With continued voltage crippling his body and voice, it sure as hell didn't belong to a damned. And neither did the stolen blood flooding my mouth. Both belonged to Kendrick.

My lids flung open and my fangs broke free. I scrambled back, letting Kendrick's body drop in a heap.

Drywall debris littered the carpet around him, having cracked from the wall above where his body had collided. He was still convulsing, eyes and lips pinned shut, and wearing nothing but boxers.

"Kendrick!" I rushed to his side in panic. After experiencing the force of my new power on inanimate objects, I knew I'd hit him with enough spark to break something. If not blast him to pieces on the inside.

Kendrick struggled through the quakes, propping himself against the wall. He groaned as I reached out to touch him. "D-d-don't t-touch me."

I pulled back feeling rejected, which I deserved a thousand times over. I'd almost blasted my best friend to kingdom come and tapped his vein like a junkie. "What can I do?" *Shit*. "Are you okay?"

Through the bond I felt his pain. Every muscle in his body was seizing, and every movement was pure agony. But he wasn't hurt beyond repair. "I'll b-be okay. I'm j-just glad I'm not a p-pillow, or—"

My bedroom door swung open and my mom glided in, cotton

and lace PJs and all. She glanced from me to Kendrick, her neat bun bouncing as her head twisted. The worry on her face morphed into suspicion. Then she registered the body-slam dent in the drywall and the scarlet staining Kendrick's neck. "What in God's name is going on?"

I backed up as she came forward, not wanting to touch her. The risk of electrocuting her was too great. And she had no idea about my power. On top of that I could smell her blood. "It was an accident."

"What was?" She paused, studying me. Then she frowned. "Kendrick, why are you in Amelia's room at this hour?"

I realized that although it looked like I'd just played a round of WWF on Kendrick, Mom was concerned about something else entirely. She actually thought something was going on between us.

"You think…" My brain flipped a does-not-compute. Mom had always been easy going whenever Kendrick had slept over in the past. She hadn't even had a problem with him sleeping in my bed after Ty and I broke up. "It's not like that. And since when do you care?"

It's not that ridiculous, Kendrick's voice echoed in my mind. *Or do I repulse you that much?*

I blinked and took a deep breath. *You know that's not what I meant.*

"You're not children anymore," Mom answered. "Plus I've noticed a change in your friendship since you got back from the Armaya. You're closer to each other than before. Due to that, we'll need to discuss house rules."

Dorian appeared through the door in nothing but flannel bottoms. He held up two bottles of blood. "Guessing you both need this." He handed a bottle to Kendrick. Then he threw one to me.

I fumbled with it, expecting the glass to shatter with a bolt of lightning. Except nothing happened. Not even a dance of blue down my arm. I carefully emptied the bottle while looking at my brother. "How'd you know?"

"Powers of deduction," Dorian said with a shrug, meaning he'd heard the ruckus and guessed.

"Will someone explain to me what is going on here?" Mom planted her hands on her hips. "Amelia?"

I needed to tell her something. And after what I'd seen, keeping this secret was no longer an option. The Council needed to be warned. I kicked at the drywall debris with my bare feet. "I had a vision."

Mom didn't flinch. Her face didn't show any sign of shock or surprise. Her mouth parted, hanging open for a moment before she spoke. "It was probably a bad dream."

"They're not dreams," Dorian said. "I've seen it."

"So have I," Kendrick added, his gaze narrowing at my mom. "And how would that be possible, Ms. Lamont? Aren't royals the only vampires who can develop elemental powers?"

My mom froze, her gaze averting and hand moving over her heart. A second later her control returned. "You are right, Kendrick. Only royals can have these gifts."

"So how can we have them?" Dorian asked.

"We?" Mom's eyes became glassy and a tear rolled down her cheek. "You have one, too?"

Dorian nodded and lifted a finger towards our mom's face, not quite touching her. The tear that was at her jawline pulled free, floating to connect with Dorian's extended finger. He shrugged. "Water."

Mom's face turned blank and her voice was a whisper. "When did this all happen?"

Instead of telling her about the many visions I'd had before knowing what they were, I settled for the one that was most shocking and relevant. "I had a vision after Caius took you to that council meeting last week." It was a partial lie. And I wasn't about to tell her it'd happened while I was spying on that council meeting. "I saw Lord Vladimir and his family...slaughtered."

Mom's face turned grim and her knees gave out before she caught herself and slid down the wall. "Oh no." Her voice was so quiet, so distraught as her tearing eyes peered up. "Amelia, all those lives lost. Why didn't you tell anyone?"

"I did!" I blurted.

"She called Marcus straight away," Kendrick said, now able to get to his feet. "But he couldn't get hold of Lord Vladimir. Then when he arrived in Russia it was already too late."

Mom shook her head in her hands. "Marcus must be so distraught. I knew he found them, all of them. But to have known about the threat beforehand..."

"Sis, what did you see tonight?" Dorian asked.

The room fell silent and Kendrick moved to my side, remaining far enough away to ward against any further shocks. The blood had repaired the damage from the shock and my bite, but he was still weak.

I crossed to the arched window and pushed open the panes. Fresh air poured in, clearing the collective blood in the air and ruffling my posters. I remembered the dank stink of clay and all those watching, obedient red eyes. "I saw the damned. Whole lines of them." I shivered and clutched my own elbows. "A vampire is leading them. He's instructing them to build their numbers in preparation."

"So they are back. The others were right." Mom seemed resigned as she got up off the floor and sat on my bed, clutching a sequined throw pillow. "Preparation for what?"

I stared up at the glowing moon. I felt unequipped and unworthy of being the bearer of these horrible fortunes. Especially when I couldn't change the futures I saw. "I don't know. But I can feel it in my bones. Something bad is coming."

Mom bit her nails, staring ahead at nothing in particular. Sudden sadness welled in her eyes as they met me at the window. "My beautiful daughter. The Oracle." She sighed, long and slow. "I did everything I could to protect you. To keep you from this world. Now I must stand aside. The decision is yours, Amelia. I will not force you either way."

"The decision?" Dorian leaned against the doorjamb.

"Whether to come out to The Council," Kendrick answered. "Being the Oracle comes with expectations. There hasn't been one for centuries."

I didn't know what these expectations were. And with what I did know, they didn't matter. Lives were at stake. Besides, The Council wouldn't just accept an anonymous warning. I needed to come forward. I needed to make them all believe.

Mom glided over with a forced smile and went to touch my shoulder. I backed away before her flesh could connect with mine. She sighed, looking truly upset as tears flooded her silver-blue eyes. "A weight of responsibility accompanies such a rare gift, sweetheart. You don't have to decide now. Take your time—"

"No. My mind's made up." I gulped at the choking, metallic wave rising up my throat. "I won't have innocent lives on my hands. The Council must be warned."

Tears spilled down Mom's face. "So it shall be. I'll call a special meeting for tomorrow. Though I'll need to get clearance from Caius."

I moved from the window as Mom headed for the door after

Kendrick and Dorian. With limited time until tomorrow's meeting, I desperately needed to be alone.

As the door swung closed, something flew in through my open window.

"Amelia. Oh my God. You're okay."

I heard Ty's worried voice a split second before I picked up his rich aroma. My bedroom door flung back open and my mom shot right back in. "What is he doing here?" Her gaze skewered Ty like a bug on a pin.

I gulped and Ty froze. Kendrick and Dorian didn't come back in, but a voice spoke in my head. *Lie. Don't tell her about the dreamscape.*

With everything that had happened I'd almost forgotten our dreamscape and being ripped from his control by my latest vision. That wasn't supposed to be possible. Ty held all power in a dream-scape, able to trap whoever he'd captured while asleep. But nothing about tonight's dream had been normal. Thinking about it all left a blanket of dark hopelessness weighing me down, like bricks under-water. This vision had forced me from Ty's dream and into someone else's body. And not Caius's. My heart felt as if it had been packed with dry ice. Caius had orchestrated the attack on the boat, and also the attempt on Kendrick and Dorian's lives at the snow. But was someone else pulling the strings? Was someone else targeting us, too?

I shook off the foreboding and stepped between Mom and Ty. "Ty, I'm okay. And Mom, we were talking on the phone earlier when I blacked out with the vision."

"You had a vision?" Ty said at the same time Mom muttered, "On the phone. Sure."

"Yeah." I glanced away from Ty, remembering how deep my fangs had plunged into Kendrick's neck. Feeling my guilt like a neon sign over my face, I stared at my bedside table. The quarter eaten block of chocolate that I'd devoured after getting Caius's note was still there. I wanted to steal a piece now. Though I knew it wouldn't lift this suffocating feeling in my chest. I'd already broken our promise to drink from Ty alone. "That's what forced me away. Someone else is commanding the damned. They're growing their numbers."

"Amelia has made a decision," my mom said, steel in her voice. "One that may force her to reside at The Council here in Portsmouth, or maybe even the Armaya. Her school and human life will be over."

So that was one expectation of being the Oracle.

"Amelia?" Ty didn't move from the arched window, but the need to be closer was written all over him. "What is she talking about?"

Seeing the worry in Ty's face was like a knife to the heart. The last thing I wanted to do was hurt him. But I couldn't change my mind now. I'd seen too much. Being selfish and letting vampires die wasn't an option. No matter how much every part of my body ached at what I was about to say.

I sank onto my bed, pulling the purple comforter over my knees. "I'm the Oracle." Saying the word out loud sent shivers down my spine. How was I supposed to carry the weight of such a rare obligation? How was I supposed to live without Ty if they forced me away? "Tomorrow Mom's taking me to the council meeting. And I'm...I'm revealing my visions."

As Ty stared at me dumbfounded, Mom spoke. "Five minutes alone. Then he's to be gone." Her hard look softened at me. "Given your decision, this may well be one of your last encounters."

When the door eased shut behind her, Ty stumbled forward. He fell to his knees, hands fisting the duvet on either side of me. "Amelia, no. Don't do this. You don't have to—"

"But I do." I held up a hand to cup his face, stopping an inch away as the sparks returned. Tears blurred my vision and my voice cracked. It felt like I was drowning, sinking lower and lower into a murky swamp. "I hate this. It's killing me." I clutched the amulet to my heart. "I won't have blood on my hands, I can't. If it were you," I said as Ty began to argue, "could you choose me if others would die because of it? Could you turn your back on who you are?"

Ty nodded and stood, his expression vacant. "No, I guess I couldn't." He smiled a dreadful, hopeless smile. "This isn't the end of us. They can't chain you inside twenty-four/seven, here or at the Armaya. We will see each other again."

The gleaming hope in his eyes made me suspicious. "Promise me you'll stay away tomorrow. That you won't do anything reckless."

When Ty didn't say anything I balled my hands into fists. "Please Ty, I can't risk you. I can't lose you."

"You never could." Ty threw one leg over the windowsill and faked a smile. "At the very least I'll see you in your dreams."

Then he was gone, nothing but moonlight replacing the now voided place on my window. And my heart.

I fell back onto my bed, curled my body into a ball and squeezed my eyes shut. "What have I done?"

CHAPTER 26

I fiddled with my long, rubber-lined gloves as I followed after Mom with Kendrick. My chest felt like it was trapped in a vice; my lungs balloons that were about to burst. This was it. The big reveal. After today my whole world would change, again. *Ty.* I could still see his face, the pain that had scarred his features at the possibility of never seeing me again. Because despite his encouraging words, he knew this could be the beginning of the end.

Kendrick nudged me. "I'm right here. Everything'll be fine. And you will see him again. I won't let them make you a prisoner."

Mom stalled before two armed guards who stood blocking the soaring entrance. They both dipped their heads at Kendrick. "Lord Baldassare." They looked to my mom in question, flicking glances at me. One rested a hand on the hilt of his sword.

"Miss Amelia Lamont." Poise and authority oozed from Mom's straight posture. "Lord Bathory has granted her entry for today."

After Mom's call to Caius, she'd managed to get him to agree to let me join this meeting. Although without revealing the why of it, Dorian wasn't included in that invitation.

The guards eyed me. After a long silent moment one nodded. "As the Lord commands."

As we passed, their heads turned to follow as we entered the large open hall of the Portsmouth Council. The pitched cathedral windows around the hall were tinted dark, letting the smallest amount of twilight through. Otherwise the room was the same as I remembered. Candles illuminated the wrought iron chandelier, and the massive marble table was packed with council members. This time there were more thrones around the table. A few lower ranked council members stood to make room for the growing group of royals. Caius headed the table, opposed by Uriel and flanked by Kendrick's mom, Serafina. She nodded when she saw her son, but made no other move to greet him.

At our entrance, Uriel's azure-blue focus shifted from the debating crowd. "Lamayli?" Her gaze shifted over me, speculative and curious. "What is this?"

Mom raised a hand for us to stop as she fronted the table. "I know this is unorthodox, but I have not brought her here without good cause."

Caius traveled around the slab of marble, gentle arms enfolding my mom. My stomach churned as his hand ran up and down her back before holding her at arm's length. He ushered a council member from the other seat beside his throne. Now noticing Kendrick and me, every set of eyes in the room slid from my mom to us. Distrust and curiosity were plain in their expressions.

"Please sit, Lamayli, and enlighten us on why your daughter is present." Caius's voice was gentle but held a distinct edge. "After your insistence last night, I am eager to understand your motives."

Mom took her position, letting her voice ring out strong and steady. "The damned, as some of us suspected, *have* returned."

Uproar exploded, council members and royals divided in belief and flat-out denial.

Caius's hands spread wide, palms down. The simple and soundless motion instantly silenced the room. "This bickering will get us nowhere. Now Lamayli, would you explain what brought you to this belief?"

Mom straightened her spine and drew back her shoulders with a nod. Then she eyed each council member. "We know with certainty that the damned have returned." Again, hushed words of venom struck out while others nodded in concurrence. "An army is being built to wage war against us. One among our own kind commands them."

"How do you come to know this?" Serafina's sharp voice cut like a knife, eyes narrowing at my mom.

Kendrick stiffened beside me, and I took his hand, the rubber glove shielding the static at my fingertips. After spending the early hours of the morning practicing how not to blow things up, I had gotten a slight handle on it. But this was an emotionally charged room, and it seemed that raw emotion fueled my sparks. Being at The Council and with this audience, the last thing I wanted was to put on an electrical show. So bravery without my special gloves was not an option, yet.

"Because you've seen it."

I scanned for the voice that'd spoken to find Uriel staring at me. Everyone in the room followed her line of sight and now watched me with mixed expressions of confusion and contempt. I twitched uncomfortably. Their piercing gazes made me feel like a frog ready to be sliced in biology.

"You," she continued, finger pointing straight at me. "Have been gifted by life and death, kissed by the power of spirit and touched by The Sight."

My stomach coiled, threatening to make me puke. I freed my hand from Kendrick's and forced myself to nod. The room fell into deafening silence, leaving my rapid-beating heart throbbing through my ears. "I—I have visions." My voice was a quiet croak. I wanted to slap myself. I sounded weak and unsure. Why would they believe anything I had to say?

"That's impossible," a middle-aged man retorted. The same one I'd seen when spying on the council meeting. "She's not even a Pure Blood."

"We have not been blessed with the power of an Oracle for centuries," Serafina added.

"We have not lost God's favor," a white-haired, elderly woman almost sang. Her words of praise were shunned by sharp whispers demanding proof.

It's okay, Kendrick sent. His fingers laced through my gloved ones and squeezed. The contact didn't make me feel any better. Because all I could think was how they wanted exactly what I couldn't give them. Proof.

The argumentative chatter grew louder, everyone becoming more distressed with every passing second. Then loud clapping rose behind us. The crowd fell silent, their gazes diverting. I turned too.

Marcus strolled in through the tall wooden doors, casually dressed in torn jeans and an open collared shirt. A haughty smile lit his face as he stood beside me, occupying the space opposite Kendrick. "So glad that we can act civilized amongst ourselves. Especially when such a volatile threat is knocking on our door."

"Marcus, what are you doing here?" I ran a gloved hand down his forearm, so badly wanting to wrap my arms around him. My warning hadn't been able to save his family and the guilt was eating me alive. "Are you okay?"

"I'm fine." Marcus sighed, but his expression remained strong under the eyes of everyone around the table. "Just keeping myself busy." His sharp focus traveled to the others. "You want proof she's the Oracle?"

The crowd murmured. Some demanded this so-called proof while others stated I had none to offer.

"What are you doing?" I spoke under my breath.

He smiled again, white teeth gleaming in the chandelier's light. "Trust me." He eyed everyone waiting and watching around the table. "The proof we need—those of you who have taken their ancestral knowledge with the importance it deserves should know— will be imprinted on her flesh."

With blurred movement Marcus bit into his wrist and pressed the punctures to my mouth. His forceful free hand found my neck, locking my lips against his flesh. Breath flooded my lungs in surprise and fear. But the voltage that I'd expected to floor Marcus didn't. Instead, his touch absorbed the power, relieving my skin of further rearing static.

Then all I tasted was his blood. That rich, peppery nectar that was distinct and individual. So similar, yet so different to Kendrick's.

As the council hall and its members faded away, Marcus's wrist tore from my lips. His hand flung my long hair over my shoulder. Then his other hand squeezed, turning my back to the now gaping crowd. "See," he said with an edge of triumph. "The Sight marks her flesh."

Through Kendrick's wide eyes I could see what everyone else could. A liquid-like, silver filigree glistened from the back of my neck. It shimmered like it was set under floodlights, not the flickering flames from chandelier candles. The tattooed picture revealed a bunch of swirls surrounding an eye. The same eye I'd seen in the elemental book Marcus had shown me at the Armaya.

My breath caught. It was...*beautiful*.

Surprised words rose around the hall, echoing through the thick columns that held up the second level balcony and pitched ceiling. Some were of disbelief, others of muted acceptance. Marcus's grip on my neck released and he spun me back to the stunned faces of everyone around the table. "Told you you were one of us," he whispered in my ear.

Caius rose from his throne and made his way to me with arms outstretched. "My dear niece." His voice was warm, a total mismatch to the disgruntled expression that darkened his face.

My body tensed, the pressure inside me building to volatile limits. If I could have done anything to stop him from touching me, I would have. But every set of eyes was focused on us, both skeptical and adoring.

Shit, shit, shit.

Caius's arms closed around me, and I held my breath. The electricity inside my body surged from my heart in veiny sparks. It didn't run along my exposed skin, but instead shot from inside to every part of me that he touched.

Caius jerked back ever so slightly, eyes wide and lips frowning. Now he knew. The power he'd engineered me for resided in my bones.

A controlled mask reset his wrinkled features as he turned back to the crowd. "Our Oracle, Miss Amelia Lamont."

As the awestruck council members began to clap, a commotion sounded from outside. I whirled on the spot to see the two guards. One guard was hauling someone through the tall open doors. The other had his sword pointed at the guy's back.

I blinked, unable to believe my eyes. Their hands were clenched around the biceps of someone I knew. My throat choked closed in disbelief at the boy being thrust forward.

Kendrick? The fight and raw determination across his face were familiar. But I'd never seen my best friend look like that. The Kendrick who still stood beside me mirrored my frozen shock.

"My Lord, he was outside." The guard with his sword aimed addressed Caius with a nod. "Though we already saw him enter the hall, and not leave."

Kendrick's double growled, struggling against the guards' vice-hard grips. Veins along his neck and arms popped against his pale skin. As he freed one arm, two more guards—ones I hadn't even noticed—rushed in from the back of the hall. They joined the restraining force, locking hands behind Kendrick's double's back and immobilizing his legs. The sword now lay kissing the flesh at his jugular.

Caius curled his fingers around the arm of the Kendrick beside me. Then he thrust him forward to face his double. "One of you is an intruder. Reveal your true form or you will both be sentenced for plotting against The Council."

Serafina vaulted to Caius's side, losing her cold control. "No, Kendrick would never." She panned back and forth between the two, bewilderment raging through her silver-blue eyes. She had no idea who the real Kendrick was, either.

But I did.

Ignoring the crawling of my skin at being so close to my murderer, I stepped forward. I took the hand of the Kendrick who had been standing beside me. The same Kendrick I'd arrived with. The same one's eyes I'd seen through when my tattoo was revealed. "This is the real Kendrick."

As the words left my mouth, fear crushed my heart. Squeezing tension threatened to burst the muscle. I pressed the amulet hidden beneath my blouse's neckline to my chest. I knew who the other boy was.

"No." The ghostly whisper of my voice barely registered through the bickering council noise. "You said you'd stay away."

Gold rippled across the boy's sad, silver eyes. Then his body began to shake, trembling and blurring. A nail gun of small snaps erupted and pain contorted his pale face. Black hair replaced golden brown, and growing muscles bulged under his once loose jeans and shirt as he morphed back to his true form. "Sorry."

Caius's smile was wicked and triumphant. "Lycan." He hissed the word through fully extended fangs. "Arrest him!"

The room jumped into chaos, council members hissing and leaping away. More guards rushed in from every angle, responding to the threat. In a matter of seconds they had their intruder incapacitated. Ty struggled as chains whipped out, locking around his wrists and ankles.

Tears muddied my sight as my mom came to Caius's side. "Caius, please," I begged. "Let him go."

Caius's smile broadened. "The wolves know our laws, and he was trespassing. I love you, Amelia." A fire grew in the pit of my stomach at his insincere words. "But I will not bestow special treatment onto him. Instead, I urge you to exhibit some restraint, lest you disgrace yourself as our Oracle."

I lifted my tear-filled eyes to my mom. "You know he's not a spy. Mom, please. Do something."

She shook her head, deep sadness cutting her lineless face. "It's not in my power. He's trespassed on council land. He's our enemy. I'm so sorry, sweetheart."

I raked my eyes over the room, searching for an escape route. There had to be some way to get us out of here alive. But there were so many guards, not just restraining Ty who continued to struggle behind me, but around the entire room, at every door and pitched window. There was no way out.

I glared at Caius, fists clenching as electricity welled beneath my gloves. "What will you do to him?"

"He will be imprisoned…until the execution."

My blood ran cold as death and I staggered. Kendrick's hand shot out to catch me, a static shock above the cover of my glove forcing him to jerk away. Instead, Marcus was the one to break my fall, pulling me up before I hit the ground. The static was again absorbed with his touch. But I couldn't think about how or why.

Staring at my former uncle, I gritted my teeth. "When?"

The prick waved a dismissive hand and the guards began hauling Ty away, swords forcing him on. "Your coronation as Oracle will commence during the next full moon. As is custom. The execution will be carried out afterward."

Dazed, I watched as Ty was dragged around a bend down the hallway. My stomach seized and I fought back the rising urge to vomit. The moon would be full in three night's time. That was all that separated Ty from death.

Caius turned back to the council members, calming their still outraged remarks. He began talking in a deep, level voice, bringing continuity back to the meeting and planning out the details for my coronation.

I heard none of it. My heart and mind felt a million miles away. My body was numb and detached.

Marcus lifted me into his arms and walked out the main doors. Kendrick remained tight behind us. "Don't worry," Marcus whispered into my ear. "He won't be executed. I have a plan."

"I wouldn't dream of calling you my friend, but—" I hesitated into my iPhone's speaker, managing to rein in the static without my gloves. "But, thank you." I hung up and shoved the phone into my hoodie. "It's done."

We were in the rec room upstairs and Dorian was perched on the edge of the leather couch in suspense. Beside him Kendrick's head was twisted over his shoulder, watching as I paced.

Marcus was lounged on an armchair. His body was relaxed, but his face was serious as hell. "Good. Now—"

"Marcus, you don't have to do this," I said, unable to stop pacing. "I mean, I appreciate it. I do. But you shouldn't be burdened with helping me save Ty."

Marcus's gaze turned vacant, staring into space. Was he remembering the moment he found his father, throat torn out in the entry of the Vladimir manor? He shook himself and clenched his jaw. "Amelia, I want to do this. I need to."

There was no talking him out of this. And really, I didn't want to. If we were going to save Ty, I needed his help. "Fine." I leaped over the back of the other armchair, needing to sit before my legs gave out.

Marcus clapped his hands together, all business as he turned to Dorian and Kendrick. "Now, Dorian, you'll be expected to arrive with your mother for the coronation, but once you've been seen by—"

"That SOB Caius," Dorian cut in.

Marcus nodded. "You'll need to slip out, without being noticed. You're our best bet for compelling the guards if needed. I'd go myself, but I have to witness the event from the Vladimir's throne on stage."

Kendrick slumped back into the couch, slinging his arms over his chest. He already knew his role, and he wasn't happy about it. "I still don't see why I can't go with Amelia to get Ty."

"You know why," I said before Marcus could reply. "You need to be our visual link to the ceremony."

"Our warning signal if the guards decide to come and get Ty early," Dorian added.

"And," Marcus cut in. "You need to hold up the facade that everything is as it should be. As long as Amelia escapes with Ty, and Dorian, you get back before the completion of the coronation, you'll all have an alibi. Caius won't be able to pin Ty's escape on any of you."

"And if we get caught?" My voice sounded like a grim shadow of the dread swimming through my veins.

Marcus grasped my hand and squeezed. "I won't let that happen."

Even though it wasn't Ty or even Kendrick, having someone touch my bare skin, even just my hand, felt nice.

Marcus came closer, his next words whispered into my ear. "I would never let any harm come to you, my—Amelia."

A sudden flame of irritation flared up my neck. Unbridled jealousy streamed from Kendrick. His eyes were fixed like flesh-burning lasers on our joined hands. I reared, about to hit him with a look that said, *c'mon, you're jealous of Marcus too*? Before I could, an eerily light tingling warmed my heart. Then the sensation split down the length of my body. My eyes rolled back and my knees gave out.

When my lids snapped open, the scene before me sent splintering ice through my veins. There was movement and shouting all around. A sound like hissing snakes.

Terror swarmed my bones. The damned. They were everywhere. Chairs were upended and black and red slicked the ground. The ground where lifeless bodies lay, cooling on the marble. They were slaughtering every vampire in sight.

A blunt force connected with my chest and I fell to my knees. My lungs ached and my breath was hard and fast.

Around me the background became a hazy rush like I was centered on a spindle. The only thing I now saw was Ty. He was across the room and snarling, fully transformed into a towering black wolf. Bunching lines creased his muzzle, bearing sharp teeth that dripped glossy black.

Before him was Caius, brandishing a silver sword that he had trained at Ty. He traced an arc with the blade, slicing through the pungent air. Its thickness was drenched with freshly spilled blood. There was another scent too. It was vile and decomposing. In any other circumstance it would have forced me to retch. But not now. I couldn't crumble with the scene before me.

Tacky red oozed from wide gashes across Ty's shoulders, legs, and back. He grunted and snarled as he weaved out of the blade's path. Then he lunged back to snap at Caius. But something was wrong, even more than everything I could see. Ty was tired. His movements had become less precise and more desperate. Every gliding arc of Caius's sword now afforded closer calls with Ty's flesh.

A surge of fear, stronger and more compelling than any I had ever experienced, had my pulse pounding through my ears. The ice in my veins thawed with a sudden surge of adrenaline. My legs began hammering without order, pounding the red and black slicked ground. I darted around and over figures—faceless people—warring around me.

Then, like a pair of tightening hands inside my chest cavity, the air was squeezed from my lungs. Everything became black. A complete body spasm shot me from the vision.

I gasped, and something pressed against my lips. Broken flesh spilled blood into my mouth. Against my will my fangs unsheathed, biting down, clamping the source like a bear trap.

"You're okay. I've got you." Marcus's lips brushed against my ear.

As my mind caught up to reality, I could feel his supporting arm, cradling me against his trembling chest. A streak of anger pierced my soul, too. I retracted my fangs, blinking against light-blinding starbursts while boiling jealousy seared up my throat.

A new set of arms tore me from Marcus's hold. "I'll take it from here." Kendrick's tone was sharp, betraying his not so latent feelings for me.

I glared up at him. How could he be possessive after what I'd just seen? "Really?"

Kendrick shrugged, his expression innocent. "What?"

"Let me down."

Before I could wriggle out of his arms, simultaneous sparks erupted from my body. Kendrick's arms shot away from me, forced by the power, and I fell. But this time no one caught me. Instead, I used Ty's training, twisting my body to plant my feet as I landed in a crouch. I stood slowly, limbs and mind still recovering as I slid back onto the armchair.

Marcus ran a finger along his healing wrist. Another person I'd used. And another time I'd broken my promise to Ty. "Why did you do that? Bottled would have been fine."

Marcus half laughed. "You're the Oracle. Bottled human blood may have cut it before, but not anymore. Once your residence is arranged, I'm sure they'll assign you a personal donor."

I stared, shocked and speechless. I wouldn't agree to it. They couldn't make me.

"Back to the fire," Dorian cut in, knowing the look on my face meant I wanted to change the subject. "So, what did you see, sis?"

Marcus seemed to flinch at the interruption. Then he knelt before me. His face was riddled with worry as he pressed a hand against my knee. "Go on."

I breathed in and out, working through the horrifying vision and feeling the shock of what I'd seen. Kendrick was already sifting through my thoughts while the others waited. I cleared my throat. "The damned are coming. It's going to happen at the Portsmouth Council."

"The night of your coronation?" Dorian guessed.

"It has to be," Kendrick answered for me, his jealousy for Marcus now replaced by fear. "The place was packed."

"So much blood…it was everywhere." I coughed, remembering the other pungent smell that had thickened the air. Damned blood. "Caius will stand against us all. I saw him."

"Then we all need to get out straight after your coronation," Kendrick spoke the words I was thinking. "Drug our moms and cart them out if need be. But it has to be done before the guards are summoned to retrieve Ty for the execution."

"Why before?" Dorian questioned.

"Because Ty was there," I said, bile exploding up my throat like little live grenades.

"And the guards won't be sent to retrieve him until you're named," Marcus said, looking at me.

"Exactly," Kendrick and I chimed in unison.

Then I added, "We can't mess this up." *Ty's life depends on it,* was my internal thought to Kendrick. "And we need to go back to The Council and force them to listen. They need to know what's coming for them, all of them."

"That could force them to postpone the coronation." Kendrick slid back onto the couch, his mind reeling with my thoughts.

"As well as the execution," I finished, feeling a gentle current of hope.

Dorian slapped his hands together. "Oh, I see. If the council grounds are evacuated, it'll be easier to break Ty out."

"Unless they decide to extradite him back to the Armaya," Marcus, being the voice of reason, spoke up. At my worried look he waved me off. "But I wouldn't expect them to. They'll have much more pressing issues to contend with than moving a prisoner when they don't care if he lives or dies."

I gulped at that, imagining the damned streaming in while we made our escape. We knew from my vision when the damned would come. But could alerting The Council alter their time of attack? There was no way to know, and even with the risk, this way was our best option.

Feeling like I was suddenly desperate for air, I sucked in a deep breath. My lungs ached in response. "Let's hope everything goes to plan."

Kendrick scrubbed a hand down his face. "What if it doesn't?"

I cracked my knuckles. The release did nothing to loosen the tension stiffening my bones. It also had no effect on the rising vengeance that had begun to throb through my veins. "We still have plan B."

CHAPTER 27

*I*n twenty minutes I'd fled the rec room, suburbia, and miles of thick forest. Still no matter how fast or far I ran, I couldn't escape the mounting shit storm that my life was becoming. The words *It's all over* by Three Days Grace pumping through my earbuds only fed my rising hate. Because I was just like a junkie. Whether it was my animalistic need for blood, being the freaking Oracle, or turning into a human lightning rod, everything I touched turned to shit. I was continually endangering not only my own life, but also everyone's I loved.

Kendrick was wrong. I was cursed.

Breaking through the tree line, I fell to my knees in crunching snow and screamed into the darkness of early night. A rustle of tree leaves from behind alerted me to Kendrick's arrival, but he had the good sense to butt out. Right now I needed to let off steam. Over-bubbling, poison pots of the stuff. And anyone who got in my way was going to fry.

With my entire body shaking with the need to release, I flung out my whip. It cracked loud as thunder in the air, my gloves relinquishing the voltage from its silver links. Again and again, I flicked the weapon out, hitting air and mulching up dirt and snow. But it wasn't helping. I needed to cause irrevocable damage, like the damage I felt in my tearing internals. Like the damage I'd brought upon Ty.

I made for a copse. The young clustering trees vibrated as if they quaked in fear with the gusty wind. My arm drew back, then surged the whip forward. The silver spikes flared out mid-air, biting into the saplings and capturing them in a bear hug of silver. I yanked back and its grip constricted, decapitating the trees halfway up. The destruction didn't relieve my pain, my heartache, or my fear. How could it? If we couldn't convince The Council, there'd be a battle to the death. Damned against vampire. Good versus evil.

I thought of Ty and the moment he'd been chained and dragged away. If my vision came true, he'd be there too, wolf form and all. Battling for survival against my sorry excuse for an uncle.

"We'll get him out." Kendrick was now behind me, far enough back to escape a lash from my whip. "Whatever happens, I promise you that."

Even with his reassurance and belief, rage suffocated me like plastic blocking my airway. "Don't make promises you can't keep."

The fight inside me was building, voltage swarming into dangerous pockets beneath my skin. It grew like wildfire, coalescing into a human-shaped bomb ready to explode. With my flesh burning up like hot coals, I tore off my gloves. Fire streamed down my arm. A thick blue fork plunged into the whip as I struck at the largest maple in sight. The hit cracked straight through the trunk, blue veins streaming from the whip's speared tip down the wood. A shockwave ricocheted off the destroyed tree, hitting our bodies like a blast and sending us flying back onto our butts.

Groggy and feeling the voltage recede, I lurch up as the tree fell. Snow dampened my jeans, but my focus was frozen. The whip in my hands was intact. The metal was heated, but otherwise unharmed.

Kendrick groaned and lifted himself up, elbows perching on his knees. He wasn't hurt, so I didn't bother asking. "That was crazy."

I shook my head, hand covering my mouth before dropping. "Check this out."

Concentrating, I gathered a few small sparks, watching the electric-blue travel to my right hand. Then I picked up the whip and rolled it out along the snow. Blue streaks shot along the silver, escaping the spikes and melting the icy white covering. As this occurred I grabbed Kendrick's hand with my free one, raising it to eye level. Not a single volt came up my other arm. "I can control it. I can channel the power."

My nerves were shot the following afternoon. Having to wait for The Council to agree to hear me out was torture, but it had given us time to put Plan B into action. Now it was half an hour past twilight as I stood before Kendrick in the back corner of the council property's parking lot. He opened the top few buttons on his shirt, revealing the mark Vanessa had etched into his chest. I reached out with my rubber-lined glove and ran a finger over the mark. It was gold, as all her tattooed markings were, a symbol resembling a drop of blood. "I hope this works," I said, glancing at Dorian behind us.

Kendrick glared down and my hand shot back. Then he licked a drop of blood from his lower lip. "I may not be on board with this whole plan, but I do trust Vanessa. If she says it'll work, it will work."

Dorian gave Kendrick a hard look, and then nodded down the gravel path to the council hall's soaring doors. "Well, there's no time like the present. Let's do this already."

The sword-armed guards nodded with respect as we passed through the thick wooden doors. Then one frowned, eyeing the stiffness that corded the muscles along Kendrick's neck. Still, in keeping with custom, he said nothing.

Once inside I fought the urge to take a breath of relief. So far so good. I led our trio up to the packed marble table. Being dark outside, bar the growing light of the almost full moon, every red velvet curtain was drawn open. The tall black panes reflected the brilliant light of the lavish candle-lit chandelier strung from the exposed-beam ceiling. And a few domed lamps created a centerline down the long marble table.

As I headed to the only spare seat, every vampire in the room turned to stare. This, of course, included Caius who headed the table's opposite end, watching me with cold wariness. From the seat beside my former uncle, Marcus nodded as if cheering me on, his smile the only warmth in this room. On the other side my mom looked nervous, her fingers intertwined and her face tight. The room fell quiet, every member waiting on me to deliver the chilling news of my latest vision. But even with Kendrick and Dorian flanking my sides, my tongue felt tied and my throat bone dry.

Caius seized the opportunity and rose. "Amelia, my dear niece. What is it you have to tell us all?"

Feeling exposed, as if I were standing there in all my naked glory, I swallowed my fear of being laughed at and labeled a liar. This was our best chance to get Ty's sentence held back. I had to try.

Feigning confidence, I let my voice ring out over The Council, filling the cathedral hall. "I've seen what is coming. We're all in grave danger. Regardless of your personal beliefs in me and the return of the damned, please don't ignore what I have to say. Your own lives and those of your families are at stake if you do." Sweat beads spouted across my forehead. I shoved my gloved hands, which had begun to shake, behind my back. "Believe me or not, but the damned have returned. I've seen them attack."

Instead of gasping in surprise or voicing outrage or disbelief, The Council stared at me. As if I'd just sprouted snakes for hair. Caius was the only one to move. He strode around his colleagues, his expression a grim shade of death. "Amelia." His tone and masked amusement as he twisted his head from the table to look at me, made my skin crawl. "Your vision has come too late. They have already attacked."

"What?" I scanned the room. Nothing was out of place. No shattered glass. No shredded drapes. No blood. Where was all the black and red blood? And what about all those dead lumps that had once been living vampires. Even the balcony was clear, the balustrade unmarked with stacked antique chairs taking up space. "How? When?"

Caius moved closer to me, now standing a foot away. He dared to lay a hesitant hand on my shoulder. I braced, trying to keep a lid on my emotions as I struggled to hold back the static growing in my heart. Every waking spare minute between visions and escape plans had been spent with Kendrick, practicing to control my new ability. Before the meeting I'd even managed to hold Kendrick's hand without shocking him. But it wasn't working now. The tension grew, alive with purpose. Because what I really wanted to do, was let my power's full force explode from every inch of my skin and into this monster. To blow him to hell where he belonged. For everything he'd already done to me, and for what he planned to do to Ty, he deserved it. Except that would cause a mega problem. We didn't need The Council knowing about my power.

Before the voltage took flight, Kendrick moved like a flash. He clutched Caius's hand and pried it from my flesh. The move was blocked from The Council's view by Caius's body, but Kendrick's vehement expression wasn't.

Whispers rose before me and I flashed Kendrick a *control your facials* scowl. The hate propelling from his face faded and he took a step back. His retraction made me feel vulnerable. I glanced nervously up at Caius's amused expression. He half turned back to his colleagues while keeping his cold-gray eyes on me. "You are too late. I am sorry to have to tell you this, my dear. The damned compromised the Armaya before dawn this morning."

What. The. Hell. When had this happened? Had there been deaths? Either way this was bad. Seriously bad. The hope was that my vision would force an evacuation. That it would lead everyone back to the Armaya and the safety of their impenetrable walls. Black dots clotted my vision, muddying the room. My knees trembled. How could the damned break into a place that was renowned as the safest of all vampire locations?

Caius is behind this. He has to be. Kendrick's thought words were clear, even though he made no move beside me. *Though I have no idea how he did it.*

Almost in answer, Caius kept on talking. "The wards were disarmed." His gray gaze slid to Marcus then back to me. "We suspect from an insider."

"Perhaps the culprit you envisioned but couldn't name in your last vision," my mom offered. She glided over to stand beside Caius.

The middle-aged man who'd been one of the first to doubt my ability spoke up. "Without a timely warning, or the protection of the wards, they walked right on in."

Uriel pointed a bony finger across the table at the guy, her azure gaze shining. "Visions aren't controlled by the viewer. They are simply received. Do you mean to insinuate that Amelia purposely withheld this information?"

The guy scoffed, but Serafina was the one to speak, taking no notice of her son as she pinned me with a stare. "How can we know when she had this vision? She hasn't told us."

All eyes turned on me, some hopeful, but most skewering. How could I tell them that this latest vision had come to me last night, and I was only now telling them about it? I had wanted to meet this morning, but the attack happened before dawn. Still, I knew the answer in my heart. Because it wasn't too late. Yes, the Armaya had been invaded, but that's not what I'd seen. The real attack would come in two night's time, straight after the Oracle ceremony.

"P-please, you have to listen to me." Most rolled their eyes or scoffed. A few had looks of dwindling hope. My head swooned, light and dizzy, but I pressed on. "My vision wasn't of the Armaya's invasion. What I saw in my vision hasn't happened yet. It happens here. After the ceremony."

Roars of disbelief erupted. The balding man's voice carried over the shouting. "How can she have a vision about a proposed attack, when she saw nothing of the Armaya's?"

"It's a diversion," Serafina called. "We all saw her reaction when the wolf was captured. They're involved."

"That's disgusting," said the old white-haired woman. She'd been one of the only ones to speak in my favor when my link to The Sight had been revealed.

"She's trying to prolong his execution," Serafina spat with disgust.

Through all the Ping-Pong arguing, my heart squeezed tighter and tighter. They didn't believe me. And if they wouldn't listen, they'd never evacuate. Ty's execution wouldn't be postponed.

"You are all being ridiculous." Uriel rose to her full willowy height, punching her knuckles into the table. The marble shook, vibrating the line of lamps. All the shouting quieted but didn't stop. Nevertheless she spoke over them. "You are all forgetting the big picture here."

"Yes," Caius said, striding back to take his throne at the far end of the table. Mom followed behind. "There is a viable threat, whether we like it or not. The Armaya was compromised. There is no doubt on that. And perhaps my niece was confused and her vision *was* of the Armaya." Daring eyes lifted to lock on mine. "Would you say that is a possibility, my dear?"

I gritted my teeth. "No. It's not. I've never been surer about anything in my life."

"It doesn't matter either which way," Uriel added, surprising me. She glanced around the table, eyeing each member as she went on. "True or not, the one thing we do know is that the damned have returned. Their thirst is for the death and destruction of all Pure Bloods."

"So what do you propose?" Marcus leaned back in his seat. As usual he appeared calm and not nearly like he was facing a war between good and evil. "Cancel the proceedings?"

"No!" Caius bellowed. "We cannot compromise our customs. We will not return to hiding, fearing the dark as we did so long ago." He ran fingers through his salt and pepper hair. Then he pointed to the stacked papers in front of him on the table. "Every still-living resident from the Armaya is on their way here. We all voted and agreed on that. So if this proposed threat is real?" His expression mocked the possibility. "*If* it is truly coming? We will have numbers above all. Even our security will shame the Armaya's."

Fan-freaking-I-need-a-truck-load-of-chocolate-stat-tastic! I'd prepared for this, but it still rocked me. Now we had no choice but to fall back on Plan B. Except I hadn't considered the possibility of a security regime that would turn this entire property and every corner into a solid fortress. I caught Marcus's eye, needing encouragement to speak up and demand that everyone listen, to somehow force them to see that evacuation *was* the best option. But Marcus's face was stiff, jaw set, telling me to keep my mouth shut.

"What about all our visitors?" Uriel demanded. "What will we tell them? How can we prepare?"

"We won't tell them anything," Serafina declared, splaying her hand across the marble table.

Uriel opened her mouth to argue, but Caius spoke over her. "That is right. We cannot tell them anything. Unless we want an uncontrollable backlash of panic on our hands."

"You cannot mean to keep them in the dark," Uriel shouted.

"Would you rather have everyone running around like beheaded chickens?" Caius rose with challenge. "Because all-out hysterics is what we will get in that event. Then they will be even more useless if this *vision* does come to fruition."

"So we tell them nothing?" My mom's voice, for the very first time, seemed to be questioning as she peered up at Caius.

He regarded her with compassion. "I am sorry, Lamayli. I do believe this is best." His focus panned over the rest of The Council. "Shall we bring this to a vote?" With murmurs and nods from around the table, Caius asked, "All in favor of doing what we can to prepare, while keeping our knowledge of this possible threat contained? Raise your hand."

Out of everyone seated around the table, every hand rose along with Caius's. This included a reluctant hand from my mom. The one person to stay their hand was Uriel.

I was on the verge of screaming that they would all be slaughtered, along with their unknowing visitors if they stayed, but pressure beside me stalled my outburst. "Amelia, you tried." It was

Marcus. I hadn't even seen him rise from Caius's side. His hand around my elbow was firm, pulling me away from the once again bickering council. Dorian and Kendrick shadowed behind. "The Council has made its choice. Nothing more you say can change that."

"But apart from The Council, everyone will be as good as sitting ducks," I said. "They won't be able to defend themselves."

A woman's commanding voice spoke over the bickering council. Uriel was on her feet, her crimson hair flawless and blue irises flashing silver with emotion. "Then we must have weapons stored all around the hall. Not just for the guards, but enough for every attendee, too. It is the only reasonable thing to do. Those in favor, raise your hands."

Caius glared at Uriel like he wanted to throttle her, but she lifted her nose indignantly. That was one fearless woman.

"Looks like we might have a fighting chance," Marcus said.

"Is a fighting chance enough?" I bit my lip and sighed. There was nothing more we could do. It was out of our hands.

"It'll have to be." Dorian shrugged, seeming less than convinced.

Leaving Marcus at the entry, we rushed along the lamp-lit path to where Dorian's Cabriolet waited. With Plan B now in full action, we had heaps to finalize and double check in the next forty-eight hours.

As we reached the car and slowed, Kendrick stepped out of the driver's side. He sighed with relief, scanning his double who'd stood by me among a council of vampires. "So, did it work?"

The second Kendrick leaned against the car, watching while the one beside me smiled. The smiling Kendrick's expression contorted. He grimaced and growled, tiny cracks splintering and remolding his face into one I knew. One I wished I could somehow never have to set eyes on again. The silver in his eyes remained, but grew dull and gray. The unlined plains of his smooth face wrinkled. An aging process on fast-forward. He shrunk half a foot, and when he spoke his voice was one that I knew as well as my own. "You tell me, my dear."

I cringed at the sight and that deep, calculating voice. Seeing a perfect mirror image of Caius right before us was uncanny. "It's flawless." I had to stop myself from touching his face to see if it was real, and from slapping it at the same time.

Dorian took a step closer to his ex-uncles likeness. "No kidding. I can't believe it worked."

The person standing before us warped again, flesh smoothing, height growing, hair darkening, and eyes rippling a magnificent gold. "Told you it would," Troy said. His voice was cocky but his expression was shadowed by exhaustion. "Just remember this truce is temporary."

"Wouldn't forget it. But will your fingerprints work?" Kendrick remained rooted in his slouched spot against the car.

It was a valid question. Because to get into the prison cells, Marcus had warned us that we'd need royal prints.

Troy arched his eyebrows. "I guess we'll have to wait and see, leech."

WHEN I AWOKE to chirping birdsong and rustling, wind swept trees, I knew two things for sure. One, I was locked inside a dreamscape in which I held no power or control. In the past, such a notion could have filled me with apprehension. But not now. Not with everything I knew. Then there was point two. This dreamscape was conjured by Ty, someone I wholeheartedly trusted without question. The one person I didn't need or want protective powers to interfere with.

J.L. MYERS

Sensing warmth and the swirl of his unmistakable scent billowing behind me, I spun. My fingers twitched, desperate to touch his chest, his face, and his lips. But the static was already dancing across my skin. I locked my hands behind my back. "Ty." I scoured his body. "Did they hurt you?"

Ty came closer, leaving an inch between our bodies. The streaming sunlight through the trees painted his skin an iridescent bronze. "They can batter me black and blue, but as long as your heart still beats for mine, they can never break my spirit."

I gulped, dreading what was to come. "Show me what they did."

Ty's chin bunched with set teeth. "No."

I made a sound between a mock laugh and a sigh. Through it all, Ty was still trying to protect me. Did he think I wasn't strong enough to see the truth? "Fine, don't. I'll see it for myself tomorrow."

Ty caught my wrist, his irises rippling alarm. "What are you talking about?"

Static bolted from my wrist. Ty grimaced but held tight.

I shrugged, focus shifting to the bird whistling above our heads. I needed to pick my words carefully. Evacuation or not, we would be busting Ty out. And I knew Ty would argue more, but he had to know the damned were coming.

With rehearsed words, I laid out my vision, every detail, excluding Ty's head to head with Caius. My hope was that when push came to shove he'd leave. But if I told him he'd have a chance to take down my enemy, I knew he'd never pass that up. Then I said simply, "So we're busting you out."

Ty's grip around my wrist hardened. "No. You're not. It's too dangerous. You need to run. Take off. Go into hiding. I couldn't live with myself if—" His words broke off with a sharp inhale as a stronger surge of static streamed from my wrist and into his hand.

368

"If they killed me too?" Ty's dark expression said everything I needed to know. He knew he would be executed tomorrow. And he planned to let it happen without a fight? Why? Just to keep me safe? I tore my electric wrist free and planted both hands on my hips. "You expect me to stand by while you're slaughtered!"

The battle would take place tomorrow night, but I didn't know if that was after or before Ty's planned execution. Him being present in the vision proved one thing to me. We had to get him out. And we would. If we didn't, this may be the first time my vision was altered, leaving Ty executed and the damned still to paint the hall with buckets of blood.

I lowered my voice to a shaky whisper. "You think I can go on living if I let them kill you?"

Ty's expression fell with utter defeat. "Of course not. You wouldn't be the girl who stole my heart if you could." He peered up with dwindling hope. "I guess there's nothing I can say to change your mind, then?"

"No."

A steady sigh whistled through Ty's lips, and he ruffled his sun-gleaming hair. "Then, you need to see this." With visible concentration he strained, body becoming statue-still. The sun and windblown trees shimmered and flashed, flickering like ghostly visions in a horror movie to reform.

I sucked in my breath. My nose wrinkled at the stink of decay that lifted in the darkness. We were no longer standing in a picturesque forest clearing. Instead, we were locked in a stone walled and iron barricaded cell. Ty stood before me, body lit by flaming torches on the wall between bars.

The sight of him caused an involuntary shudder to undulate down my body. He wasn't battered or bruised like I expected him to be. Still, it was clear he was far from okay. His wrists were shackled.

Chains fell from those cuffs and trailed the ground before rising to anchor points in the stone wall. The chains were twice as thick as the ones that had held me. Twice as thick as the ones the guards had used to haul Ty away. The sight renewed my full-body shudder at recalling my own hell and close brush with death. I forced myself to look more closely at Ty's restraints. A mixture of repeating symbols had been engraved into each individual link. My gaze dropped to the uneven stone floor. His captors weren't taking any chances when it came to escaping. A second set of shackles trapped his ankles, also bolted to the wall.

My heart felt hollow. Blossoming tears glazed my vision and I reached for his face, restraining myself before I could shock him. "I'm sorry. I'm so sorry. I'll fix this. I'll get you out."

Ty nodded past my shoulder at the thick, iron bars. "This is what you need to see."

Without squinting, I refocused along the dark hall that led from the left of Ty's cell. Empty cells lined the opposing walls and a door ended the hallway.

With a rattle I felt Ty's warmth closing in behind me. The heat of his breath brushed against my neck as he spoke. "There's always one guard straight outside the door at all times. Posts change every four hours. On the dot."

"Then we only have to incapacitate one guard. That should be easy—"

"No. There's more," Ty interrupted, his voice deep and commanding. "Look above the doorway."

Above the door was a mechanical box. On its face a small red light blinked at me. "Dammit. Video surveillance?"

"Yes," Ty breathed. His hand squeezed mine then let go before the voltage could reach him. "From what I've overheard, there's a command center. I'm pretty sure it's manned twenty-four/seven."

"Okay," I said with a nod. "What else?"

Ty spun me around to face him, expression set and solemn. "There's a print register at the door, and I'm guessing at every locked door down to this point. It's the only way to gain access. So, you know what you're going to have to do?"

Marcus had already let us in on that little hiccup. I nodded again and half smiled. "A truce has been struck. They've already agreed to help."

"You're serious?" Ty brows arched. "Great, good. I mean, this could actually work." He then lifted his shackled wrists up between us. "I need you to remember the symbols."

I frowned. "Why?"

"They prevent the chains from being broken." Ty dropped his wrists as if they were weighted by concrete cinder blocks. "I've seen the symbols in a book of Vanessa's. She might have something we can use to break them. Another symbol or something."

Ty sounded far from certain. But I needed to think positive. I needed to believe that no matter what obstacles were thrown at us, we would find a way to save Ty.

"We're going there in the afternoon to stock up on weapons and whatever we can use to get you out. I'll show her the symbols." I went to lift Ty's dropped chin with my hand before stopping myself. I sighed. Not being able to touch him killed me. But it was better than hurting him. "Ty, we will find a way to break them. We'll get out of this, I promise. I won't let you die."

CHAPTER 28

I stood by one of Vanessa's workbenches, checking out all the bubbling potions in multi-sized beakers. As I bent to examine a purple liquid with vapor rising off its surface, my elbow bumped a rack of test tubes. A single drop of red liquid splashed from a tube, burning a small, sizzling hole through the bench top.

I backed away and turned my attention to Dorian across the basement at the weaponry wall. He raised a brand new, one-of-a-kind crossbow to eye level. The weapon was fitted with a removable CO_2 cartridge, and rather than taking arrows that needed to be nocked, it took a canister of bolts. It was also covered in alchemist marks that boosted the firing speed to lightning fast. Dorian was a natural, and after practicing all morning with it, the confident look in his flirtatious eyes said so. "Reckon I could sneak this one in?"

Vanessa pursed her lips, looking cheeky. Then she snatched the bow from his grasp and pulled a lever. The cartridge and canister dislodged and the crossbow's arms folded back, rendering the weapon into a neat, concealable rectangle. She handed the weapon back with a smile. "If you can figure out how to reassemble it, you can keep it." She picked up and flung a canister of bolts at him. "Oh, and these are better. Silver-coated bolts."

Not needing any further encouragement, Dorian began to fiddle with the device, all the while giving her cheeky glances.

Kendrick nudged me. "Give them some privacy."

I *humphed* but couldn't look away. Watching them in the past I'd suspected something was going on. Now there was no question. So during Dorian's disappearances and late beach walks, he'd been catching up with Vanessa. The look on his face now stopped the warning brewing on my lips. He was smitten. Still, despite their budding relationship, we had things to do. We still had so many bases to cover, and after spending the day training and practicing to control my voltage, it was almost sundown. At best our time was limited. "Dorian, that's enough playing. We're here for a reason."

"Right," Vanessa said, back to being all work. "More weapons." She crossed the room and pressed the silver button that began the loud rattling of chains. Then the eight foot long section of the wall spun on its axis.

"Not just weapons," I said, freezing Vanessa who had pulled a large black duffel bag from under the stainless steel bench. "There are other obstacles we need help with."

"Like what?" Vanessa dropped the bag with a clank.

"They have Ty in chains," Kendrick said. "Each link is engraved with these symbols." He fished into his pocket and retrieved a piece of paper with a set of symbols drawn in thick marker.

"They're binding symbols," Vanessa said. "The first weakens the flesh of anything it touches. The second makes the chains unbreakable. And the third prevents a lycan or werewolf from being able to shift into wolf form."

"But they can be broken, right?" I moved in closer, cooling the new static coursing through my body.

Vanessa looked resigned. "No. They can't. They're unbreakable. Only a key with an opposing symbol can unlock the cuffs."

Unbreakable. The word was final but not without wiggle room, I hoped.

"You think?" Kendrick asked.

Dorian and Vanessa perked up, turning their full attention on us as I nodded. "You said the second symbol made the chains unbreakable?"

Vanessa frowned with annoyance. "Yeah, so?"

"So," I hedged. "We won't break them. Well not at first." I strode across the room and carefully lifted the test tube filled with the thin, red liquid. The need to spark warmed my veins but I held it back. "We'll burn the symbols off."

For the first time ever, Vanessa seemed impressed. "You know," she said thoughtfully. "That could work."

Dorian smiled as we walked over, still holding the disassembled bow. "Who would have guessed that you were the smart one?"

"Ha, very funny," I said, minding not to spill the liquid again as I jabbed an elbow into his ribs.

Behind us, Kendrick had begun shoveling an arsenal of stakes, blades, and canisters into the duffel bag. "Now on to the marks..."

"Marks?" Vanessa questioned with amusement. "And what marks could I possibly give to a group of vampires?"

"Well," I said. "You can create a mark that repels compulsion. But can you create one that boosts its effects?"

Vanessa went to her workbench and sighed. She popped the locks on a thick, dusty book and held it against her chest. "All the marks I know are in this book. Every page is imprinted on my memory." She sighed again. "But there isn't any mark that can boost a vampire's compulsion ability. It would go against everything we try to prevent."

There was a creak and Vanessa's grandfather appeared, hobbling down the rickety wooden stairs. One hand clutched the wonky railing while the other curled tight around a small thick-bound book. "My granddaughter is right," Mr. Aquinas said. "Such a marking would go against everything we as alchemists dedicate our lives to. But you are also wrong, Vanessa."

She ran to his side as he met the concrete landing, and strung a supporting arm around his free elbow. After a few pain-filled steps he paused, holding open the book to a page near the back. The pages were stained and wrinkled like they had been drench in tea then dried in the sun. Centering the left page was a large symbol that had been hand drawn with charcoal. It was an eye, perfectly symmetrical with a pupil that had eaten away the iris, and whites that were struck by a dozen tiny, delicate sparks.

"This mark will boost any living vampire's ability to compel, as much as ten-fold. Though it only lasts for about forty-eight hours, *if* you're lucky." He looked to Vanessa. "Would you like me to administer the marks?"

"No, Grandfather. I can do this." Vanessa took him by the arm again and began leading him back to the stairs. "Besides, you look like you need a rest."

Mr. Aquinas's rebuttal was gruff as she helped him clamber up the stairs. "I may be old, granddaughter, but I'm not dead."

After five minutes of stuffing more weaponry into the duffel bag, Vanessa re-emerged, bounding down the creaky stairs. She dug into a drawer below the workbench before placing a glass jar filled with a glittering gold liquid on its top. A menacing tool followed that resembled a medieval tattoo gun with various markings etched into the metal casing. "Who's first?"

"Is that a real tattoo gun?" Dorian, looking apprehensive and excited all at the same time, sidled up beside her.

"Homemade." Vanessa plugged the gun's cord into the socket on the top corner of the bench and flicked the trigger. The machine made a terrible, ear-drumming noise, more jackhammer than needle-pointed gun. "What did you expect?" she asked, turning the contraption off. "A magical feather that painted pretty gold lines on your flesh?"

"Well kinda," I replied, unable to help myself. With all the ability these marks could bestow? I had expected the process to be a little more magical than mechanical.

Vanessa laughed while Kendrick smiled. "She's an alchemist, Amelia. Not a witch."

"You're right about that," Vanessa chimed, seeming to appreciate the distinction. "We don't work hocus pocus. We challenge the limitations of physical substances."

At Dorian's and my dumb look she explained. "We experiment with any and all substances, manipulating their essence until we reach the outcome we desire. There is no magic involved in what we do, just good hard work, patience, and above all, science. We are the centuries old scientists who didn't cave to modern beliefs. We don't accept that something can't be done just because someone else says so. We challenge the rules and create new ones."

"So what's in the gold liquid?" I asked.

Vanessa smiled a wry and self-important smile. "If I told you that," she said with a wink, "I'd have to kill you." Without preamble she unscrewed the lid from the jar and pulled up a stool. "So, who's first?"

Dorian and Kendrick received their marks with manly control, keeping the cursing to a minimum while their faces strained. There was a mark to boost their ability to compel and also repel compulsion. One increased their physical strength and speed. Another sped up the healing process.

Now it was my turn. I slid onto the stool and removed my tank top to expose my left shoulder, flinging my hair forward to clear the space. This would be a real test of my control—being in pain while trying not to send sparks firing into that horrible-looking device.

"Ready?" Vanessa slapped on rubber gloves for good measure.

She had already fired up the gun, and its malicious drumming sent waves of panic through me. I forced myself to remain motionless, focusing all my attention on keeping the electricity at bay while biting my lip. "As I'll ever be."

Without any further invitation, the gun's needle tips bit into my flesh in a repetitive and scraping fashion. My teeth, clamped over my bottom lip, released. The tension in my body retreated. The feel of having five needles pierce my skin wasn't the agony I had psyched myself into expecting. It was more like tiny pinches that almost tickled more than anything, healing numbing my skin before pain could take over.

Vanessa took a sharp breath behind me. Then I felt her go over the same spot again, and again, and again. Dorian and Kendrick edged closer. Through the bond I saw through Kendrick's eyes. He was peering over Vanessa at my exposed shoulder, hidden behind the enormous gun still drumming away into my flesh.

"What's wrong?" I asked, itching to turn and see what the problem was.

Then the gun snapped off. The stool spun around, putting me face to face with Vanessa who was flustered and perspiring. She blew a thick, curly strand of hair from her face. "The tattoo," she said, looking both frustrated and confused at the same time. "It's kinda...disappearing."

My hand flung over my shoulder and my neck craned. I zeroed

in on the reddened, irritated flesh across the back of my shoulder. "How is that possible?"

Kendrick moved behind me and ran a light thumb across the raw but healing and totally unmarked flesh. Not a single spark erupted at his touch. "Well I'm not sure about this, but Marcus and I were taught about some of the practices in alchemy at the Armaya. And..."

"Only someone who is one hundred percent alive," Vanessa interrupted, "can be marked."

It felt like the world had suddenly stopped spinning and I had stepped right into the epicenter of an alternate universe. *I'm part dead?* In total contradiction my heart drummed with the anxiety that streamed through my veins. I raised a sweating palm to my chest as if making sure the heart palpitations were real. They were real. The feel was so strong and forceful against my flattened hand. "But I am alive."

Vanessa pursed her lips, while Kendrick's thoughts whirled at one hundred miles a minute. His thoughts were too jumbled and incoherent to make sense of. In the drowning silence he spluttered, "The silver potion Caius poisoned you with. It contained damned blood."

"And the damned are dead," I added.

But before I could fall back on that explanation, Dorian said something to bring it all crashing back down. "No. It's not possible."

Vanessa was flicking through books but shot a curious glance at my brother. "What do you mean?"

"You said Caius pretty much drained all but a few drops of your blood, the blood he had been poisoning. And then," he continued, ignoring my dumbfounded look, "you drank Kendrick's blood. Vampire blood that can kill off damned blood and its poison."

Dorian's explanation brought me back to the moment I had

forced Ty to drink from me after being slashed to ribbons by the damned vampire on the cruise. I could so clearly remember my total fear when I realized that Ty wasn't healing. The damned hadn't managed to bite him, but Ty had still ingested a fair amount of their disgusting, dead blood. Feeding him *my* blood had allowed him to heal.

My brother remained quiet, waiting for me to piece it all together. "Kendrick's blood cleansed what was left of my own, removing any remnants of the poison. There isn't any damned blood left in me."

"So, it can't be damned blood that is making it impossible for Vanessa to mark you," Kendrick added.

Vanessa's eyes brightened like she'd had a light bulb idea. She slammed shut the book she'd had her nose buried in. "Caius's poison worked on a cellular level—it's in your DNA."

LATER THAT NIGHT I fell asleep to meet Ty in his promised dreamscape. And I couldn't wait. With tomorrow's ceremony and breakout plan, this would be our last time together before all hell broke loose. And I wasn't about to let hours of practice go to waste.

When my eyelids lifted I was in Ty's cell. His face lit up and he came forward, lifting his arms to embrace me. Then they came down and he sighed. "It's so good to see you."

Those simple words coupled with defeat said he wanted to do so much more than that.

Ignoring the putrid space and the danger to come, I smiled and held up my hands to show off their innocence. Then I placed them on his chest, loving the feel of his hot flesh through the thin material of his shirt. Ty looked wary but didn't step back. "I think I can control the sparks." I pressed slightly parted lips to his collarbone, breathing him in. "See."

A gentle rumble vibrated Ty's chest as he dipped his head. "I've missed this," he said against my lips. "You have no idea how much."

Nerves for tomorrow built inside me along with unrestrainable desire that would never be fulfilled if tomorrow went horribly wrong. Time wasn't on our side.

I took Ty's bottom lip between my teeth, fangs pressing down, then let go after a playful nip. "I don't want to wait anymore. I want to be with you, Ty. I'm ready. I'm so, so ready."

"Amelia." The way he spoke my name caressed every inch of my body, and I shivered. "I do too. More than anything." He inched back, emotion saddening his eyes. "But it's not real. You know it's not."

I shook my head and my hair fell over my shoulders. Tension began to build within me. "I don't care. I won't let another thing get between us. I *want* this." Self-doubt colored my thoughts for a second. After everything, was Ty reluctant to take our relationship to the next level? To physically join our bodies in an act that could never be undone or forgotten? My heart grew heavy. "Don't you?"

"Amelia, I want you. Every single part of you. I've never wanted anything more in my entire life. But…"

There was no other invitation I needed. In a flash I reared on my toes and cut off his words, pressing my lips with abandon against his. "No buts. Just kiss me."

Ty flinched, then the tension tightening his body melted. His lips pressed harder against mine and he groaned, a pained and needy sound. His arm circled my waist, drawing me against the curve of his chest. A perfect fit. His free hand curled around my neck, pinning me close.

Around us the dingy cell warped and faded, replaced in a flash by a gentle fall of water that dusted over us. It was the softest, purest waterfall I could ever imagine, reminding me of our real encounter not so long ago. Yet here the gentle mist felt like the caress of angel wings over my skin.

Electric current streamed through me, growing wilder and more intense and erratic. Each kiss against my lips, cheek, jaw, and neck pushed me closer to the edge. But I held it back, wanting more, needing more.

Ty's hands found my waist and began to rise, caressing, exploring. My skin came alive under his fingertips, every touch sending an electric spark through my veins. My own hands lowered with intent, gliding down his shirt and over the ripples of his chest then abs. Then they met the smooth muscles that ran below the barrier of his pants. Ty flinched again, growling into my mouth.

A distinct warning went off, like a switch that couldn't be unflicked. I knew what was about to come. I jerked out of Ty's hungry embrace. Too late. Current flowed like a dead line instantly reconnected to live power, racing to every inch of my flesh. It crackled, breaking free to shoot into every point that Ty's flesh connected with mine.

As if in fast-forward, Ty's hands flung from my body and he flew back through the air. He connected with a cracking thud against an invisible wall that flickered and changed. Now back inside Ty's dank cell, he fell to the rotting cot. A squeal of protest cried out as the metal frame warped and he tumbled to the stone ground.

I rushed forward, pulling back my hands as fresh waves of blue lightning shot from my fingers. "Oh my God. Ty."

Ty groaned and with great effort levered his body up. His blood's strong aroma poisoned the dank air, making my fangs ache. Voices taunted me to taste him, but I locked them down. Then I gasped, lungs squeezing at the sudden gush of air. Any and all hunger was forgotten.

Ty was still getting to his feet, but I could already see the damage I'd somehow caused. The flaming torches beyond the cell's bars highlighted them as if on display. His face was a mosaic of amber, purple, blue, and black bruises. A gash ran from his top lip down to his bottom lip. It was thick and deep, but somehow it was already scabbed over. A second semi-healed gash ran across one side of his forehead. Even more gruesome and fresh cuts painted his chest with raw scarlet stripes beneath his slashed shirt. The pants he wore were dirty and torn. Below them his knees were shredded almost to the bone. And his toes and fingernails... I swallowed the urge to heave. They were gnarled and cracked. Like he had been using them to scrape a way out of this stone prison.

"I—I did this?"

Ty stumbled and doubled over, catching his breath. Then he straightened, drawing in a slow lungful of air. When he let it out he appeared so drained that I could hardly believe he was standing upright. "No. I didn't want you to see. I tried to hide it. But the shock..."

Sharp focus knocked my own breath from my lungs. It wasn't my sudden electric shock that had caused these physical injuries. It was the guards, either of their own volition and hate for lycans. Or under the order of a higher power that was intent on inflicting torture to get the information they desired. "They did this to you?"

When Ty forced a weak smile, his lip split. Fresh blood oozed from the cut. "It's not as bad as it looks."

Like hell it wasn't. I clenched my teeth to keep from screaming. "If that's true, then why aren't you healing?"

Ty sighed again and dropped onto the mangled cot behind him. As if keeping up the charade of stability now that his cover had blown was just too much work. "Caius paid me a visit. I tried to resist, but the guards had just flogged me and I was weak. Once they left, he drugged me. The liquid was thick and black. It stunk like only one thing I've ever smelled before."

"Damned blood," I whispered. Ty's injuries on the boat when he'd come so close to dying crowded my mind. I fought the need to shudder. "That's why you're not regenerating." Without even a glimmer of hesitation I bit into wrist, fangs and teeth tearing flesh. The wound bled freely and I held it up to Ty's lips. "Here, take my vein."

Ty slouched further down on the cot. "It won't work."

I stared at him then at my wrist. "What do you mean? It has to."

"It's a dream, remember?" Ty's dulling gold eyes were filled with even more exhaustion than a moment ago. "It's not real."

I gaped at him in disbelief. Minutes ago I had shocked him with electric current and sent him flying into the wall of his cell. "But I shocked you. I felt it. And I know you didn't fly across this shit hole on your own accord. How do you explain that?"

Ty took my hand and I almost pulled away, fearing I'd shock him again. But there was nothing. No tingles. No blue light. Just two people holding hands. Had shocking Ty temporarily snuffed my electric power?

"Amelia," Ty said. His voice was so unwavering and certain that I peered down into his eyes that showed no ability to gleam with the gold that I longed to see. "Your lightning power may not be restricted by space..." He sighed, as though speaking were a hard task. "But the physical limits of your flesh and blood are."

CHAPTER 29

"*M*om, stop fussing." I fidgeted in the white lace and silk-layered gown as she pinned miniature black orchids to my braided hair.

We were in one of the rooms behind the second story balcony, readying for the evening's ceremony. In this room everything was pristine white. The walls, carpet, chiffon draped bed, massive dresser, and draping curtains. This room was supposed to be mine after the ceremony. A room I desperately wanted to escape from so I could rescue Ty.

The ticking from the white, wall-hung clock pressed in on me. "I don't see why all this is necessary."

"It is necessary." Mom peered over my shoulder at our reflection in the gold-framed cheval mirror. Her hands came up to squeeze my shoulders and I channeled the lightning down to my fingertips. Her expression was a mask of resolution. Yet her eyes glistened with the promise of tears. A betrayal that showed how much she wished I'd chosen differently. How much she wanted to protect me even though

I was the Oracle. "To all vampires, especially royals, your ability proves that our struggles to do what's right haven't been in vain." She pinned another two lilies to my hair and with a slight nudge twirled me to face her. "Sweetheart, are you ready to take your place as our true Oracle?"

Feeling like I'd swallowed a brick, I tugged at the dress's high neckline. I wanted to say *no, of course I'm not ready. I'm nobody. A turned vampire. Not important or worthy.* But knowing what we had to accomplish by using this situation kept my true feelings masked. Instead I said, "I'm as ready as I'll ever be. Though I'd like a minute alone." I opened the white-painted door for Mom to step outside. "Tell The Council I'm on my way."

With a slow nod and a tight-lipped smile, she glided away and I eased the door shut. An audible creak pricked my ears. I flew to the night blackened, pitched window as it slid up and open. An agile girl swung through the opening to land feet first before me.

"Could you be noisier?"

"Bloody guard city out there. I was trying to get in without being seen." Marika threw me a small vial tinged with red. "Don't see Ty's fascination. You taste like shit."

Ignoring the jab at having to drink my blood to sneak onto council grounds, I frowned. She had on leather knee-high boots, a pair of tight-fitting black shorts, and a busty, aqua tank. "What the hell are you wearing? I said black, concealing clothes. Not 'look at me I'm a skank' clothes. What if someone saw you?"

Marika sneered, moving forward so that our faces were inches apart. "You are not in charge here. And I am not your pawn to boss around. I am here to rescue Ty. It's entirely your fault that he's facing death. No one else's." A pointed finger came up and jabbed my collarbone. "You made him fall in love with you." She jabbed again. "You made it impossible for him to stay away when you put yourself in danger." And again. "So if you don't want me—and by me I mean me and Troy—to back out of your life-threatening play, show a little damn respect."

Every part of me was rearing to lunge at this poor substitute for a lifeline and belt out my frustration. But I couldn't. We needed their help. Doing this without them wasn't an option. More than that, I knew she was right. Guilt lit within me and swelled. If it weren't for me, Ty would never have been in this mess.

With great effort I put a lid on my guilt and rising irritation. Because in spite of the risk to her own life, Marika was still on board. I swallowed back the spike of acid in my throat. When the plan had been made to involve the wolves to save Ty, my initial vision had made sense. Caius hadn't been calling me a traitor. He'd been calling Marika one. Hesitating to drink the blood-filled chalice during the ceremony was proof enough.

"Fine, thank you. Just remember what's at stake."

Marika flashed her wicked-long canines. "I won't let Ty down."

I began to unbutton the beads down my back. "Let's get this over with."

We both stripped and I handed over my ceremonial dress. Thank God I'd packed black jeans, a tank, Vans, and my hoodie from home, all in black, or I'd be donning Marika's nightclub getup. In minutes we stood before each other. Marika was now stuffed into my slim-line coronation dress and I was incognito in full black. "Now what?" I asked.

Without preamble Marika stepped forward and clasped my fore-arm. Unable to hold back any longer, sparks flew through the connection. I went to pull away as Marika grimaced, but she yanked me back and held tight. "No. It'll be more accurate this way."

As the firing currents dulled to tiny sparks, a distinct crack echoed around the square, white room. Marika's clasp on my hand tightened, manicured nails digging into my flesh as her ribs buckled and shrunk. Her face twisted, every muscle along her arms and neck twitching. Her height shot an inch taller with another crack. Then her expression, a mask of agony, warped with the smaller breaks of facial bones. Her paling complexion stretched as her cheekbones grew sharper and her chin became more pronounced. The length of her black hair faded to golden blond, growing down to the small of her back. With a final all over body quake her head lifted, and her irises—now a silver-blue that I could never confuse—gazed into mine.

Marika checked herself out in the cheval mirror, rearranging the dress's bodice to fit her new, less curvy figure. "How do I look?"

I shuddered at the memory of her imprinted with my likeness beneath Ty's sex-ready body and hungry lips. The day of that auction had been one of the worst of my life. Besides the day my uncle had tried to kill me. Now I could fully understand how this mirror copy had fooled Ty.

I shrugged and took my spark-shielding gloves from the dresser and pulled them on, covering their length with my hoodie's sleeves. "It's flawless." I began pulling the pinned flowers from my hair. "It just needs one little touch."

BENEATH THE SHADOWED shelter of a moss-draping oak tree, I scanned my surroundings. Guards, ten in total, positioned at even intervals along the east wall of the council building. Five on the ground with swords sheathed at their backs and guns holstered at their sides. Five sniper shooters at each top level window.

Getting past them even in my comfy Vans hadn't been easy, but somehow I made it.

Now all that stood between me and access to the back door—and the corridors that would lead to Ty—were two guards who paced from either end to meet in the center. The door was shielded from view of the other guards. But that wouldn't make getting in any easier.

The plan had been to use Caius's likeness to talk our way inside, leaving Dorian's compulsion as a way to erase our passing. But now neither of those would work. Not with the latest obstacle that was panning left to right and blinking with a red light. Mounted on both the east and west corner of the brick exterior were surveillance cameras.

There was also surveillance inside the main hall, watching over the ceremony. It would now be underway, with the entire Royal Council present along with the real Caius.

A gentle rustle of tree leaves above me drew my eye. Dorian was perched on a lower branch with his arm outstretched. "Get up here."

I took his hand and allowed him to hoist me up to his level. On a higher and thicker branch, a perfectly suited and formidable figure sat. Troy, ready to take Caius's appearance. He peered around the secluding tree trunk, frowning at the back door. "You didn't mention anything about cameras outside, leech."

"And their guards are all connected through hand-held radios," Dorian added in a hushed whisper. "They do a verbal security check every fifteen minutes of every guard stationed outside."

"So we need to get inside without being caught on camera," I said, thinking out loud. "When's the next security check?"

"About five minutes," Troy answered, attaching a silencer to his gun before holstering it to his belt. "And they're always on the dot."

Thoughts of any and all ways to get through this first obstacle inundated my thoughts. Troy and Dorian both looked to me as if I had all the answers. A whirlwind of stupid suggestions flooded my thoughts. Knock out the two guards. Smash the cameras. Don't get caught.

We were all fast, Dorian and Troy especially after the marks Vanessa had given them to boost their speed and strength. But what would happen when the next security check came? If the guards were unconscious, there would be no one to complete it. And worse, if they came to, the head of security would be alerted and all The Council's armed power would come after us.

I slumped against the curved trunk and sighed. As if heaven sent, a critical piece of information pulsed through my ears. *The cameras run on a separate circuit to the rest of the building,* Kendrick said.

Like a light bulb going off in my brain, my muse finally kicked in. *I can short out the cameras.*

But you'll only have three minutes max to get in before the main guard reboots the power box.

I lifted my chin. "I can take out the cameras, but we still need to get in without being remembered. And talking our way in will take too long."

"We're packed and ready to go." Dorian patted the backpack at his shoulder with excitement. He glanced at Troy. "You know what to do."

There was a stiff nod from Troy. Then they braced their feet against the trunk, ready to leap. The wood creaked under their weight.

Now it was my turn. I peeled off my gloves and focused on my last encounter with Ty. I saw with gut-turning clarity the bruises and the slashed flesh seeping with blood that wouldn't clot and heal. Then I saw his resolve to let himself die in place of risking an escape. Rage at it all bubbled inside me, boiling my blood and turning it into an instant scalding steam that shot through my veins.

The two guards had met in the middle and stopped to exchange a few words. Now was the perfect time.

As I lifted my hands the blue sparks that had sizzled across my skin rushed to collect at my fingertips. A bolt split from both palms, striking out at each camera.

The two guards spun towards the quiet but distinct noise. In the same instant Dorian and Troy sprung from their positions. They both moved in a blur of speed, each restraining a guard up against the wall.

Dorian, with both hands working to stop the guard from lashing out, stared into the guard's eyes. "Shut up and don't move." The guard's expression fell slack. "You heard and saw nothing."

Static crackled over the radios. *'Control room. Cameras down. Check one.'* Checks began to ring out through the speaker. *'Station one secure. Out. Station two secure...'*

Shit. We hadn't expected an instant security check.

Down the gravel path, Troy struggled to keep the second guard under control. He had one hand over the guy's mouth to keep him quiet. Still with one free hand the guard lashed out with everything he had.

"Once we're inside," Dorian rushed on. "You will resume your post, and voice your security check."

He released the guard and we ran at Troy. But it was too late. The guard managed to tug free his gun and unloaded a shot into Troy's side. Troy knocked the gun to the ground and went to swing. Before he hit, I leaped onto his back, pulling at his punch-ready arm with all my might.

Dorian shot in front of Troy just in time, covering the guard's mouth with his hand. "Stop fighting and don't scream for help." The guard's flailing arms dropped to his sides and Dorian removed the cover over his mouth. "Tell me the code to access the back door."

"Three, two, nine, six, eight, one," he mumbled, eyes rolling like marbles.

More checks rang out over the radio. *'Station ten secure, over...'*

"We're running out of time." Troy continued to struggle against me, and damn was he strong. In less than a second he'd have his arm back and would be bludgeoning the guard to a bloody pulp. "You can't leave a mark," I hissed. "It will only jeopardize Ty." Feeling his fight subside I released his arms, shoved him to the door, and punched in the code.

"You heard and saw nothing," Dorian said as the door clicked open. "Resume your post in three seconds."

With that Dorian shot like a flash, swooping up Troy's gun and entering the building after us. The door closed behind him with a distinct click of the lock. Then one of the guards completed the security check. A short burst of static followed, then the control guard's voice. *'Exiting post to reboot cameras. Repeat security check in three minutes.'*

"Get it out!" Troy slammed back against the stone wall while something sizzled. He tore open his suit, exposing his chest and stomach.

I stood frozen before Troy, my stare locked on the bullet hole seeping sweet, delicious blood. With my fangs long and throbbing, I bit my tongue, hard. The taste of my own blood filled my mouth, but it did nothing to dull my desire. The one thing that distracted my hunger was that sizzling. It was coming from the blood-gurgling hole in his side.

I tore my gaze away. The corridor was dark, scarcely lit by dim red bulbs. One marked the doorway and another sat above the bend ahead, which Dorian was striding toward.

Troy grunted, stealing my focus. Excruciation scrunched his hard face. But I couldn't remove the bullet. If I did, the outcome was set. Already the images were toying with my mind. Me, nails puncturing his sides while I lapped up that shiny red torrent. "I—I can't. You have to…"

With a glare, Troy shoved two fingers inside the hole and dug around. Then he cursed, ripping his prodding fingers free. Through the blood coating his digits the smell of singed flesh lifted in the air. "I can't touch it. It's charmed. Probably engraved with some anti-wolf and damned symbol. You have to get it out."

I wanted to help. Really I did. And I wanted to stop that flow of tempting crimson. I pulled my gloves back on, but I still couldn't do it. The temptation to turn Troy into an evening meal while forgetting our plans to save Ty was something I couldn't risk. "Troy, I…"

Dorian appeared right beside me and dropped his backpack with a clatter. "Stand still," he hissed at Troy. His silvery gaze fell to the gurgling blood leaking from Troy's ribs. Then his hand rose, shaking with strain. The torrent slowed, the leaking turning off like a tap. Then it receded, climbing back up Troy's side and disappearing into the bullet hole. "Now," he said, glancing at me. "Take out the bullet." As I went to argue he pinned me with a firm stare. "No, I can't do both. And it's silver since they're armed for the damned."

Struck by his harsh tone, my gloved hand shot out, fingers plunging in deep. Inside the squishy wetness, I found the solid cylindrical bullet. Pinched the sides, and pulled. A muted grunt escaped Troy as I fell back on my butt.

The retracting hold Dorian had on Troy's blood released and a fresh stream spilled out. "About time," Troy snapped.

I scrambled back, hitting the opposing wall, fixated as the leaking blood slowed and the wound began to heal.

"We don't have time for this." Dorian grabbed the backpack and my hand and dragged me down the corridor.

Looking back I saw Troy taking after us while covering the

wound by re-buttoning his suit. A twist to the left then another to the right had us as close to the security control room as we could get without being seen. It was a square room bordered by four walls of clear glass. It was also at the epicenter of the corridor we stood in as well as three other corridors that met in the middle.

The next phase of our plan was to restrain the guard, long enough for Dorian to compel him to believe we were here to collect the prisoner for execution. Troy appearing as Caius would make the task easier.

Footsteps echoed from one of the forking corridors. Then a guard appeared, about to enter the glass room when he stalled. His chin lifted and he drew in a testing breath through his nose.

Something nudged me in the ribs. I turned to see Dorian pointing to the bloodstains still wet across Troy's suit. I could smell it too, had been able to smell the provoking scent since the wound was inflicted. Troy may have been marked to have his scent blocked. But that clearly didn't cover spilled blood. Now this small overlook was about to cost us our cover.

The guard peered up the dark corridor in our direction. One hand found the gun at his belt, and the other located his radio. He stepped forward, lifting the radio to his mouth...

Troy whipped past so fast I couldn't track him. A split second later he'd collided with the guy to drive him back against the glass wall. A crack shattered one whole glass panel, the shards falling like red diamonds.

Dorian and I ran forward, but it was too late. Troy battered his fists into the guard's face, turning it black and blue. The guy slumped into unconsciousness, falling slack over the glittering shards of shattered glass across the control boards.

When my hand found Troy's shoulder he staggered back, releasing his fist from the guy's shirt. "What the hell did you do?"

Still red with the flush of attack and the lighting of red bulbs, Troy glared at me with gold-rippling eyes. "What I had to."

On his other side Dorian fished into his black backpack, creating a clatter of musical noise. Then he reared and handed an armful of iron circlets to Troy. "Hurry up and get these on him."

I had noticed the backpack outside but had assumed it was filled with weapons and things we could use. Not these... "What are you doing?"

Troy began unclipping the circlets and fastening them around the unconscious guard's wrists and ankles. "Restraining him."

"I suppose there are chains in that bag too, then?" I directed my accusing glare from the bag and up to Dorian.

His face cracked. It almost looked like he was about to laugh, but then thought better of it. Clearing his throat he said, "The bands will do enough. They're inscribed. See..." He pointed to the last circlet as Troy clipped it around the guard's neck. Each band was engraved with symbols, some repeating and others individual.

"What will they do?"

Troy stepped back and dusted off his hands. "The ones on his wrists and ankles will keep him immobile. The one around his neck will stop him from breathing a single word."

I couldn't believe my ears. Had they both conspired to have this happen? Had this been the plan all along? I huffed and ran a hand over my face then glanced down at the lifeless guard. "Now how is he going to initiate the next security check that was..." My accusing glare lifted to Troy. "Oh I don't know, supposed to be happening right now?"

Troy ignored my look and smiled with self-satisfaction. "Like this..."

A succession of cracks erupted with his resetting bones. His entire form melted, shrinking in size and stature. When the transformation was complete, what stood before me was not at all what I expected. Still covered in the suit, which had complimented his tall and broad stature, was a much smaller and more wiry figure. His face now perfectly matched the unconscious guard draped across the control board.

In his new skin, Troy reached out and unclipped the radio transmitter from the guard and pressed the intercom button. Then in a voice that matched the person we'd heard over the intercom earlier, he said, "Control room. Cameras up. Check one."

CHAPTER 30

*a*fter a torturous second that seemed to stretch on forever, static crackled over the line. The first of the checks rang through the speaker. With a dizzying sigh, I allowed myself to breathe. "That was too close."

Troy smiled with cocky confidence. "But it worked." He dragged the unconscious guard from the control board and propped him against the far wall.

In the meantime, Dorian had moved into the glass room. With a sweeping hand he brushed the glass shards from the many screens that surrounded the horseshoe-shaped desk. To my right were screens covering the council property's perimeter. Right in front of me six screens overlooked various angles of the main hall. The space was packed. Every seat in the house was taken and not an inch of floor space was left visible. Font rows were occupied by the pristine dressed. They sported lavish gowns, expensive suits, and jewelry that sparkled under the chandelier's candlelight. These attendees had to be extended family to the royals in power.

An elevated dais had been erected before the crowd. Each reigning royal occupied one of the seven wooden and velvet-swathed thrones. Caius took up the center position being the eldest. Uriel and Serafina flanked him, and Marcus being the youngest but not yet sworn in, was positioned at the last throne to the left. Before them was my double. The resemblance was flawless, a perfect mirror image.

"Damn," Dorian said. "I can see how Ty was tricked."

I flinched, a flash of her wearing my appearance beneath Ty invading my thoughts. "Don't remind me."

Kendrick stood to the side of the dais, having been commissioned by his mother to lead any rituals that were to take place. His relief at where we were was stained by urgency.

How long do we have? I sent out the silent words to my best friend.

His gaze shifted sideways to Caius. *You've got fifteen, maybe twenty minutes before the ceremony concludes and the guards are sent to retrieve Ty.*

Fifteen minutes... Thanks to Marcus we'd seen the blueprints. Though we still had to get down another level, and through one guarded and locked door to gain access to the lower prison cells. If that wasn't already enough, once we found him, we still had to steal a key to unlock Ty's cell. Then we had to break through his shackles and get the hell out. All this without raising any alarm to notify The Council straight above our heads of our actions. It was almost impossible. But it was our only hope.

"We've got fifteen minutes," I said, determination edging my words. With the limited time we would have to act fast and be ruthless. Compelling our way through the blocks was no longer an option. "When we reach the block I need you both to incapacitate the guard. Fast."

Dorian, who had been kneeling before me, rose. In his hand was a pile of folded black material. "There's another way."

In seconds, Dorian and I stripped off our own clothes and yanked on the spare guard uniforms. The uniforms matched the guards' outfits outside and had belts with loops for holding stakes, a loop to sheath a sword or thick knife, plus holsters at each hip to carry a gun. A few strapped holsters to hold daggers from Dorian's backpack were concealed at our shins. My whip clipped onto a loop at the small of my back.

With Dorian and I armed and dressed the part, and Troy the spitting image of Caius, we set off. A flight of stairs down and a turn to the left led us to our block. One guard was seated by a solid iron door. Above him was a blinking surveillance camera that we'd managed to turn off at the switchboard.

As we approached, the guard stood to attention then frowned and glanced at his watch. "Is it time already?"

Troy with Caius's set expression tipped his head. "It is."

The guard stepped aside, resuming his seat and burying his nose back into the pages of a magazine. Behind where he'd been standing was a touchpad attached to the wall. It was black with a blue-lit screen, and two solid red lights set into the black metal cover.

Troy threw a quick sidelong look my way then stepped forward. His thumb planted over the screen. A chime sounded and the first red light flashed green. A buzzing followed as a slender needle emerged from a tiny hole in the bottom of the device. The words *Blood Check* flashed up on the screen.

Troy's head whipped around to me, his scowl venomous and accusing. But I didn't know about this any more than he did. We'd only known about the thumbprint. Nothing else. Especially not blood. And whose blood did the device need? Did it have to be Caius's? A royal's? A guard's?

The screen beeped like it was reminding us that the final step had not yet been completed. The guard looked up from his magazine. His hand hovered over the radio at his waist and his mouth opened.

Before he could speak, Dorian leaped between the guard and Troy, sending a loaded elbow at the guard's face. The impact cracked bone and the guard cried out. But he didn't go down.

Instead he kicked out, connecting with my hip. The booted kick hit with a sting, feeling like my flesh had been torn. I ignored the raw tearing as his hand closed over his gun, removing it from the holster.

Before the guard could cock or aim, Dorian swiped the loaded metal and pumped a single shot into the guard's abdomen. Another shot like a spear into his forearm.

"Dorian, no!" I went to stop him. "Don't kill him!"

Troy, wearing Caius's meat suit, locked my arms behind my back. "He's not."

Another two shots rang out, one each into the guard's thighs. The guard slumped over with an agonized scream, falling back onto the seat, unconscious.

In a blur, Dorian strung out a long chain and coiled it around the guard until he was tied down to the metal chair. A huge padlock with engraved symbols connected the two opposing ends of the chain. These chains couldn't easily be broken, and anyone restricted by them would be powerless to escape.

Troy convulsed with an all-over body quake, returning to his own form. He kicked the out-cold guard's leg. "Now what?"

Dorian eyed the vicious needle pointing out of the print scanner. "If you become Caius again, will your blood work?"

"No. The imprint changes how I look and sound. My insides,

blood and DNA make-up, or whatever you want to call it, remains the same. My blood won't work."

"What if I zap it?" I said out loud.

Amidst Dorian and Troy's vote of agreement, Kendrick's voice rang through my ears. *No! It'll be alarm wired. Any power break could set it off. It's probably on a timer, too.*

Dammit! "Scratch that," I said, pulling at my braid in frustration. "Kendrick says it'll set off the alarm."

Then something a council member had exclaimed when Mom announced my Oracle visions rang through my ears. *That's impossible. She's not even a Pure Blood.*

Suspect excitement rushed through my veins. I stared at my own hands. The answer had been right in front of me this whole time, way before my power was revealed. Right back when I'd realized that the rarest ability bestowed onto Pure Bloods, coursed through every fiber of my being. It was part of me. Part of my blood. Part of who I really was. If damned blood coursed through my veins and had altered my DNA, then so did Pure Blood.

I removed one glove and extended my index finger as Kendrick screamed internally for me to stop. But this was our only chance. Whether I was right or wrong would all be set in place right after…

The needle pierced my finger with a sharp sting. A crimson drop fell as the needle recessed back into the touch pad. A heart-stopping second later the device beeped and the second red light flashed green. The distinct sound of deadlock bars slid free.

It had worked. More than that, it had answered the question I had sought out since fleeing the Armaya and Caius. Now without any resignation I knew the truth. I knew exactly what I was. *A manufactured Pure Blood.*

Beyond the once-bolted, three-inch solid steel door, we found a corridor lined with cells. Ty's cell was the last on the left. With my glove back on, I channeled the sparks to my fingers and rushed ahead as two chained, dirty arms reached through the bars. Ty took hold of me, wrapping his arms around my waist as mine reached through the bars to encase him.

"You made it," he said, voice gruff and tinged by surprise.

"Told you we would." I fought back the tears at having done it, having broken through every obstacle. Though being able to physically touch Ty in a way that I hadn't been able to since his imprisonment, had a few wet drops sliding free.

Troy clearing his throat had Ty's arms receding back into the cell. "Enough with the reunion. If I die in this hole, I'm taking you all down with me."

Dorian stood at the cell's barred door, slotting the large iron key we'd commandeered from the last guard into the thick lock. "I'd argue, but he's right. Let's blow this shit hole before it's too late." A loud clank announced the release and the door swung open with a slight push.

I weaved past Dorian and threw myself into Ty's arms. Though his arms flung around me, he staggered and groaned. I jerked away, pain striking my chest at the unaltered sight of him. Still shackled and through the shredded fabric of what had been his shirt and pants, I could see everything. Elongated welts covered his skin. Each was deep and wide and seeped blood. Bruises of every color stained his once tan flesh. His lip was split too. It was as swollen as his right eye that was completely closed and oozing yellowish muck. Without being able to heal, each injury must have been killing him. And that wasn't all. His left arm dangled at an entirely awkward angle, the bone broken and jutting through his forearm's flesh.

My stomach dropped. I'd just rushed into his arms, and he had hugged me back. Doing so must have been pure agony.

With a gentle hand I led Ty back, easing him down onto the

rotten cot. Then I reached for the vial. My hand slid into the pocket of my pants, feeling openness as my fingers dipped through a hole in the bottom. "Shit!"

"What's wrong," Troy demanded, hovering like the hulk over my shoulder.

I turned to expose the damage of my stolen guard's pants. The pocket was burnt through and ragged. Now I knew what that stinging pain had been. My skin below the material was mottled and edged white, with darker, uneven patches where fleshy holes had already healed. "When the guard kicked me, it broke the acid vial."

"What's...the acid for?" Ty asked in a weary voice. Even sitting his body swayed, bordering on unconsciousness.

"To break your chains." Dorian moved to my other side. He picked up Ty's non-broken arm and began pulling at the shackle.

As he tugged and grunted, my thoughts raced. Whispers that we'd failed, that we'd never get out of this alive, struck me. But I couldn't give up. I wouldn't. If we failed, I'd at least die trying.

"That won't work," Troy said. He stripped the backpack from Dorian's back and fished through it. His face was set with hard lines and desperation. The expression was unlike any I had ever seen on him before, and it set one thing in black and white. Freeing Ty meant as much to him as it did to either of us.

An idea hit me like a slap in the face. *Kendrick, will my blood give him some strength even with the restraints intact?*

What? Oh. I'm not sure, he answered, sounding distracted. *It's possible. But that still won't free...*

Kendrick's response stopped short as my idea registered in his mind. I knelt beside Ty, rolled one glove down to my wrist, and bit down, creating a deep gouge in the flesh. Crimson pooled at the punctures.

Troy's head whipped up from his bag tampering. With a

disgusted snarl he shot forward, pinning me against the far wall. "What the hell are you doing?"

"Troy, please," I pleaded, coughing at the shock of being slammed against rough stone. "You have to let me go. We don't have time for this."

"Get your hands off her!" Dorian shot up behind Troy, fangs out and arms around the guy's neck.

"Not on your life." Troy threw a back swing while keeping his other arm pinned across my neck. The hit met Dorian's chest, sending him flying back into the bars. He raised a closed fist to my face, disgust painting his expression black. "Infect him with your blood?"

Small sparks did nothing to ease the pressure of his arm against my throat. "It's the only way to get us out of here alive," I croaked.

Troy pushed harder, his canines like threatening spears poking from his mouth. "By turning him?"

"No." A raspy voice sounded from the cot. Ty coughed, spluttering on what sounded like blood. With a groan he pushed himself up into a slumped sitting position. "That's not what Amelia's trying to do. Let. Her. Go."

Troy glared, sending a bolt of daggers at me. Then his arm released and he stepped back.

Free, I scrambled forward and reopened the healing punctures before holding out my wrist. Any voltage was redirected down to my other hand. Ty's eyes met mine for a moment, trusting and hopeful. He took my arm and pressed the bleeding wound to his lips. Scarlet dripped from the corners of his hot lips, sending a current of gooseflesh all the way down to my toes.

Troy paced behind me, clearly fighting the impulse to tear my bleeding flesh from his alpha. Dorian was deceptively leaning against the cell's back wall, his knee propped up. His unblinking eyes were zoned in on Troy and a dagger was in his hand. He wasn't about to let Troy get the upper hand again.

After what seemed like minutes but couldn't have even been thirty seconds, Ty released my wrist and winced. He glanced down, face pinching at his bloody, bone-protruding arm. "It's not working." He rattled the chains hanging from his wrists. "Your blood can't heal me. Not with these."

"I know. The symbols prevent it." I straightened and took Ty's hand. There was no way to know if my idea would work, expect to test it. "But don't you feel something?" Desperate hope tightened my chest. "Somehow different?"

Ty pressed his free hand against the center of his chest. "Yeah. Like there's a ball of energy trapped in here."

This was as close to a sign that my idea could work as we were going to get. I lifted Ty to his feet, staring into his dull honey-glazed eyes. "I need you to try to imprint me."

"Imprint you? Why? What good…" His words broke off with understanding, eyes shining with the briefest glint of possibility. "You mean…"

"That's ridiculous," Troy cut in. "He can barely stand. He can't even heal. We're just wasting time we don't have. We need to consider amputation."

"You want to mutilate your own alpha?" Dorian's leg fell off the wall with a look of sheer disbelief.

"With what we have to work with?" Troy sneered over his shoulder at my brother. "It's our only hope to get out of here alive."

"No. It's not," I said, imagining Ty with gory stumped legs and arms. "It's torture. And it's not necessary."

Troy stalked forward so that his seething face was a breath away from mine. "What if it doesn't work?"

To that I didn't have a comeback. What would we do? What could we?

Before I could utter my total blank response, Ty's hand tightened around mine. A succession of cracks erupted between us. I stared wide-eyed, pain from a cracked bone in my hand shooting up my arm. Ty was doing it. He was actually doing it.

Deep growls reverberated from his throat as his entire shell vibrated, blurring and changing right before our eyes. His head fell and his height slanted with a crack of one leg. The breaking of the second leveled it. His complexion paled, tan turning porcelain. Black as night hair lengthened and streamed down from the roots in a blond wave. The hand still holding so tight to mine became soft as cashmere, no longer broad and marked with callouses from his many years of fighting experience. When Ty's body had stopped shaking, still draped and scarcely covered by his torn clothes, his head rose.

"It worked." My hand came up, marveling at the face I had known my entire life. My own silver-blue irises, pale lips, and porcelain skin.

Ty stared down at himself, head shaking as if he couldn't believe it. His hand released mine then his arms dropped. The shackles slid straight from his wrists, clattering to the ground. He swayed and dropped back onto the chain-strung cot, his back hitting the wall. Watching him and seeing my own likeness, I almost felt the stone wall's hard connection. It was eerie and surreal, but I couldn't dwell on it.

I dropped to the ground and began tugging at the shackle around his now slender right ankle. Dorian fell to my other side, and with a little edging and pulling we managed to free both restraints without inflicting too much pain.

As they fell to the floor, a harsh noise tore from Ty's throat. He fell sideways, hitting the thin, soiled mattress and tucking into a ball.

Seconds later and after a torturous cry, Ty had returned to his former self. He rolled to his back, heaving as if the air was thin of oxygen. A glimmer of gold flashed in his glassy eyes. "We did it."

"He needs more." I sent a quick glance at Troy. Needing his approval wasn't the issue. But I wanted to prevent another bust-up.

Fury at my statement blotted his face red. Still he nodded as if to say *do it.*

I slashed a nail across my wrist and dropped to my knees, pressing the bloody gash to Ty's mouth. He coughed then swallowed. After a few seconds he lifted his hands to clutch my arm. Déjà vu washed over me. Ty had tasted my blood this way when he'd needed to heal on the cruise after being wounded by the damned. That time and the one just before, my blood had flowed freely with my pulse. This time Ty's unbroken suction drew it from me, faster and faster. I gasped at the sensation and Ty broke his hold. His irises rippled for the briefest moment with that glorious gold.

"Are you okay?" Worry that he'd hurt me creased his face. Yet as he said the words, the black and purple bruises maiming his face began to fade. The puffiness to his eye and lip receded.

"You're healing," I cried. Total relief brightened what had minutes ago been a dire situation.

In the back corner of my mind I became acutely aware of Marika repeating the sworn oath as the vampires' recognized their Oracle. The oath that would bind her to deliver the truth of her visions. During the words her ruse held, her voice matching my own, her copycat features determined. She was pulling it off. When she'd completed the oath, Kendrick's sight slid from my double. He threw a quick look at the blood-filled chalice in his hands. Then his gaze lifted to the ticking clock poised below the second level balcony. The time didn't matter, but his message was clear.

"The coronation is almost complete." My vision returned to the dank cell and Ty. "The guards will be sent to retrieve you any minute. We need to leave. Now."

With a look of determination, Troy reached between us and straightened out Ty's broken arm. "Ready?"

Ty's lips thinned and he nodded. Before I could ask *ready for what?* Troy gripped above and below the exposed bone in Ty's forearm and twisted. A wicked crack broke the air as the bone snapped back into one straight piece. The pain must have been unbearable, but Ty didn't cry out or even curse. Instead he squeezed his lids shut and clenched his jaw with a screeching grind of his teeth. When it was over, my blood had worked as much of its healing power as it could.

Ty got up with a helping hand from Troy and Dorian. "Let's blow this dump."

We all bolted through the cell's door, making for the first exit we'd need to clear. Figuring our way out of the building and past the army of guards marking the exterior would be a play-by-play.

As we passed the body of the last guard we'd rendered unconscious, an electric current shot into my chest. Panic crippled my soul. I froze, hand bracing against the stone wall. "Wait!"

The other three stalled at the high shrill tone of my voice. "What's wrong?" Dorian asked.

Breathing wasn't an option, and my brain swam without oxygen. "Something's wrong. Marika—"

CHAPTER 31

My mind shifted, occupying Kendrick's and seeing through his eyes. On the elevated dais before him were six seated royals, all donning long cloaks.

The seventh was Caius, standing before my double and holding out the chalice filled with peppery Pure Blood.

Each reigning royal had donated their own blood to fill the chalice as part of the ritual to recognize and bless their new Oracle. All Marika, still perfectly masked as me, had to do was drink it. All of it.

Now in her hands, the chalice lifted inch by slow inch until its cold edge grazed her lower lip.

There was an instantaneous hush all around as she tipped the cup, not wavering even a nanosecond. Yet as the blood flowed into her mouth, an unmissable flash of gold crossed my mirrored eyes.

That was all he needed to see.

Caius took back the empty chalice, stepping back to place it on the altar. He scrutinized my double. Then his unwavering voice rose over the dense crowd of eager vampires. "This is not my niece."

Caius unsheathed the sword at his back and gasps rang out over the crowd. It was the same sword that had been used to bleed out each royal's blood for the offering. He pointed the gleaming edge at my double's heart. His eyes blazed, incredulous and crazed. "Traitor!"

My mom jumped up from the front row, clearing the rise to the dais to land between Caius and his readying sword. "Caius, stop! What in the world are you doing?"

"Caius knows I'm not me," I said, while still watching through Kendrick's eyes.

A hot, calloused hand gripped mine and pulled, forcing me along a path I couldn't see. Rushing words blew through my ears, but I couldn't make sense of them. My total focus was a level above us, watching the horror unfold.

Caius retracted his sword a few inches and regarded my mom with a hard look. "Lamayli, this is not your daughter. This is an—" He moved with blurred speed, his wielding arm burying the sword in Marika's stomach. "Imposter!"

Uproar exploded and guards closed in on the stage.

Kendrick rushed forward as Caius's sword drew free, glistening blade dripping bright with crimson. He caught Marika right before she collapsed to the ground and hauled her sideways.

My mom screamed with violent disbelief. She threw herself onto Caius as guards stood by, waiting for a command.

Marcus rose and strode toward Kendrick, while the rest of The Council sat in unmoving shock.

Except for Uriel. She flung off her cloak to reveal silver stakes strapped to her sides. Among the growing panic rising from the crowd, she was the only one to speak. "In heaven's name, what have you done?" She pinned Caius with a piercing stare, curling a gloved hand around one of the stakes.

My mom continued beating her fists into Caius who seemed unperturbed by her onslaught. "That is not Miss Amelia Lamont," he bellowed loud enough to cover the noise of everyone watching as he pointed his stained sword. "She is not even a vampire."

As the word *vampire* rang out the audience hushed.

Kendrick's sight dropped, looking at my double who had pulsing blood pouring from her abdomen. Just as fast as Ty had morphed back to himself after imprinting me, so did Marika. Her blond hair receded, turning black and glossy. Her body bulged, tight once again in my coronation dress. And with tearing hazel eyes, and skin a tan contrast to the almost translucent porcelain it had been seconds before, the recession to her former self was complete.

With Caius's clarifying words, "She's a lycan!" the entire court swarmed into anarchy.

"What's happening?" Dorian's voice came from behind me. His hand pressed against my back, helping guide the way while Ty hauled me relentlessly forward. "Are they okay?"

"It's M-Marika." My vision merged back to the corridors we were speeding through. The image of blood pouring from Marika's abdomen rose every time I blinked. I clutched at the phantom pain lancing through my own stomach and gagged, swallowing the rise of vomit. "Caius's...sword. He..." The words died on my tongue, too horrific to spit out. But they had to know. "He ran her through."

Ty's grip on my hand tightened, forcing me on even faster. "I'll kill him."

"Is she dead?" Troy's snarl was more animal than human, his inner wolf threatening to break free.

With a slow blink, I saw the chaos. A maelstrom of volatile wind had formed. Inside it, Kendrick had managed to drag Marika to the back corner stairs leading to the second level balcony. Blood continued to leak from her healing wound, but her complexion had grown pale. She would die before the blood flow stopped. She coughed and crimson pooled from her mouth and ran down her chin. Kendrick used a blade to score his forearm and forced it to her mouth.

All of a sudden I was forced to a standstill. The hall blacked out like a light and the red-tinted corridor appeared. We had cleared the lower level and were now a corridor's length from the glass security station.

"I asked you a question, leech." Troy pressed an arm against my windpipe, pinning me against the wall.

My mouth opened, but nothing came out. Pressure tightened my chest and striking pain pierced my neck. A gentle push down is all it would take to crush bone.

Quick as a flash, two figures shot to either side of us. Ty had his hands around Troy's neck, and Dorian belted into the guy's chest while tearing his arm back from my throat. They threw him at the opposite stone wall.

With murder in his eyes, Ty's face tilted, huge canines sliding free. "Touch her again," he snarled, blocking the space between Troy and me, "and I will tear out your fucking throat."

Keeping them in his line of sight, Dorian came to my side to inspect the damage. "Anything broken?"

I rubbed the blazing flesh while my focus remained on the wolves. "No." Troy looked milliseconds from taking on Ty's threat. And I couldn't have it. I went to Ty's side and tugged on his shoulder. "Stop it. Both of you." I tried not to let Troy's radiating hatred poison my expression. "Lives are at stake and we need to work together."

Ty released his hold but didn't move or retract his canines.

"I know you're worried about Marika, but she's okay. Kendrick's with her. He's helping her heal."

Troy breathed through flared nostrils. Then he pushed off the wall. Quiet cracks erupted with the elongation of his mouth, and his teeth grew to razor-sharp canines. "With his blood?" His mouth twisted while his hazel eyes raged with golden flecks. A succession of louder cracks erupted with the outraged cry of a human voice turning wild.

"Kendrick's doing what's needed to save her life," Dorian cut in.

But no words could stop what was already set in motion. In seconds Troy had transformed into a dark-chocolate-colored wolf. Ty blocked his way before he could take off. "Touch Kendrick and I'll let her," he flashed his hard stare at me, "kill you. You get them out and that's it. No casualties."

Troy snarled then let out a bark. His skull dipped and tilted, then he took off, paws pelting the ground as he ran. Without pause we shot after him.

As we reached the cross paths that split from the station, Kendrick's voice rang through my ears. *Amelia, left!*

"This way." I tugged on Ty's hand, redirecting the three of us along the corridor that snaked left from the glass station. "Troy will catch up." Kendrick was sending us directly to the council hall. And we needed every second we could get. If my vision was right, and my gut told me it was, the damned would be busting in any second now.

Part of me needed to stay for the fight. Everyone in that hall was here to see me. Their Oracle. Caius may have brought them here, but attendance wasn't mandatory. I couldn't abandon them. Not when I knew of the mortal danger to come. But if I stayed?

I'd seen Ty bleeding and weak, being cut up by Caius's sword. I didn't know the outcome, and I didn't want to stick around to find out.

As we reached the last bend before immersing ourselves in the loud riot that poured through the arched entrance, I tugged Ty back. With forceful hands, I shoved his shoulders back against the wall. "Wait!" Dorian paused, and I nodded him on. "Get to Kendrick and move Marika to the second level balcony. We'll be right behind you."

Dorian disappeared around the bend, pulling the folded crossbow from his backpack and flinging it out into operation.

"Amelia, we don't have time for this." Ty watched after my brother, body twitching to take after him. "They need our help."

"I know. But I need you to promise me something." At Ty's raised eyebrows I went on. "Promise me that we'll get to our friends and you'll get out."

"That's the plan, isn't it?" Ty's expression shifted, speculation drawing his lips open. "Amelia, what aren't you telling me?"

That Caius will come gunning for you. I gulped and bit my lip.

Before I could speak, a crash of glass imploding split through the air.

In a flash we appeared at the arched opening to the council hall and stood frozen in horror. Every glimmering glass pane surrounding the hall had been smashed in. Streaming through them and filling the hall were countless figures, a moving wall of vicious-ness closing in on all the vampires below. All draped in black with gray translucent flesh, their piercing red pupils shone with starvation.

Shouts came from the dais, instruction for all living vampires to arm themselves. The shock of having a lycan impersonating their Oracle was easily forgotten. Every vampire inside the hall was moving. Some made for the exits, while others scrambled over each other to arm themselves with the many weapons that had been stowed beneath boxed benches lining the hall.

Still positioned on the dais was the Royal Vampire Council. Every one of them was armed to the teeth. Some clutched silver stakes while the rest unsheathed gleaming silver swords from the backs of their thrones.

Before the RVC were their immediate family members. These ones had clearly been alerted to the possible attack because they were now all brandishing an assortment of weapons. They leaped into battle, weapons swinging past those still rushing to get armed. But they weren't fast enough. The damned moved like lightning, their blurred figures rendering bodies lifeless quicker than they could be taken down. In the melee one thing was glaringly apparent. Caius was nowhere to be seen and neither was my mom.

Kendrick hauled an almost unconscious Marika up the stairs to the balcony. Dorian covered them, firing off rounds from his crossbow at the swarming damned. I shuddered as they reached the balcony railing. Damned were crawling up the walls like spiders.

Desperation and fear clung to my heart and soul. We didn't have long. "Ty, will you leave with them?"

"Will *I*?" His jaw clenched, reading between the lines. "What about you?"

There was no backing out of this now. "I'm staying." Fully accepted as the Oracle or not, the vampires needed me. I couldn't leave them to die. Not when I could help. A cold knot unfurled in my gut. "I can't abandon them."

Clear determination rippled through Ty's eyes. Without even a glimmer of hesitation he said, "Then I stay, too."

I knew that fierce look from the threats Ty had given Troy. Nothing I could say would make him change his mind. Just like nothing he'd said could have kept me from endangering us all to rescue him. I could never have left him to be executed. And he would never leave me here alone. He'd never abandon me. So there was no way to alter the future. I had done everything to escape the inevitable, but it couldn't be controlled or changed any more than my love for Ty could.

"Okay." I pressed a soft kiss to his lips that was over and done with way too soon. Tears blurred my vision but I held them back. "But promise you'll stay away from Caius." I paused for the briefest moment, but he had to know the fate I'd seen. "He's going to try to kill you."

With a roar and the crack of reforming bones, Ty transformed into the wolf. The strongest and most equipped form he had for battle. He threw a glance at me before leaping into the fray, canines bared and ready to tear flesh.

I bounded after him with my stake in hand and got caught in the mass of vampires and damned fighting to the death. Keeping low, I weaved between those already feuding and managed to take out a few damned with the tactic of surprise. As I staked my third damned, I sensed Kendrick watching me over the balcony. The spider-climbing damned were scaling up to their level. The only thing holding them back was Kendrick's whirlwind and Dorian's firing crossbow.

Kendrick. Get Marika and Dorian out. And don't come back.

If you think I'm leaving you down there alone, you've lost your mind.

Kendrick lifted Marika and edged back with Dorian to the pitched window ending the balcony. As he went to kick the glass out, a damned broke through the maelstrom. Dorian pulled the crossbow trigger, but the canister was empty.

At the same instant, I swept under the clawed hands of a damned, my foot striking out to bring him down. Though not before he'd rent tracks across my ribs. My stake came down, piercing his heart.

When my eyes shot up from the exploding ash, I almost froze. Dorian had his hands out in front of him. The concentration straining his face was do or die. Then it happened. The damned stalking forward fell to its knees. Black oozed from its eyes, streaming down its murderous-turned-panicked face. As its mouth twisted open in agony, more blood gurgled up. Then it fell flat on its face.

Overwhelmed, but seeing more damned begin to break the wind barrier, I rushed my words. *Kendrick, please. I can't lose you, too.* My stake pierced another attacker's chest before my heart could skip a beat. The damned's face contorted and then her entire body combusted into a smoldering pile of burning ash.

I'll be back, Kendrick's promise echoed through my ears.

Before I could argue, he leaped from the window with Marika slung over his shoulder. Dorian was right behind them, reloading his crossbow.

My instant relief at their escape came crashing down. They'd landed amongst a black and gray sea of damned. My mind screamed out to Kendrick. But it was no use. The link to his mind closed like a tunnel caving in on itself.

CHAPTER 32

orn. Like my body wanted to split in half and take off in opposite directions.

Before me, the damned had taken so many already that lifeless bodies littered the floor, slicking the marble with glossy red puddles. I wanted to make a run for it, to get past these walls to see if Kendrick and my brother were okay. But I couldn't leave these people. And I couldn't abandon Ty or Troy who were both now fighting for their lives because of me.

Caius was still MIA, but that wouldn't last. Because this *was* the scene from my vision. The blood, the bodies, the damned. It was reality now. One I couldn't change if I ran.

No, I needed to stay and fight. I needed to believe that if Kendrick or Dorian's lives were destined to end that I would have seen it coming.

Decision made, I panned across the room, taking in the damage. Ty centered the assault, all muscle and raw animal power. Troy now flanked his side, snarling fiercely. For the moment they held their ground, dropping damned like bags of wet sand.

Outrage for the lycans from living vampires was lost to their screams as they fell to the ground. So many of them, although they were armed, had no idea how to wield their weapons.

I saw Marcus before me, his face streaked with black and red blood, fighting off the advances of two damned. And he was losing ground.

I sprung to his side, peeling off one glove. Then I freed my spiked whip from my back and rolled it out with the flick of my wrist. Static crackled along the silver weapon. "Got your back."

Marcus smiled, total relief to see me brightening his face. "Perfect timing."

The first damned surged forward. Its fangs snapped for my jugular, dripping red with someone else's blood. I spun around, using my free arm to dodge his attack as I recoiled part of the whip. Then I snapped out the shorter length to curl around his throat. A little tug and the spikes embedded with a twisting squeeze, and voltage sparked down its length.

Behind me I could hear Marcus battling the second damned. But I couldn't turn around. Already another damned was rushing my way.

With the first damned writhing on the ground, sizzling hands tugging at my embedded whip, I snatched a stake from my belt and pierced the launching damned straight through the heart. Ash exploded around me and I spun before inhaling its charcoal remains.

The first damned got free from my whip with burned and black-oozing hands. He leaped mid-air and I recoiled my whip. But I wasn't fast enough.

The damned landed on my chest, drooling fangs snapping for my neck as we tumbled to the ground. Its claws tunneled into my shoulders, touching bone. The only thing holding back his bite was my arm locked against his chest. An arm that let out borrowed sparks from my whip-clutching hand.

Time seemed to slow to an almost standstill. My arm began to give with crippling muscle spasms. Then my resistance failed. The damned had me.

Except his fangs never reached my neck. Only the cold saliva of his anticipation did as his face froze, twisting before bursting into ash.

A broad, pale hand caught mine and pulled me up. Marcus, with a wide gash coming back together across his forehead, dusted off his hands. "Same fate goes to anyone who tries to kill you. I'll take down this whole room if I have to."

I let out the breath I hadn't realized I'd been holding. "Three more down. How many to go?"

A devilish smile crossed his face, the kind that made me wonder if he'd ever felt true fear.

A careless damned attempted to rush past and he sliced through her without blinking. "That's six on my count." His teal-flecked eyes shifted to the battling crowd. "The genetics of being warriors is coming back to them."

It was true. Though unprepared and forced into battle, the vampires had gained some ground. Many of their bodies littered the veined marble, each new one piling on top of another fallen. Yet the number of ashen piles was growing faster by the minute, too.

I holstered my stake and held my whip ready. "Let's even the odds."

With a powerful jump, I immersed myself in the belly of battle, flanking Ty's other side. Cuts and gashes tacked up both wolves' fur, but they continued to fight strong as if their lives and everyone's in this hall rested on their shoulders alone. They were an unstoppable force, protecting a race that hated them.

My heart swelled with relief and determination to get us all out of this alive. "Time to make it rain black."

I swear Ty grinned, wolf canines and all. He licked my hand then struck out, saving a vampire from having her neck shredded like soft fruit.

The relentless battle went on, more bodies and ash falling every minute. With our combined force and the perseverance of the living vampires, we were slowly making ground. With every dropped damned I felt a little lighter, a little more hopeful that we could make it out of this alive.

A close fighting royal, the balding council member, sneered over his shoulder at Ty and Troy. "They don't belong here."

I glared at him in disbelief. Full on battle still hadn't curbed his racism. "We need them. Unless you'd prefer to die."

Indignant, the royal turned up his nose. Then almost like I'd called down a curse from heaven, a damned girl with blue-black hair and bloody fangs shot forward. She launched, taking the royal with such ferocious speed that all that was left was a shredded, bloody throat and dead eyes.

Then she turned on me. I cracked my whip out and missed. The damned ducked and the spikes curled around her wrist rather than her neck.

And then she was leaping, straight through the air...at me.

Ty shot between us and clamped onto her arm. She shrieked, turning to slice her extending talons through his side.

My whip released and I cracked it out again. It sailed, tip snaking around the damned's neck and pulling her off Ty.

But it was too late.

Her fangs had already plunged into Ty's thigh. They ripped free with another yank of my whip to tear a fleshy chunk away. A howl scored through others' cries as her extended fangs aimed for his neck. Troy returned the howl but was barricaded behind his own advancing damned.

I went to yank the damned backward again, but a falling vampire knocked the whip from my grasp.

With no time to think, my hand darted to my belt and my sliver stake. I cleared the bodies on the floor and collided with the girl, knocking us both to the ground.

Craze-blinded she flipped me onto my back, cold wetness soaking my clothes. The blood of the fallen.

Her mouth opened wide and her fingernails bit into my neck and chest, pinning me. "You're dead." Her mouth opened wide, her fangs closing in.

As her rank, cold breath touched my neck, my bare hand shot up. It drove the stake home into her cold, dead heart. An electric burst erupted through the silver, sending her flying back off my stake and into a heap of dead bodies. "No. You are."

Far from needing to witness another body combust, I jumped up from the pool of blood and surrounding dead bodies. My sight skittered.

There.

Ty was on four paws, muzzle twisting to crunch around a damned's stomach. Crimson leaked from his thigh where the chunk had been torn out. But he was alive.

As if sensing my gaze, his wolf eyes met mine and he let out a howl.

At that instant a fresh band of damned encroached, forcing me back and separating us. Over their heads I glimpsed Ty and Troy's wolf backs. The beta was back at his side. More blood made Ty's black fur glisten. But he was still on his feet, movements advancing with continued attack. "Ty!"

A level howl rose from the noise of battle. He was okay. For now.

I tried to rush forward, but I had to fend off my own attackers. Five in total. Snatching up my whip from between torn bodies, I struck out sure and true. But my static voltage was gone, snuffed like a flame under water.

My free hand ripped a dagger from the holster at my calf, lashing out.

The blows from my attackers came flying, and I returned each with the punishment for striking me. In what felt like hours of ducking, leaping, and lashing out with my weapons, I managed to drop two of the five damned.

I weaved on my feet, fighting exhaustion that filled my bones like putty. The unrelenting energy of the remaining damned held strong, and they struck out with as much force as they had started with.

One thing was dauntingly clear. I no longer had the strength to outfight my enemies, much less the speed. So I needed to be cunning. It was time to switch tactics.

One of the three sprung forward, cracking an elbow into my jaw. I dropped, feigning unconsciousness. My ears peeled past the endless warring around me. There were footsteps first, tracking through sticky blood. Bones crunched as the fallen were walked over like forgotten garbage. Raspy breathing neared, growing louder with anticipation. At last the chill of putrid breath brushed my cheek.

My knee shot up, connecting with the attacker's groin. Dead or not, that still had to freaking hurt. And it did. The damned cried out, surprised red eyes turning even more vibrant with the pain.

But the true surprise was yet to come.

My arms shot up, releasing the concealed stake from my sleeve and driving it home. Smoldering ash exploded around me and I leaped through its wake, ready to take on the two remaining damned.

But one was already behind me. Its arms curled around my own, locking them behind my back. "You first," it hissed at the damned in front of me.

The other snarled in response, seething with the need to tear me to pieces.

A distant voice drew my eye to the dais, where heavy thrones lay cracked and upturned. "Caius," my mom cried out. "My children need me. Let me out!"

Caius slammed the steel door below the dais shut and bolted it. He mumbled something while dusting off his clothes. My mouth gaped at his words, *"I will not let you die. You will be safe here."*

Before I could comprehend any reason for his act of protection, the damned stepped forward, hissing. "You'll pay for that, bitch."

A direct voice stopped his advance. The same voice I'd just heard, now loud and commanding. "Don't kill her!" Caius stood on the edge of the dais. As if he'd been watching the whole battle take place from the start. Not hiding out to lock up my mom. "Restrain her!"

"Caius!" Uriel stared over the thinning swarm of battlers, mystified. She sliced a damned in two with a wicked-looking sword with a wavy edge and serrated tip. Now she advanced on him, the sword a warning in her steady hand. "What in heaven's name are you doing?"

"Taking what is mine." Caius's wrinkled face flared with rage. Outing himself clearly hadn't been the plan. With a single-handed motion, he set a band of three damned on his colleague.

Other vampires gaped, shocked at his treachery, but he ignored them.

With a point of his sword, he set another four damned on me and began weaving through the fallen bodies. "I need her alive."

Caius still needed my blood to become immortal. And every drop he could drain from my veins was no use if I was already dead. Due to that underlying fact, for the moment *I* held the upper hand. I didn't need to escape the vicious fangs of however many damned that now had their hungry red eyes focused on me. I just had to stay conscious enough to kill every last one that came my way.

With the soles of my feet aching in my Vans, an idea came to mind. I struggled against my restrainer and kicked out. The base of my Vans flew like a mallet into the damned's stomach before me. The force sent him sailing back until he crashed into his advancing back up.

Without hesitation, I threw my head back. My skull connected with the damned's nose with a splitting crack. His grip loosened.

Exactly what I needed.

With some motion to my arms returned, I spun, swinging the butt of the whip around the damned's torso and catching it as it came around. I gripped the length and crossed the whip over itself, pulling hard. He wailed as the spikes sank into his chest and back. Black blood gurgled out from the countless silver punctures.

The shock caught him by surprise, but I didn't have a second to waste. The fallen damned were back on their feet and making a beeline for me.

I centered my stance, ready to lash out with my dagger in one hand and my retracted whip in the other. As I went to rush forward, Kendrick and Dorian appeared at my side.

"Oh my god." I couldn't believe it. "You're alright!"

Since they'd jumped into the swarm lurking outside, my connection to Kendrick had been severed. I'd had no idea if they were okay, let alone alive. Now they stood right beside me. Both looked far worse for wear but were still in once piece. Still breathing.

"We kicked some undead butt!" Dorian's silver eyes were as wild as his mussed hair. His guard's uniform was torn, and I could smell blood on him. Damned and his own. Still, beneath the torn fabric I saw healing lacerations.

Kendrick, in similar shape, ducked out of a damned's way. As he dropped he stabbed through the creature's back with a stake. A pile of crackling embers was all that was left in his wake. "Here to save your ass, by the looks of it."

The remaining four damned closed in, surrounding us. We answered every attack with our trained line of defense, ducking, weaving, using each other as leverage, and striking out with every opportunity. Our attackers minded their kill strikes when coming at me, but were ruthless against Kendrick and Dorian. Still, even with their attempt to kill, Kendrick and Dorian's *kill or be killed* response was in clear action.

While the battle forged on, I caught glimpses of Kendrick's memories. Outside and swarmed by damned, their powers had been the striking queen on a chessboard. Whirlpools of wind cocooned Marika in safety while she healed. Batting gusts assaulted the damned, throwing them off balance or up against the outside of the building. Strong swirls, made visible with rock and tree debris, launched them up into the air, only to drop them from a splattering height. Dorian's crossbow and ability to bleed out his opponents, along with Kendrick's stake, made most of the kill shots, cutting their enemy's numbers. The entire throng of damned outside had been slayed, all while managing to keep Marika unharmed.

Their powers were MIA after the exhausting expulsion, leaving weapons as their last defense. Still, they weren't about to give in now.

As the fourth damned fell, another even larger group set on us. Around us, the ratio of damned to vampires was gradually leveling. Our resistance was almost on par with theirs. Uriel was among those still standing, fierce battlers. Marcus, who I'd just spotted for the first time since he'd incinerated the damned that had decked me, wasn't far from her. Two damned were taking him on, but their attacks seemed weak and somehow deliberate. Around them other royal and turned vampires fought on, still consumed with the never-ending advances of remaining enemies.

Then I saw something that distracted my attack of the female damned I was about to stake. A blunt force connected with my chest and I fell to my knees. My lungs ached and my breath came hard and fast.

Kendrick and Dorian covered my fallen body, but they couldn't stop me from seeing my nightmare unfolding before my very eyes.

Ty snarled across the room, still a towering menace in his magnificent wolf form. His muzzle creased up into bunching lines. His bared canines glistened with black blood that pooled from his mouth.

Before him was Caius. In his hand was his silver sword, and it was trained at Ty. The blade sliced through the pungent air, thickened with the scent of both fresh and damned blood.

Tacky red oozed from new, wide gashes across Ty's shoulders, legs, and back. He grunted and snarled as he ducked and weaved out of Caius's blade's path while lunging and snapping bites.

He was tired, I realized, his movements less precise and more desperate than earlier.

The disadvantage left Caius's sword affording closer calls with Ty's flesh with every arching swing.

A surge of fear, stronger and more compelling than any I had ever experienced, had my pulse pounding through my ears. The ice in my veins melted with a sudden spike of electric adrenaline.

I sprung up, pushing Dorian and Kendrick away as my whip struck out. It slashed through the damned before me, a relentless and unforgiving weapon that didn't fail as I forged a path through the fallen bodies and still-encroaching damned. All the while my focus remained lasered ahead.

Ty dodged a fresh strike from Caius. In the leap back his paws caught on a crumpled body that had fallen at his feet. He tripped, losing his footing for a split second.

That second lapse was all Caius needed. He lanced forward, sword slicing into Ty's shoulder.

A high-pitched howl erupted as Ty fell, the deep gash pulsing fiery sweet blood. Ty struggled to stand, legs giving way on the slick marble.

Caius closed in and raised his scarlet-painted sword. The point trained at Ty's skull. "Time to die, mongrel."

A shrill cry pulsated through the air. The hairs along the back of my neck rose. And it took me a second to realize that *I* had been the one to scream. In the same instant my hands lifted, reaching and stretching, palms flexed forward. Two blue bolts broke free, connecting to become one. They crackled through the air and around everything in their path, like a missile locked on its target.

But it was too late.

Caius's sword came down with the force of a guillotine. Ty rolled back, the deadly point missing his skull and piercing straight through his heart.

CHAPTER 33

Ty's wolf body slid from the sword, crumpling to the ground in a vibration that returned him to human form.

Then the lightning bolt found its target.

It connected with Caius's chest and sent him flying backward, skidding across the slick ground until he hit a mountain of bodies. Shock crippled his menacing expression and he dropped the sword, which skittered away with a clank.

Most of the remaining damned scattered, seeing their leader fall under the force of my power. The battle was over, and they knew it. The still living royals and their guards moved to take on any stragglers.

The cries of the remaining damned and resulting ash explosions meant nothing to me. I had a score to settle.

With uncontainable rage bursting inside me, I strode to Caius. One hand pressed over the other, pointing my palms forward. Tiny threads of blue electricity danced down my arms, collecting at my desperate call. I needed to make this monster pay for what he'd taken from me. Pay for Ty's life with his own. But the sparks were residual, not strong enough to stream the same powerful voltage from me and into him. I strained harder and the sparks retracted, running back up my arms and disappearing.

I roared and swiped Caius's sword from the ground. It was so wet with Ty's blood that it dripped from the end. I sniffed back tears and pointed the tip straight at Caius's heart. "You'll pay for what you did."

"You will not do it." Caius stared up at me, almost daring me to disobey. "You cannot kill your own flesh and blood."

"You're not my fucking blood! You're nothing to me."

I pressed the tip to his flesh. Crimson bloomed from the slice, staining his white shirt. It made me smile and fed my need for revenge. My need for owed justice. "You ordered the deaths of Marcus's family and unleashed genocide on this council. You *killed...*"

I couldn't finish the sentence. Couldn't believe that Ty was gone while this monster was still alive and breathing. Clutching the hilt harder, my hands rose, ready to deliver divine justice by driving the sword straight through his black heart. "Go to hell!"

Before the sword could claim my revenge, a crack of metal and wood rang out. A shrill cry pierced my ears. Racing from where she'd been locked beneath the dais, my mom leaped in front of me, blocking my kill shot. "Amelia, stop!"

"Move!" Blinded by fury I could barely see her. My mom or not, no one would stop this. "Or meet his fate!"

"Amelia, no." She clung to my arms, splitting my hands apart and forcing the sword to clatter to the ground. "Stop. Amelia, please. You can't kill him."

Behind her Caius got to his feet, a bemused smile animating his old face. "And why might that be, Lamayli?"

Mom's teary eyes rose to meet mine. An expression that was as painful as it was unreadable scored her face. "Because he *is* your flesh and blood."

"Liar!" I pushed her away and kicked the sword up, catching it in my shaking hand. I aimed at Caius again, glaring at him. If looks could kill, his heart would already have stopped. "Tell her it's not true. You compelled my mom. You even marked her flesh so your lies would stick. Tell her the truth!"

Caius smiled, his expression self-important. "You know the truth, my dear."

A gentle hand cupped over mine holding the sword. "I was compelled, and marked," my mom spoke softly. "At my own request. So I could lie. To you and your brother. Before I knew of your power, I saw you change. You both became curious. And I couldn't have that."

I held my grip on the sword, ready to plunge it in deep. My whole body shook. "It's not true."

Mom stepped in front of me, pushing the weapon aside. "Sweetheart, it is. Caius is your father."

It felt like the world around me had just imploded. The reality of this hall and everything I ever thought I knew smashed to smithereens. The world was like a haze that couldn't quite reach me. Guards continued to restrain any damned that hadn't fled with my electric outburst. There was shouting, instructions, and debate. But I couldn't hear it, any of it. Blood pounded through my heart that felt like it wanted to explode. My legs turned to jello and gave out. Something broke my fall, but I didn't know what. Corpse or survivor, it didn't matter. I didn't care. All I could see was a band of black-clad guards dragging Caius away. My mom scurried after, her flapping mouth directing questions I couldn't hear at…*my father.*

Splitting pain struck through my body. Knowing what that

monster had stolen from me tore never-ending strips off my ragged heart, as if the organ were an orange being peeled. I had failed, and it had cost me the one thing I didn't think I could live without. I clutched the amulet to my heart as morbid reality dawned. *Ty is dead.*

The thing that had broken my fall shifted, lifting my weight and pulling us up from the slippery mess of spilled blood. Kendrick's voice began to lift the fog from my mind. *Amelia.* He spun me on the spot until all that encompassed my entire line of sight was Ty. *He's not dead.*

I sucked in a sharp breath, sending a blowout of pins through my lungs.

Ty lay a few unmoving bodies away. Having morphed back into human form, he was naked, his body hunched in on itself. Black and crimson covered every inch of his battered, slashed, and bleeding flesh. An ugly opening scored his back.

The place where Caius's sword had struck through.

It was cleanly sliced, a mouth spitting scarlet pulses. But Kendrick was right. He was still alive. An uncontrollable shiver had his entire body quaking. In the surrounding noise, I could hear the repetitive, harsh sound of air being sucked into wet lungs. In, in, in, out. In, in, in, out.

"Ty!"

Without direction my body responded, legs moving and arms outstretched. I stumbled and crashed to the floor. The expulsion of my electric bolt, the strongest I had ever created, had left me weak. Still I couldn't, I wouldn't, stop. With every muscle and every last ounce of strength in me, I dragged my body through a mound of ash until I had Ty within reach.

"Ty," I croaked. I clung to his arms, pulling with all my might to draw him to me. Another two sets of hands appeared, pale and stained—I wasn't sure whose. They lifted Ty so that he was draped across my lap.

Ty coughed, spluttering on blood that swelled from his mouth. His eyelids cracked, but couldn't open all the way. "Amelia?"

"Yes." I sniffed back tears and wiped a shaking hand over his forehead, clearing his claggy hair from his face. "I'm here. Everything's going to be okay."

The wounds that covered his exposed body were countless. Each oozed a mixture of red and black tacky blood. The black was the ingested damned blood. He must have swallowed a bucket-load while taking them down. The tar-thick stuff was like poison, preventing his countless wounds from healing. Among the gashes were uglier patches of skin that had been punctured and serrated... by teeth. Ty had been bitten, over and over, flesh torn from his limbs and damned venom injected with every puncture. But the wound killing him was the gaping hole through his chest.

I pressed my hands over the entry, feeling the dying beat of his sliced heart. It was impossible for Ty to heal; we'd learned that when rescuing him. But there was an antidote, a way to reverse the effects of damned blood. A way to begin healing his broken body. My blood.

"Amelia." Kneeling behind me, Kendrick placed a broad hand across my shoulder. "He's too badly injured. You can't cure him. And even if you could, after all his injuries, you could..." The words *damn him* floated on the air through our bond.

"So I should let him die?" I threw a venomous look behind my back, then to every other face that surrounded us. There was Dorian, Marcus, and Troy who held up a worse-for-wear but alive Marika at his side.

"He's better dead than one of them," Troy said, kicking at a pile of ash. Somehow he was in human form, wearing a shredded pair of jeans.

"Troy's right." Marika coughed, expression sympathetic as if she were imagining Troy in that position. "The damned are so much worse than rogues. Ty's life has been devoted to hunting the lesser of the two."

Dorian spoke up but looked like he hated what he had to say. "It would destroy him to become everything he was raised to hate."

Marcus stepped forward and knelt before us. "There's no guarantee that he'll turn damned. He's a lycan. He'd likely die first." The look on his face spoke volumes. Part vampire or not, a lycan had never been turned damned. He touched my hand and a glint of encouraging hope passed between us. "Though Amelia is different. No one can deny that. She could cure him."

"And if he turns?" Troy glared at Marcus, canines peeking through parted lips. "Then what?"

I gulped. If I did nothing, Ty would die. Acting could kill him too, or worse. Either way it might already be too late. Still, I needed to believe that this wasn't the end. I could save him, somehow. "If he turns, we find a way to reverse it." That had been Caius's plan all along. Restore his damned mother and sisters to living vampires. And I was the key. "There's a way. I know there is. I can't lose him."

Ty shifted with a groan, growing heavier across my lap. His eyelids fluttered open and a weak smile curved his split lips. "Do—" he croaked around a rising mouthful of blood, "—it." He coughed and crimson sprayed from his mouth, speckling my face and chest. "I know you can save me."

Debate escalated from the others, but I didn't care. What they thought didn't matter. Right here and now there was only me and Ty, lost in each other's eyes. Without breaking our gaze I lifted my wrist and bit down, then I pressed the bleeding punctures to Ty's lips. My blood pooled, mixing with his own until his mouth was so full that it spilled out the corners of his lips. Vibrant torrents ran down either side of his face. I fought back the tears that clouded my vision. "Ty, please. You have to swallow."

Ty's expression pinched. His eyes rolled back and his body began convulsing. All the blood that had filled his mouth came streaming out in a river, not a single drop taken in. My free arm held tighter to him, willing his body to become still. And then it did. Every muscle that had been so taut and rapt with uncontrollable spasms released. I began to extend my wrist, to make him drink again, but then I stopped.

Ty's head twitched, shaking almost indiscernibly left to right. "No." His voice was so quiet, a voided echo of the power I knew his tone could carry. "It's t-too late."

"What?" It suddenly seemed like Ty was so far away from me. Like he was fading into a tunnel before my very eyes. "No. You can't mean that. You're not dead. There's still time."

I looked up, pleading with everyone that had stopped bickering to stare at me with morbid pity. Each of their expressions said, *you can't save him, he's as good as dead.*

The feel of a warm and shaking hand pressing against my cheek stole my gaze. Ty's face was a mirror of agony as breath rasped from his throat. It became even shallower and rattly with the tremors that rushed like a flood back through his entire body. Yet even in this state, his hand somehow remained against my jaw, thumb grazing my bottom lip. His mouth parted with the shadow of a smile. "I-I… l-love you, Amelia. I w-will always…l-love you."

"Ty, no!" I screamed, clutching his shoulder and shaking. "Don't say that. Don't say goodbye."

In my violently shaking hands Ty's entire body turned limp. I watched his eyes roll back to the whites. Then I heard the breath release from his throat and lungs. Suddenly his body felt as if it weighed more than a freight train. He slipped from my grasp and his skull hit the marble with a crack.

I leaped onto his chest. "Don't leave me!"

With the heel of my palm I began compressions. An innate sense washed over me as even more black-stained red blood streamed from Ty's wounds. I needed voltage. I needed the electricity that sparked from my body and hands. Like a defibrillator to jump-start his heart. But there was nothing. All of its force had been used to blast Caius from Ty.

A rib cracked under my palms as my compressions became desperate. "Wake up!"

"Amelia. Sweetheart." My mom had come up behind, resurfacing since she took after Caius and the guards. Her fingers curled around my arms, pulling me back. "He's gone. It's time to let go."

I tore my arms free and beat my fists against Ty's chest. "No! I can bring him back. I can save him. It's not too late!"

Pressure squeezed around both my arms and hauled me off Ty. Even though I was aware that one of the two was Kendrick, I lashed out with nails and feet. Thrashing to get free, thrashing to get back to Ty. "Let me fucking go!"

"Amelia." Dorian's grip on my arm tightened. "It's too late. There's nothing you can do."

The tunnel grew longer and Ty's lifeless body became smaller. "You're not dead. Move. Speak. *Do* something, Ty!"

In my relentless thrashing I managed to release one of my arms. My freed hand curled around the dagger's hilt at my thigh and struck out, connecting with flesh and bone.

Dorian's resistance failed and my mom cried out, rushing to his side.

Kendrick caught my armed hand and squeezed, cracking bone

until I released the dagger. As it clattered to the floor someone appeared before me. A flash of light reflected off the gun rising in Troy's hands. A whistle sounded and something sharp sank into my throat.

Legs and arms failed. Eyes rolled.

Then there was nothing but cold darkness.

CHAPTER 34

"We can't tell her." I heard my mom's voice as though she were speaking under water. She sounded impossibly far away. "She's been through enough already."

Arms supported my weight, cradling me against a firm chest. Light sent flickering pins of shining beams through my closed lids. But I couldn't open them. Invisible weights pinned them shut, preventing sight. The same drowning weight had hold of my body, bones, and muscles. I couldn't move. Then there was darkness again.

In the darkness, a cone of light opened up before me. What I focused on was the last event I ever wanted to relive.

"Time to die, mongrel." Caius's sword had struck its target, a knife through butter slicing straight through Ty's heart. Ty's head dropped, wolf eyes almost wide at the hilt of a thick silver sword protruding from his chest. A noise of surprise escaped his muzzle, almost sounding human. The gruesome and wide gaping hole pulsed hiccups of rich blood as Ty's body slid from the sword. He crumpled, a wolf-shaped ragdoll falling to the ground. Bones turned to liquid. Then his body vibrated with a convulsing shudder. His human and naked form lay bleeding out between the fallen.

Agony scored my own heart, as if I'd been the one run through. As if my heart was a gaping hole of pulsing blood. So I was dead, and this was hell. It had to be. Nothing else could be so cruel.

The shattering reenactment faded and fresh voices danced on a wave around me. *Ty!* I fought against the fading memory. The blood, the scene…Ty's death. Hell or not, letting go wasn't an option. I wanted to stay here, in this never-ending torture. So long as I could see him. But it was no use. Ty was gone, and the fresh voices kept growing louder.

"She should have woken by now," Dorian muttered. I could hear shuffling. No, not shuffling. Pacing. Then a distinct thud followed by something shattering against a solid surface. "Have you even left this room in the last two days?"

"No." A broad hand cupped over mine, squeezing. "Troy said the tranquilizer should have worn off by now." Kendrick's voice, and he was speaking right beside me. The hand covering mine squeezed again. "But that's under normal circumstances."

"Her injuries weren't that bad." Dorian sounded like he wanted to hit someone.

The pacing started back up as a door creaked open. Someone barefoot padded over soft carpet. "That's true," Mom said, her voice broken. Her steps neared my other side. "Her physical injuries have long since healed with the blood transfusions. Though no amount of blood can heal a broken heart. Only time can do that."

Behind my eyelids, I saw Ty. His body was draped over my lap, his face a mirror of pain, his breath a rasp from his throat. Against my cheek his hand lay. It trembled like a leaf in a gentle breeze while his thumb grazed my bottom lip. A ghostly smile parted his lips. "I-I…l-love you, Amelia. I w-will always…l-love you."

"Ty, no!" I clutched his shoulders and shook violently. "Don't say that. Don't say goodbye." Yet as my words swirled on a repeating echo around me, Ty's face began to fade. His body had turned limp in my hands and his eyes rolled back to the whites. With the release of breath from his throat, the sudden compacting weight of his body followed. The sight of him disappeared like a puff of black smoke.

"Ty!" I screamed, throat raw as ground meat. The heaviness of my body was returning, the light of reality hauling me back. Striking pain pierced my heart, like a lance spearing through my chest to come out clean on the other side. In its wake was a gaping hole that would never heal. One that would never close up. Excruciating pain crippled my entire body, flourishing like flesh-eating acid from my shattered heart outward. It engulfed every bone, every vein, and every inch of my flesh. I knew what was about to happen. I was waking up, my conscious mind forcing my lids to flutter against dim room light. Forcing me to leave the horrific memories of Ty's death. There was nothing I wanted less than to wake, to leave this dream-like state behind. What awaited was a world that had been robbed of Ty. My life would never be the same without him. To know that I would never be able to see Ty's face, or hear his voice like I just had in these heartbreaking but lucid dreams? It was worse than reliving the scene of his death over, and over. I wasn't ready to leave, to let go. I wasn't ready to give Ty or his vivid memory up.

"No!" I screamed and flailed, striking and fighting. "Don't leave me. Ty!"

Hands pressed my wrists back, pinning them against soft pillows. "Amelia, it's okay."

"NO!" Using my whole body, I thrashed out. "Ty, no!"

The restraints against my wrists released. Arms flung in a split second to wrap around my body, drawing me close and squeezing. Lips found the crown of my hair and pressed down. "Shh." Kendrick's cool breath ruffled my eyelashes. "I've got you."

My body's thrashing was useless. Against Kendrick's strong arms, mine were as weak as a child's. I stopped fighting, limbs trembling with exertion and the excruciating pain that radiated from my shredded heart. Tears filled my eyes and I squeezed them shut, clinging to Kendrick's sides with desperate hands. "He's gone." I struggled to breathe and clutched the amulet in a tight fist. "He's dead."

A smaller and more delicate hand found my back and began moving in slow circles. "I know, sweetheart. I know…"

We stayed like that for a long while, Kendrick's arms holding me, and Mom's hand continuing its gentle support. After what felt like an eternity of struggling through the incessant waves of pain, I somehow slowed my hyperventilation and took a steady breath. I drew from Kendrick's hold, still crying unending tears. We were in my bedroom, dark-purple drapes drawn and chandelier extinguished. Light glowed from the black-velvet lamp at my bedside. Kendrick was on the edge of my bed, his arms loosened but still holding me. Mom sat on my other side, expression riddled with relief and grief all at the same time. Her eyes were puffy as hell. Dorian stood across the carpeted space at the door, hand gripping tight to a manila envelope. Behind him, my mirrored dresser was crammed with bouquets of flowers. There were red and white roses, purple lupines, and white and black calla lilies. More flower pieces decorated the floor space around the dresser, growing outward like a living garden. There was also a smashed vase beside Dorian's bare feet. The smash I'd heard earlier.

"Who are all the flowers from?" My voice sounded hollow and far away.

Mom leaned forward and patted my knee. "They're from your true followers. The ones that came to witness your coronation, and…" Her words broke off with a deep unsettled sigh.

I knew what she had been about to say. "The ones who didn't die at the hands of the damned."

"Yes." Kendrick drew me back against his chest.

Tears kept rolling down my face, an unending supply that refused to stop. I swiped them away and looked from Dorian to Kendrick, then to my mom. "I want to see him. I want to see Ty."

Dorian moved closer, looking at Kendrick then Mom, an evident question cast from his eyes. His concern shifted to me. "Amelia, don't you remember?"

Kendrick's grip around me tightened and his lips met my hair again. "He died."

I jerked away and shook my head. Like I hadn't been there when it had happened? Like I hadn't just relived the torture in my own nightmares? My fists clenched. "I know that." Then they unclenched. I wasn't angry with them. "I do. I just…"

Using the back of my hand, I wiped the wetness from my face and jaw. Fresh billowing pain surged from my heart, rawness swamping down to my stomach. So much of me wanted to believe that he wasn't gone, that there was still something I could do to…*save him.* I choked on a sob, tasting acid spike my throat. *I know you can save me.* Ty's faith in me hadn't even wavered with his dying breaths. And I had failed him.

I cleared my phlegm and acid-filled throat and sniffed back the snot that clogged up my nose. My blurry vision rose to Mom. "Please, I need to see his body."

There was a moment of tension-fueled silence. Mom's expression strained while she shared a tight-lipped frown with Dorian and then Kendrick. "Ty's funeral is today," she said, her gaze returning to me. "You're not invited."

KENDRICK DIVERTED his lingering gaze from the rearview mirror, where Dorian sat, silent and motionless. That was at least ten on my count since we snuck out of the house. A conspicuous look came my way. "You know your mom will kill you when she finds out you're gone."

Beyond the moving car it was daylight. Gated properties rushed past on one side and ocean scenery was a blur on the other. For once it wasn't raining or snowing.

"We'll be back before she wakes up. She's not going to find out," I said, tone narrowing on a warning. "Isn't that right, Dorian?"

On the outside I was a reflection of strength and stability. But inside? I was drowning, organs swimming in acid that made my head, stomach, bones, and heart feel as though they were being eaten alive, melted slowly from the inside out. The agony had been escalating from the second I woke, from the second I remembered exactly what I had lost. Kendrick, of course, could feel the depth of my emotional wounds. They radiated like poison through our bond. Still he knew me, maybe even better than I knew myself. Now wasn't the time to talk things out. Instead we were heading to Ty's funeral, against my mom's forbidding command.

A tidal wave rolled my stomach and I strained my throat in an attempt to keep rising vomit from pouring up. *Ty is dead.* The horrific reality made me wonder if this could just be a terrible nightmare. My worst fear come to life. But I wasn't that lucky. The pain of his loss alone proved that.

I threw a glance over my shoulder to my brother. Since my insistence to see Ty to say goodbye before his body was surrendered to the ground, he hadn't spoken a word. "Dorian?"

My brother flinched, eyes straining harder than they had been the second before. He frowned, focus tearing from the blank A4 envelope in his hands and up to me. "Huh?"

"I said…" Then I stalled. Dorian's expression was guarded and his fingers were clinging to that envelope in his tight hands for dear life. I twisted further in my seat and pointed a finger. Giving into my slight curiosity, I pleaded, to who or what, I wasn't sure, that whatever was in his hands would distract a twinge of the torture I was living. "What is that, anyway?"

Dorian's gaze slid up to the rearview mirror then back down. His expression tightened. As if looking at me caused him physical pain. In the same instant I saw Kendrick exchange a cautionary look with my brother. Then the link to his thoughts and feelings shut off. "Nothing you need to worry about," Dorian said.

"Yeah," Kendrick chimed in, voice way too cheery to be anything but put on. "Let's focus on getting through today. We can worry about everything else, later."

There's more? The vicious blow of accepting that Ty was dead was already more than I could take. My continued involvement with him had been the catalyst that had delivered him into the vengeful path of Caius's sword. It was more than I could live with. More than I wanted to live with. And now there was more? Would it upheave our lives further? Did it have to do with…*Ty?*

With widened eyes, I shot a look at Kendrick. His focus was trained intently through the windshield at the sun-speckled road. His thoughts were still unreadable, a vault closed and the dial spun. Still there was no way in hell I was about to let this go. And if either Kendrick or Dorian thought I would, then they had seriously forgotten who I was. I glared at my brother. "I have a right to know. Tell me what's in that envelope."

"Not now," Kendrick warned. His narrowed eyes flared as he glowered into the rearview mirror at my brother. Then they softened to settle on me. His hand shifted from the leather steering wheel to cup my knee. "Amelia, please. There will be plenty of time for this, later. Right now you need to mourn, to think of and remember Ty." At my venomous look, his hand retracted, palm up. "I know how painful this is for you. You know I do. And the question you're asking has nothing to do with him. I promise you that."

I gritted my teeth. Whether the information was related to Ty or not, it clearly had something to do with me. Good or bad—probably the latter given the distant look in Dorian's eyes—I needed to know. I snatched the envelope from Dorian. It came from his grasp that had seemed so tight and desperate, as easily as if he hadn't been holding it at all. We may never have had that eerie connection twins shared, but I still knew him. He wanted me to know what hid within this flimsy yellow covering that couldn't have held more than a few single pages. "Tell me what's in here," I said to Dorian. "Or I'll find out myself."

Dorian drew in a long breath and expelled it. "The envelope holds blood test results."

I thought of Ty, wondering if they had tested his blood after his death and discovered he was a hybrid. Though I couldn't think of any reason they would want or need to test his blood in the first place. "Whose results are they?"

Dorian yanked at the navy scarf around his neck, worrying at the frayed end. "They're Caius's, Mom's, mine, and yours."

I frowned. *Why test our blood?* My brain felt sluggish, unable to conjure the answers. All I could see when I kept thinking back was Ty, his chest sliding free from Caius's scarlet-painted sword before crumpling to the red and black slicked council ground. I fought the need to shudder. There was no turning back now. He had to tell me. "Why?" I demanded. "I don't understand."

Kendrick pried my hand from the edge of the envelope. "The Council needed to prove or discount your mother's claim." A grimace pinched his face. "Don't you remember?"

The fragmented pieces of memory splintered, then shot back together. Mom had leaped between Caius and me. I screamed at her to move, threatening to kill her too if she didn't. Still my unwavering threat hadn't dispelled her, hadn't freed my attack of Caius's sword ready in my hand. Instead she had clung to my arms, pleading for me not to kill him. *But why?* My internals lifted, as if I'd plunged off a cliff, free falling. I clutched at my throat, struggling to find air in the Cabriolet's small cab. "My father is…is Caius."

At my words, Dorian turned a ghastly shade of gray. The deadpan look on his face was alien and terrifying. I had never seen him look so vacant before, so totally lost. Dropping the envelope I spun on my seat, knees pressing into the backrest. Desperation made me want to reach out to him, to soothe his turmoil. But the stillness of him sitting there, not looking at me, not looking at anything, kept my fingers pried around the edge of the leather seat. "My God, Dorian. What is it? What's wrong? Please, you have to tell me."

Dorian didn't even budge, and it was Kendrick who spoke. "The tests proved that you are both natural-born royals. You were never turned vampires."

After all the obstacles we had needed to break through, especially when Pure Blood had been required to open the locked door to the cell corridor below the Portsmouth Council, I had suspected that I was somehow a royal. Though I'd only thought Caius's experiments had modified my DNA and blood. Being a born royal hadn't even crossed my mind. Now I knew the truth. Caius was my biological father. My stomach churned like milk turning to butter. Had Caius forced himself on our mom all those years ago? I recalled her trust in him, the way she gained strength at his touch when she'd revealed us all to be vampires. Then I remembered Caius locking her away during the battle. There was something between them. There always had been. I'd seen it in my vision of Dorian's and my birth.

Another revelation hit me like a bullet between the eyes. "A-Athobry," I stammered. It was the name our mom had said was our fathers. Which wasn't a total lie—if you rearranged the letters. How could we all have been so blind? "It's an anagram for Bathory."

With this new sickening notion to deal with, on top of everything else that should have rendered me crazed and screaming, a question formed on my lips. Part of it came from Dorian's statue-stiff form. The rest resulted from feeling the roadblocks in Kendrick's mind that remained as solid as a foot-thick fortress of steel. "Kendrick? Dorian? What aren't you telling me?"

Dorian's chin rose, expression lost and alone. Trepidation tightened my chest. His silver-blue eyes were glazed, but not reddened with tears. His grief here was bigger than the day I'd revealed Marika's treachery. It was personal and forever life changing. "Caius is your father," he said on the breath of a whisper, holding up the results for me to see. "But he's not mine. And that's not all…"

Bewildered by stiff silence, I sat staring through the windshield but seeing nothing. Dorian wasn't Caius's son. If that were the only drowning revelation, it would have been enough. But there was more. So much more. There had been a fourth set of blood results that had been rushed after the first three were reported. This fourth blood test was my mom's. It revealed a number of interesting facts. One confirmed that she was, in fact, a turned vampire. This corroborated Caius's claims that he had turned her, as did my vision of the act. Still I wanted to believe he'd somehow compelled her to think it was necessary. Yet after everything we now knew, it couldn't be true. Mom had to have been involved.

The second and much more gripping reveal, was that our mom's maternal genetic markers which matched my DNA, were not even close to matching Dorian's. Dorian, my twin, the boy who'd been my brother since my first breath of life, was not even related to me. He wasn't biologically my brother. Our mom wasn't our mom. She was mine. Only mine.

Shaking my brain free of cobwebs, I twisted, reaching out to clasp Dorian's hand. "I don't care what those stupid results say." I glared at the envelope now repositioned on his lap, as if it were the culprit for this chasm between us. "Blood or not, you *are* my brother. Nothing can ever change that."

Dorian shrugged. His expression wasn't as blank as before, but it was just as wary. "Sure. Whatever."

CHAPTER 35

*W*ith a crunch of gravel the scenery surrounding us cleaved into focus. The Cabriolet had stopped moving. Surrounding us were parked cars, a church...and a hearse. The two brick levels with spear-shaped windows reflected the doom-lacking, fluffy clouds above.

Without a word, I exited the car and slid around the side of the building. We hadn't been invited to the funeral and wouldn't be welcomed, even if hell did freeze over. With Kendrick and Dorian waiting, shielded by a canopy of magnolia trees, I scaled the outer wall to the second level. Each sliding step tightened my lungs, like a vice was closing around them. I wanted so badly to slip through one of the speared windows that marked the church's entire west side. I wanted to get as close as possible to Ty's gold coffin. To see his human face and run my fingers across his cheek. To imagine he was just sleeping and not a decomposing shell of the boy I still and always would love.

From this position, I could make out the open lid over the heads of people lining up to pay their respects. But I couldn't risk it. Couldn't get close enough to whisper those three powerful and undying words to him, hoping he'd hear it beyond. A werewolf's sense of smell was second to none. It would only take a whiff to alert them of my presence. And the soaring church was packed to the brim with them. From what I could see, everyone had honey-glazed irises marking them as werewolves. Yet to my surprise, not all were black haired and tan.

"Are they all...?" I whispered, throwing a glance down at Kendrick and Dorian. It was late afternoon and the wintery sun, though weakened, was clear from any shielding clouds as it dipped low. Lace-work shadowed over them from magnolia branches, and I could feel the tingle that touched Kendrick's flesh at the ultraviolet light. "Werewolves?"

From where they stood, Kendrick had a clear view of a number of faces inside through a lower window. He shook his head while prodding fingers trampled over my brain. *I can't believe he never explained it to you.*

For a second I thought he was about to give me another lecture on things Ty had kept from me when alive. But no. He was simply surprised that the clarification had never come up.

Ty was a lycanthrope, a form of werewolf. The kind that is born, not created. The more general term werewolf refers to humans who contracted the lycanthropy disease, through the bite of either a natural-born lycan or a werewolf. All wolves morph during a full moon, but only lycans can do it on command.

I studied the people inside. Apart from their eyes, most of them appeared more or less human. They didn't have the same excess of overdeveloped muscle. Though most were still toned and built to fight. Beyond that, their other physical features didn't hold any distinct pattern that would mark them as unique or part of an elite group.

My forehead pressed against the cool glass, desperately hoping to catch a glimpse of Ty. Minutes passed. Then the lined up people paying their respects fanned out. I held my breath. My shaking fingers lifted to the glass, as if reaching out that few inches would bring me closer to him. Still I couldn't see Ty. An overflowing arrangement of vibrant orange, yellow, and white flowers blocked my view of what the coffin held. Sudden relief washed over me. It traveled from Kendrick down on the ground and magically through our bond. At the same moment Ty's father appeared on the stage, unshaven and looking like he'd just rolled out of bed. He clumsily rearranged a set of cards in his hands as he stood at a glass podium, dull eyes downcast.

I gave neither him nor Kendrick a second thought. My Vans, toes squished into the front of my shoes, began edging along the tiny ridge that jutted out below the line of windows. Pressure constricted my chest. I couldn't breathe. Couldn't let my breath out to take a fresh one in until I was close enough to see him.

"Amelia, stop," Dorian rasped from below the trees. "They'll see you."

Kendrick's relief vanished. He launched from the ground and up twenty feet to block me on the ridge. In what seemed to be a reoccurring event, his thoughts and emotions became blocked. Yet what he could hide from me mentally, he couldn't keep concealed physically. His eyes were wide and unblinking. His heart drummed with the fear that froze his expression. "Amelia, please. It's time to go."

"What?" I breathed out in surprise rather than allowance. "No. I want to see him. I need to say…" The feeling of waking during heart surgery with no anesthetic, my ribcage cracked open and a scalpel cutting into my heart, sent volumes of pain flooding my body. My

Vans slipped on the ridge and Kendrick caught at my elbow, keeping me from plummeting to the ground. I winced, trying to think past the agony. "I need this, Kendrick. And I can't promise that I'll be able to go on afterward. But ever since waking, ever since remembering *his* death," I said while thinking, *and failing to save him.* "I've just had one thing that kept me breathing. One thing that kept me from giving up, on everything. Please understand. I need to say *goodbye.*"

Kendrick grimaced, feeling my pain and love for Ty collectively. He sighed. "I know you do. But I also know you trust me." He glanced at Dorian then back at me with hope. "I need you to trust me now. You don't want to see this. It won't help anything. It will only…" He broke off, staring away from me and squinting at the lowering sun. His teeth gritted. "Amelia, please…"

"No," I snapped. Today of all days he wasn't going to pull this crap with me. "And it will only what?" I pinched his jaw and forced his face back to me. "Kendrick, you're hiding your thoughts from me. What I don't know is why. You say to trust you, and I do. You know that. But you also know that I'm not leaving until you tell me what's going on."

Kendrick sighed, the resolve to keep his mind locked from mine waning. "Something happened after Troy knocked you out with that tranq. The council hall was cleared out, bar the guards and a few others. We came back to help clear out the…" he paused, shuddering, "*bodies.*" His eyes, so filled with fear and yet so honest, rose to mine. "I was certain you'd want to see Ty when you woke, and I wanted to make sure you could."

"But when you got back, the wolves had come to claim him," I said, finding the words in Kendrick's head before he'd decided how to deliver them.

A surreal reenactment played snippets through my mind. Mr. Malau stalking into the Portsmouth Council, rage bulging every corded muscle. Two lycans flanked his side along with Troy and Marika, still in human form. Guards intercepted them. Then the threats started. "Give me my son," Mr. Malau had snarled, body vibrating, canines sliding past lips, and eyes glowing with hate. The next second the anger was gone. Vacancy replaced it and Troy and Marika moved to support the solid man's crushing weight.

I blinked away the snippets. There was something important there, but I wasn't getting it. "Was there a fight?" I asked. Then a terrifying thought occurred to me. "Oh no. The Council wanted to keep Ty's body to run tests on him, experiments. Didn't they?"

Kendrick's brows arched in surprise. "No. And even if they did…" He sighed again, long and hard. But he didn't seem able to get the words out.

Behind me I sensed someone's presence. The shadow of their body blocked the warm sunlight from my back. "Amelia." It was Dorian, balanced on the ridge, his voice a murmur of emotional control. "There was nothing for them to fight over."

Whipping my head sideways, blood pulsed through my ears. Dorian's words echoed like a taunting threat. Below I saw the backs of Mr. Malau and his son, Harper, along with Troy and Marika. Harper's shoulders were shaking, and his hand lifted to scrub his face. Troy's face was painted by frozen anger as they closed in on Ty's coffin. Marika lifted the flower arrangement, sniffing back free-falling tears. She shifted it to the stage, leaving a clear view of the coffin and the white satin padding within.

The coffin was empty.

Before Kendrick or Dorian could stop me, I fell to the grass, landing as quiet as a panther. In less than a second I sped around the external wall of the church and burst through the heavy wooden doors and into the werewolf-filled hall. The group of four carrying the now shut coffin froze. Every pair of honey-glazed eyes settled on me and rippled with threatening gold. Everyone seated on the pews shot up, bodies tensing and stances readying because a threat, one of their sworn mortal enemies, had busted into a very exclusive and private funeral.

Mr. Malau's face didn't show any surprise to see me, only agitation, eyes narrowing into hardened gold chips. "How dare you come here." He held the coffin with one hand and raised his other, stalling the encroachment of his werewolf-turning lycans. "Haven't you already done enough?"

Aware of Kendrick and Dorian right behind me, I rushed forward and leaped onto the back half of the coffin. I flung the top half of the lid open. Inside the satin was white, but not quite as empty as it had appeared from the upper-level window. On the cushioned surface lay a trophy, the current state championship award Ty had won for swimming. There was also a small frame that housed a smaller version of the family photo that hung on the wall in the Malau dining room. Last was a solitary item that couldn't be confused. A glittering, silver stake. The same one I'd found in Ty's backpack on the cruise. The same one I'd tried to wield before I knew how to. Still the one thing that mattered, the one thing I'd notice from the upper window, hadn't changed. My eyes hadn't been playing tricks on me. Ty wasn't here. He wasn't cold and stiff and without breath, with pallor graying as he began to decompose.

"Where the hell is he?" My vision blurred with tears as I clawed into the satin. My fingers scraped the base, splinters biting into my flesh. "Tell me where the fuck he is!"

Kendrick and Dorian paused well before the raised coffin, shooting nervous glances around. Wind lifted around them like a cocoon, and a separate whirling tunnel enveloped the coffin, me, and its carriers. Werewolves surrounded them from every angle.

"Amelia," Kendrick said, voice warning and low while he scouted left to right. "We need to go. Now."

At my wild look Dorian said, "We won't leave without you."

"You shouldn't be here," Marika said with a rush. She was at my back left, holding the last handle on the coffin. But she wouldn't be for long.

The coffin tipped as Troy released the front left handle. Then the whole wooden death-bed free fell. As it hit the ground, shattering beneath me into jagged, golden splinters, Troy leaped to land before me. His face was a hardened flush, eyes blazing and lips curled back over growing canines. "Not unless you want to be killed," he said. Then he grinned wickedly. "On second thought..."

He launched, faster than I had time to react to. In a flash he had me pinned to the ground, wood splinters piercing my back and drawing blood. "I've been waiting for this day."

I struggled against his unwavering strength, forearms shoved against his chest to hold back his snapping canines. Voltage surged from my skin and into him, but it didn't help. The expelled power was no more than a zap you'd get from touching a small battery to your tongue.

Over Troy's head I could see Kendrick and Dorian's panicked faces, both trapped behind a thick line of barricading werewolves. They were screaming, but over the shouts of limitless werewolves I couldn't make out their words. Mr. Malau stood before the barricade, his face alight with satisfaction. Marika and Harper were on either side of the wood explosion, staring in frozen horror.

Then the satisfaction melted from Mr. Malau's face. He made a choking noise as veins struck his eyes. With shock his hands came up, crimson leaking from his eyes and nose and rolling down his face.

"Get off my sister, or he's dead."

I caught sight of Dorian through the startled crowd. His hands were lifted and shaking while Kendrick held up the wind barricade. Hearing him call me his sister after all we'd learned would normally have touched my heart. But not now. The electric silver in his irises sparked with conviction. He meant every word of his threat.

I called out for him to stop, but the crowd was too loud.

Troy's arms came around my blocking forearms, hands clutching my neck. "She'll be dead first. Then I'm gunning for you, leech."

As my resistance began to fade, Troy's spittle-glistening teeth and lengthening snout neared my collarbone. I closed my eyelids and let my consciousness shift to Ty. After what I had caused him, his family, and his kind, I deserved to die. An eye for an eye. Isn't that what they say? The sooner this was over with, the more chance Mr. Malau had to survive. Because if Dorian succeeded, they'd never get out alive.

I let my arms fall from Troy's chest, ready to take what I deserved.

"Amelia, no!"

Beyond Kendrick's scream a girl's voice cursed. Then a loud, ear-punching sound struck the air. Troy let out a yelping cry and landed to my side.

A hand appeared before me, open and waiting. I locked my fingers around the wrist—small boned, delicate, and yet strong all at the same time—and allowed them to haul me upright.

"Are you okay?"

A girl stepped before me, dressed in black gear that both hugged her body and appeared movable at the same time. She wore a utility belt with an empty gun holster at her left side. In her hand was the gun itself, barrel smoking. Her red hair was pulled back into a high ponytail that flashed an array of golden filigrees across her collarbone and neck. Vanessa.

My focus shot to Troy who was clutching at his right leg. A drizzle of tacky liquid oozed from a small hole in his thigh, staining his soot-colored pants red. "You shot Troy for me?"

She smiled, but Mr. Malau stalked forward before she could speak. His hands curled into beefy fists. "What do you think you're doing?"

Vanessa twirled to face him, her free hand meeting her hip, the other loose on her gun. "I'm preventing you from allowing your own to harm an innocent."

"Innocent?" Troy scoffed. Then he groaned as he ripped the leg of his pants to expose his wounded flesh. He began digging into the hole in his leg, trying to remove the bullet. "No leech is innocent. Especially not her."

Mr. Malau now stood right before Vanessa in her stiletto boots. He towered over her, eyes lasered down into hers. "My son is dead because of her," he said through clenched teeth. "She deserves to pay for his life."

"Ty made his own decisions," Kendrick called out, still stuck with Dorian behind the wolves. The wind tunnel was holding, but its spinning drive had slowed.

"Just like Marika and Troy did," Dorian added, shooting a glare at Troy who had managed to finger the bullet free from his leg. His unwavering strength, despite the threat surrounding them, was as heroic as it was blind. "They all had a choice and they all decided to stay and fight."

"It's true," Marika said, taking Harper's hand while keeping him behind her. "We all made our own choices." Her gaze met Dorian then Kendrick, and she flushed.

The argument between wolves and vampires continued with Vanessa the only point of reason between the two. Yet I couldn't hear their words, couldn't concentrate on anything they were saying while my thoughts raced a million miles.

There was nothing for them to fight over. Dorian's words throbbed through my mind, over and over. What did it mean? Where was Ty? How could they have a funeral without his body?

Numbly I stepped forward, suspicions rising. Still my mind refused to acknowledge the possibility. The shouting had become a contest, louder with every spat word back and forth. I didn't register any of it. My hand lifted, curling around Vanessa's wrist. She spun with a start and then relaxed at seeing me. "Tell me, please. I have to know. Where is Ty's…" I fought the all over body quake that threatened to floor me. "Where is his body?"

Vanessa motioned for me to wait and swiveled back to Mr. Malau. "Stop this now," she warned. "Unless you want their council to come after you and all of yours. You do know who she is, don't you? Their Oracle. The first one they've had in centuries. Do you think they'll let her murder slide?"

The arguing stopped as Mr. Malau came forward, pushing past Vanessa to face me. "The funeral is over. Everyone out." His hardened scowl didn't leave mine as dispute exploded all around. As the cacophony rose, he twisted his head, fixing the collection of werewolves and lycans with a hard stare. "These vampires are no threat to me. Now, get out."

His booming voice vibrated the speared windows. Then a tide of anger left as the wolves departed. All that remained was our group and the five of them.

Returning his venomous glare to me, Mr. Malau's nostrils flared with audible breath. His body towered over mine, arms tense at his sides. "His body is gone. All because of you."

The wind barricading Kendrick and Dorian cut off, and then they were at my sides. The speared, wooden doors swung shut as the last of the werewolves left. Upended and skewed pews littered the hall around us.

"That's what we were trying to tell you," Dorian said from my left. He edged forward, as if in protection of any advance Mr. Malau may suddenly decide to take.

Mr. Malau shook his head, aggression melting into despairing disgust. "They took it."

I looked from him to Kendrick, who stared blankly at the wood chips covering the ground. "They who? Took what?" Nausea rolled my stomach. "No. Not Ty."

"Yes." Kendrick's face pinched with the magnitude of what he was about to reveal. "The Council thinks looming damned came back after the battle to..."

At his cut-off words, Marika appeared between Dorian and Mr. Malau. Her eyes were still puffy, but no more tears fell. "They took his body."

"What?" My voice sounded like it was miles away. My head twisted side to side, and my eyelids pinned shut. Behind my lids I saw the expression fall from Ty's face the moment he had died. Heard the breath escape his lungs for the last time. Felt the compacting weight of his dead body. I clutched the amulet and didn't let go. "Why would they do that? Why—"

"They're scavenging creatures, the damned." Troy reared up off the floor, dusting off wood splinters. "Just like the rest of you leeches." His leg was bare from where he'd ripped the material from his pants off, but the bullet hole was closed, scabbing and no longer bleeding. "Probably took him to feed."

I fell to my knees and heaved, but all the came out was a dribble of acid. Kendrick's broad hand found my back, rubbing circles while he knelt beside me. *They took him to feed?* I gagged at the sickening thought. The image of a crowd of red-eyed monsters devouring the boy I loved imprinted on my mind and soul. A stain that would never wash out. Though something that was almost like a little light within my heart, beamed at the same time. *There was no body.*

Weak from mental strain, I forced myself up to my feet. Kendrick rose with me, hand under my elbow. "What if they didn't?"

Mr. Malau pegged me with a hard stare. "What if they didn't what?"

I forced down the shudder verging up my spine and leveled my voice. "What if they didn't take his body to feed?"

"Why else would they take it?" Dorian questioned. "He was one of a handful of bodies that disappeared."

"Yeah, and we all witnessed it…Ty dying." Marika gulped, face paling. "What other use would the damned have for a dead lycan?"

"Experiments?" Vanessa fastened her gun back in her holster. "Considering the other bodies they took."

"They don't think that way," Kendrick said. "They're about death and destruction. They're already stronger, faster, and more ruthless than either of our races. They have no need to experiment."

Everyone had said their piece and now had their eyes trained on me, waiting for my ground-shattering answer. And it would be ground shattering. If I was right, and I hoped more than anything I had ever hoped for in my life that I was, then this single piece of information could change the lives of not just me, but also this small mismatched group before me. I drew in a long breath. "What if they took Ty and the others, knowing or suspecting that…" I took another breath and bit my lip. "That they weren't dead. That they would wake. Not as they were. Not really alive in any way. But…damned."

My hand fell from the amulet and it bounced against my black and purple tank. Mr. Malau snarled and caught the heavy stone in a clenched fist. "Where did you get this?"

Dorian tensed, hand rising, and a current of wind began to blow around the airtight room.

"Ty gave it to her." Vanessa's stilettos clinked as she stepped forward. Her hand rested on the butt of her holstered gun, but she made no move to pull it free.

I stood my ground, even though Mr. Malau was breathing down my neck. "Your wife, his mother, left it with him the night she died. Ty wanted me to have it." The words I was about to say broke my heart all over again. "His heart in stone, forever."

Mr. Malau sighed and dropped the amulet. His hands covered his face before falling slack at his sides. "He truly trusted you. He told you everything."

Though they weren't questions, I nodded. "If he's out there, I'll find him. Damned, soulless, I don't care. If I can bring him home to you—" I glanced around at everyone, my heart brimming with hope that I prayed wasn't false "—to all of you, I will. Or I'll die trying."

Mr. Malau sighed, quietly studying my face. "I can see what my son saw in you. You're so much like his mother. My dear Selena." A determined smile curved his full mouth. "You're a fighter, just like she was." He held out his arm, hand sideways, eyes piercing. "If you're going to succeed, you need leads and hardcore training. Do we have an alliance?"

As Kendrick and Dorian called out their disagreement, I stepped forward, my hand clutching the alpha's.

"To saving Ty. No matter what it takes."

Will Amelia ever find Ty or is she searching for a dead man?
Turn the page to find out in Web of Lies…

465

THANK YOU FOR READING!

Dear Reader,

Thank you for reading *Made By Design (Blood Bound Series Book 2)*. If you enjoyed this book please turn to the last page an select a star rating, or if you have a moment to spare, you can leave a review. It doesn't have to be long—one or two sentences would be amazing. The more reviews a book has the more Amazon is willing to put it in front of potential readers. As an indie author, I don't have a big publishing company promoting my work, so every little bit helps and I'd love for my audience to be a part of it. I read every one of my reviews and completely appreciate the thoughts and opinions of all my readers.

http://bit.ly/reviewmbd

Thank you, J.L. Myers

Continue reading for a sneak peek at the Blood Bound Series Book 3, *Web of Lies*.

AMELIA, TY, AND KENDRICK'S STORY
CONTINUES IN…

Web of Lies - Blood Bound #3

*D*esperation lit like fire in my bones, threatening to ignite my world and shatter it to hell. Again. The spilled combination of blood that had filled once-living vampires and the damned choked up my throat. But my tears were reserved for the fast-fading life bleeding out before me. Lying in a growing pool of his own blood, Ty clenched his teeth, molars grinding. A seizure rode his body and his arms flung up, unable to stop the shakes. Unable to cover the leaking slice in his chest. Fear and longing drenched his golden irises as they met mine, cut off as his lids slammed shut. Horror seeped through my chest.

Time wasn't on our side.

Not now. Not then.

Because this wasn't the first reenactment and it sure as hell wouldn't be the last. The broken bodies and black and red smeared hall with all its shattered glass proved that. I couldn't stop the events from playing out any more than I could change the outcome. And I couldn't save my breaking heart from shattering all over again.

The second the seizure released, I tore into my wrist and pressed the bleeding punctures to Ty's lips. Vampire blood to heal a lycan, like our long-ago ancestors used to do before the two races became enemies. My blood pooled, mixing with his own until his mouth was so full that it overflowed. A vibrant torrent ran down either side of his face and I fought back tears. "Ty, *please*. You have to swallow."

Ty's pinched expression released, lids flinging open only to have his eyes roll back. His trembling body began convulsing. All the blood in his mouth streamed out like a river breaking its banks. My free arm clung tighter to him, willing his body to become still.

And then it did.

Every muscle that had been so taut and rapt with spasm released. My breath caught. Not in relief, but in fear. I knew what was next and I couldn't stop it. My arm shook as I extended my bleeding wrist.

"No. It's t-too late."

Despair drowned me as Ty faded into that dark tunnel. He was slipping away again, right before my very eyes. "No. You can't mean that. You're not dead. There's still time."

Ty's rough and warm hand shook as he pressed it against my cheek. Death mirrored across his face and wet breath rasped from his throat. It became shallower as tremors flooded back through his body. Yet his hand remained glued to my jaw, muscles bunching with dying strain up his arm. His thumb grazed my bottom lip. Resolve of the inevitable stole the sad longing from his stare. His mouth parted with the shadow of a smile. "I-I…l-love you, Amelia. I w-will always…l-love you."

"Ty, no!" I screamed, that same helplessness flooring my heart like a tidal wave. I clutched his shoulders and shook him. "Don't say that. Don't say goodbye."

In my violently shaking hands Ty's entire body turned limp. His eyes rolled back to the whites and the breath released from his lungs. Without warning, his body felt as if it weighed more than a freight train. He slipped from my grasp and his skull cracked against the marble.

I threw a leg over his hips. "Don't leave me!"

With the heel of my palm, I began compressions. But it wasn't enough. I needed voltage. The spark from my own hands like a defibrillator to jump-start his heart.

But there was nothing.

A rib cracked under my palms as my compressions became desperate. "Wake up!"

There was speaking and hands trying to pull me away. Faces I refused to register. Then screams. My own as I fought to stay with him. "Let me fucking go!"

The tunnel grew longer and Ty's lifeless body became smaller. "You're not dead. Move. Speak. *Do* something, Ty!"

All of a sudden, everything went quiet. All the talking and faces that had surrounded me were gone. Only the shattered windows remained, the bodies and the blood. Quiet peaceful carnage after the battle had run its course.

But this wasn't normal. This extension of time after his death. Something had changed. But I wasn't about to complain. Time was time. Even if it wasn't the way you wanted it.

Lost in the silence, I ran my hand down Ty's handsome face. A face that would never smile at me again. At those perfect lips that would never press against mine with unrestrained passion. I sniffed back tears, refusing to lose this clear view of him as my fingers stilled across his cheek.

Then the surroundings flickered, slow like a faulty bulb at first, then faster. No. Too soon. Not yet. The flashes strobed until there was nothing but light.

The surroundings were gone. Only Ty's body straddled beneath me remained.

Color and definition crept in: three dark walls, a curtain-covered doorway, and a daybed beneath me. Ty's skin was no longer shredded and soaked by black and red patches. Blood no longer painted his chin and neck. His old scars remained, but the hole in his chest was gone. Despite the lack of sound from a beating heart, his pale face held clear muscle control. He looked peaceful. Sleeping rather than dead.

Oh, God. *"Ty?"*

Ty's eyelids flung open and his crimson pupils drilled straight into my soul. In a flash, he arched up on the bed, ice-cold lips capturing mine. I kissed him back, consumed by the taste of him. A wish come true. Even in a warped dream. I let myself get lost in the moment. Lost in the fact that this was Ty and he was kissing me. That when I couldn't control my dreams, this could be the last physical connection beyond replaying his death.

Suddenly his cold, hard hands shot to my waist and flipped me onto my back. Now straddling me in nothing but jeans, Ty smiled, long fangs peeking through his pale lips. "Hello, beautiful."

Continue Amelia's epic journey here: http://bit.ly/wolbb3

CONNECT WITH J.L. MYERS

If you want to stay updated about my latest book releases and get freebies or exclusive review offers, join my VIP list!
Visit : www.jlmyers.com and enter your email address. You can unsubscribe at any time and your email will be kept 100% private.

Come check out my author page on Facebook. I'd love to hear from you:
https://www.facebook.com/author.jlmyers

Come say hi on twitter or Connect with me on Goodreads!
https://twitter.com/authorjlmyers
https://www.goodreads.com/author/show/7178370.J_L_Myers

Don't miss my new releases. Follow me on Amazon & Bookbub
https://www.amazon.com/J.L.-Myers/e/B00DK4P0EO/
https://www.bookbub.com/authors/j-l-myers

ABOUT THE AUTHOR

Jessica L Myers' vivid imagination and quiet demeanor as a child led her to the imaginary worlds of books. Even at a young age, her love for the supernatural was prevalent, with her first loved books being R.L. Stine's *Goosebumps* series. Following that she took an interest in other non-fantasy fiction, including Virginia C. Andrews series *Flowers in the Attic*.

In her teen years, Jessica spent many school hours writing poetry and dark short stories and took up sketching some of the terrifying things that came from the graphic night terrors she'd grown up with.

As an adult and after meeting the love of her life, Jessica got married and started a small construction business with her husband. With the birth of her son, Jessica suffered PPD and found escape in her books and their fantasy landscapes. It was during this time that her need to write flourished. In 2009 the decision was made and the first words to her YA novel *What Lies Inside* were written.

When Jessica isn't immersed in writing about extraordinary characters with dangerous and deadly obstacles to overcome, she likes to spend time with her two kids and husband, curl up with a good book, or watch anything and everything supernatural.

Contact J.L. directly:
www.jlmyers.com

facebook.com/author.jlmyers

twitter.com/authorjlmyers

instagram.com/authorjlmyers